Superna

Supernatural Short Stories,
Tales of Murder

and

Letters on Demonology
and Witchcraft

Sir Walter Scott

ALMA CLASSICS

ALMA CLASSICS
an imprint of

ALMA BOOKS LTD
Thornton House
Thornton Road
Wimbledon Village
London SW19 4NG
United Kingdom
www.almaclassics.com

This collection first published by Alma Classics in 2024

For publication details of the tales in this volume, see the first note for each story

Cover: David Wardle

Printed in Great Britain by CPI Group (UK) Ltd, Croydon CR0 4YY

ISBN: 978-1-84749-930-1

All rights reserved. No part of this publication may be reproduced, stored in or introduced into a retrieval system, or transmitted, in any form or by any means (electronic, mechanical, photocopying, recording or otherwise), without the prior written permission of the publisher. This book is sold subject to the condition that it shall not be resold, lent, hired out or otherwise circulated without the express prior consent of the publisher.

Contents

SUPERNATURAL SHORT STORIES   1
AND TALES OF MURDER

    THE FORTUNES OF MARTIN WALDECK   3

    PHANTASMAGORIA   13

    WANDERING WILLIE'S TALE   19

    THE HIGHLAND WIDOW   35

    THE TWO DROVERS   91

    MY AUNT MARGARET'S MIRROR   117

    THE TAPESTRIED CHAMBER   149

    DONNERHUGEL'S NARRATIVE   163

    THE BRIDAL OF JANET DALRYMPLE   175

LETTERS ON DEMONOLOGY   181
AND WITCHCRAFT

    Note on the Texts   211
    Notes   211
    Glossary   257

SUPERNATURAL SHORT STORIES
AND
TALES OF MURDER

The Fortunes of Martin Waldeck*

The solitudes of the Harz forest in Germany,* but especially the mountains called Blocksberg, or rather Brockenberg, are the chosen scenes for tales of witches, demons and apparitions. The occupation of the inhabitants, who are either miners or foresters, is of a kind that renders them peculiarly prone to superstition, and the natural phenomena which they witness in pursuit of their solitary or subterraneous profession are often set down by them to the interference of goblins or the power of magic. Among the various legends current in that wild country, there is a favourite one which supposes the Harz to be haunted by a sort of tutelar demon in the shape of a wild man, of huge stature, his head wreathed with oak leaves, and his middle cinctured with the same, bearing in his hand a pine torn up by the roots. It is certain that many persons profess to have seen such a form traversing, with huge strides, in a line parallel to their own course, the opposite ridge of a mountain, when divided from it by a narrow glen, and indeed the fact of the apparition is so generally admitted that modern scepticism has only found refuge by ascribing it to optical deception.*

In elder times, the intercourse of the demon with the inhabitants was more familiar, and, according to the traditions of the Harz, he was wont, with the caprice usually ascribed to these earth-born powers, to interfere with the affairs of mortals, sometimes for their weal, sometimes for their woe. But it was observed that even his gifts often turned out, in the long run, fatal to those on whom they were bestowed, and it was no uncommon thing for the pastors, in their care of their flocks, to compose long sermons, the burden whereof was a warning against having any intercourse, direct or indirect, with the Harz demon. The fortunes of Martin Waldeck have been often quoted by the aged to their giddy children, when they were heard to scoff at a danger which appeared visionary.

A travelling Capuchin* had possessed himself of the pulpit of the thatched church at a little hamlet called Morgenbrodt, lying in the Harz district, from which he declaimed against the wickedness of the inhabitants, their communication with fiends, witches and fairies, and, in particular, with the woodland goblin of the Harz. The doctrines of Luther had already begun to spread among the peasantry (for the incident is placed under the reign of Charles V),* and they laughed to scorn the zeal with which the venerable man insisted upon his topic. At length, as his vehemence increased with opposition, so their opposition rose in proportion to his vehemence. The inhabitants did not like to hear an accustomed quiet demon who had inhabited the Brockenberg for so many ages summarily confounded with Baal-peor, Ashtaroth and Beelzebub himself, and condemned without reprieve to the bottomless Tophet.* The apprehensions that the spirit might avenge himself on them for listening to such an illiberal sentence added to their national interest in his behalf. A travelling friar, they said, that is here today and away tomorrow, may say what he pleases, but it is we, the ancient and constant inhabitants of the country, that are left at the mercy of the insulted demon, and must, of course, pay for all. Under the irritation occasioned by these reflections, the peasants from injurious language betook themselves to stones, and, having pebbled the priest pretty handsomely, they drove him out of the parish to preach against demons elsewhere.

Three young men, who had been present and assisting on this occasion, were upon their return to the hut where they carried on the laborious and mean occupation of preparing charcoal for the smelting furnaces. On the way, their conversation naturally turned upon the demon of the Harz and the doctrine of the Capuchin. Max and George Waldeck, the two elder brothers, although they allowed the language of the Capuchin to have been indiscreet and worthy of censure, as presuming to determine upon the precise character and abode of the spirit, yet contended it was dangerous in the highest degree to accept of his gifts or hold any communication with him. He was powerful, they allowed, but wayward and capricious, and those who had intercourse with him seldom came to a good end. Did he not give the brave knight Ecbert of Rabenwald that famous black steed, by means of which he vanquished all the champions at the great tournament at Bremen? And did not the same steed afterwards precipitate itself with its rider into an abyss so steep and fearful that neither horse nor man were ever seen more? Had he not given to Dame Gertrude Trodden a curious spell for making butter come? And was she not burnt for a witch by the grand criminal judge of the Electorate* because she availed herself of his gift? But these, and many other instances which they quoted of mischance and ill luck ultimately attending on the apparent benefits conferred by the Harz spirit, failed to make any impression upon Martin Waldeck, the youngest of the brothers.

Martin was youthful, rash and impetuous, excelling in all the exercises which distinguish a mountaineer, and brave and undaunted from his familiar intercourse with the dangers that attend them. He laughed at the timidity of his brothers. "Tell me not of such folly," he said. "The demon is a good demon – he lives among us as if he were a peasant like ourselves, haunts the lonely crags and recesses of the mountains like a huntsman or goatherd, and he who loves the Harz forest and its wild scenes cannot be indifferent to the fate of the hardy children of the soil. But, if the demon were as malicious as you would make him, how should he derive power over mortals, who barely avail themselves of his gifts, without binding themselves to submit to his pleasure? When you carry your charcoal to the furnace, is not the money as good that is paid you by blaspheming Blaize, the old reprobate overseer, as if you got it from the pastor himself? It is not the goblin's gifts which can endanger you, then, but it is the use you shall make of them that you must account for. And were the demon to appear to me at this moment and indicate to me a gold or silver mine, I would begin to dig away even before his back were turned – and I would consider myself as under protection of a much Greater than he, while I made a good use of the wealth he pointed out to me."

To this the elder brother replied that wealth ill won was seldom well spent, while Martin presumptuously declared that the possession of all the treasures of the Harz would not make the slightest alteration on his habits, morals or character.

His brother entreated Martin to talk less wildly upon the subject, and with some difficulty contrived to withdraw his attention by calling it to the consideration of the approaching boar chase. This talk brought them to their hut, a wretched wigwam, situated upon one side of a wild, narrow and romantic dell in the recesses of the Brockenberg. They released their sister from attending upon the operation of charring the wood, which requires constant attention, and divided among themselves the duty of watching it by night, according to their custom, one always waking, while his brothers slept.

Max Waldeck, the eldest, watched during the first two hours of the night, and was considerably alarmed by observing, upon the opposite bank of the glen, or valley, a huge fire surrounded by some figures that appeared to wheel around it with antic gestures. Max at first bethought him of calling up his brothers, but, recollecting the daring character of the youngest and finding it impossible to wake the elder without also disturbing Martin – conceiving also what he saw to be an illusion of the demon, sent perhaps in consequence of the venturous expressions used by

Martin on the preceding evening – he thought it best to betake himself to the safeguard of such prayers as he could murmur over, and to watch in great terror and annoyance this strange and alarming apparition. After blazing for some time, the fire faded gradually away into darkness, and the rest of Max's watch was only disturbed by the remembrance of its terrors.

George now occupied the place of Max, who had retired to rest. The phenomenon of a huge blazing fire, upon the opposite bank of the glen, again presented itself to the eye of the watchman. It was surrounded as before by figures, which, distinguished by their opaque forms, being between the spectator and the red glaring light, moved and fluctuated around it as if engaged in some mystical ceremony. George, though equally cautious, was of a bolder character than his elder brother. He resolved to examine more nearly the object of his wonder, and, accordingly, after crossing the rivulet which divided the glen, he climbed up the opposite bank and approached within an arrow's flight of the fire, which blazed apparently with the same fury as when he first witnessed it.

The appearance of the assistants who surrounded it resembled those phantoms which are seen in a troubled dream, and at once confirmed the idea he had entertained from the first: that they did not belong to the human world. Amongst these strange unearthly forms, George Waldeck distinguished that of a giant overgrown with hair, holding an uprooted fir in his hand, with which, from time to time, he seemed to stir the blazing fire, and having no other clothing than a wreath of oak leaves around his forehead and loins. George's heart sank within him at recognizing the well-known apparition of the Harz demon, as he had been often described to him by the ancient shepherds and huntsmen who had seen his form traversing the mountains. He turned, and was about to fly, but upon second thoughts, blaming his own cowardice, he recited mentally the verse of the Psalmist, "All good angels, praise the Lord!"* – which is in that country supposed powerful as an exorcism – and turned himself once more towards the place where he had seen the fire. But it was no longer visible.

The pale moon alone enlightened the side of the valley, and when George, with trembling steps, a moist brow and hair bristling upright under his collier's cap, came to the spot on which the fire had been so lately visible, marked as it was by a scathed oak tree, there appeared not on the heath the slightest vestiges of what he had seen. The moss and wild flowers were unscorched, and the branches of the oak tree, which had so lately appeared enveloped in wreaths of flame and smoke, were moist with the dews of midnight.

George returned to his hut with trembling steps, and, arguing like his elder brother, resolved to say nothing of what he had seen, lest he should awake in Martin that daring curiosity which he almost deemed to be allied with impiety.

It was now Martin's turn to watch. The household cock had given his first summons, and the night was well-nigh spent. Upon examining the state of the furnace in which the wood was deposited in order to its being coked or charred, he was surprised to find that the fire had not been sufficiently maintained – for in his excursion and its consequences, George had forgot the principal object of his watch. Martin's first thought was to call up the slumberers, but, observing that both his brothers slept unwontedly deep and heavily, he respected their repose, and set himself to supply the furnace with fuel without requiring their aid. What he heaped upon it was apparently damp and unfit for the purpose, for the fire seemed rather to decay than revive. Martin next went to collect some boughs from a stack which had been carefully cut and dried for this purpose, but, when he returned, he found the fire totally extinguished. This was a serious evil, and threatened them with loss of their trade for more than one day. The vexed and mortified watchman set about to strike a light in order to rekindle the fire, but the tinder was moist, and his labour proved in this respect also ineffectual. He was now about to call up his brothers, for circumstances seemed to be pressing, when flashes of light glimmered not only through the window, but through every crevice of the rudely built hut, and summoned him to behold the same apparition which had before alarmed the successive watches of his brethren. His first idea was that the Muhllerhaussers, their rivals in trade, and with whom they had had many quarrels, might have encroached upon their bounds for the purpose of pirating their wood, and he resolved to awake his brothers, and be revenged on them for their audacity. But a short reflection and observation on the gestures and manner of those who seemed to "work in the fire" induced him to dismiss this belief, and, although rather sceptical in such matters, to conclude that what he saw was a supernatural phenomenon. "But be they men or fiends," said the undaunted forester, "that busy themselves yonder with such fantastical rites and gestures, I will go and demand a light to rekindle our furnace." He relinquished at the same time the idea of awaking his brethren. There was a belief that such adventures as he was about to undertake were accessible only to one person at a time; he feared also that his brothers, in their scrupulous timidity, might interfere to prevent his pursuing the investigation he had resolved to commence – and therefore, snatching his boar spear from the wall, the undaunted Martin Waldeck set forth on the adventure alone.

With the same success as his brother George, but with courage far superior, Martin crossed the brook, ascended the hill and approached so near the ghostly assembly that he could recognize, in the presiding figure, the attributes of the Harz demon. A cold shuddering assailed him for the first time in his life, but the recollection that he had at a distance dared and even courted the intercourse which was now about to take place confirmed his staggering courage, and, pride supplying what he wanted in resolution, he advanced with tolerable firmness towards the fire, the figures which surrounded it appearing still more wild, fantastical and supernatural the more near he approached to the assembly. He was received with a loud shout of discordant and unnatural laughter, which, to his stunned ears, seemed more alarming than a combination of the most dismal and melancholy sounds that could be imagined. "Who art thou?" said the giant, compressing his savage and exaggerated features into a sort of forced gravity, while they were occasionally agitated by the convulsion of the laughter which he seemed to suppress.

"Martin Waldeck, the forester," answered the hardy youth. "And who are you?"

"The King of the Waste and of the Mine," answered the spectre. "And why hast thou dared to encroach on my mysteries?"

"I came in search of light to rekindle my fire," answered Martin hardily, and then resolutely asked in his turn: "What mysteries are those that you celebrate here?"

"We celebrate," answered the complaisant demon, "the wedding of Hermes with the Black Dragon* – but take thy fire that thou camest to seek, and begone! No mortal may look upon us and live."

The peasant struck his spear point into a large piece of blazing wood, which he heaved up with some difficulty, and then turned round to regain his hut, the shouts of laughter being renewed behind him with treble violence, and ringing far down the narrow valley. When Martin returned to the hut, his first care, however much astonished with what he had seen, was to dispose the kindled coal among the fuel so as might best light the fire of his furnace, but after many efforts, and all exertions of bellows and fire prong, the coal he had brought from the demon's fire became totally extinct, without kindling any of the others. He turned about, and observed the fire still blazing on the hill, although those who had been busied around it had disappeared. As he conceived the spectre had been jesting with him, he gave way to the natural hardihood of his temper, and, determining to see the adventure to an end, resumed the road to the fire, from which, unopposed by the demon, he brought off in the same manner a blazing piece of charcoal, but still without being able to succeed in lighting his fire. Impunity having increased his rashness, he resolved upon a third experiment, and was as successful as before in reaching the fire, but when he had again appropriated a piece of burning coal and had turned to depart, he heard the harsh and supernatural voice which had before accosted him pronounce these words: "Dare not return hither a fourth time!"

The attempt to kindle the fire with this last coal having proved as ineffectual as on the former occasions, Martin relinquished the hopeless attempt and flung himself on his bed of leaves, resolving to delay till the next morning the communication of his supernatural adventure to his brothers. He was awakened from a heavy sleep into which he had sunk, from fatigue of body and agitation of mind, by loud exclamations of surprise and joy. His brothers, astonished at finding the fire extinguished when they awoke, had proceeded to arrange the fuel in order to renew it, when they found in the ashes three huge metallic masses, which their skill (for most of the peasants in the Harz are practical mineralogists) immediately ascertained to be pure gold.

It was some damp upon their joyful congratulations when they learnt from Martin the mode in which he had obtained this treasure, to which their own experience of the nocturnal vision induced them to give full credit. But they were unable to resist the temptation of sharing in their brother's wealth. Taking now upon him as head of the house, Martin Waldeck bought lands and forests, built a castle, obtained a patent of nobility, and, greatly to the indignation of the ancient aristocracy of the neighbourhood, was invested with all the privileges of a man of family. His courage in public war, as well as in private feuds, together with the number of retainers whom he kept in pay, sustained him for some time against the odium which was excited by his sudden elevation and the arrogance of his pretensions.

And now it was seen in the instance of Martin Waldeck, as it has been in that of many others, how little mortals can foresee the effect of sudden prosperity on their own disposition. The evil propensities in his nature, which poverty had checked and repressed, ripened and bore their unhallowed fruit under the influence of temptation and the means of indulgence. As deep calls unto deep,* one bad passion awakened another: the fiend of avarice invoked that of pride, and pride was to be supported by cruelty and oppression. Waldeck's character, always bold and daring, but rendered harsh and assuming by prosperity, soon made him odious – not to the nobles only, but likewise to the lower ranks, who saw, with double dislike, the oppressive rights of the feudal nobility of the empire so remorselessly exercised by one who had risen from the very dregs of the people. His adventure, although carefully concealed, began likewise to be whispered abroad, and the clergy already stigmatized as a wizard and accomplice of fiends the wretch who, having acquired so huge a treasure in so strange a manner, had not sought to sanctify it by dedicating a considerable portion to the use of the Church. Surrounded by enemies, public and private, tormented by a thousand feuds, and threatened by the Church with excommunication, Martin Waldeck – or, as we must now call him, the Baron von Waldeck – often regretted bitterly the labours and sports of his unenvied poverty. But his courage failed him not under all these difficulties, and seemed rather to augment in proportion to the danger which darkened around him, until an accident precipitated his fall.

A proclamation by the reigning Duke of Brunswick had invited to a solemn tournament all German nobles of free and honourable descent, and Martin Waldeck, splendidly armed, accompanied by his two brothers and a gallantly equipped retinue, had the arrogance to appear among the chivalry of the province and demand permission to enter the lists.* This was considered as filling up the measure of his presumption. A thousand voices exclaimed, "We will have no cinder-sifter mingle in our games of chivalry." Irritated to frenzy, Martin drew his sword and hewed down the herald who, in compliance with the general outcry, opposed his entry into the lists. An hundred swords were unsheathed to avenge what was in those days regarded as a crime only inferior to sacrilege or regicide. Waldeck, after defending himself like a lion, was seized, tried on the spot by the judges of the lists and condemned, as the appropriate punishment for breaking the peace of his sovereign and violating the sacred person of a herald-at-arms, to have his right hand struck from his body, to be ignominiously deprived of the honour of nobility, of which he was unworthy, and to be expelled from the city. When he had been stripped of his arms, and sustained the mutilation imposed by this severe sentence, the unhappy victim of ambition was abandoned to the rabble, who followed him with threats and outcries levelled alternately against the necromancer and oppressor, which at length ended in violence. His brothers (for his retinue were fled and dispersed) at length succeeded in rescuing him from the hands of the populace, when, satiated with cruelty, they had left him half dead through loss of blood and through the outrages he had sustained. They were not permitted, such was the ingenious cruelty of their enemies, to make use of any other means of removing him, excepting such a collier's cart as they had themselves formerly used, in which they deposited their brother on a truss of straw, scarcely expecting to reach any place of shelter ere death should release him from his misery.

When the Waldecks, journeying in this miserable manner, had approached the verge of their native country, in a hollow way* between two mountains, they perceived a figure advancing towards them which at first sight seemed to be an aged man. But as he approached, his limbs and stature increased, the cloak fell from his shoulders, his pilgrim's staff was changed into an uprooted pine tree, and the gigantic figure of the Harz demon passed before them in his terrors. When he came opposite to the cart which contained the miserable Waldeck, his huge features dilated into a grin of unutterable contempt and malignity, as he asked the sufferer, "How like you the fire *my* coals have kindled?" The power of motion, which terror suspended in his two brothers, seemed to be restored to Martin by the energy of his courage. He raised himself on the cart, bent his brows and, clenching his fist, shook it at the spectre with a ghastly look of hate and defiance. The goblin vanished with his usual tremendous and explosive laugh, and left Waldeck exhausted with this effort of expiring nature.

The terrified brethren turned their vehicle towards the towers of a convent which arose in a wood of pine trees beside the road. They were charitably received by a barefooted and long-bearded Capuchin, and Martin survived only to complete the first confession he had made since the day of his sudden prosperity, and to receive absolution from the very priest whom, precisely on that day three years, he had assisted to pelt out of the hamlet of Morgenbrodt. The three years of precarious prosperity were supposed to have a mysterious correspondence with the number of his visits to the spectral fire upon the hill.

The body of Martin Waldeck was interred in the convent where he expired, in which his brothers, having assumed the habit of the order, lived and died in the performance of acts of charity and devotion. His lands, to which no one asserted any claim, lay waste until they were reassumed by the emperor as a lapsed fief, and the ruins of the castle, which Waldeck had called by his own name, are still shunned by the miner and forester as haunted by evil spirits. Thus were the miseries attendant upon wealth hastily attained and ill employed exemplified in the fortunes of Martin Waldeck.

Phantasmagoria*

"Come like shadows – so depart"*

The incident which I am about to narrate came to your present correspondent through the most appropriate channel for such information: by the narration, namely, of an old woman. I must, however, add that though this old lady literally wore the black silk gown, small haunch-hoop and triple ruffles which form the apparel most proper to her denomination,* yet in sense, spirit, wit and intelligence she greatly exceeded various individuals of her own class who have been known to me, although their backs were clothed with purple robes or military uniforms, and their heads attired with cocked hats or three-tailed periwigs. I have not, in my own mind, the slightest doubt that she told the tale to me in the precise terms in which she received it from the person principally concerned. Whether it was to be believed in its full extent as a supernatural visitation, she did not pretend to determine, but she strongly averred her conviction that the lady to whom the event happened was a woman not easily to be imposed upon by her own imagination, however excited, and that the whole tone of her character, as well as the course of her life, exempted her from the slightest suspicion of an attempt to impose on others. Without further preface, and without any effort at ornament or decoration, I proceed to my narration, only premising that though I suppress the name of the lady out of respect to surviving relations, yet it is well known to me.

A lady, wife to a gentleman of respectable property on the borders of Argyllshire, was, about the middle of the last century, left a widow, with the management of an embarrassed estate and the care of an only son. The young gentleman approached that period of life when it was necessary that he should be sent into the world in some active professional line. The natural inclination of the youth, like most others of that age and country, was to enter into the army, a disposition which his mother saw with anxiety, as all the perils of the military profession were aggravated to her imagination by maternal tenderness and a sense of her own desolate situation. A circumstance however occurred which induced her to grant her consent to her son's embracing this course of life with less reluctance than it would otherwise have been given.

A Highland gentleman named Campbell (we suppress his designation), and nearly related to Mrs ——, was about this time named to the command of one of the independent companies levied for protecting the peace of the Highlands and preventing the marauding parties in which the youth of the wilder clans were still occasionally exercised. These companies were called *sidier dhu*, i.e. black soldiers, to distinguish them from the *sidier roy*, or red soldiers, of the regular army, and hence, when embodied into a marching regiment (the well-known Forty-Second), the corps long retained, and still retains, the title of the Black Watch.* At the period of the story the independent companies retained their original occupation, and were generally considered as only liable to do duty in their native country.* Each of these corps consisted of about three hundred men, using the Highland garb and arms, and commanded by such gentlemen as the Brunswick government* imagined they might repose confidence in. They were understood to engage only to serve in the Highlands and nowhere else, and were looked upon rather as a kind of volunteers than as regular soldiers.

A service of this limited nature, which seemed to involve but little risk of actual danger, and which was to be exercised in his native country alone, was calculated to remove many of the objections which a beloved mother might be supposed to have against her only son entering into the army. She had also the highest reliance on the kindness and affection of her kinsman, Captain Campbell, who, while he offered to receive the young gentleman as a cadet into his independent company, gave her his solemn assurance to watch over him in every respect as his own son, and to prevent his being exposed to any unnecessary hazard until he should have attained the age and experience necessary for his own guidance. Mrs —— greatly reconciled to parting with her son, in consequence of these friendly assurances on the part of his future commander, it was arranged that the youth should join the company at a particular time, and in the meanwhile Mrs ——, who was then residing at Edinburgh, made the necessary preparations for his proper equipment.

These had been nearly completed when Mrs —— received a piece of melancholy intelligence, which again unsettled her resolution, and, while it filled her with grief on account of her relation, awakened in the most cruel manner all the doubts and apprehensions which his promises had lulled to sleep. A body of katerns, or freebooters, belonging, if I mistake not, to the country of Lochiel, had made a descent upon a neighbouring district of Argyllshire, and driven away a considerable *creagh*, or spoil, of cattle. Captain Campbell, with such of his independent company as he could assemble upon a sudden alarm, set off in pursuit of the depredators, and after a fatiguing march came up with them. A slight skirmish took place, in course of which the cattle were recovered, but not before Captain Campbell had received a severe wound. It was not immediately, perhaps not necessarily, mortal, but was rendered so by want of shelter and surgical assistance, and the same account which brought to Edinburgh an account of the skirmish communicated to Mrs —— the death of her affectionate kinsman. To grief for his loss she had now to add the painful recollection that her son, if he pursued the line which had been resolved on, would be deprived of the aid, countenance and advice of the person to whose care, as to that of a father, she had resolved to confide him. And the very event which was otherwise so much attended with grief and perplexity served to show that the service of the independent companies, however limited in extent, did not exempt those engaged in it from mortal peril. At the same time, there were many arguments against retracting her consent, or altering a plan in which so much progress had been already made, and she felt as if, on the one hand, she sacrificed her son's life if she permitted him to join the corps – on the other, that his honour or spirit might be called in question by her obliging him to renounce the situation. These contending emotions threw her – a widow, with no one to advise her, and the mother of an only son whose fate depended upon her resolving wisely – into an agony of mind which many readers may suppose will account satisfactorily for the following extraordinary apparition.

I need not remind my Edinburgh friends that in ancient times their forefathers lived, as they do still in Paris, in flats, which have access by a common stair. The apartments occupied by Mrs —— were immediately above those of a family with whom she was intimate, and she was in the habit of drinking tea with them every evening. It was duskish, and she began to think that her agitation of mind had detained her beyond the hour at which she should have joined her friends, when, opening the door of her little parlour to leave her own lodging, she saw standing directly opposite to her in the passage the exact resemblance of Captain Campbell, in his complete Highland dress, with belted plaid, dirk, pistols, pouch and broadsword. Appalled at this vision, she started back, closed the door of the room, staggered backwards to a chair and endeavoured to convince herself that the apparition she had seen was only the effect of a heated imagination. In this, being a woman of a strong mind, she partly succeeded, yet could not prevail upon herself again to open the door which seemed to divide her from the shade of her deceased relation, until she heard a tap on the floor beneath, which was the usual signal from her friendly neighbours to summon her to tea. On this she took courage, walked firmly to the door of the apartment flung it open, and... again beheld the military spectre of the deceased officer of the Black Watch. He seemed to stand within a yard of her, and held his hand stretched out, not in a menacing manner, but as if to prevent her passing him. This was too much for human fortitude to endure, and she sank down on the floor, with a noise which alarmed her friends below for her safety.

On their hastening upstairs and entering Mrs ——'s lodging, they saw nothing extraordinary in the passage, but in the parlour found the lady in strong hysterics. She was recalled to herself with difficulty, but concealed the extraordinary cause of her indisposition. Her friends naturally imputed it to the late unpleasant intelligence from Argyllshire, and remained with her till a late hour, endeavouring to amuse and relieve her mind. The hour of rest however arrived, and there was a necessity (which Mrs —— felt an alarming one) that she should go to her solitary apartment. She had scarce set down the light which she held in her hand, and was in the act of composing her mind ere addressing the Deity for protection during the perils of the night, when, turning her head, the vision she had seen in the passage was standing in the apartment. On this emergency she summoned up her courage, and, addressing him by his name and surname, conjured him in the name of Heaven to tell her wherefore he thus haunted her. The apparition instantly answered, with a voice and manner in no respect differing from those proper to him while alive, "Cousin, why did you not speak sooner?... My visit is but for your good... Your grief disturbs me in my grave... and it is by permission of the Father of the fatherless and Husband of the widow* that I come to tell you not to be disheartened by my fate, but to pursue the line which, by my advice, you adopted for your son. He will find a protector more efficient, and as kind as I would have been – will rise high in the military profession, and live to close your eyes." With these words the figure representing Captain Campbell completely vanished.

Upon the point of her being decidedly awake and sensible, through her eyes and ears, of the presence and words of this apparition, Mrs —— declared herself perfectly convinced. She said, when minutely questioned by the lady who told me the story, that his general appearance differed in no respect from that which he presented when in full life and health, but that in the last occasion, while she fixed her eyes on the spectre in terror and anxiety, yet with a curiosity which argued her to be somewhat familiarized with his presence, she observed a speck or two of blood upon his breast, ruffle and band, which he seemed to conceal with his hand when he observed her looking at him. He changed his attitude more than once, but slightly, and without altering his general position.

The fate of the young gentleman in future life seemed to correspond with the prophecy. He entered the army, rose to considerable rank and died in peace and honour, long after he had closed the eyes of the good old lady who had determined, or at least professed to have determined, his destination in life upon this marvellous suggestion.

It would have been easy for a skilful narrator to give this tale more effect by a slight transference or trifling exaggeration of the circumstances. But the author has determined in this and future communications to limit himself strictly to his authorities, and rests your humble servant,

SIMON SHADOW

Wandering Willie's Tale*

Ye maun have heard of Sir Robert Redgauntlet* of that ilk, who lived in these parts before the dear years.* The country will lang mind him, and our fathers used to draw breath thick if ever they heard him named. He was out wi' the Hielandmen in Montrose's time, and again he was in the hills wi' Glencairn in the saxteen hundred and fifty-twa,* and sae when King Charles II came in, wha was in sic favour as the Laird of Redgauntlet? He was knighted at Lonon court, wi' the king's ain sword, and being a red-hot prelatist, he came down here, rampauging like a lion, with commissions of lieutenancy (and of lunacy, for what I ken), to put down a' the Whigs* and Covenanters in the country. Wild wark they made of it, for the Whigs were as dour as the Cavaliers were fierce, and it was which should first tire the other. Redgauntlet was aye for the strong hand, and his name is kend as wide in the country as Claverhouse's or Tam Dalyell's.* Glen, nor dargle, nor mountain, nor cave, could hide the puir hill folk* when Redgauntlet was out with bugle and bloodhound after them, as if they had been sae mony deer. And troth, when they fand them, they didna mak muckle mair ceremony than a Hielandman wi' a roebuck – it was just, "Will ye tak the test?"* If not: "Make ready... present... fire!" – and there lay the recusant.

Far and wide was Sir Robert hated and feared. Men thought he had a direct compact with Satan; that he was proof against steel, and that bullets happed aff his buff coat* like hailstanes from a hearth; that he had a mear that would turn a hare* on the side of Carrifra-gawns* – and muckle to the same purpose, of whilk mair anon. The best blessing they wared on him was, "Deil scowp wi' Redgauntlet!" He wasna a bad master to his ain folk, though, and was weel aneugh liked by his tenants, and as for the lackies and troopers that rade out wi' him to the persecutions, as the Whigs caa'd those killing times,* they wad hae drunken themsells blind to his health at ony time.

Now, you are to ken that my gudesire lived on Redgauntlet's grund – they ca' the place Primrose Knowe. We had lived on the grund, and under the Redgauntlets, since the riding days, and lang before. It was a pleasant bit, and I think the air is callerer and fresher there than onywhere else in the country. It's a' deserted now, and I sat on the broken door cheek three days since, and was glad I couldna see the plight the place was in, but that's a' wide o' the mark. There dwelt my gudesire, Steenie Steenson, a rambling, rattling chiel' he had been in his young days, and could play weel on the pipes: he was famous at 'Hoopers and Girders' – a' Cumberland couldna touch him at 'Jockie Lattin'* – and he had the finest finger for the back-lill between Berwick and Carlisle. The like o' Steenie wasna the sort that they made Whigs o'. And so he became a Tory, as they ca' it, which we now ca' Jacobites,* just out of a kind of needcessity, that he might belang to some side or other. He had nae ill will to the Whig bodies, and liked little to see the blude rin, though, being obliged to follow Sir Robert in hunting and hoisting, watching and warding, he saw muckle mischief, and maybe did some, that he couldna avoid.

Now, Steenie was a kind of favourite with his master, and kend a' the folks about the castle, and was often sent for to play the pipes when they were at their merriment. Auld Dougal MacCallum, the butler, that had followed Sir Robert through gude and ill, thick and thin, pool and stream, was specially fond of the pipes, and aye gae my gudesire his gude word wi' the laird, for Dougal could turn his master round his finger.

Weel, round came the Revolution,* and it had like to have broken the hearts baith of Dougal and his master. But the change was not a'thegether sae great as they feared and other folk thought for. The Whigs made an unco crawing what they wad do with their auld enemies, and in special wi' Sir Robert Redgauntlet. But there were ower many great folks dipped in the same doings, to mak a spick-and-span new warld. So Parliament passed it a' ower easy, and Sir Robert, bating that he was held to hunting foxes instead of Covenanters, remained just the man he was.* His revel was as loud, and his hall as weel lighted, as ever it had been, though maybe he lacked the fines of the nonconformists that used to come to stock his larder and cellar,* for it is certain he began to be keener about the rents than his tenants used to find him before, and they behoved to be prompt to the rent day, or else the laird wasna pleased. And he was sic an awsome body that naebody cared to anger him, for the oaths he swore, and the rage that he used to get into, and the looks that he put on, made men sometimes think him a devil incarnate.

Weel, my gudesire was nae manager – no that he was a very great misguider – but he hadna the saving gift, and he got twa terms' rent in arrear. He got the first brash at Whitsunday put ower wi' fair word and piping, but when Martinmas* came, there was a summons from the grund officer to come wi' the rent on a day preceese, or else Steenie behoved to flit. Sair wark he had to get the siller, but he was weel freended, and at last he got the haill scraped thegether – a thousand merks – the maist of it was from a neighbour they caa'd Laurie Lapraik, a sly tod. Laurie had walth o' gear – could hunt wi' the hound and rin wi' the hare – and be Whig or Tory, saunt or sinner, as the wind stood. He was a professor in this Revolution warld, but he liked an orra sough of this warld, and a tune on the pipes weel aneugh at a bytime,* and abune a', he thought he had gude security for the siller he lent my gudesire ower the stocking at Primrose Knowe.

Away trots my gudesire to Redgauntlet Castle wi' a heavy purse and a light heart, glad to be out of the laird's danger. Weel, the first thing he learnt at the castle was that Sir Robert had fretted himsell into a fit of the gout, because he did not appear before twelve o'clock. It wasna a'thegether for sake of the money, Dougal thought, but because he didna like to part wi' my gudesire aff the grund. Dougal was glad to see Steenie, and brought him into the great oak parlour, and there sat the laird his leesome lane, excepting that he had beside him a great, ill-favoured jackanape that was a special pet of his: a cankered beast it was, and mony an ill-natured trick it played – ill to please it was, and easily angered: ran about the haill castle, chattering and yowling, and pinching, and biting folk, specially before ill weather, or disturbances in the state. Sir Robert caa'd it Major Weir, after the warlock that was burnt,* and few folk liked either the name or the conditions of the creature – they thought there was something in it by ordinar – and my gudesire was not just easy in mind when the door shut on him and he saw himself in the room wi' naebody but the laird, Dougal MacCallum and the Major, a thing that hadna chanced to him before.

Sir Robert sat – or, I should say, lay – in a great armchair, wi' his grand velvet gown, and his feet on a cradle, for he had baith gout and gravel,* and his face looked as gash and ghastly as Satan's. Major Weir sat opposite to him, in a red laced coat, and the laird's wig on his head, and aye as Sir Robert girned wi' pain, the jackanape girned too, like a sheep's head between a pair of tangs* – an ill-faured, fearsome couple they were. The laird's buff coat was hung on a pin behind him, and his broadsword and his pistols within reach, for he keepit up the auld fashion of having the weapons ready and a horse saddled day and night, just as he used to do when he was able to loup on horseback and away after ony of the hill folk he could get speerings of. Some said it was for fear of the Whigs taking vengeance, but I judge it was just his auld custom – he wasna gien to fear onything. The rental book, wi' its black cover and brass clasps, was lying beside him, and a book of sculduddry sangs was put betwixt the leaves, to keep it open at the place where it bore evidence against the goodman of Primrose Knowe, as behind the hand with his mails and duties. Sir Robert gave my gudesire a look as if he would have withered his heart in his bosom. Ye maun ken he had a way of bending his brows that men saw the visible mark of a horseshoe in his forehead, deep dinted, as if it had been stamped there.

"Are ye come light-handed, ye son of a toom whistle?" said Sir Robert. "Zounds! If you are…"

My gudesire, with as gude a countenance as he could put on, made a leg and placed the bag of money on the table wi' a dash, like a man that does something clever. The laird drew it to him hastily. "Is it all here, Steenie, man?"

"Your Honour will find it right," said my gudesire.

"Here, Dougal," said the laird, "gie Steenie a tass of brandy downstairs, till I count the siller and write the receipt."

But they werena weel out of the room when Sir Robert gied a yelloch that garr'd the castle rock. Back ran Dougal, in flew the liverymen – yell on yell gied the laird, ilk ane mair awfu' than the ither. My gudesire knew not whether to stand or flee, but he ventured back into the parlour, where a' was gaun hirdy-girdy – naebody to say "Come in" or "Gae out". Terribly the laird roared for cauld water to his feet and wine to cool his throat, and "Hell, hell, hell, and its flames" was aye the word in his mouth. They brought him water, and when they plunged his swollen feet into the tub, he cried out it was burning, and folks say that it *did* bubble and sparkle like a seething caldron. He flung the cup at Dougal's head and said he had given him blood instead of burgundy – and, sure aneugh, the lass washed clotted blood aff the carpet the neist day. The jackanape they caa'd Major Weir, it jibbered and cried as if it was mocking its master; my gudesire's head was like to turn – he forgot baith siller and receipt, and downstairs he banged, but as he ran, the shrieks came faint and fainter; there was a deep-drawn shivering groan, and word gaed through the castle that the laird was dead.

Weel, away came my gudesire wi' his finger in his mouth, and his best hope was that Dougal had seen the money bag and heard the laird speak of writing the receipt. The young laird, now Sir John, came from Edinburgh to see things put to rights. Sir John and his father never gree'd weel. Sir

John had been bred an advocate, and afterwards sat in the last Scots Parliament and voted for the Union,* having gotten, it was thought, a rug of the compensations – if his father could have come out of his grave, he would have brained him for it on his awn hearthstane. Some thought it was easier counting with the auld rough knight than the fair-spoken young ane – but mair of that anon.

Dougal MacCallum, poor body, neither grat nor grained, but gaed about the house looking like a corpse, but directing, as was his duty, a' the order of the grand funeral. Now, Dougal looked aye waur and waur when night was coming, and was aye the last to gang to his bed, whilk was in a little round just opposite the chamber of dais, whilk his master occupied while he was living, and where he now lay in state, as they caa'd it, weel-a-day! The night before the funeral, Dougal could keep his awn counsel nae langer; he came doun with his proud spirit, and fairly asked auld Hutcheon to sit in his room with him for an hour. When they were in the round, Dougal took ae tass of brandy to himsell and gave another to Hutcheon, and wished him all health and lang life, and said that, for himsell, he wasna lang for this world, for that every night since Sir Robert's death, his silver call had sounded from the state chamber, just as it used to do at nights in his lifetime, to call Dougal to help to turn him in his bed. Dougal said that being alone with the dead on that floor of the tower (for naebody cared to wake Sir Robert Redgauntlet like another corpse), he had never daured to answer the call, but that now his conscience checked him for neglecting his duty – for, "Though death breaks service," said MacCallum, "it shall never break my service to Sir Robert, and I will answer his next whistle, so be you will stand by me, Hutcheon."

Hutcheon had nae will to the wark, but he had stood by Dougal in battle and broil, and he wad not fail him at this pinch, so down the carles sat ower a stoup of brandy, and Hutcheon, who was something of a clerk, would have read a chapter of the Bible, but Dougal would hear naething but a blaud of Davie Lindsay,* whilk was the waur preparation.

When midnight came and the house was quiet as the grave, sure enough the silver whistle sounded as sharp and shrill as if Sir Robert was blowing it, and up got the twa auld serving men, and tottered into the room where the dead man lay. Hutcheon saw aneugh at the first glance, for there were torches in the room, which showed him the foul fiend, in his ain shape, sitting on the laird's coffin! Ower he couped as if he had been dead. He could not tell how lang he lay in a trance at the door, but when he gathered himself, he cried on his neighbour, and getting nae answer raised the house, when Dougal was found lying dead within twa steps of the bed where his master's coffin was placed. As for the whistle, it was gane anes and aye, but mony a time was it heard at the top of the house on the bartisan, and amang the auld chimneys and turrets where the howlets have their nests. Sir John hushed the matter up, and the funeral passed over without mair bogle wark.

But when a' was ower and the laird was beginning to settle his affairs, every tenant was called up for his arrears, and my gudesire for the full sum that stood against him in the rental book. Weel, away he trots to the castle to tell his story, and there he is introduced to Sir John, sitting in his father's chair, in deep mourning, with weepers and hanging cravat, and a small walking rapier by his side, instead of the auld broadsword that had a hunderweight of steel about it, what with blade, chape and basket hilt. I have heard their communings so often tauld ower that I almost think I was there myself, though I couldna be born at the time. (In fact, Alan,* my companion mimicked, with a good deal of humour, the flattering, conciliating tone of the tenant's address and the hypocritical melancholy of the laird's reply. His grandfather, he said, had, while he spoke, his eye fixed on the rental book, as if it were a mastiff dog that he was afraid would spring up and bite him.)

"I wuss ye joy, sir, of the head seat, and the white loaf, and the braid lairdship. Your father was a kind man to friends and followers: muckle grace to you, Sir John, to fill his shoon – his boots, I suld say, for he seldom wore shoon, unless it were muils when he had the gout."

"Ay, Steenie," quoth the laird, sighing deeply and putting his napkin to his een, "his was a sudden call, and he will be missed in the country; no time to set his house in order – weel prepared Godward, no doubt, which is the root of the matter, but left us behind a tangled hesp to wind, Steenie. Hem! Hem! We maun go to business, Steenie – much to do, and little time to do it in."

Here he opened the fatal volume. I have heard of a thing they call Domesday Book* – I am clear it has been a rental of back-ganging tenants.

"Stephen," said Sir John, still in the same soft, sleekit tone of voice, "Stephen Stephenson, or Steenson, ye are down here for a year's rent behind the hand – due at last term."

Stephen: "Please Your Honour, Sir John, I paid it to your father."

Sir John: "Ye took a receipt, then, doubtless, Stephen, and can produce it?"

Stephen: "Indeed, I hadna time, an it like Your Honour, for nae sooner had I set doun the siller, and just as His Honour, Sir Robert, that's gaen, drew it till him to count it and write out the receipt, he was taen wi' the pains that removed him."

"That was unlucky," said Sir John after a pause. "But ye maybe paid it in the presence of somebody. I want but a *talis qualis* evidence,* Stephen. I would go ower strictly to work with no poor man."

Stephen: "Troth, Sir John, there was naebody in the room but Dougal MacCallum the butler. But, as Your Honour kens, he has e'en followed his auld master."

"Very unlucky again, Stephen," said Sir John without altering his voice a single note. "The man to whom ye paid the money is dead, and the man who witnessed the payment is dead too – and the siller, which should have been to the fore, is neither seen nor heard tell of in the repositories. How am I to believe a' this?"

Stephen: "I dinna ken, Your Honour, but there is a bit memorandum note of the very coins, for – God help me! – I had to borrow out of twenty purses, and I am sure that ilka man there set down will take his grit oath for what purpose I borrowed the money."

Sir John: "I have little doubt ye *borrowed* the money, Steenie. It is the *payment* to my father that I want to have some proof of."

Stephen: "The siller maun be about the house, Sir John. And since Your Honour never got it, and His Honour that was canna have taen it wi' him, maybe some of the family may have seen it."

Sir John: "We will examine the servants, Stephen – that is but reasonable."

But lackey and lass, and page and groom, all denied stoutly that they had ever seen such a bag of money as my gudesire described. What was waur, he had unluckily not mentioned to any living soul of them his purpose of paying his rent. Ae quean had noticed something under his arm, but she took it for the pipes.

Sir John Redgauntlet ordered the servants out of the room and then said to my gudesire, "Now, Steenie, ye see ye have fair play, and, as I have little doubt ye ken better where to find the siller than any other body, I beg in fair terms, and for your own sake, that you will end this fasherie, for, Stephen, ye maun pay or flit."

"The Lord forgie your opinion," said Stephen, driven almost to his wits' end. "I am an honest man."

"So am I, Stephen," said His Honour, "and so are all the folks in the house, I hope. But if there be a knave amongst us, it must be he that tells the story he cannot prove." He paused, and then added, mair sternly, "If

I understand your trick, sir, you want to take advantage of some malicious reports concerning things in this family, and particularly respecting my father's sudden death, thereby to cheat me out of the money, and perhaps take away my character, by insinuating that I have received the rent I am demanding. Where do you suppose this money to be? I insist upon knowing."

My gudesire saw everything look so muckle against him that he grew nearly desperate – however, he shifted from one foot to another, looked to every corner of the room and made no answer.

"Speak out, sirrah," said the laird, assuming a look of his father's, a very particular ane, which he had when he was angry – it seemed as if the wrinkles of his frown made that selfsame fearful shape of a horse's shoe in the middle of his brow. "Speak out, sir! I *will* know your thoughts – do you suppose that I have this money?"

"Far be it frae me to say so," said Stephen.

"Do you charge any of my people with having taken it?"

"I wad be laith to charge them that may be innocent," said my gudesire, "and if there be anyone that is guilty, I have nae proof."

"Somewhere the money must be, if there is a word of truth in your story," said Sir John. "I ask where you think it is – and demand a correct answer."

"In hell, if you *will* have my thoughts of it," said my gudesire, driven to extremity. "In hell! With your father, his jackanape and his silver whistle."

Down the stairs he ran (for the parlour was nae place for him after such a word), and he heard the laird swearing blood and wounds, behind him, as fast as ever did Sir Robert, and roaring for the bailie and the baron officer.*

Away rode my gudesire to his chief creditor (him they caa'd Laurie Lapraik), to try if he could make onything out of him, but when he tauld his story, he got but the worst word in his wame – thief, beggar and dyvour were the saftest terms, and to the boot of these hard terms Laurie brought up the auld story of dipping his hand in the blood of God's saunts, just as if a tenant could have helped riding with the laird, and that a laird like Sir Robert Redgauntlet. My gudesire was, by this time, far beyond the bounds of patience, and, while he and Laurie were at Deil speed the liars, he was wanchancy aneugh to abuse Lapraik's doctrine as weel as the man, and said things that garr'd folks' flesh grue that heard them – he wasna just himsell, and he had lived wi' a wild set in his day.

At last they parted, and my gudesire was to ride hame through the wood of Pitmurkie, that is a' fou of black firs, as they say. I ken the wood, but the firs may be black or white for what I can tell. At the entry of the wood there is a wild common, and on the edge of the common a little lonely change house, that was keepit then by an ostler wife – they suld hae caa'd her* Tibbie Faw – and there puir Steenie cried for a mutchkin of brandy, for he had had no refreshment the haill day. Tibbie was earnest wi' him to take a bite of meat, but he couldna think o't, nor would he take his foot out of the stirrup, and took off the brandy wholly at twa draughts, and named a toast at each: the first was the memory of Sir Robert Redgauntlet, and might he never lie quiet in his grave till he had righted his poor bond-tenant, and the second was a health to Man's Enemy, if he would but get him back the pock of siller, or tell him what came o't, for he saw the haill world was like to regard him as a thief and a cheat, and he took that waur than even the ruin of his house and hauld.

On he rode, little caring where. It was a dark night turned, and the trees made it yet darker, and he let the beast take its ain road through the wood, when all of a sudden, from tired and wearied that it was before, the nag began to spring and flee and stend, that my gudesire could hardly keep the saddle – upon the whilk a horseman, suddenly riding up beside him, said, "That's a mettle beast of yours, freend. Will you sell him?" So saying, he touched the horse's neck with his riding wand, and it fell into its auld heigh-ho of a stumbling trot. "But his spunk's soon out of him, I think," continued the stranger, "and that is like mony a man's courage, that thinks he wad do great things till he come to the proof."

My gudesire scarce listened to this but spurred his horse, with "Gude e'en to you, freend".

But it's like the stranger was ane that doesna lightly yield his point, for, ride as Steenie liked, he was aye beside him at the selfsame pace. At last my gudesire, Steenie Steenson, grew half angry, and to say the truth, half feared.

"What is it that you want with me, freend?" he said. "If ye be a robber, I have nae money; if ye be a leal man wanting company, I have nae heart to mirth or speaking, and if ye want to ken the road, I scarce ken it mysell."

"If you will tell me your grief," said the stranger, "I am one that, though I have been sair miscaa'd in the world, am the only hand for helping my freends."

So my gudesire, to ease his ain heart, mair than from any hope of help, told him the story from beginning to end.

"It's a hard pinch," said the stranger, "but I think I can help you."

"If you could lend the money, sir, and take a lang day – I ken nae other help on earth," said my gudesire.

27

"But there may be some under the earth," said the stranger. "Come, I'll be frank wi' you: I could lend you the money on bond, but you would maybe scruple my terms. Now, I can tell you that your auld laird is disturbed in his grave by your curses and the wailing of your family, and if ye daur venture to go to see him, he will give you the receipt."

My gudesire's hair stood on end at this proposal, but he thought his companion might be some humoursome child that was trying to frighten him, and might end with lending him the money. Besides, he was bauld wi' brandy, and desperate wi' distress, and he said he had courage to go to the gate of hell and a step farther for that receipt. The stranger laughed.

Weel, they rode on through the thickest of the wood, when, all of a sudden, the horse stopped at the door of a great house, and, but that he knew the place was ten miles off, my father* would have thought he was at Redgauntlet Castle. They rode into the outer courtyard, through the muckle faulding yetts, and aneath the auld portcullis, and the whole front of the house was lighted, and there were pipes and fiddles, and as much dancing and deray within as used to be at Sir Robert's house at Pace and Yule, and such high seasons. They lap off, and my gudesire, as seemed to him, fastened his horse to the very ring he had tied him to that morning, when he gaed to wait on the young Sir John.

"God!" said my gudesire. "If Sir Robert's death be but a dream!"

He knocked at the ha' door just as he was wont, and his auld acquaintance, Dougal MacCallum – just after his wont, too – came to open the door, and said, "Piper Steenie, are ye there, lad? Sir Robert has been crying for you."

My gudesire was like a man in a dream – he looked for the stranger, but he was gane for the time. At last he just tried to say, "Ha! Dougal Driveower, are you living? I thought ye had been dead."

"Never fash yourself wi' me," said Dougal, "but look to yourself, and see ye tak naething frae onybody here – neither meat, drink or siller – except just the receipt that is your ain."

So saying, he led the way out through halls and trances that were weel kend to my gudesire, and into the auld oak parlour – and there was as much singing of profane sangs, and birling of red wine, and speaking blasphemy and sculduddry, as had ever been in Redgauntlet Castle when it was at the blithest.

But, Lord take us in keeping, what a set of ghastly revellers they were that sat around that table! My gudesire kend mony that had long before gane to their place, for often had he piped to the most part in the hall of Redgauntlet. There was the fierce Middleton, and the dissolute Rothes, and the crafty Lauderdale, and Dalyell, with his bald head and a beard to his girdle, and Earlshall, with Cameron's blude on his hand, and wild Bonshaw, that tied blessed Mr Cargill's limbs till the blude sprang, and Dunbarton Douglas, the twice-turned traitor baith to country and king. There was the Bluidy Advocate MacKenyie, who, for his worldly wit and wisdom had been to the rest as a god. And there was Claverhouse, as beautiful as when he lived, with his long, dark, curled locks streaming down over his laced buff coat, and with his left hand always on his right spule blade, to hide the wound that the silver bullet had made.* He sat apart from them all, and looked at them with a melancholy, haughty countenance, while the rest hallooed and sung and laughed, that the room rang. But their smiles were fearfully contorted from time to time, and their laugh passed into such wild sounds as made my gudesire's very nails grow blue, and chilled the marrow in his banes.

They that waited at the table were just the wicked serving men and troopers that had done their work and cruel bidding on earth. There was the Lang Lad of the Nethertown, that helped to take Argyll, and the bishop's summoner, that they called the Deil's Rattle-Bag, and the wicked guardsmen in their laced coats, and the savage Highland Amorites,* that shed blood like water, and mony a proud serving man, haughty of heart and bloody of hand, cringing to the rich and making them wickeder than they would be, grinding the poor to powder, when the rich had broken them to fragments. And mony, mony mair were coming and ganging, a' as busy in their vocation as if they had been alive.

Sir Robert Redgauntlet, in the midst of a' this fearful riot, cried, wi' a voice like thunder, on Steenie Piper to come to the board head where he was sitting, his legs stretched out before him, and swathed up with flannel, with his holster pistols aside him, while the great broadsword rested against his chair, just as my gudesire had seen him the last time upon earth; the very cushion for the jackanape was close to him, but the creature itsell was not there – it wasna its hour, it's likely, for he heard them say, as he came forward, "Is not the Major come yet?" And another answered, "The jackanape will be here betimes the morn." And when my gudesire came forward, Sir Robert, or his ghaist, or the deevil in his likeness, said, "Weel, piper, hae ye settled wi' my son for the year's rent?"

With much ado my father gat breath to say that Sir John would not settle without His Honour's receipt.

"Ye shall hae that for a tune of the pipes, Steenie," said the appearance of Sir Robert. "Play us up 'Weel Hoddled, Luckie'."*

Now, this was a tune my gudesire learnt frae a warlock, that heard it when they were worshipping Satan at their meetings, and my gudesire had sometimes played it at the ranting suppers in Redgauntlet Castle, but never very willingly, and now he grew cauld at the very name of it, and said, for excuse, he hadna his pipes wi' him.

"MacCallum, ye limb of Beelzebub," said the fearfu' Sir Robert, "bring Steenie the pipes that I am keeping for him!"

MacCallum brought a pair of pipes might have served the piper of Donald of the Isles.* But he gave my gudesire a nudge as he offered them, and, looking secretly and closely, Steenie saw that the chanter was of steel, and heated to a white heat, so he had fair warning not to trust his fingers with it. So he excused himself again, and said he was faint and frightened, and had not wind aneugh to fill the bag.

"Then ye maun eat and drink, Steenie," said the figure, "for we do little else here, and it's ill speaking between a fou man and a fasting."

Now, these were the very words that the bloody Earl of Douglas said to keep the king's messenger in hand while he cut the head off MacLellan of Bombie at the Threave Castle,* and that put Steenie mair and mair on his guard. So he spoke up like a man, and said he came neither to eat or drink or make minstrelsy, but simply for his ain: to ken what was come o' the money he had paid, and to get a discharge for it – and he was so stout-hearted by this time that he charged Sir Robert for conscience's sake (he had no power to say the holy name), and as he hoped for peace and rest, to spread no snares for him, but just to give him his ain.

The appearance gnashed its teeth and laughed, but it took from a large pocketbook the receipt and handed it to Steenie. "There is your receipt, ye pitiful cur – and for the money, my dog whelp of a son may go look for it in the Cat's Cradle."

My gudesire uttered mony thanks, and was about to retire when Sir Robert roared aloud, "Stop, though, thou sackdoudling son of a whore! I am not done with thee. *Here* we do nothing for nothing, and you must return on this very day twelvemonth to pay your master the homage that you owe me for my protection."

My father's tongue was loosed of a suddenly, and he said aloud, "I refer mysell to God's pleasure, and not to yours."

He had no sooner uttered the word than all was dark around him, and he sunk on the earth with such a sudden shock that he lost both breath and sense.

How lang Steenie lay there he could not tell, but when he came to himself, he was lying in the auld kirkyard of Redgauntlet parochine, just at the door of the family aisle, and the scutcheon of the auld knight, Sir Robert, hanging over his head. There was a deep morning fog on grass and gravestane around him, and his horse was feeding quietly beside the minister's twa cows. Steenie would have thought the whole was a dream, but he had the receipt in his hand fairly written and signed by the auld laird – only, the last letters of his name were a little disorderly, written like one seized with sudden pain.

Sorely troubled in his mind, he left that dreary place, rode through the mist to Redgauntlet Castle, and with much ado he got speech of the laird.

"Well, you dyvour bankrupt," was the first word, "have you brought me my rent?"

"No," answered my gudesire, "I have not, but I have brought Your Honour Sir Robert's receipt for it."

"How, sirrah? Sir Robert's receipt! You told me he had not given you one."

"Will Your Honour please to see if that bit line is right?"

Sir John looked at every line, and at every letter, with much attention, and, at last, at the date, which my gudesire had not observed: "'From my appointed place,'" he read, "'this twenty-fifth of November.' What! That is yesterday! Villain, thou must have gone to hell for this!"

"I got it from Your Honour's father – whether he be in heaven or hell, I know not," said Steenie.

"I will delate you for a warlock to the Privy Council!" said Sir John. "I will send you to your master, the Devil, with the help of a tar barrel and a torch!"

"I intend to debate myself to the Presbytery," said Steenie, "and tell them all I have seen last night, whilk are things fitter for them to judge of than a borrel man like me."

Sir John paused, composed himself and desired to hear the full history, and my gudesire told it him from point to point, as I have told it you – word for word, neither more nor less.

Sir John was silent again for a long time, and at last he said, very composedly, "Steenie, this story of yours concerns the honour of many a noble family besides mine, and if it be a leasing-making to keep yourself out of my danger, the least you can expect is to have a red-hot iron driven through your tongue, and that will be as bad as scauding your fingers wi' a red-hot chanter. But yet it may be true, Steenie, and if the money cast up, I shall not know what to think of it. But where shall we find the Cat's Cradle? There are cats enough about the old house, but I think they kitten without the ceremony of bed or cradle."

"We were best ask Hutcheon," said my gudesire. "He kens a' the odd corners about as weel as... another serving man that is now gane, and that I wad not like to name."

Aweel, Hutcheon when he was asked told them that a ruinous turret, lang disused, next to the clock house, only accessible by a ladder, for the opening was on the outside, and far above the battlements, was called of old the Cat's Cradle.

"There will I go immediately," said Sir John, and he took (with what purpose Heaven kens) one of his father's pistols from the hall table, where they had lain since the night he died, and hastened to the battlements.

It was a dangerous place to climb, for the ladder was auld and frail, and wanted ane or twa rounds. However, up got Sir John, and entered at the turret door, where his body stopped the only little light that was in the bit turret. Something flees at him wi' a vengeance, maist dang him back ower – bang gaed the knight's pistol, and Hutcheon, that held the ladder, and my gudesire that stood beside him, hears a loud skelloch. A minute after, Sir John flings the body of the jackanape down to them, and cries that the siller is fund, and that they should come up and help him. And there was the bag of siller sure eneugh, and mony orra thing besides that had been missing for mony a day. And Sir John, when he had riped the turret weel, led my gudesire into the dining parlour, and took him by the hand, and spoke kindly to him, and said he was sorry he should have doubted his word, and that he would hereafter be a good master to him to make amends.

"And now, Steenie," said Sir John, "although this vision of yours tend, on the whole, to my father's credit as an honest man, that he should, even after his death, desire to see justice done to a poor man like you, yet you are sensible that ill-dispositioned men might make bad constructions upon it concerning his soul's health. So, I think, we had better lay the haill dirdum on that ill-deedie creature, Major Weir, and say naething about your dream in the wood of Pitmurkie. You had taken ower muckle brandy to be very certain about onything, and, Steenie, this receipt" – his hand shook while he held it out – "it's but a queer kind of document, and we will do best, I think, to put it quietly in the fire."

"Od, but for as queer as it is, it's a' the voucher I have for my rent," said my gudesire, who was afraid, it may be, of losing the benefit of Sir Robert's discharge.

"I will bear the contents to your credit in the rental book, and give you a discharge under my own hand," said Sir John, "and that on the spot. And, Steenie, if you can hold your tongue about this matter, you shall sit, from this time downward, at an easier rent."

"Mony thanks to Your Honour," said Steenie, who saw easily in what corner the wind was. "Doubtless I will be conformable to all Your Honour's commands, only I would willingly speak wi' some powerful minister on the subject, for I do not like the sort of soumons of appointment whilk Your Honour's father—"

"Do not call the phantom my father!" said Sir John, interrupting him.

"Well, then, the thing that was so like him," said my gudesire. "He spoke of my coming back to see him this time twelvemonth, and it's a weight on my conscience."

"Aweel, then," said Sir John, "if you be so much distressed in mind, you may speak to our minister of the parish – he is a douce man, regards the honour of our family, and the mair that he may look for some patronage from me."

Wi' that, my father readily agreed that the receipt should be burnt, and the laird threw it into the chimney with his ain hand. Burn it would not for them though, but away it flew up the lum, wi' a lang train of sparks at its tail, and a hissing noise like a squib.

My gudesire gaed down to the manse, and the minister, when he had heard the story, said it was his real opinion that though my gudesire had gaen very far in tampering with dangerous matters, yet, as he had refused the Devil's arles (for such was the offer of meat and drink), and had refused to do homage by piping at his bidding, he hoped that if he held a circumspect walk hereafter, Satan could take little advantage by what was come and gane. And, indeed, my gudesire, of his ain accord, lang forswore baith the pipes and the brandy – it was not even till the year was out, and the fatal day past, that he would so much as take the fiddle, or drink usquebaugh or tippeny.

Sir John made up his story about the jackanape as he liked himself, and some believe till this day there was no more in the matter than the filching nature of the brute. Indeed, ye'll no hinder some to threap that it was nane o' the auld Enemy that Dougal and Hutcheon saw in the laird's room, but only that wanchancy creature the Major capering on the coffin, and that, as to the blawing on the laird's whistle that was heard after he was dead, the filthy brute could do that as weel as the laird himself, if no better. But Heaven kens the truth, whilk first came out by the minister's wife, after Sir John and her ain gudeman were baith in the moulds. And then my gudesire, wha was failed in his limbs, but not in his judgement or memory – at least nothing to speak of – was obliged to tell the real narrative to his friends, for the credit of his good name. He might else have been charged for a warlock.*

The Highland Widow*

CHAPTER I

> It wound as near as near could be,
> But what it is she cannot tell;
> On the other side it seemed to be
> Of the huge broad-breasted old oak tree.
>
> COLERIDGE*

Mrs Bethune Baliol's memorandum begins thus.*

It is five-and-thirty, or perhaps nearer forty, years ago* since, to relieve the dejection of spirits occasioned by a great family loss sustained two or three months before, I undertook what was called "the short Highland tour". This had become in some degree fashionable, but though the military roads* were excellent, yet the accommodation was so indifferent that it was reckoned a little adventure to accomplish it. Besides, the Highlands, though now as peaceable as any part of King George's dominions, was a sound which still carried terror while so many survived who had witnessed the insurrection of 1745 – and a vague idea of fear was impressed on many as they looked from the towers of Stirling northward to the huge chain of mountains which rises like a dusky rampart to conceal in its recesses a people whose dress, manners and language differed still very much from those of their Lowland countrymen. For my part, I come of a race not greatly subject to apprehensions arising from imagination only. I had some Highland relatives, knew several of their families of distinction, and, though only having the company of my bower-maiden, Mrs Alice Lambskin, I went on my journey fearless.

But then I had a guide and cicerone almost equal to Greatheart in the *Pilgrim's Progress*,* in no less a person than Donald MacLeish, the postilion* whom I hired at Stirling, with a pair of able-bodied horses, as steady as Donald himself, to drag my carriage, my duenna and myself wheresoever it was my pleasure to go.

Donald MacLeish was one of a race of post boys whom, I suppose, mail coaches and steamboats have put out of fashion. They were to be found chiefly at Perth, Stirling or Glasgow, where they and their horses were usually hired by travellers or tourists to accomplish such journeys of business or pleasure as they might have to perform in the land of the Gael. This class of persons approached to the character of what is called abroad a *conducteur*, or might be compared to the sailing master on board a British ship of war, who follows out after his own manner the course which the captain commands him to observe. You explained to your postilion the length of your tour and the objects you were desirous it should embrace, and you found him perfectly competent to fix the places of rest or refreshment, with due attention that those should be chosen with reference to your convenience, and to any points of interest which you might desire to visit.

The qualifications of such a person were necessarily much superior to those of the "first ready", who gallops thrice a day over the same ten miles. Donald MacLeish, besides being quite alert at repairing all ordinary accidents to his horses and carriage, and in making shift to support them where forage was scarce with such substitutes as bannocks and cakes, was likewise a man of intellectual resources. He had acquired a general knowledge of the traditional stories of the country which he had traversed so often, and, if encouraged (for Donald was a man of the most decorous reserve), he would willingly point out to you the site of the principal clan battles, and recount the most remarkable legends by which the road, and the objects which occurred in travelling it, had been distinguished. There was some originality in the man's habits of thinking and expressing himself, his turn for legendary lore strangely contrasting with a portion of the knowing shrewdness belonging to his actual occupation, which made his conversation amuse the way well enough.

Add to this, Donald knew all his peculiar duties in the country which he traversed so frequently. He could tell, to a day, when they would be "killing lamb" at Tyndrum or Glenuilt, so that the stranger would have some chance of being fed like a Christian, and knew to a mile the last village where it was possible to procure a wheaten loaf, for the guidance of those who were little familiar with the Land of Cakes.* He was acquainted with the road every mile, and could tell to an inch which side of a Highland bridge was passable, which decidedly dangerous.* In short, Donald MacLeish was not only our faithful attendant and steady servant, but our humble and obliging friend, and though I have known the half-classical cicerone of Italy, the talkative French *valet-de-place* and even the muleteer of Spain, who piques himself on being a maize-eater,* and whose honour is not to be questioned without danger, I do not think I have ever had so sensible and intelligent a guide.

Our motions were, of course, under Donald's direction, and it frequently happened, when the weather was serene, that we preferred halting to rest his horses even where there was no established stage, and taking our refreshment under a crag from which leapt a waterfall, or beside the verge of a fountain enamelled with verdant turf and wild flowers. Donald had an eye for such spots, and though he had, I dare say, never read *Gil Blas* or *Don Quixote*,* yet he chose such halting places as Lesage or Cervantes would have described. Very often, as he observed the pleasure I took in conversing with the country people, he would manage to fix our place of rest near a cottage where there was some old Gael whose broadsword had blazed at Falkirk or Preston,* and who seemed the frail yet faithful record of times which had passed away. Or he would contrive to quarter us, as far as a cup of tea went, upon the hospitality of some parish minister of worth and intelligence, or some country family of the better class, who mingled with the wild simplicity of their original manners and their ready and hospitable welcome, a sort of courtesy belonging to a people the lowest of whom are accustomed to consider themselves as being, according to the Spanish phrase, "as good gentlemen as the king, only not quite so rich".

To all such persons Donald MacLeish was well known, and his introduction passed as current as if we had brought letters from some high chief of the country.

Sometimes it happened that the Highland hospitality, which welcomed us with all the variety of mountain fare, preparations of milk and eggs and girdle cakes of various kinds, as well as more substantial dainties, according to the inhabitant's means of regaling the passenger, descended rather too exuberantly on Donald MacLeish in the shape of mountain dew.* Poor Donald! He was on such occasions like Gideon's fleece, moist with the noble element,* which, of course, fell not on us. But it was his only fault, and when pressed to drink *doch-an-dorroch* to my ladyship's good health, it would have been ill taken to have refused the pledge, nor was he willing to do such discourtesy. It was, I repeat, his only fault, nor had we any great right to complain, for if it rendered him a little more talkative, it augmented his ordinary share of punctilious civility, and he only drove slower, and talked longer and more pompously, than when he had not come by a drop of usquebaugh. It was, we remarked, only on such occasions that Donald talked with an air of importance of the family of

MacLeish, and we had no title to be scrupulous in censuring a foible the consequences of which were confined within such innocent limits.

We became so much accustomed to Donald's mode of managing us that we observed with some interest the art which he used to produce a little agreeable surprise by concealing from us the spot where he proposed our halt to be made, when it was of an unusual and interesting character. This was so much his wont that when he made apologies at setting off for being obliged to stop in some strange, solitary place till the horses should eat the corn which he brought on with them for that purpose, our imagination used to be on the stretch to guess what romantic retreat he had secretly fixed upon for our noontide baiting place.*

We had spent the greater part of the morning at the delightful village of Dalmally, and had gone upon the lake under the guidance of the excellent clergyman who was then incumbent at Glenorquhy,* and had heard a hundred legends of the stern chiefs of Loch Awe,* Duncan with the thrum bonnet and the other lords of the now mouldering towers of Kilchurn.* Thus it was later than usual when we set out on our journey, after a hint or two from Donald concerning the length of the way to the next stage, as there was no good halting place between Dalmally and Oban.

Having bid adieu to our venerable and kind cicerone, we proceeded on our tour, winding round the tremendous mountain called Cruachan Ben,* which rushes down in all its majesty of rocks and wilderness on the lake, leaving only a pass, in which, notwithstanding its extreme strength, the warlike clan of MacDougall of Lorn were almost destroyed by the sagacious Robert Bruce.* That king, the Wellington* of his day, had accomplished by a forced march the unexpected manoeuvre of forcing a body of troops round the other side of the mountain, and thus placed them in the flank and in the rear of the men of Lorn, whom at the same time he attacked in front. The great number of cairns yet visible, as you descend the pass on the westward side, shows the extent of the vengeance which Bruce exhausted on his inveterate and personal enemies. I am, you know, the sister of soldiers, and it has since struck me forcibly that the manoeuvre which Donald described resembled those of Wellington or of Bonaparte. He was a great man, Robert Bruce, even a Baliol must admit that,* although it begins now to be allowed that his title to the crown was scarce so good as that of the unfortunate family with whom he contended. But let that pass. The slaughter had been the greater as the deep and rapid River Awe is disgorged from the lake just in the rear of the fugitives, and encircles the base of the tremendous mountain, so that the retreat of the unfortunate flyers was intercepted on all sides by the inaccessible character of the country, which had seemed to promise them defence and protection.*

Musing, like the Irish lady in the song, "upon things which are long enough a-gone",* we felt no impatience at the slow and almost creeping pace with which our conductor proceeded along General Wade's military road, which never or rarely condescends to turn aside from the steepest ascent, but proceeds right up- and downhill, with the indifference to height and hollow, steep or level, indicated by the old Roman engineers.* Still, however, the substantial excellence of these great works – for such are the military highways in the Highlands – deserved the compliment of the poet, who, whether he came from our sister kingdom and spoke in his own dialect, or whether he supposed those whom he addressed might have some national pretension to the second sight, produced the celebrated couplet:

Had you but seen these roads *before* they were made,
You would hold up your hands, and bless General Wade.*

Nothing indeed can be more wonderful than to see these wildernesses penetrated and pervious in every quarter by broad accesses of the best possible construction, and so superior to what the country could have demanded for many centuries for any pacific purpose of commercial intercourse. Thus the traces of war are sometimes happily accommodated to the purposes of peace. The victories of Bonaparte have been without results, but his road over the Simplon* will long be the communication betwixt peaceful countries, who will apply to the ends of commerce and friendly intercourse that gigantic work which was formed for the ambitious purpose of warlike invasion.

While we were thus stealing along, we gradually turned round the shoulder of Ben Cruachan, and, descending the course of the foaming and rapid Awe, left behind us the expanse of the majestic lake which gives birth to that impetuous river. The rocks and precipices which stooped down perpendicularly on our path on the right hand exhibited few remains of the wood which once clothed them, but which had, in latter times, been felled to supply, Donald MacLeish informed us, the iron foundries at the Bunawe.* This made us fix our eyes with interest on one large oak, which grew on the left hand towards the river. It seemed a tree of extraordinary magnitude and picturesque beauty, and stood just where there appeared to be a few roods of open ground lying among huge stones which had rolled down from the mountain. To add to the romance of the situation, the spot of clear ground extended round the foot of a proud-browed rock, from the summit of which leapt a mountain stream in a fall of sixty feet, in which it was dissolved into foam and dew. At the bottom of the fall the rivulet with difficulty collected, like a routed general, its dispersed forces, and, as if tamed by its descent, found a noiseless passage through the heath to join the Awe.

I was much struck with the tree and waterfall, and wished myself nearer them – not that I thought of sketchbook or portfolio (for, in my younger days, misses were not accustomed to blacklead pencils, unless they could use them to some good purpose), but merely to indulge myself with a closer view. Donald immediately opened the chaise door, but observed it was rough walking down the brae, and that I would see the tree better by keeping the road for a hundred yards further, when it passed closer to the spot, for which he seemed, however, to have no predilection. He knew, he said, a far bigger tree than that nearer Bunawe, and it was a place where there was flat ground for the carriage to stand, which it could jimply do on these braes – but just as My Leddyship liked.

My ladyship did choose rather to look at the fine tree before me than to pass it by in hopes of a finer, so we walked beside the carriage till we should come to a point from which, Donald assured us, we might, without scrambling, go as near the tree as we chose – though he "wadna advise us to go nearer than the high road".

There was something grave and mysterious in Donald's sun-browned countenance when he gave us this intimation, and his manner was so different from his usual frankness that my female curiosity was set in motion. We walked on the whilst, and I found the tree, of which we had now lost sight by the intervention of some rising ground, was really more distant than I had at first supposed. "I could have sworn now," said I to my cicerone, "that yon tree and waterfall was the very place where you intended to make a stop today."

"The Lord forbid!" said Donald hastily.

"And for what, Donald? Why should you be willing to pass so pleasant a spot?"

"It's ower near Dalmally, my leddy, to corn the beasts: it would bring their dinner ower near their breakfast, poor things – an', besides, the place is not canny."

"Oh! Then the mystery is out. There is a bogle or a brownie, a witch or a gyre-carlin, a bodach or a fairy in the case?"

"The ne'er a bit, my leddy: ye are clean aff the road, as I may say. But if Your Leddyship will just hae patience and wait till we are by the place and out of the glen, I'll tell ye all about it. There is no much luck in speaking of such things in the place they chanced in."

I was obliged to suspend my curiosity, observing that if I persisted in twisting the discourse one way while Donald was twining it another, I should make his objection, like a hempen cord, just so much the tougher. At length the promised turn of the road brought us within fifty paces of the tree which I desired to admire, and I now saw to my surprise that there was a human habitation among the cliffs which surrounded it. It was a hut of the least dimensions and most miserable description that I ever saw even in the Highlands. The walls of sod, or "divot", as the Scotch call it, were not four feet high; the roof was of turf, repaired with reeds and sedges; the chimney was composed of clay, bound round by straw ropes, and the whole walls, roof and chimney were alike covered with the vegetation of houseleek, ryegrass and moss, common to decayed cottages formed of such materials. There was not the slightest vestige of a kaleyard, the usual accompaniment of the very worst huts, and of living things we saw nothing save a kid which was browsing on the roof of the hut, and a goat, its mother, at some distance, feeding betwixt the oak and the River Awe.

"What man," I could not help exclaiming, "can have committed sin deep enough to deserve such a miserable dwelling?"

"Sin enough," said Donald MacLeish with a half-suppressed groan, "and God He knoweth, misery enough too, and it is no man's dwelling neither, but a woman's."

"A woman's!" I repeated. "And in so lonely a place. What sort of a woman can she be?"

"Come this way, my leddy, and you may judge that for yourself," said Donald. And by advancing a few steps and making a sharp turn to the left, we gained a sight of the side of the great broad-breasted oak, in the direction opposed to that in which we had hitherto seen it.

"If she keeps her old wont, she will be there at this hour of the day," said Donald, but immediately became silent and pointed with his finger, as one afraid of being overheard. I looked, and beheld, not without some sense of awe, a female form seated by the stem of the oak, with her head drooping, her hands clasped and a dark-coloured mantle drawn over her head, exactly as Judah is represented in the Syrian medals as seated under her palm tree.* I was infected with the fear and reverence which my guide seemed to entertain towards this solitary being, nor did I think of advancing towards her to obtain a nearer view until I had cast an enquiring look on Donald, to which he replied in a half-whisper: "She has been a fearfu' bad woman, my leddy."

"Mad woman, said you?" replied I, hearing him imperfectly. "Then she is perhaps dangerous?"

"No, she is not mad," replied Donald, "for then it may be she would be happier than she is, though when she thinks on what she has done and caused to be done, rather than yield up a hair-breadth of her ain wicked will, it is not likely she can be very well settled. But she is neither mad nor mischievous – and yet, my leddy, I think you had best not go nearer to her." And then, in a few hurried words, he made me acquainted with the story which I am now to tell more in detail. I heard the narrative with a mixture of horror and sympathy, which at once impelled me to approach the sufferer and speak to her the words of comfort, or rather of pity, and at the same time made me afraid to do so.

This indeed was the feeling with which she was regarded by the Highlanders in the neighbourhood, who looked upon Elspat MacTavish (or the Woman of the Tree, as they called her) as the Greeks considered those who were pursued by the Furies* and endured the mental torment consequent on great criminal actions. They regarded such unhappy beings as Orestes and Oedipus* as being less the voluntary perpetrators of their crimes than as the passive instruments by which the terrible decrees of Destiny had been accomplished, and the fear with which they beheld them was not unmingled with veneration.

I also learnt further from Donald MacLeish that there was some apprehension of ill luck attending those who had the boldness to approach too near or disturb the awful solitude of a being so unutterably miserable – that it was supposed that whosoever approached her must experience in some respect the contagion of her wretchedness.

It was therefore with some reluctance that Donald saw me prepare to obtain a nearer view of the sufferer, and that he himself followed to assist me in the descent down a very rough path. I believe his regard for me conquered some ominous feelings in his own breast, which connected his duty on this occasion with the presaging fear of lame horses, lost linchpins, overturns and other perilous chances of the postilion's life.

I am not sure if my own courage would have carried me so close to Elspat, had he not followed. There was in her countenance the stern abstraction of hopeless and overpowering sorrow, mixed with the contending feelings of remorse and of the pride which struggled to conceal it. She guessed, perhaps, that it was curiosity, arising out of her uncommon story, which induced me to intrude on her solitude, and she could not be pleased that a fate like hers had been the theme of a traveller's amusement. Yet the look with which she regarded me was one of scorn instead of embarrassment. The opinion of the world and all its children could not add or take an iota from her load of misery, and, save from the half-smile that seemed to intimate the contempt of a being rapt by the very intensity of her affliction above the sphere of ordinary humanities, she seemed as indifferent to my gaze as if she had been a dead corpse or a marble statue.

Elspat was above the middle stature; her hair, now grizzled, was still profuse, and it had been of the most decided black. So were her eyes, in which, contradicting the stern and rigid features of her countenance, there shone the wild and troubled light that indicates an unsettled mind. Her hair was wrapped round a silver bodkin with some attention to neatness, and her dark mantle was disposed around her with a degree of taste, though the materials were of the most ordinary sort.

After gazing on this victim of guilt and calamity till I was ashamed to remain silent, though uncertain how I ought to address her, I began to express my surprise at her choosing such a desert and deplorable dwelling. She cut short these expressions of sympathy by answering in a stern voice, without the least change of countenance or posture: "Daughter of the stranger, he has told you my story." I was silenced at once, and felt how little all earthly accommodation must seem to the mind which had such subjects as hers for rumination. Without again attempting to open the conversation, I took a piece of gold from my purse, for Donald had intimated she lived on alms, expecting she would at least stretch her hand to receive it. But she neither accepted nor rejected the gift – she did not even seem to notice it, though twenty times as valuable, probably, as was usually offered. I was obliged to place it on her knee, saying involuntarily, as I did so: "May God pardon you, and relieve you!" I shall never forget the look which she cast up to heaven, nor the tone in which she exclaimed, in the very words of my old friend, John Home,

"My beautiful – my brave!"*

It was the language of nature, and arose from the heart of the deprived mother, as it did from that gifted imaginative poet while furnishing with appropriate expressions the ideal grief of Lady Randolph.

CHAPTER II

> Oh, I'm come to the Low Country,
> Och, och, ohonochie,
> Without a penny in my pouch
> To buy a meal for me.
> I was the proudest of my clan,
> Long, long may I repine;
> And Donald was the bravest man,
> And Donald, he was mine.
>
> OLD SONG*

Elspat had enjoyed happy days, though her age had sunk into hopeless and inconsolable sorrow and distress. She was once the beautiful and happy wife of Hamish MacTavish, for whom his strength and feats of prowess had gained the title of MacTavish Mhor.* His life was turbulent and dangerous, his habits being of the old Highland stamp, which esteemed it shame to want anything that could be had for the taking. Those in the Lowland line* who lay near him and desired to enjoy their lives and property in quiet were contented to pay him a small composition, in name of protection money, and comforted themselves with the old proverb that it was better to "fleech the Deil than fight him". Others who accounted such composition dishonourable were often surprised by MacTavish Mhor and his associates and followers, who usually inflicted an adequate penalty either in person or property, or both. The creagh is yet remembered in which he swept one hundred and fifty cows from Monteith in one drove, and how he placed the laird of Ballybught naked in a slough for having threatened to send for a party of the Highland Watch* to protect his property.

Whatever were occasionally the triumphs of this daring cateran, they were often exchanged for reverses, and his narrow escapes, rapid flights and the ingenious stratagems with which he extricated himself from imminent danger were no less remembered and admired than the exploits in which he had been successful. In weal or woe, through every species of fatigue, difficulty and danger, Elspat was his faithful companion. She enjoyed with him the fits of occasional prosperity, and when adversity pressed them hard, her strength of mind, readiness of wit and courageous endurance of danger and toil are said often to have stimulated the exertions of her husband.

Their morality was of the old Highland cast, faithful friends and fierce enemies: the Lowland herds and harvests they accounted their own, whenever they had the means of driving off the one or of seizing upon the other – nor did the least scruple on the right of property interfere on such occasions. Hamish Mhor argued like the old Cretan warrior:

> My sword, my spear, my shaggy shield,
>   They make me lord of all below;
> For he who dreads the lance to wield
>   Before my shaggy shield must bow;
> His lands, his vineyards must resign,
> And all that cowards have is mine.*

But those days of perilous, though frequently successful depredation began to be abridged after the failure of the expedition of Prince Charles Edward.* MacTavish Mhor had not sat still on that occasion, and he was outlawed, both as a traitor to the state and as a robber and cateran. Garrisons were now settled in many places where a redcoat had never before been seen, and the Saxon war drum resounded among the most hidden recesses of the Highland mountains. The fate of MacTavish became every day more inevitable, and it was the more difficult for him to make his exertions for defence or escape that Elspat, amid his evil days, had increased his family with an infant child, which was a considerable encumbrance upon the necessary rapidity of their motions.

At length the fatal day arrived. In a strong pass on the skirts of Ben Cruachan, the celebrated MacTavish Mhor was surprised by a detachment of the *sidier roy*.* His wife assisted him heroically, charging his piece from time to time, and as they were in possession of a post that was nearly unassailable, he might have perhaps escaped if his ammunition had lasted. But at length his balls were expended, although it was not until he had fired off most of the silver buttons from his waistcoat, and the soldiers, no longer deterred by fear of the unerring marksman who had slain three and wounded more of their number, approached his stronghold and, unable to take him alive, slew him, after a most desperate resistance.

All this Elspat witnessed and survived, for she had, in the child which relied on her for support, a motive for strength and exertion. In what manner she maintained herself it is not easy to say. Her only ostensible means of support were a flock of three or four goats, which she fed wherever she pleased on the mountain pastures, no one challenging the intrusion. In the general distress of the country, her ancient acquaintances had little to bestow, but what they could part with from their own necessities they willingly devoted to the relief of others. From Lowlanders she sometimes demanded tribute, rather than requested alms. She had not forgotten she was the widow of MacTavish Mhor, or that the child who trotted by her knee might, such were her imaginations, emulate one day the fame of his father and command the same influence which he had once exerted without control. She associated so little with others, went so seldom and so unwillingly from the wildest recesses of the mountains, where she usually dwelt with her goats, that she was quite unconscious of the great change which had taken place in the country around her, the substitution of civil order for military violence, and the strength gained by the law and its adherents over those who were called in Gaelic song "the stormy sons of the sword".* Her own diminished consequence and straitened circumstances she indeed felt, but for this the death of MacTavish Mhor was, in her apprehension, a sufficing reason, and she doubted not that she should rise to her former state of importance when Hamish Bean (or Fair-Haired James) should be able to wield the arms of his father. If, then, Elspat was repelled rudely when she demanded anything necessary for her wants, or the accommodation of her little flock, by a churlish farmer, her threats of vengeance, obscurely expressed, yet terrible in their tenor, used frequently to extort, through fear of her maledictions, the relief which was denied to her necessities, and the trembling goodwife who gave meal or money to the widow of MacTavish Mhor wished in her heart that the stern old carline had been burnt on the day her husband had his due.

Years thus ran on, and Hamish Bean grew up, not indeed to be of his father's size or strength, but to become an active, high-spirited, fair-haired youth, with a ruddy cheek, an eye like an eagle and all the agility, if not all the strength, of his formidable father, upon whose history and achievements his mother dwelt in order to form her son's mind to a similar course of adventures. But the young see the present state of this changeful world more keenly than the old. Much attached to his mother, and disposed to do all in his power for her support, Hamish yet perceived, when he mixed with the world, that the trade of the cateran was now alike dangerous and discreditable, and that, if he were to emulate his father's prowess, it must be in some line of warfare more consonant to the opinions of the present day.

As the faculties of mind and body began to expand, he became more sensible of the precarious nature of his situation, of the erroneous views of his mother, and her ignorance respecting the changes of the society with which she mingled so little. In visiting friends and neighbours, he became aware of the extremely reduced scale to which his parent was limited, and learnt that she possessed little or nothing more than the absolute necessaries of life, and that these were sometimes on the point of failing. At times his success in fishing and the chase was able to add something to her subsistence, but he saw no regular means of contributing to her support, unless by stooping to servile labour, which, if he himself could have endured it, would, he knew, have been like a death's wound to the pride of his mother.

Elspat, meanwhile, saw with surprise that Hamish Bean, although now tall and fit for the field, showed no disposition to enter on his father's scene of action. There was something of the mother at her heart, which prevented her from urging him in plain terms to take the field as a cateran, for the fear occurred of the perils into which the trade must conduct him, and when she would have spoken to him on the subject, it seemed to her heated imagination as if the ghost of her husband arose between them in his bloody tartans, and, laying his finger on his lips, appeared to prohibit the topic. Yet she wondered at what seemed his want of spirit, sighed as she saw him from day to day lounging about in the long-skirted Lowland coat, which the legislature had imposed upon the Gael instead of their own romantic garb,* and thought how much nearer he would have resembled her husband had he been clad in the belted plaid and short hose, with his polished arms gleaming at his side.

Besides these subjects for anxiety, Elspat had others arising from the engrossing impetuosity of her temper. Her love of MacTavish Mhor had been qualified by respect, and sometimes even by fear, for the cateran was not the species of man who submits to female government, but over his son she had exerted, at first during childhood, and afterwards in early youth, an imperious authority, which gave her maternal love a character of jealousy. She could not bear when Hamish, with advancing life, made repeated steps towards independence, absented himself from her cottage at such season and for such length of time as he chose, and seemed to consider, although maintaining towards her every possible degree of respect and kindness, that the control and responsibility of his actions rested on himself alone. This would have been of little consequence could she have concealed her feelings within her own bosom, but the ardour and impatience of her passions made her frequently show her son that she conceived herself neglected and ill-used. When he was absent for any length of time from her cottage without giving intimation of his purpose, her resentment on his return used to be so unreasonable that it naturally suggested to a young man fond of independence, and desirous to amend his situation in the world, to leave her, even for the very purpose of enabling him to provide for the parent whose egotistical demands on his filial attention tended to confine him to a desert in which both were starving in hopeless and helpless indigence.

Upon one occasion, the son having been guilty of some independent excursion, by which the mother felt herself affronted and disobliged, she had been more than usually violent on his return, and awakened in Hamish a sense of displeasure which clouded his brow and cheek. At length, as she persevered in her unreasonable resentment, his patience became exhausted, and, taking his gun from the chimney corner and muttering to himself the reply which his respect for his mother prevented him from speaking aloud, he was about to leave the hut which he had but barely entered.

"Hamish," said his mother, "are you again about to leave me?"

But Hamish only replied by looking at and rubbing the lock of his gun.

"Ay, rub the lock of your gun," said his parent bitterly. "I am glad you have courage enough to fire it, though it be but at a roe deer."

Hamish started at this undeserved taunt, and cast a look of anger at her in reply.

She saw that she had found the means of giving him pain. "Yes," she said, "look fierce as you will at an old woman, and your mother – it would be long ere you bent your brow on the angry countenance of a bearded man."

"Be silent, Mother, or speak of what you understand," said Hamish, much irritated, "and that is of the distaff and the spindle."

"And was it of spindle and distaff that I was thinking when I bore you away on my back, through the fire of six of the Saxon soldiers, and you a wailing child? I tell you, Hamish, I know a hundredfold more of swords and guns than ever you will, and you will never learn so much of noble war by yourself as you have seen when you were wrapped up in my plaid."

"You are determined at least to allow me no peace at home, Mother, but this shall have an end," said Hamish as, resuming his purpose of leaving the hut, he rose and went towards the door.

"Stay, I command you," said his mother. "Stay! Or may the gun you carry be the means of your ruin – may the road you are going be the track of your funeral!"

"What makes you use such words, Mother?" said the young man, turning a little back. "They are not good, and good cannot come of them. Farewell just now, we are too angry to speak together – farewell: it will be long ere you see me again." And he departed, his mother, in the first burst of her impatience, showering after him her maledictions, and in the next invoking them on her own head so that they might spare her son's. She passed that day and the next in all the vehemence of impotent and yet unrestrained passion, now entreating Heaven, and such powers as were familiar to her by rude tradition, to restore her dear son, "the calf of her heart", now in impatient resentment, meditating with what bitter terms she should rebuke his filial disobedience upon his return, and now studying the most tender language to attach him to the cottage – which, when her boy was present, she would not, in the rapture of her affection, have exchanged for the apartments of Taymouth Castle.*

Two days passed, during which, neglecting even the slender means of supporting nature which her situation afforded, nothing but the strength of a frame accustomed to hardships and privations of every kind could have kept her in existence, notwithstanding the anguish of her mind prevented her being sensible of her personal weakness. Her dwelling, at this period, was the same cottage near which I had found her, but then more habitable by the exertions of Hamish, by whom it had been in a great measure built and repaired.

It was on the third day after her son had disappeared, as she sat at the door rocking herself, after the fashion of her countrywomen when in distress or in pain, that the then unwonted circumstance occurred of a passenger being seen on the high road above the cottage. She cast but one glance at him: he was on horseback, so that it could not be Hamish, and Elspat cared not enough for any other being on earth to make her turn her eyes towards him a second time.

The stranger, however, paused opposite to her cottage, and, dismounting from his pony, led it down the steep and broken path which conducted to her door.

"God bless you, Elspat MacTavish!" She looked at the man, as he addressed her in her native language, with the displeased air of one whose reverie is interrupted, but the traveller went on to say: "I bring you tidings of your son Hamish." At once, from being the most uninteresting object, in respect to Elspat, that could exist, the form of the stranger became awful in her eyes, as that of a messenger descended from heaven expressly to pronounce upon her death or life. She started from her seat, and with hands convulsively clasped together and held up to heaven, eyes fixed on the stranger's countenance and person stooping forward to him, she looked those enquiries which her faltering tongue could not articulate. "Your son sends you his dutiful remembrance and this," said the messenger, putting into Elspat's hand a small purse containing four or five dollars.

"He is gone – he is gone," exclaimed Elspat. "He has sold himself to be the servant of the Saxons, and I shall never more behold him! Tell me, Miles MacPhadraick, for now I know you, is it the price of the son's blood that you have put into the mother's hand?"

"Now, God forbid!" answered MacPhadraick, who was a tacksman, and had possession of a considerable tract of ground under his chief, a proprietor who lived about twenty miles off. "God forbid I should do wrong or say wrong to you, or to the son of MacTavish Mhor! I swear to you by the hand of my chief that your son is well, and will soon see you, and the rest he will tell you himself." So saying, MacPhadraick hastened back up the pathway, gained the road, mounted his pony and rode upon his way.

CHAPTER III

Elspat MacTavish remained gazing on the money, as if the impress of the coin could have conveyed information how it was procured.

"I love not this MacPhadraick," she said to herself. "It was his race of whom the bard hath spoken, saying: 'Fear them not when their words are loud as the winter's wind, but fear them when they fall on you like the sound of the thrush's song.'* And yet this riddle can be read but one way: my son hath taken the sword to win that, with strength like a man, which churls would keep him from with the words that frighten children." This idea, when once it occurred to her, seemed the more reasonable, that MacPhadraick, as she well knew, himself a cautious man, had so far encouraged her husband's practices as occasionally to buy cattle of MacTavish, although he must have well known how they were come by, taking care, however, that the transaction was so made as to be accompanied with great profit and absolute safety. Who so likely as MacPhadraick to indicate to a young cateran the glen in which he could commence his perilous trade with most prospect of success, who so likely to convert his booty into money? The feelings which another might have experienced on believing that an only son had rushed forward on the same path in which his father had perished were scarce known to the Highland mothers of that day. She thought of the death of MacTavish Mhor as that of a hero who had fallen in his proper trade of war, and who had not fallen unavenged. She feared less for her son's life than for his dishonour. She dreaded on his account the subjection to strangers and the death-sleep of the soul which is brought on by what she regarded as slavery.

The moral principle which so naturally and so justly occurs to the mind of those who have been educated under a settled government of laws that protect the property of the weak against the incursions of the strong was to poor Elspat a book sealed and a fountain closed. She had been taught to consider those whom they called Saxons as a race with whom the Gael were constantly at war, and she regarded every settlement of theirs within the reach of Highland incursion as affording a legitimate object of attack and plunder. Her feelings on this point had been strengthened and confirmed not only by the desire of revenge for the death of her husband, but by the sense of general indignation entertained, not unjustly, through the Highlands of Scotland on account of the barbarous and violent conduct of the victors after the Battle of Culloden.* Other Highland clans, too, she regarded as the fair objects of plunder when that was possible, upon the score of ancient enmities and deadly feuds.

The prudence that might have weighed the slender means which the times afforded for resisting the efforts of a combined government,* which had, in its less compact and established authority, been unable to put down the ravages of such lawless caterans as MacTavish Mhor, was unknown to a solitary woman whose ideas still dwelt upon her own early times. She imagined that her son had only to proclaim himself his father's successor in adventure and enterprise, and that a force of men as gallant as those who had followed his father's banner would crowd around to support it when again displayed. To her, Hamish was the eagle who had only to soar aloft and resume his native place in the skies, without her being able to comprehend how many additional eyes would have watched his flight, how many additional bullets would have been directed at his bosom. To be brief, Elspat was one who viewed the present state of society with the same feelings with which she regarded the times that had passed away. She had been indigent, neglected, oppressed, since the days that her husband had no longer been feared and powerful, and she thought that the term of her ascendance would return when her son had determined to play the part of his father. If she permitted her eye to glance further into futurity, it was but to anticipate that she must be for many a day cold in the grave, with the coronach of her tribe cried duly over her, before her fair-haired Hamish could, according to her calculation, die with his hand on the basket hilt of the red claymore. His father's hair was grey ere, after a hundred dangers, he had fallen with his arms in his hands. That she should have seen and survived the sight was a natural consequence of the manners of that age. And better it was – such was her proud thought – that she had seen him so die than to have witnessed his departure from life in a smoky hovel, on a bed of rotten straw, like an over-worn hound or a bullock which died of disease. But the hour of her young, her brave Hamish was yet far distant. He must succeed – he must conquer, like his father. And when he fell at length, for she anticipated for him no bloodless death, Elspat would ere then have lain long in the grave, and could neither see his death struggle nor mourn over his grave-sod.

With such wild notions working in her brain, the spirit of Elspat rose to its usual pitch, or rather to one which seemed higher. In the emphatic language of Scripture, which in that idiom does not greatly differ from her own, she arose, she washed and changed her apparel, and ate bread, and was refreshed.*

She longed eagerly for the return of her son, but she now longed not with the bitter anxiety of doubt and apprehension. She said to herself that much must be done ere he could in these times arise to be an eminent and dreaded leader. Yet when she saw him again, she almost expected him at the head of a daring band, with pipe playing and banners flying, the noble tartans fluttering free in the wind, in despite of the laws which had suppressed, under severe penalties, the use of the national garb, and all the appurtenances of Highland chivalry. For all this, her eager imagination was content only to allow the interval of some days.

From the moment this opinion had taken deep and serious possession of her mind, her thoughts were bent upon receiving her son at the head of his adherents in the manner in which she used to adorn her hut for the return of his father.

The substantial means of subsistence she had not the power of providing, nor did she consider that of importance. The successful caterans would bring with them herds and flocks. But the interior of her hut was arranged for their reception; the usquebaugh was brewed or distilled in a larger quantity than it could have been supposed one lone woman could have made ready. Her hut was put into such order as might, in some degree, give it the appearance of a day of rejoicing. It was swept and decorated with boughs of various kinds, like the house of a Jewess upon what is termed the Feast of the Tabernacles.* The produce of the milk of her little flock was prepared in as great variety of forms as her skill admitted, to entertain her son and his associates, whom she expected to receive along with him.

But the principal decoration, which she sought with the greatest toil, was the cloudberry, a scarlet fruit, which is only found on very high hills, and there only in small quantities. Her husband, or perhaps one of his forefathers, had chosen this as the emblem of his family, because it seemed at once to imply by its scarcity the smallness of their clan, and by the places in which it was found the ambitious height of their pretensions.

For the time that these simple preparations of welcome endured, Elspat was in a state of troubled happiness. In fact, her only anxiety was that she might be able to complete all that she could do to welcome Hamish and the friends who she supposed must have attached themselves to his band before they should arrive, and find her unprovided for their reception.

But when such efforts as she could make had been accomplished, she once more had nothing left to engage her save the trifling care of her goats, and when these had been attended to, she had only to review her little preparations, renew such as were of a transitory nature, replace decayed branches and fading boughs, and then to sit down at her cottage door and watch the road as it ascended on the one side from the banks of the Awe and on the other wound round the heights of the mountain with such a degree of accommodation to hill and level as the plan of the military engineer permitted. While so occupied, her imagination, anticipating the future from recollections of the past, formed out of the morning mist or the evening cloud the wild forms of an advancing band, which were then called *sidier dhu** (dark soldiers), dressed in their native tartan, and so named to distinguish them from the scarlet ranks of the British army. In this occupation she spent many hours of each morning and evening.

CHAPTER IV

It was in vain that Elspat's eyes surveyed the distant path, by the earliest light of the dawn and the latest glimmer of the twilight. No rising dust awakened the expectation of nodding plumes or flashing arms; the solitary traveller trudged listlessly along in his brown Lowland greatcoat, his tartans dyed black or purple to comply with or evade the law which prohibited their being worn in their variegated hues. The spirit of the Gael, sunk and broken by the severe though perhaps necessary laws that proscribed the dress and arms which he considered as his birthright, was intimated by his drooping head and dejected appearance. Not in such depressed wanderers did Elspat recognize the light and free step of her son, now, as she concluded, regenerated from every sign of Saxon thraldom. Night by night, as darkness came, she removed from her unclosed door to throw herself on her restless pallet – not to sleep, but to watch. "The brave and the terrible," she said, "walk by night: their steps are heard in darkness, when all is silent save the whirlwind and the cataract; the timid deer comes only forth when the sun is upon the mountain's peak, but the bold wolf walks in the red light of the harvest moon." She reasoned in vain: her son's expected summons did not call her from the lowly couch where she lay dreaming of his approach. Hamish came not.

"Hope deferred," saith the royal sage, "maketh the heart sick"* – and, strong as was Elspat's constitution, she began to experience that it was unequal to the toils to which her anxious and immoderate affection subjected her, when early one morning the appearance of a traveller on the lonely mountain road revived hopes which had begun to sink into listless despair. There was no sign of Saxon subjugation about the stranger. At a distance she could see the flutter of the belted plaid that drooped in graceful folds behind him, and the plume that, placed in the bonnet, showed rank and gentle birth. He carried a gun over his shoulder, the claymore was swinging by his side, with its usual appendages, the dirk, the pistol and the *sporran mollach*.* Ere yet her eye had scanned all these particulars, the light step of the traveller was hastened, his arm was waved in token of recognition; a moment more, and Elspat held in her arms her darling son, dressed in the garb of his ancestors, and looking, in her maternal eyes, the fairest among ten thousand!

The first outpouring of affection it would be impossible to describe. Blessings mingled with the most endearing epithets which her energetic language affords in striving to express the wild rapture of Elspat's joy. Her board was heaped hastily with all she had to offer, and the mother watched the young soldier, as he partook of the refreshment, with feelings how similar to, yet how different from, those with which she had seen him draw his first sustenance from her bosom!

When the tumult of joy was appeased, Elspat became anxious to know her son's adventures since they parted, and could not help greatly censuring his rashness for traversing the hills in the Highland dress in the broad sunshine, when the penalty was so heavy, and so many red soldiers were abroad in the country.

"Fear not for me, Mother," said Hamish in a tone designed to relieve her anxiety, and yet somewhat embarrassed. "I may wear the *breacan** at the gate of Fort Augustus,* if I like it."

"Oh, be not too daring, my beloved Hamish, though it be the fault which best becomes thy father's son – yet be not too daring! Alas! They fight not now as in former days, with fair weapons and on equal terms, but take odds of numbers and of arms, so that the feeble and the strong are alike levelled by the shot of a boy. And do not think me unworthy to be called your father's widow and your mother because I speak thus, for God knoweth that, man to man, I would peril thee against the best in Breadalbane and broad Lorn* besides."

"I assure you, my dearest mother," replied Hamish, "that I am in no danger. But have you seen MacPhadraick, Mother, and what has he said to you on my account?"

"Silver he left me in plenty, Hamish, but the best of his comfort was that you were well, and would see me soon. But beware of MacPhadraick, my son, for when he called himself the friend of your father, he better loved the most worthless stirk in his herd than he did the lifeblood of MacTavish Mhor. Use his services, therefore, and pay him for them, for it is thus we should deal with the unworthy. But take my counsel, and trust him not."

Hamish could not suppress a sigh, which seemed to Elspat to intimate that the caution came too late. "What have you done with him?" she continued, eager and alarmed. "I had money of him, and he gives not that without value: he is none of those who exchange barley for chaff. Oh, if you repent you of your bargain, and if it be one which you may break off without disgrace to your truth or your manhood, take back his silver, and trust not to his fair words."

"It may not be, Mother," said Hamish. "I do not repent my engagement, unless that it must make me leave you soon."

"Leave me! How leave me? Silly boy, think you I know not what duty belongs to the wife or mother of a daring man? Thou art but a boy yet, and when thy father had been the dread of the country for twenty years, he did not despise my company and assistance, but often said my help was worth that of two strong gillies."

"It is not on that score, Mother, but since I must leave the country—"

"Leave the country!" replied his mother, interrupting him. "And think you that I am like a bush, that is rooted to the soil where it grows and must die if carried elsewhere? I have breathed other winds than these of Ben Cruachan. I have followed your father to the wilds of Ross and the impenetrable deserts of Y Mac Y Mhor.* Tush, man, my limbs, old as they are, will bear me as far as your young feet can trace the way."

"Alas, Mother," said the young man with a faltering accent, but to cross the sea—"

"The sea! Who am I that I should fear the sea? Have I never been in a birling in my life – never known the Sound of Mull, the Isles of Treshornish and the rough rocks of Harris?"*

"Alas, Mother, I go far, far from all of these. I am enlisted in one of the new regiments, and we go against the French in America."*

"Enlisted!" uttered the astonished mother. "Against *my* will – without *my* consent? You could not... you would not" – then, rising up and assuming a posture of almost imperial command: "Hamish, you DARED not!"

"Despair, Mother, dares everything," answered Hamish in a tone of melancholy resolution. "What should I do here, where I can scarce get bread for myself and you, and when the times are growing daily worse? Would you but sit down and listen, I would convince you I have acted for the best."

With a bitter smile Elspat sat down, and the same severe, ironical expression was on her features as, with her lips firmly closed, she listened to his vindication.

Hamish went on, without being disconcerted by her expected displeasure. "When I left you, dearest Mother, it was to go to MacPhadraick's house, for, although I knew he is crafty and worldly, after the fashion of the Sassenach, yet he is wise, and I thought how he would teach me, as it would cost him nothing, in which way I could mend our estate in the world."

"Our estate in the world!" said Elspat, losing patience at the word. "And went you to a base fellow with a soul no better than that of a cowherd to ask counsel about your conduct? Your father asked none, save of his courage and his sword."

"Dearest Mother," answered Hamish, "how shall I convince you that you live in this land of our fathers as if our fathers were yet living? You walk as it were in a dream, surrounded by the phantoms of those who have been long with the dead. When my father lived and fought, the great respected the man of the strong right hand, and the rich feared him. He had protection from MacAllan Mhor* and from Caberfae,* and tribute from meaner men. That is ended, and his son would only earn a disgraceful and unpitied death by the practices which gave his father credit and power among those who wear the *breacan*. The land is conquered, its lights are quenched – Glengarry, Lochiel, Perth, Lord Lewis,* all the high chiefs, are dead or in exile. We may mourn for it, but we cannot help it. Bonnet, broadsword and sporran, power, strength and wealth, were all lost on Drummossie Muir."*

"It is false!" said Elspat fiercely. "You, and suchlike dastardly spirits, are quelled by your own faint hearts, not by the strength of the enemy – you are like the fearful waterfowl, to whom the least cloud in the sky seems the shadow of the eagle."

"Mother," said Hamish proudly, "lay not faint heart to my charge. I go where men are wanted who have strong arms and bold hearts too. I leave a desert for a land where I may gather fame."

"And you leave your mother to perish in want, age and solitude," said Elspat, essaying successively every means of moving a resolution which she began to see was more deeply rooted than she had at first thought.

"Not so neither," he answered. "I leave you to comfort and certainty, which you have yet never known. Barcaldine's son is made a leader, and with him I have enrolled myself; MacPhadraick acts for him, and raises men, and finds his own in doing it."

"That is the truest word of the tale, were all the rest as false as hell," said the old woman bitterly.

"But we are to find our good in it also," continued Hamish, "for Barcaldine is to give you a shieling in his wood of Letterfindreight, with grass for your goats, and a cow, when you please to have one, on the common, and my own pay, dearest Mother, though I am far away, will do more than provide you with meal, and with all else you can want. Do not fear for me. I enter a private gentleman, but I will return, if hard fighting and regular duty can deserve it, an officer, and with half a dollar a day."

"Poor child!" replied Elspat in a tone of pity mingled with contempt. "And you trust MacPhadraick?"

"I might, Mother," said Hamish, the dark-red colour of his race crossing his forehead and cheeks, "for MacPhadraick knows the blood which flows in my veins, and is aware that, should he break trust with you, he might count the days which could bring Hamish back to Breadalbane, and number those of his life within three suns more. I would kill him at his own hearth, did he break his word with me – I would, by the great Being who made us both!"

The look and attitude of the young soldier for a moment overawed Elspat: she was unused to see him express a deep and bitter mood which reminded her so strongly of his father, but she resumed her remonstrances in the same taunting manner in which she had commenced them.

"Poor boy!" she said. "And you think that at the distance of half the world your threats will be heard or thought of! But go... go... place your neck under him of Hanover's* yoke, against whom every true Gael fought to the death. Go, disown the royal Stuart, for whom your father, and his fathers, and your mother's fathers, have crimsoned many a field with their blood. Go, put your head under the belt of one of the race of Dermid, whose children murdered... yes," she added with a wild shriek, "murdered your mother's father in their peaceful dwellings in Glencoe!* Yes," she again exclaimed, with a wilder and shriller scream, "I was then unborn, but my mother has told me, and I attended to the voice of *my* mother – well I remember her words! They came in peace, and were received in friendship, and blood and fire arose, and screams and murder!"*

"Mother," answered Hamish mournfully, but with a decided tone, "all that I have thought over; there is not a drop of the blood of Glencoe on the noble hand of Barcaldine – with the unhappy house of Glenlyon* the curse remains, and on them God hath avenged it."

"You speak like the Saxon priest already," replied his mother. "Will you not better stay and ask a kirk from MacAllan Mhor, that you may preach forgiveness to the race of Dermid?"

"Yesterday was yesterday," answered Hamish, "and today is today. When the clans are crushed and confounded together, it is well and wise that their hatreds and their feuds should not survive their independence and their power. He that cannot execute vengeance like a man should not harbour useless enmity like a craven. Mother, young Barcaldine is true and brave; I know that MacPhadraick counselled him that he should not let me take leave of you lest you dissuaded me from my purpose, but he said, 'Hamish MacTavish is the son of a brave man, and he will not break his word.' Mother, Barcaldine leads an hundred of the bravest of the sons of the Gael in their native dress, and with their fathers' arms, heart to heart, shoulder to shoulder. I have sworn to go with him. He has trusted me, and I will trust him."

At this reply, so firmly and resolvedly pronounced, Elspat remained like one thunderstruck and sunk in despair. The arguments which she had considered so irresistibly conclusive had recoiled like a wave from a rock. After a long pause, she filled her son's quaigh and presented it to him with an air of dejected deference and submission.

"Drink," she said, "to thy father's roof-tree ere you leave it for ever, and tell me, since the chains of a new king and of a new chief, whom your fathers knew not save as mortal enemies, are fastened upon the limbs of your father's son – tell me, how many links you count upon them?"

Hamish took the cup, but looked at her as if uncertain of her meaning. She proceeded in a raised voice. "Tell me," she said, "for I have a right to know, for how many days the will of those you have made your masters permits me to look upon you? In other words, how many are the days of my life? For when you leave me, the earth has naught besides worth living for."

"Mother," replied Hamish MacTavish, "for six days I may remain with you, and if you will set out with me on the fifth, I will conduct you in safety to your new dwelling. But if you remain here, then I will depart on the seventh by daybreak; then, as at the last moment, I must set out for Dumbarton,* for if I appear not on the eighth day, I am subject to punishment as a deserter, and am dishonoured as a soldier and a gentleman."

"Your father's foot," she answered, "was free as the wind on the heath – it were as vain to say to him 'Where goest thou?' as to ask that viewless driver of the clouds 'Wherefore blowest thou?' Tell me, under what penalty thou must – since go thou must and go thou wilt – return to thy thraldom?"

"Call it not thraldom, Mother: it is the service of an honourable soldier – the only service which is now open to the son of MacTavish Mhor."

"Yet say, what is the penalty if thou shouldst not return?" replied Elspat.

"Military punishment as a deserter," answered Hamish, writhing, however, as his mother failed not to observe, under some internal feelings, which she resolved to probe to the uttermost.

"And that," she said, with assumed calmness, which her glancing eye disowned, "is the punishment of a disobedient hound, is it not?"

"Ask me no more, Mother," said Hamish. "The punishment is nothing to one who will never deserve it."

"To me it is something," replied Elspat, "since I know better than thou that, where there is power to inflict, there is often the will to do so without cause. I would pray for thee, Hamish, and I must know against what evils I should beseech Him who leaves none unguarded to protect thy youth and simplicity."

"Mother," said Hamish, "it signifies little to what a criminal may be exposed if a man is determined not to be such. Our Highland chiefs used also to punish their vassals, and, as I have heard, severely. Was it not Lachlan MacIan, whom we remember of old, whose head was struck off by order of his chieftain for shooting at the stag before him?"

"Ay," said Elspat, "and right he had to lose it, since he dishonoured the father of the people even in the face of the assembled clan. But the chiefs were noble in their ire: they punished with the sharp blade, and not with the baton. Their punishments drew blood, but they did not infer dishonour. Canst thou say the same for the laws under whose yoke thou hast placed thy freeborn neck?"

"I cannot, Mother – I cannot," said Hamish mournfully. "I saw them punish a Sassenach for deserting, as they called it, his banner. He was scourged, I own it – scourged like a hound who had offended an imperious master. I was sick at the sight, I confess it. But the punishment of dogs is only for those worse than dogs, who know not how to keep their faith."

"To this infamy, however, thou hast subjected thyself, Hamish," replied Elspat, "if thou shouldst give, or thy officers take, measure of offence against thee. I speak no more to thee on thy purpose. Were the sixth day from this morning's sun my dying day, and thou wert to stay to close mine eyes, thou wouldst run the risk of being lashed like a dog at a post – yes! Unless thou hadst the gallant heart to leave me to die alone, and, upon my desolate hearth, the last spark of thy father's fire and of thy forsaken mother's life to be extinguished together!"

Hamish traversed the hut with an impatient and angry pace. "Mother," he said at length, "concern not yourself about such things. I cannot be subjected to such infamy, for never will I deserve it, and were I threatened with it, I should know how to die before I was so far dishonoured."

"There spoke the son of the husband of my heart!" replied Elspat, and she changed the discourse, and seemed to listen in melancholy acquiescence when her son reminded her how short the time was which they were permitted to pass in each other's society, and entreated that it might be spent without useless and unpleasant recollections respecting the circumstances under which they must soon be separated.

Elspat was now satisfied that her son, with some of his father's other properties, preserved the haughty masculine spirit which rendered it impossible to divert him from a resolution which he had deliberately adopted. She assumed, therefore, an exterior of apparent submission to their inevitable separation, and if she now and then broke out into complaints and murmurs, it was either that she could not altogether suppress the natural impetuosity of her temper, or because she had the wit to consider that a total and unreserved acquiescence might have seemed to her son constrained and suspicious, and induced him to watch and defeat the means by which she still hoped to prevent his leaving her. Her ardent, though selfish, affection for her son, incapable of being qualified by a regard for the true interests of the unfortunate object of her attachment, resembled the instinctive fondness of the animal race for their offspring, and diving further into futurity than one of the inferior creatures, she only felt that to be separated from Hamish was to die.

In the brief interval permitted them, Elspat exhausted every art which affection could devise to render agreeable to him the space which they were apparently to spend with each other. Her memory carried her far back into former days, and her stores of legendary history, which furnish at all times a principal amusement of the Highlander in his moments of repose, were augmented by an unusual acquaintance with the songs of ancient bards and traditions of the most approved seannachies and tellers of tales. Her officious attentions to her sons' accommodation, indeed, were so unremitted as almost to give him pain, and he endeavoured quietly to prevent her from taking so much personal toil in selecting the blooming heath for his bed, or preparing the meal for his refreshment. "Let me alone, Hamish," she would reply on such occasions. "You follow your own will in departing from your mother – let your mother have hers in doing what gives her pleasure while you remain."

So much she seemed to be reconciled to the arrangements which he had made in her behalf that she could hear him speak to her of her removing to the land of Green Colin, as the gentleman was called on whose estate he had provided her an asylum. In truth, however, nothing could be further from her thoughts. From what he had said during their first violent dispute, Elspat had gathered that, if Hamish returned not by the appointed time permitted by his furlough, he would incur the hazard of corporal punishment. Were he placed within the risk of being thus dishonoured, she was well aware that he would never submit to the disgrace by a return to the regiment where it might be inflicted. Whether she looked to any further probable consequences of her unhappy scheme cannot be known, but the partner of MacTavish Mhor in all his perils and wanderings was familiar with a hundred instances of resistance or escape by which one brave man, amidst a land of rocks, lakes and mountains, dangerous passes and dark forests, might baffle the pursuit of hundreds. For the future, therefore, she feared nothing – her sole engrossing object was to prevent her son from keeping his word with his commanding officer.

With this secret purpose, she evaded the proposal which Hamish repeatedly made that they should set out together to take possession of her new abode, and she resisted it upon grounds apparently so natural to her character that her son was neither alarmed nor displeased. "Let me not," she said, "in the same short week, bid farewell to my only son and to the glen in which I have so long dwelt. Let my eye, when dimmed with weeping for thee, still look around, for a while at least, upon Loch Awe and on Ben Cruachan."

Hamish yielded the more willingly to his mother's humour in this particular: that one or two persons who resided in a neighbouring glen, and had given their sons to Barcaldine's levy, were also to be provided for on the estate of the chieftain – and it was apparently settled that Elspat was to take her journey along with them when they should remove to their new residence. Thus, Hamish believed that he had at once indulged his mother's humour and ensured her safety and accommodation. But she nourished in her mind very different thoughts and projects!

The period of Hamish's leave of absence was fast approaching, and more than once he proposed to depart in such time as to ensure his gaining easily and early Dumbarton, the town where were the headquarters of his regiment. But still his mother's entreaties, his own natural disposition to linger among scenes long dear to him and, above all, his firm reliance in his speed and activity induced him to protract his departure till the sixth day, being the very last which he could possibly afford to spend with his mother, if indeed he meant to comply with the conditions of his furlough.

CHAPTER V

But for your son, believe it – oh, believe it –
Most dangerously you have with him prevailed,
If not most mortal to him.

CORIOLANUS*

On the evening which preceded his proposed departure, Hamish walked down to the river with his fishing rod to practise in the Awe for the last time, a sport in which he excelled, and to find, at the same time, the means for making one social meal with his mother on something better than their ordinary cheer. He was as successful as usual, and soon killed a fine salmon. On his return homeward, an incident befell him which he afterwards related as ominous, though probably his heated imagination, joined to the universal turn of his countrymen for the marvellous, exaggerated into superstitious importance some very ordinary and accidental circumstance.

In the path which he pursued homeward, he was surprised to observe a person who, like himself, was dressed and armed after the old Highland fashion. The first idea that struck him was that the passenger belonged to his own corps, who, levied by government and bearing arms under royal authority, were not amenable for breach of the statutes against the use of the Highland garb or weapons. But he was struck on perceiving, as he mended his pace to make up to his supposed comrade, meaning to request his company for the next day's journey, that the stranger wore a white cockade,* the fatal badge which was proscribed in the Highlands. The stature of the man was tall, and there was something shadowy in the outline which added to his size, and his mode of motion, which rather resembled gliding than walking, impressed Hamish with superstitious fears concerning the character of the being which thus passed before him in the twilight. He no longer strove to make up to the stranger, but contented himself with keeping him in view, under the superstition common to the Highlanders that you ought neither to intrude yourself on such supernatural apparitions as you may witness nor avoid their presence, but leave it to themselves to withhold or extend their communication, as their power may permit or the purpose of their commission require.

Upon an elevated knoll by the side of the road, just where the pathway turned down to Elspat's hut, the stranger made a pause, and seemed to await Hamish's coming up. Hamish, on his part, seeing it was necessary he should pass the object of his suspicion, mustered up his courage and approached the spot where the stranger had placed himself, who first pointed to Elspat's hut and made, with arm and head, a gesture prohibiting Hamish to approach it, then stretched his hand to the road which led to the southward, with a motion which seemed to enjoin his instant departure in that direction. In a moment afterwards, the plaided form was gone – Hamish did not exactly say vanished, because there were rocks and stunted trees enough to have concealed him, but it was his own opinion that he had seen the spirit of MacTavish Mhor, warning him to commence his instant journey to Dumbarton without waiting till morning or again visiting his mother's hut.

In fact, so many accidents might arise to delay his journey, especially where there were many ferries, that it became his settled purpose, though he could not depart without bidding his mother adieu, that he neither could nor would abide longer than for that object, and that the first glimpse of next day's sun should see him many miles advanced towards Dumbarton. He descended the path, therefore, and, entering the cottage, he communicated, in a hasty and troubled voice which indicated mental agitation, his determination to take his instant departure. Somewhat to his surprise, Elspat appeared not to combat his purpose, but she urged him to take some refreshment ere he left her for ever. He did so hastily, and in silence thinking on the approaching separation, and scarce yet believing it would take place without a final struggle with his mother's fondness. To his surprise she filled the quaigh with liquor for his parting cup.

"Go," she said, "my son, since such is thy settled purpose, but first stand once more on thy mother's hearth, the flame on which will be extinguished long ere thy foot shall again be placed there."

"To your health, Mother!" said Hamish. "And may we meet again in happiness, in spite of your ominous words."

"It were better not to part," said his mother, watching him as he quaffed the liquor, of which he would have held it ominous to have left a drop.

"And now," she said, muttering the words to herself, "go – if thou canst go."

"Mother," said Hamish as he replaced on the table the empty quaigh, "thy drink is pleasant to the taste, but it takes away the strength which it ought to give."

"Such is its first effect, my son," replied Elspat, "but lie down upon that soft heather couch, shut your eyes but for a moment and, in the sleep of an hour, you shall have more refreshment than in the ordinary repose of three whole nights, could they be blended into one."

"Mother," said Hamish, upon whose brain the potion was now taking rapid effect, "give me my bonnet; I must kiss you and begone – yet it seems as if my feet were nailed to the floor."

"Indeed," said his mother, "you will be instantly well if you will sit down for half an hour – but half an hour: it is eight hours to dawn, and dawn were time enough for your father's son to begin such a journey."

"I must obey you, Mother – I feel I must," said Hamish inarticulately, "but call me when the moon rises."

He sat down on the bed, reclined back and almost instantly was fast asleep. With the throbbing glee of one who has brought to an end a difficult and troublesome enterprise, Elspat proceeded tenderly to arrange the plaid of the unconscious slumberer, to whom her extravagant affection was doomed to be so fatal, expressing, while busied in her office, her delight in tones of mingled tenderness and triumph. "Yes," she said, "calf of my heart, the moon shall arise and set to thee, and so shall the sun, but not to light thee from the land of thy fathers, or tempt thee to serve the foreign prince or the feudal enemy. To no son of Dermid shall I be delivered to be fed like a bondswoman, but he who is my pleasure and my pride shall be my guard and my protector. They say the Highlands are changed, but I see Ben Cruachan rear his crest as high as ever into the evening sky – no one hath yet herded his kine on the depth of Loch Awe, and yonder oak does not yet bend like a willow. The children of the mountains will be such as their fathers, until the mountains themselves shall be levelled with the strath. In these wild forests, which used to support thousands of the brave, there is still surely subsistence and refuge left for one aged woman and one gallant youth of the ancient race and the ancient manners."

While the misjudging mother thus exalted in the success of her stratagem, we may mention to the reader that it was founded on the acquaintance with drugs and simples which Elspat, accomplished in all things belonging to the wild life which she had led, possessed in an uncommon degree, and which she exercised for various purposes. With the herbs, which she knew how to select as well as how to distil, she could relieve more diseases than a regular medical person could easily believe. She applied some to dye the bright colours of the tartan; from others she compounded draughts of various powers, and unhappily possessed the secret of one which was strongly soporific. Upon the effects of this last concoction, as the reader doubtless has anticipated, she reckoned with security on delaying Hamish beyond the period for which his return was appointed, and she trusted to his horror for the apprehended punishment to which he was thus rendered liable to prevent him from returning at all.

Sound and deep, beyond natural rest, was the sleep of Hamish MacTavish on that eventful evening, but not such the repose of his mother. Scarce did she close her eyes from time to time, but she awakened again with a start, in the terror that her son had arisen and departed, and it was only on approaching his couch and hearing his deep-drawn and regular breathing that she reassured herself of the security of the repose in which he was plunged.

Still, dawning, she feared, might awaken him, notwithstanding the unusual strength of the potion with which she had drugged his cup. If there remained a hope of mortal man accomplishing the journey, she was aware that Hamish would attempt it, though he were to die from fatigue upon the road. Animated by this new fear, she studied to exclude the light by stopping all the crannies and crevices through which, rather than through any regular entrance, the morning beams might find access to her miserable dwelling, and this in order to detain amid its wants and wretchedness the being on whom, if the world itself had been at her disposal, she would have joyfully conferred it.

Her pains were bestowed unnecessarily. The sun rose high above the heavens, and not the fleetest stag in Breadalbane, were the hounds at his heels, could have sped to save his life, so fast as would have been necessary to keep Hamish's appointment. Her purpose was fully attained: her son's return within the period assigned was impossible. She deemed it equally impossible that he would ever dream of returning, standing, as he must now do, in the danger of an infamous punishment. By degrees, and at different times, she had gained from him a full acquaintance with the predicament in which he would be placed by failing to appear on the day appointed, and the very small hope he could entertain of being treated with lenity.

It is well known that the great and wise Earl of Chatham prided himself on the scheme by which he drew together for the defence of the colonies those hardy Highlanders who, until his time, had been the objects of doubt, fear and suspicion on the part of each successive administration.* But some obstacles occurred from the peculiar habits and temper of this people to the execution of his patriotic project. By nature and habit, every Highlander was accustomed to the use of arms, but at the same time totally unaccustomed to, and impatient of, the restraints imposed by discipline upon regular troops. They were a species of militia, who had no conception of a camp as their only home. If a battle was lost, they dispersed to save themselves and look out for the safety of their families; if won, they went back to their glens to hoard up their booty and attend to their cattle and their farms. This privilege of going and coming at pleasure they would not be deprived of even by their chiefs, whose authority was in most other respects so despotic. It followed as a matter of course that the new-levied Highland recruits could scarce be made to comprehend the nature of a military engagement which compelled a man to serve in the army longer than he pleased, and perhaps, in many instances, sufficient care was not taken at enlisting to explain to them the permanency of the engagement which they came under, lest such a disclosure should induce them to change their mind. Desertions were therefore become numerous from the newly raised regiment, and the veteran general who commanded at Dumbarton saw no better way of checking them than by causing an unusually severe example to be made of a deserter from an English corps. The young Highland regiment was obliged to attend upon the punishment, which struck a people peculiarly jealous of personal honour with equal horror and disgust, and not unnaturally indisposed some of them to the service. The old general, however, who had been regularly bred in the German wars,* stuck to his own opinion, and gave out in orders that the first Highlander who might either desert or fail to appear at the expiry of his furlough should be brought to the halberds,* and punished like the culprit whom they had seen in that condition. No man doubted that General —— would keep his word rigorously whenever severity was required – and Elspat, therefore, knew that her son, when he perceived that due compliance with his orders was impossible, must at the same time consider the degrading punishment denounced against his defection as inevitable, should he place himself within the general's power.*

When noon was well passed, new apprehensions came on the mind of the lonely woman. Her son still slept under the influence of the draught – but what if, being stronger than she had ever known it administered, his health or his reason should be affected by its potency? For the first time, likewise, notwithstanding her high ideas on the subject of parental authority, she began to dread the resentment of her son, whom her heart told her she had wronged. Of late, she had observed that his temper was less docile, and his determinations, especially upon this late occasion of his enlistment, independently formed, and then boldly carried through. She remembered the stern wilfulness of his father when he accounted himself ill-used, and began to dread that Hamish, upon finding the deceit she had put upon him, might resent it even to the extent of casting her off and pursuing his own course through the world alone. Such were the alarming and yet the reasonable apprehensions which began to crowd upon the unfortunate woman after the apparent success of her ill-advised stratagem.

It was near evening when Hamish first awoke, and then he was far from being in the full possession either of his mental or bodily powers. From his vague expressions and disordered pulse, Elspat at first experienced much apprehension, but she used such expedients as her medical knowledge suggested, and in the course of the night she had the satisfaction to see him sink once more into a deep sleep, which probably carried off the greater part of the effects of the drug, for about sunrising she heard him arise and call to her for his bonnet. This she had purposely removed, from a fear that he might awaken and depart in the night-time without her knowledge.

"My bonnet – my bonnet," cried Hamish. "It is time to take farewell. Mother, your drink was too strong. The sun is up, but with the next morning I will still see the double summit of the ancient dun.* My bonnet – my bonnet! Mother, I must be instant in my departure." These expressions made it plain that poor Hamish was unconscious that two nights and a day had passed since he had drained the fatal quaigh, and Elspat had now to venture on what she felt as the almost perilous, as well as painful, task of explaining her machinations.

"Forgive me, my son," she said, approaching Hamish and taking him by the hand with an air of deferential awe, which perhaps she had not always used to his father, even when in his moody fits.

"Forgive you, Mother?... For what?" said Hamish, laughing. "For giving me a dram that was too strong, and which my head still feels this morning, or for hiding my bonnet to keep me an instant longer? Nay, do *you* forgive *me*? Give me the bonnet, and let that be done which now must be done. Give me my bonnet, or I go without it – surely I am not to be delayed by so trifling a want as that, I who have gone for years with only a strap of deer's hide to tie back my hair. Trifle not, but give it me, or I must go bareheaded, since to stay is impossible."

"My son," said Elspat, keeping fast hold of his hand, "what is done cannot be recalled; could you borrow the wings of yonder eagle, you would arrive at the dun too late for what you purpose – too soon for what awaits you there. You believe you see the sun rising for the first time since you have seen him set, but yesterday beheld him climb Ben Cruachan, though your eyes were closed to his light."

Hamish cast upon his mother a wild glance of extreme terror, then, instantly recovering himself, said, "I am no child to be cheated out of my purpose by such tricks as these. Farewell, Mother, each moment is worth a lifetime."

"Stay," she said, "my dear – my deceived son! Rush not on infamy and ruin. Yonder I see the priest upon the high road on his white horse: ask him the day of the month and week – let him decide between us."

With the speed of an eagle, Hamish darted up the acclivity and stood by the minister of Glenorquhy, who was pacing out thus early to administer consolation to a distressed family near Bunawe.

The good man was somewhat startled to behold an armed Highlander, then so unusual a sight, and apparently much agitated, stop his horse by the bridle and ask him with a faltering voice the day of the week and month. "Had you been where you should have been yesterday, young man," replied the clergyman, "you would have known that it was God's Sabbath, and that this is Monday, the second day of the week, and twenty-first of the month."

"And this is true?" said Hamish.

"As true," answered the surprised minister, "as that I yesterday preached the Word of God to this parish. What ails you, young man? Are you sick? Are you in your right mind?"

Hamish made no answer, only repeated to himself the first expression of the clergyman: "Had you been where you should have been yesterday" – and, so saying, he let go the bridle, turned from the road and descended the path towards the hut, with the look and pace of one who was going to execution. The minister looked after him with surprise, but although he knew the inhabitant of the hovel, the character of Elspat had not invited him to open any communication with her, because she was generally reputed a papist, or rather one indifferent to all religion, except some superstitious observances which had been handed down from her parents. On Hamish the Reverend Mr Tyrie had bestowed instructions when he was occasionally thrown in his way, and if the seed fell among the brambles and thorns of a wild and uncultivated disposition, it had not yet been entirely checked or destroyed. There was something so ghastly in the present expression of the youth's features that the good man was tempted to go down to the hovel and enquire whether any distress had befallen the inhabitants in which his presence might be consoling and his ministry useful. Unhappily he did not persevere in this resolution, which might have saved a great misfortune, as he would have probably become a mediator for the unfortunate young man, but a recollection of the wild moods of such Highlanders as had been educated after the old fashion of the country prevented his interesting himself in the widow and son of the far-dreaded robber MacTavish Mhor, and he thus missed an opportunity, which he afterwards sorely repented, of doing much good.

When Hamish MacTavish entered his mother's hut, it was only to throw himself on the bed he had left and, exclaiming "Undone – undone!", to give vent, in cries of grief and anger, to his deep sense of the deceit which had been practised on him, and of the cruel predicament to which he was reduced.

Elspat was prepared for the first explosion of her son's passion, and said to herself, "It is but the mountain torrent, swelled by the thunder shower. Let us sit and rest us by the bank – for all its present tumult, the time will soon come when we may pass it dryshod." She suffered his complaints and his reproaches, which were, even in the midst of his agony, respectful and affectionate, to die away without returning any answer – and when, at length, having exhausted all the exclamations of sorrow which his language, copious in expressing the feelings of the heart, affords to the sufferer, he sank into a gloomy silence, she suffered the interval to continue near an hour ere she approached her son's couch.

"And now," she said at length, with a voice in which the authority of the mother was qualified by her tenderness, "have you exhausted your idle sorrows, and are you able to place what you have gained against what you have lost? Is the false son of Dermid your brother, or the father of your tribe, that you weep because you cannot bind yourself to his belt, and become one of those who must do his bidding? Could you find in yonder distant country the lakes and the mountains that you leave behind you here? Can you hunt the deer of Breadalbane in the forests of America, or will the ocean afford you the silver-scaled salmon of the Awe? Consider, then, what is your loss, and, like a wise man, set it against what you have won."

"I have lost all, Mother," replied Hamish, "since I have broken my word and lost my honour. I might tell my tale, but who – oh, who would believe me?" The unfortunate young man again clasped his hands together, and, pressing them to his forehead, hid his face upon the bed.

Elspat was now really alarmed, and perhaps wished the fatal deceit had been left unattempted. She had no hope or refuge saving in the eloquence of persuasion, of which she possessed no small share, though her total ignorance of the world as it actually existed rendered its energy unavailing. She urged her son, by every tender epithet which a parent could bestow, to take care for his own safety.

"Leave me," she said, "to baffle your pursuers. I will save your life – I will save Your Honour. I will tell them that my fair-haired Hamish fell from the *corrie dhu*" (black precipice) "into the gulf, of which human eye never beheld the bottom. I will tell them this, and I will fling your plaid on the thorns which grow on the brink of the precipice, that they may believe my words. They will believe, and they will return to the dun of the double crest, for though the Saxon drum can call the living to die, it cannot recall the dead to their slavish standard. Then will we travel together far northward to the salt lakes of Kintail,* and place glens and mountains betwixt us and the sons of Dermid. We will visit the shores of the dark lake, and my kinsman – for was not my mother of the children of Kenneth,* and will they not remember us with the old love? – my kinsmen will receive us with the affection of the olden time, which lives in those distant glens, where the Gael still dwell in their nobleness, unmingled with the churl Saxons, or with the base brood that are their tools and their slaves."

The energy of the language, somewhat allied to hyperbole, even in its most ordinary expressions, now seemed almost too weak to afford Elspat the means of bringing out the splendid picture which she presented to her son of the land in which she proposed to him to take refuge. Yet the colours were few with which she could paint her Highland paradise. The hills, she said, were higher and more magnificent than those of Breadalbane – Ben Cruachan was but a dwarf to Skooroora.* The lakes were broader and larger, and abounded not only with fish, but with the enchanted and amphibious animal which gives oil to the lamp.* The deer were larger and more numerous; the white-tusked boar, the chase of which the brave loved best, was yet to be roused in those western solitudes; the men were nobler, wiser and stronger than the degenerate brood who lived under the Saxon banner. The daughters of the land were beautiful, with blue eyes and fair hair, and bosoms of snow, and out of these she would choose a wife for Hamish, of blameless descent, spotless fame, fixed and true affection, who should be in their summer bothy as a beam of the sun, and in their winter abode as the warmth of the needful fire.

Such were the topics with which Elspat strove to soothe the despair of her son, and to determine him, if possible, to leave the fatal spot on which he seemed resolved to linger. The style of her rhetoric was poetical, but in other respects resembled that which, like other fond mothers, she had lavished on Hamish while a child or a boy, in order to gain his consent to do something he had no mind to, and she spoke louder, quicker and more earnestly in proportion as she began to despair of her words carrying conviction.

On the mind of Hamish her eloquence made no impression. He knew far better than she did the actual situation of the country, and was sensible that, though it might be possible to hide himself as a fugitive among more distant mountains, there was now no corner in the Highlands in which his father's profession could be practised, even if he had not adopted, from the improved ideas of the time when he lived, the opinion that the trade of the cateran was no longer the road to honour and distinction. Her words were therefore poured into regardless ears, and she exhausted herself in vain in the attempt to paint the regions of her mother's kinsmen in such terms as might tempt Hamish to accompany her thither. She spoke for hours, but she spoke in vain. She could extort no answer save groans and sighs, and ejaculations expressing the extremity of despair.

At length, starting on her feet and changing the monotonous tone in which she had chanted, as it were, the praises of the province of refuge into the short, stern language of eager passion: "I am a fool," she said, "to spend my words upon an idle, poor-spirited, unintelligent boy who crouches like a hound to the lash. Wait here, and receive your taskmasters, and abide your chastisement at their hands, but do not think your mother's eyes will behold it. I could not see it and live. My eyes have looked often upon death, but never upon dishonour. Farewell, Hamish! We never meet again."

She dashed from the hut like a lapwing, and perhaps for the moment actually entertained the purpose which she expressed of parting with her son for ever. A fearful sight she would have been that evening to any who might have met her wandering through the wilderness like a restless spirit, and speaking to herself in language which will endure no translation. She rambled for hours, seeking rather than shunning the most dangerous paths. The precarious track through the morass, the dizzy path along the edge of the precipice or by the banks of the gulfing river, were the roads which, far from avoiding, she sought with eagerness and traversed with reckless haste. But the courage arising from despair was the means of saving the life which (though deliberate suicide was rarely practised in the Highlands) she was perhaps desirous of terminating. Her step on the verge of the precipice was firm as that of the wild goat. Her eye, in that state of excitation, was so keen as to discern, even amid darkness, the perils which noon would not have enabled a stranger to avoid.

Elspat's course was not directly forward, else she had soon been far from the bothy in which she had left her son. It was circuitous, for that hut was the centre to which her heartstrings were chained, and though she wandered around it, she felt it impossible to leave the vicinity. With the first beams of morning, she returned to the hut. Awhile she paused at the wattled door, as if ashamed that lingering fondness should have brought her back to the spot which she had left with the purpose of never returning, but there was yet more of fear and anxiety in her hesitation – of anxiety, lest her fair-haired son had suffered from the effects of her potion; of fear, lest his enemies had come upon him in the night. She opened the door of the hut gently and entered with noiseless step. Exhausted with his sorrow and anxiety, and not entirely relieved, perhaps, from the influence of the powerful opiate, Hamish Bean again slept the stern sound sleep by which the Indians are said to be overcome during the interval of their torments.* His mother was scarcely sure that she actually discerned his form on the bed, scarce certain that her ear caught the sound of his breathing. With a throbbing heart, Elspat went to the fireplace in the centre of the hut, where slumbered, covered with a piece of turf, the glimmering embers of the fire, never extinguished on a Scottish hearth until the indwellers leave the mansion for ever.

"Feeble *greishogh*,"* she said as she lighted, by the help of a match, a splinter of bog pine which was to serve the place of a candle, "weak *greishogh*, soon shalt thou be put out for ever, and may Heaven grant that the life of Elspat MacTavish have no longer duration than thine!"

While she spoke she raised the blazing light towards the bed, on which still lay the prostrate limbs of her son, in a posture that left it doubtful whether he slept or swooned. As she advanced towards him, the light flashed upon his eyes – he started up in an instant, made a stride forward with his naked dirk in his hand, like a man armed to meet a mortal enemy, and exclaimed, "Stand off! On thy life, stand off."

"It is the word and the action of my husband," answered Elspat, "and I know by his speech and his step the son of MacTavish Mhor."

"Mother," said Hamish, relapsing from his tone of desperate firmness into one of melancholy expostulation, "oh, dearest Mother, wherefore have you returned hither?"

"Ask why the hind comes back to the fawn," said Elspat. "Why the cat of the mountain returns to her lodge and her young. Know you, Hamish, that the heart of the mother only lives in the bosom of the child."

"Then will it soon cease to throb," said Hamish, "unless it can beat within a bosom that lies beneath the turf. Mother, do not blame me – if I weep, it is not for myself but for you, for my sufferings will soon be over, but yours... Oh, who but Heaven shall set a boundary to them?"

Elspat shuddered and stepped backward, but almost instantly resumed her firm and upright position and her dauntless bearing.

"I thought thou wert a man but even now," she said, "and thou art again a child. Hearken to me yet, and let us leave this place together. Have I done thee wrong or injury? If so, yet do not avenge it so cruelly. See, Elspat MacTavish, who never kneeled before even to a priest, falls prostrate before her own son and craves his forgiveness." And at once she threw herself on her knees before the young man, seized on his hand and, kissing it an hundred times, repeated as often, in heartbreaking accents, the most earnest entreaties for forgiveness. "Pardon," she exclaimed, "pardon for the sake of your father's ashes – pardon for the sake of the pain with which I bore thee, the care with which I nurtured thee! Hear it, Heaven, and behold it, Earth – the mother *asks* pardon of her child, and she is refused!"

It was in vain that Hamish endeavoured to stem this tide of passion by assuring his mother, with the most solemn asseverations, that he forgave entirely the fatal deceit which she had practised upon him.

"Empty words," she said, "idle protestations, which are but used to hide the obduracy of your resentment. Would you have me believe you, then leave the hut this instant, and retire from a country which every hour renders more dangerous. Do this, and I may think you have forgiven me; refuse it, and again I call on moon and stars, heaven and earth, to witness the unrelenting resentment with which you prosecute your mother for a fault which, if it be one, arose out of love of you."

"Mother," said Hamish, "on this subject you move me not. I will fly before no man. If Barcaldine should send every Gael that is under his banner, here and in this place will I abide them, and when you bid me fly, you may as well command yonder mountain to be loosened from its foundations. Had I been sure of the road by which they are coming hither, I had spared them the pains of seeking me, but I might go by the mountain, while they perchance came by the lake. Here I will abide my fate – nor is there in Scotland a voice of power enough to bid me stir from hence, and be obeyed."

"Here, then, I also stay," said Elspat, rising up and speaking with assumed composure. "I have seen my husband's death – my eyelids shall not grieve to look on the fall of my son. But MacTavish Mhor died as became the brave, with his good sword in his right hand – my son will perish like the bullock that is driven to the shambles by the Saxon owner who has bought him for a price."

"Mother," said the unhappy young man, "you have taken my life – to that you have a right, for you gave it – but touch not my honour. It came to me from a brave train of ancestors, and should be sullied neither by man's deed nor woman's speech. What I shall do, perhaps I myself yet know not, but tempt me no further by reproachful words: you have already made wounds more than you can ever heal."

"It is well, my son," said Elspat in reply. "Expect neither further complaint nor remonstrance from me, but let us be silent and wait the chance which Heaven shall send us."

The sun arose on the next morning, and found the bothy silent as the grave. The mother and son had arisen, and were engaged each in their separate task – Hamish in preparing and cleaning his arms with the greatest accuracy, but with an air of deep dejection. Elspat, more restless in her agony of spirit, employed herself in making ready the food which the distress of yesterday had induced them both to dispense with for an unusual number of hours. She placed it on the board before her son so soon as it was prepared, with the words of a Gaelic poet: "Without daily food, the husbandman's ploughshare stands still in the furrow; without daily food, the sword of the warrior is too heavy for his hand. Our bodies are our slaves, yet they must be fed if we would have their service. So spake in ancient days the Blind Bard to the warriors of Fionn."*

The young man made no reply, but he fed on what was placed before him, as if to gather strength for the scene which he was to undergo. When his mother saw that he had eaten what sufficed him, she again filled the fatal quaigh, and proffered it at the conclusion of the repast. But he started aside with a convulsive gesture, expressive at once of fear and abhorrence.

"Nay, my son," she said, "this time surely thou hast no cause of fear."

"Urge me not, Mother," answered Hamish, "or put the leprous toad into a flagon, and I will drink, but from that accursed cup, and of that mind-destroying potion, never will I taste more!"

"At your pleasure, my son," said Elspat haughtily, and began, with much apparent assiduity, the various domestic tasks which had been interrupted during the preceding day. Whatever was at her heart, all anxiety seemed banished from her looks and demeanour. It was but from an overactivity of bustling exertion that it might have been perceived, by a close observer, that her actions were spurred by some internal cause of painful excitement, and such a spectator, too, might also have observed how often she broke off the snatches of songs or tunes which she hummed, apparently without knowing what she was doing, in order to cast a hasty glance from the door of the hut. Whatever might be in the mind of Hamish, his demeanour was directly the reverse of that adopted by his mother. Having finished the task of cleaning and preparing his arms, which he arranged within the hut, he sat himself down before the door of the bothy and watched the opposite hill like the fixed sentinel who expects the approach of an enemy. Noon found him in the same unchanged posture, and it was an hour after that period when his mother, standing beside him, laid her hand on his shoulder and said, in a tone indifferent, as if she had been talking of some friendly visit, "When dost thou expect them?"

"They cannot be here till the shadows fall long to the eastward," replied Hamish, "that is, even supposing the nearest party, commanded by Sergeant Allan Breack Cameron, has been commanded hither by express from Dumbarton, as it is most likely they will."

"Then enter beneath your mother's roof once more – partake the last time of the food which she has prepared. After this, let them come, and thou shalt see if thy mother is a useless encumbrance in the day of strife. Thy hand, practised as it is, cannot fire these arms so fast as I can load them – nay, if it is necessary, I do not myself fear the flash or the report, and my aim has been held fatal."

"In the name of Heaven, Mother, meddle not with this matter!" said Hamish. "Allan Breack is a wise man and a kind one, and comes of a good stem. It may be he can promise for our officers that they will touch me with no infamous punishment, and if they offer me confinement in the dungeon, or death by the musket, to that I may not object."

"Alas, and wilt thou trust to their word, my foolish child? Remember the race of Dermid were ever fair and false, and no sooner shall they have gyves on thy hands than they will strip thy shoulders for the scourge."

"Save your advice, Mother," said Hamish sternly. "For me, my mind is made up."

But though he spoke thus, to escape the almost persecuting urgency of his mother, Hamish would have found it, at that moment, impossible to say upon what course of conduct he had thus fixed. On one point alone he was determined: namely, to abide his destiny, be it what it might, and not to add to the breach of his word, of which he had been involuntarily rendered guilty, by attempting to escape from punishment. This act of self-devotion he conceived to be due to his own honour and that of his countrymen. Which of his comrades would in future be trusted if he should be considered as having broken his word and betrayed the confidence of his officers? And whom but Hamish Bean MacTavish would the Gael accuse for having verified and confirmed the suspicions which the Saxon general was well known to entertain against the good faith of the Highlanders? He was, therefore, bent firmly to abide his fate. But whether his intention was to yield himself peaceably into the hands of the party who should come to apprehend him, or whether he purposed, by a show of resistance, to provoke them to kill him on the spot, was a question which he could not himself have answered. His desire to see Barcaldine and explain the cause of his absence at the appointed time urged him to the one course; his fear of the degrading punishment and of his mother's bitter upbraidings strongly instigated the latter and the more dangerous purpose. He left it to chance to decide when the crisis should arrive – nor did he tarry long in expectation of the catastrophe.

Evening approached, the gigantic shadows of the mountains streamed in darkness towards the east, while their western peaks were still glowing with crimson and gold. The road which winds round Ben Cruachan was fully visible from the door of the bothy when a party of five Highland soldiers, whose arms glanced in the sun, wheeled suddenly into sight from the most distant extremity, where the highway is hidden behind the mountain. One of the party walked a little before the other four, who marched regularly and in files, according to the rules of military discipline. There was no dispute, from the firelocks which they carried, and the plaids and bonnets which they wore, that they were a party of Hamish's regiment, under a non-commissioned officer, and there could be as little doubt of the purpose of their appearance on the banks of Loch Awe.

"They come briskly forward," said the widow of MacTavish Mhor. "I wonder how fast or how slow some of them will return again! But they are five, and it is too much odds for a fair field. Step back within the hut, my son, and shoot from the loophole beside the door. Two you may bring down ere they quit the high road for the footpath; there will remain but three, and your father, with my aid, has often stood against that number."

Hamish Bean took the gun which his mother offered, but did not stir from the door of the hut. He was soon visible to the party on the high road, as was evident from their increasing their pace to a run – the files, however, still keeping together like coupled greyhounds, and advancing with great rapidity. In far less time than would have been accomplished by men less accustomed to the mountains, they had left the high road, traversed the narrow path and approached within pistol shot of the bothy, at the door of which stood Hamish, fixed like a statue of stone, with his firelock in his hand, while his mother, placed behind him and almost driven to frenzy by the violence of her passions, reproached him in the strongest terms which despair could invent for his want of resolution and faintness of heart. Her words increased the bitter gall which was arising in the young man's own spirit as he observed the unfriendly speed with which his late comrades were eagerly making towards him, like hounds towards the stag when he is at bay. The untamed and angry passions which he inherited from father and mother were awakened by the supposed hostility of those who pursued him, and the restraint under which these passions had been hitherto held by his sober judgement began gradually to give way.

The sergeant now called to him: "Hamish Bean MacTavish, lay down your arms and surrender."

"Do *you* stand, Allan Breack Cameron, and command your men to stand, or it will be the worse for us all."

"Halt, men," said the sergeant, but continuing himself to advance. "Hamish, think what you do, and give up your gun – you may spill blood, but you cannot escape punishment."

"The scourge – the scourge, my son – beware the scourge!" whispered his mother.

"Take heed, Allan Breack," said Hamish. "I would not hurt you willingly, but I will not be taken unless you can assure me against the Saxon lash."

"Fool!" answered Cameron. "You know I cannot. Yet I will do all I can. I will say I met you on your return, and the punishment will be light – but give up your musket. Come on, men."

Instantly he rushed forward, extending his arm as if to push aside the young man's levelled firelock. Elspat exclaimed: "Now, spare not your father's blood to defend your father's hearth!" Hamish fired his piece, and Cameron dropped dead. All these things happened, it might be said, in the same moment of time. The soldiers rushed forward and seized Hamish, who, seeming petrified with what he had done, offered not the least resistance. Not so his mother, who, seeing the men about to put handcuffs on her son, threw herself on the soldiers with such fury that it required two of them to hold her, while the rest secured the prisoner.

"Are you not an accursed creature," said one of the men to Hamish, "to have slain your best friend, who was contriving, during the whole march, how he could find some way of getting you off without punishment for your desertion?"

"Do you hear *that*, Mother?" said Hamish, turning himself as much towards her as his bonds would permit – but the mother heard nothing and saw nothing. She had fainted on the floor of her hut. Without waiting for her recovery, the party almost immediately began their homeward march towards Dumbarton, leading along with them their prisoner. They thought it necessary, however, to stay for a little space at the village of Dalmally, from which they dispatched a party of the inhabitants to bring away the body of their unfortunate leader, while they themselves repaired to a magistrate to state what had happened, and require his instructions as to the further course to be pursued. The crime being of a military character, they were instructed to march the prisoner to Dumbarton without delay.

The swoon of the mother of Hamish lasted for a length of time, the longer perhaps that her constitution, strong as it was, must have been much exhausted by her previous agitation of three days' endurance. She was roused from her stupor at length by female voices, which cried the coronach, or lament for the dead, with clapping hands and loud exclamations, while the melancholy note of a lament, appropriate to the Clan Cameron, played on the bagpipe, was heard from time to time.

Elspat started up like one awakened from the dead, and without any accurate recollection of the scene which had passed before her eyes. There were females in the hut, who were swathing the corpse in its bloody plaid before carrying it from the fatal spot. "Women," she said, starting up and interrupting their chant at once and their labour, "tell me, women, why sing you the dirge of MacDhonuil Dhu* in the house of MacTavish Mhor?"

"She-wolf, be silent with thine ill-omened yell," answered one of the females, a relation of the deceased, "and let us do our duty to our beloved kinsman! There shall never be coronach cried or dirge played for thee or thy bloody wolf-burd.* The ravens shall eat him from the gibbet, and the foxes and wildcats shall tear thy corpse upon the hill. Cursed be he that would sain your bones, or add a stone to your cairn!"

"Daughter of a foolish mother," answered the widow of MacTavish Mhor, "know that the gibbet with which you threaten us is no portion of our inheritance. For thirty years the 'black tree of the law', whose apples are dead men's bodies, hungered after the beloved husband of my heart, but he died like a brave man, with the sword in his hand, and defrauded it of its hopes and its fruit."

"So shall it not be with thy child, bloody sorceress," replied the female mourner, whose passions were as violent as those of Elspat herself. "The ravens shall tear his fair hair to line their nests before the sun sinks beneath the Treshornish islands."

These words recalled to Elspat's mind the whole history of the last three dreadful days. At first, she stood fixed as if the extremity of distress had converted her into stone, but in a minute the pride and violence of her temper, outbraved as she thought herself on her own threshold, enabled her to reply: "Yes, insulting hag, my fair-haired boy may die, but it will not be with a white hand: it has been dyed in the blood of his enemy, in the best blood of a Cameron, remember that – and when you lay your dead in his grave, let it be his best epitaph that he was killed by Hamish Bean for essaying to lay hands on the son of MacTavish Mhor on his own threshold. Farewell – the shame of defeat, loss and slaughter remain with the clan that has endured it!"

The relative of the slaughtered Cameron raised her voice in reply, but Elspat, disdaining to continue the objurgation, or perhaps feeling her grief likely to overmaster her power of expressing her resentment, had left the hut, and was walking forth in the bright moonshine.

The females who were arranging the corpse of the slaughtered man hurried from their melancholy labour to look after her tall figure as it glided away among the cliffs. "I am glad she is gone," said one of the younger persons who assisted. "I would as soon dress a corpse when the great Fiend himself – God sain us! – stood visibly before us, as when Elspat of the Tree is amongst us. Ay, ay – even overmuch intercourse hath she had with the Enemy in her day."

"Silly woman," answered the female who had maintained the dialogue with the departed Elspat, "thinkest thou that there is a worse fiend on earth, or beneath it, than the pride and fury of an offended woman, like yonder bloody-minded hag? Know that blood has been as familiar to her as the dew to the mountain daisy. Many and many a brave man has she caused to breathe their last for little wrong they had done to her or hers. But her hough-sinews are cut, now that her wolf-burd must, like a murderer as he is, make a murderer's end."

Whilst the women thus discoursed together as they watched the corpse of Allan Breack Cameron, the unhappy cause of his death pursued her lonely way across the mountain. While she remained within sight of the bothy, she put a strong constraint on herself, that by no alteration of pace or gesture she might afford to her enemies the triumph of calculating the excess of her mental agitation – nay, despair. She stalked, therefore, with a slow rather than a swift step, and, holding herself upright, seemed at once to endure with firmness that woe which was passed and bid defiance to that which was about to come. But when she was beyond the sight of those who remained in the hut, she could no longer suppress the extremity of her agitation. Drawing her mantle wildly round her, she stopped at the first knoll and, climbing to its summit, extended her arms up to the bright moon, as if accusing Heaven and earth for her misfortunes, and uttered scream on scream, like those of an eagle whose nest has been plundered of her brood. Awhile she vented her grief in these inarticulate cries, then rushed on her way with a hasty and unequal step, in the vain hope of overtaking the party which was conveying her son a prisoner to Dumbarton. But her strength, superhuman as it seemed, failed her in the trial, nor was it possible for her, with her utmost efforts, to accomplish her purpose.

Yet she pressed onward, with all the speed which her exhausted frame could exert. When food became indispensable, she entered the first cottage. "Give me to eat," she said. "I am the widow of MacTavish Mhor, I am the mother of Hamish MacTavish Bean – give me to eat, that I may once more see my fair-haired son." Her demand was never refused, though granted in many cases with a kind of struggle between compassion and aversion in some of those to whom she applied, which was in others qualified by fear. The share she had had in occasioning the death of Allan Breack Cameron, which must probably involve that of her own son, was not accurately known, but, from a knowledge of her violent passions and former habits of life, no one doubted that in one way or other she had been the cause of the catastrophe, and Hamish Bean was considered, in the slaughter which he had committed, rather as the instrument than as the accomplice of his mother.

This general opinion of his countrymen was of little service to the unfortunate Hamish. As his captain, Green Colin, understood the manners and habits of his country, he had no difficulty in collecting from Hamish the particulars accompanying his supposed desertion and the subsequent death of the non-commissioned officer. He felt the utmost compassion for a youth who had thus fallen a victim to the extravagant and fatal fondness of a parent. But he had no excuse to plead which could rescue his unhappy recruit from the doom which military discipline and the award of a court martial denounced against him for the crime he had committed.

No time had been lost in their proceedings, and as little was interposed betwixt sentence and execution. General —— had determined to make a severe example of the first deserter who should fall into his power, and here was one who had defended himself by main force and slain in the affray the officer sent to take him into custody. A fitter subject for punishment could not have occurred, and Hamish was sentenced to immediate execution. All which the interference of his captain in his favour could procure was that he should die a soldier's death, for there had been a purpose of executing him upon the gibbet.

The worthy clergyman of Glenorquhy chanced to be at Dumbarton, in attendance upon some Church courts, at the time of this catastrophe. He visited his unfortunate parishioner in his dungeon, found him ignorant indeed, but not obstinate, and the answers which he received from him, when conversing on religious topics, were such as induced him doubly to regret that a mind naturally pure and noble should have remained unhappily so wild and uncultivated.

When he ascertained the real character and disposition of the young man, the worthy pastor made deep and painful reflections on his own shyness and timidity, which, arising out of the evil fame that attached to the lineage of Hamish, had restrained him from charitably endeavouring to bring this strayed sheep within the great fold. While the good minister blamed his cowardice in times past, which had deterred him from risking his person to save, perhaps, an immortal soul, he resolved no longer to be governed by such timid counsels, but to endeavour by application to his officers to obtain a reprieve, at least, if not a pardon, for the criminal, in whom he felt so unusually interested, at once from his docility of temper and his generosity of disposition.

Accordingly the divine sought out Captain Campbell at the barracks within the garrison. There was a gloomy melancholy on the brow of Green Colin, which was not lessened but increased when the clergyman stated his name, quality and errand. "You cannot tell me better of the young man than I am disposed to believe," answered the Highland officer. "You cannot ask me to do more in his behalf than I am of myself inclined, and have already endeavoured to do. But it is all in vain. General —— is half a Lowlander, half an Englishman. He has no idea of the high and enthusiastic character which in these mountains often brings exalted virtues in contact with great crimes – which, however, are less offences of the heart than errors of the understanding. I have gone so far as to tell him that in this young man he was putting to death the best and the bravest of my company, where all, or almost all, are good and brave. I explained to him by what strange delusion the culprit's apparent desertion was occasioned, and how little his heart was accessory to the crime which his hand unhappily committed. His answer was, 'These are Highland visions, Captain Campbell, as unsatisfactory and vain as those of the second sight. An act of gross desertion may, in any case, be palliated under the plea of intoxication – the murder of an officer may be as easily coloured over with that of temporary insanity. The example must be made, and if it has fallen on a man otherwise a good recruit, it will have the greater effect.' Such being the general's unalterable purpose," continued Captain Campbell with a sigh, "be it your care, reverend sir, that your penitent prepare by break of day tomorrow for that great change which we shall all one day be subjected to."

"And for which," said the clergyman, "may God prepare us all, as I in my duty will not be wanting to this poor youth."

Next morning, as the very earliest beams of sunrise saluted the grey towers which crown the summit of that singular and tremendous rock, the soldiers of the new Highland regiment appeared on the parade within the Castle of Dumbarton, and, having fallen into order, began to move downward by steep staircases and narrow passages towards the external barrier gate which is at the very bottom of the rock. The wild wailings of the pibroch were heard at times, interchanged with the drums and fifes which beat the dead march.

The unhappy criminal's fate did not, at first, excite that general sympathy in the regiment which would probably have arisen had he been executed for desertion alone. The slaughter of the unfortunate Allan Breack had given a different colour to Hamish's offence, for the deceased was much beloved, and besides belonged to a numerous and powerful clan, of whom there were many in the ranks. The unfortunate criminal, on the contrary, was little known to, and scarcely connected with, any of his regimental companions. His father had been, indeed, distinguished for his strength and manhood, but he was of a broken clan, as those names were called who had no chief to lead them to battle.

It would have been almost impossible in another case to have turned out of the ranks of the regiment the party necessary for execution of the sentence, but the six individuals selected for that purpose were friends of the deceased, descended, like him, from the race of MacDhonuil Dhu, and while they prepared for the dismal task which their duty imposed, it was not without a stern feeling of gratified revenge. The leading company of the regiment began now to defile from the barrier gate, and was followed by the others, each successively moving and halting according to the orders of the adjutant, so as to form three sides of an oblong square, with the ranks faced inwards. The fourth or blank side of the square was closed up by the huge and lofty precipice on which the castle rises. About the centre of the procession, bareheaded, disarmed and with his hands bound, came the unfortunate victim of military law. He was deadly pale, but his step was firm and his eye as bright as ever. The clergyman walked by his side; the coffin which was to receive his mortal remains was borne before him. The looks of his comrades were still, composed and solemn. They felt for the youth, whose handsome form and manly yet submissive deportment had, as soon as he was distinctly visible to them, softened the hearts of many, even of some who had been actuated by vindictive feelings.

The coffin destined for the yet living body of Hamish Bean was placed at the bottom of the hollow square, about two yards distant from the foot of the precipice, which rises in that place as steep as a stone wall to the height of three or four hundred feet. Thither the prisoner was also led, the clergyman still continuing by his side, pouring forth exhortations of courage and consolation, to which the youth appeared to listen with respectful devotion. With slow and, it seemed, almost unwilling steps, the firing party entered the square and were drawn up facing the prisoner, about ten yards distant. The clergyman was now about to retire. "Think, my son," he said, "on what I have told you, and let your hope be rested on the anchor which I have given. You will then exchange a short and miserable existence here for a life in which you will experience neither sorrow nor pain. Is there aught else which you can entrust me to execute for you?"

The youth looked at his sleeve buttons. They were of gold, booty perhaps which his father had taken from some English officer during the civil wars.* The clergyman disengaged them from his sleeves.

"My mother!" he said with some effort. "Give them to my poor mother! See her, good father, and teach her what she should think of all this. Tell her Hamish Bean is more glad to die than ever he was to rest after the longest day's hunting. Farewell, sir – farewell!"

The good man could scarce retire from the fatal spot. An officer afforded him the support of his arm. At his last look towards Hamish, he beheld him alive and kneeling on the coffin; the few that were around him had all withdrawn. The fatal word was given, the rock rung sharp to the sound of the discharge, and Hamish, falling forward with a groan, died, it may be supposed, without almost a sense of the passing agony.

Ten or twelve of his own company then came forward and laid with solemn reverence the remains of their comrade in the coffin, while the dead march was again struck up, and the several companies, marching in single files, passed the coffin one by one, in order that all might receive from the awful spectacle the warning which it was peculiarly intended to afford. The regiment was then marched off the ground and reascended the ancient cliff, their music, as usual on such occasions, striking lively strains, as if sorrow, or even deep thought, should as short a while as possible be the tenant of the soldier's bosom.

At the same time the small party which we before mentioned bore the bier of the ill-fated Hamish to his humble grave in a corner of the churchyard of Dumbarton, usually assigned to criminals. Here, among the dust of the guilty, lies a youth whose name, had he survived the ruin of the fatal events by which he was hurried into crime, might have adorned the annals of the brave.

The minister of Glenorquhy left Dumbarton immediately after he had witnessed the last scene of this melancholy catastrophe. His reason acquiesced in the justice of the sentence, which required blood for blood, and he acknowledged that the vindictive character of his countrymen required to be powerfully restrained by the strong curb of social law. But still he mourned over the individual victim. Who may arraign the bolt of Heaven when it bursts among the sons of the forest? Yet who can refrain from mourning when it selects for the object of its blighting aim the fair stem of a young oak that promised to be the pride of the dell in which it flourished? Musing on these melancholy events, noon found him engaged in the mountain passes, by which he was to return to his still-distant home.

Confident in his knowledge of the country, the clergyman had left the main road to seek one of those shorter paths which are only used by pedestrians or by men, like the minister, mounted on the small but sure-footed, hardy and sagacious horses of the country. The place which he now traversed was in itself gloomy and desolate, and tradition had added to it the terror of superstition, by affirming it was haunted by an evil spirit, termed "Cloght-dearg", that is, Redmantle, who at all times, but especially at noon and at midnight, traversed the glen, in enmity both to man and the inferior creation, did such evil as her power was permitted to extend to and afflicted with ghostly terrors those whom she had not licence otherwise to hurt.

The minister of Glenorquhy had set his face in opposition to many of these superstitions, which he justly thought were derived from the dark ages of popery, perhaps even from those of paganism, and unfit to be entertained or believed by the Christians of an enlightened age. Some of his more attached parishioners considered him as too rash in opposing the ancient faith of their fathers, and though they honoured the moral intrepidity of their pastor, they could not avoid entertaining and expressing fears that he would one day fall a victim to his temerity, and be torn to pieces in the glen of the Cloght-dearg, or some of those other haunted wilds which he appeared rather to have a pride and pleasure in traversing alone on the days and hours when the wicked spirits were supposed to have especial power over man and beast.

These legends came across the mind of the clergyman, and, solitary as he was, a melancholy smile shaded his cheek as he thought of the inconsistency of human nature, and reflected how many brave men, whom the yell of the pibroch would have sent headlong against fixed bayonets, as the wild bull rushes on his enemy, might have yet feared to encounter those visionary terrors which he himself, a man of peace, and in ordinary perils no way remarkable for the firmness of his nerves, was now risking without hesitation.

As he looked around the scene of desolation, he could not but acknowledge, in his own mind, that it was not ill chosen for the haunt of those spirits which are said to delight in solitude and desolation. The glen was so steep and narrow that there was but just room for the meridian sun to dart a few scattered rays upon the gloomy and precarious stream which stole through its recesses, for the most part in silence, but occasionally murmuring sullenly against the rocks and large stones which seemed determined to bar its further progress. In winter, or in the rainy season, this small stream was a foaming torrent of the most formidable magnitude, and it was at such periods that it had torn open and laid bare the broad-faced and huge fragments of rock which, at the season of which we speak, hid its course from the eye and seemed disposed totally to interrupt its course. "Undoubtedly," thought the clergyman, "this mountain rivulet, suddenly swelled by a waterspout or thunderstorm, has often been the cause of those accidents which, happening in the glen called by her name, have been ascribed to the agency of the Cloght-dearg."

Just as this idea crossed his mind, he heard a female voice exclaim, in a wild and thrilling accent, "Michael Tyrie – Michael Tyrie!" He looked round in astonishment, and not without some fear. It seemed for an instant as if the evil being whose existence he had disowned was about to appear for the punishment of his incredulity. This alarm did not hold him more than an instant, nor did it prevent his replying in a firm voice, "Who calls, and where are you?"

"One who journeys in wretchedness, between life and death," answered the voice – and the speaker, a tall female, appeared from among the fragments of rocks which had concealed her from view.

As she approached more closely, her mantle of bright tartan, in which the red colour much predominated, her stature, the long stride with which she advanced and the writhen features and wild eyes which were visible from under her curch, would have made her no inadequate representative of the spirit which gave name to the valley. But Mr Tyrie instantly knew her as the Woman of the Tree, the widow of MacTavish Mhor, the now childless mother of Hamish Bean. I am not sure whether the minister would not have endured the visitation of the Cloght-dearg herself, rather than the shock of Elspat's presence, considering her crime and her misery. He drew up his horse instinctively, and stood endeavouring to collect his ideas, while a few paces brought her up to his horse's head.

"Michael Tyrie," said she, "the foolish women of the clachan* hold thee as a god; be one to me, and say that my son lives. Say this, and I too will be of thy worship: I will bend my knees on the seventh day in thy house of worship, and thy God shall be my God."

"Unhappy woman," replied the clergyman, "man forms not pactions with his Maker as with a creature of clay like himself. Thinkest thou to chaffer with Him who formed the earth and spread out the heavens, or that thou canst offer aught of homage or devotion that can be worth acceptance in His eyes? He hath asked obedience, not sacrifice – patience under the trials with which He afflicts us, instead of vain bribes, such as man offers to his changeful brother of clay, that he may be moved from his purpose."

"Be silent, priest!" answered the desperate woman. "Speak not to me the words of thy white book. Elspat's kindred were of those who crossed themselves and knelt when the sacring bell* was rung, and she knows that atonement can be made on the altar for deeds done in the field. Elspat had once flocks and herds, goats upon the cliffs and cattle in the strath. She wore gold around her neck and on her hair – thick twists as those worn by the heroes of old. All these would she have resigned to the priest, all these – and if he wished for the ornaments of a gentle lady or the sporran of a high chief, though they had been great as MacAllan Mhor himself, MacTavish Mhor would have procured them if Elspat had promised them. Elspat is now poor, and has nothing to give. But the Black Abbot of Inchaffray* would have bidden her scourge her shoulders and macerate her feet by pilgrimage, and he would have granted his pardon to her when he saw that her blood had flowed, and that her flesh had been torn. These were the priests who had indeed power even with the most powerful: they threatened the great men of the earth with the word of their mouth, the sentence of their book, the blaze of their torch, the sound of their sacring bell. The mighty bent to their will, and unloosed at the word of the priests those whom they had bound in their wrath, and set at liberty, unharmed, him whom they had sentenced to death, and for whose blood they had thirsted. These were a powerful race, and might well ask the poor to kneel, since their power could humble the proud. But you! Against whom are ye strong but against women who have been guilty of folly and men who never wore sword? The priests of old were like the winter torrent which fills this hollow valley and rolls these massive rocks against each other as easily as the boy plays with the ball which he casts before him. But you! You do but resemble the summer-stricken stream, which is turned aside by the rushes and stemmed by a bush of sedges. Woe worth you, for there is no help in you!"

The clergyman was at no loss to conceive that Elspat had lost the Roman Catholic faith without gaining any other, and that she still retained a vague and confused idea of the composition with the priesthood, by confession, alms and penance, and of their extensive power, which, according to her notion, was adequate, if duly propitiated, even to effecting her son's safety.

Compassionating her situation, and allowing for her errors and ignorance, he answered her with mildness. "Alas, unhappy woman! Would to God I could convince thee as easily where thou oughtest to seek, and art sure to find, consolation, as I can assure you with a single word that, were Rome and all her priesthood once more in the plenitude of their power, they could not, for largesse or penance, afford to thy misery an atom of aid or comfort. Elspat MacTavish, I grieve to tell you the news."

"I know them without thy speech," said the unhappy woman. "My son is doomed to die."

"Elspat," resumed the clergyman, "he *was* doomed, and the sentence has been executed."

The hapless mother threw her eyes up to heaven and uttered a shriek so unlike the voice of a human being that the eagle which soared in middle air answered it as she would have done the call of her mate.

"It is impossible!" she exclaimed. "It is impossible! Men do not condemn and kill on the same day! Thou art deceiving me. The people call thee holy – hast thou the heart to tell a mother she has murdered her only child?"

"God knows," said the priest, the tears falling fast from his eyes, "that, were it in my power, I would gladly tell better tidings. But these which I bear are as certain as they are fatal. My own ears heard the death shot, my own eyes beheld thy son's death – thy son's funeral. My tongue bears witness to what my ears heard and my eyes saw."

The wretched female clasped her hands close together and held them up towards heaven like a sibyl announcing war and desolation, while, in impotent yet frightful rage, she poured forth a tide of the deepest imprecations. "Base Saxon churl!" she exclaimed. "Vile, hypocritical juggler! May the eyes that looked tamely on the death of my fair-haired boy be melted in their sockets with ceaseless tears, shed for those that are nearest and most dear to thee! May the ears that heard his death knell be dead hereafter to all other sounds save the screech of the raven and the hissing of the adder! May the tongue that tells me of his death and of my own crime be withered in thy mouth – or better, when thou wouldst pray with thy people, may the Evil One guide it and give voice to blasphemies instead of blessings, until men shall fly in terror from thy presence and the thunder of heaven be launched against thy head, and stop for ever thy cursing and accursed voice! Begone, with this malison! Elspat will never, never again bestow so many words upon living man."

She kept her word: from that day the world was to her a wilderness, in which she remained without thought, care or interest, absorbed in her own grief, indifferent to everything else.

With her mode of life, or rather of existence, the reader is already as far acquainted as I have the power of making him. Of her death, I can tell him nothing. It is supposed to have happened several years after she had attracted the attention of my excellent friend, Mrs Bethune Baliol. Her benevolence, which was never satisfied with dropping a sentimental tear when there was room for the operation of effective charity, induced her to make various attempts to alleviate the condition of this most wretched woman. But all her exertions could only render Elspat's means of subsistence less precarious – a circumstance which, though generally interesting even to the most wretched outcasts, seemed to her a matter of total indifference. Every attempt to place any person in her hut to take charge of her miscarried, through the extreme resentment with which she regarded all intrusion on her solitude, or by the timidity of those who had been pitched upon to be inmates with the terrible Woman of the Tree. At length, when Elspat became totally unable (in appearance, at least) to turn herself on the wretched settle which served her for a couch, the humanity of Mr Tyrie's successor sent two women to attend upon the last moments of the solitary, which could not, it was judged, be far distant, and to avert the possibility that she might perish for want of assistance or food before she sank under the effects of extreme age or mortal malady.

It was on a November evening that the two women appointed for this melancholy purpose arrived at the miserable cottage which we have already described. Its wretched inmate lay stretched upon the bed, and seemed almost already a lifeless corpse, save for the wandering of the fierce dark eyes, which rolled in their sockets in a manner terrible to look upon, and seemed to watch with surprise and indignation the motions of the strangers, as persons whose presence was alike unexpected and unwelcome. They were frightened at her looks, but, assured in each other's company, they kindled a fire, lighted a candle, prepared food and made other arrangements for the discharge of the duty assigned them.

The assistants agreed they should watch the bedside of the sick person by turns, but, about midnight, overcome by fatigue, for they had walked far that morning, both of them fell fast asleep. When they awoke, which was not till after the interval of some hours, the hut was empty and the patient gone. They rose in terror, and went to the door of the cottage, which was latched as it had been at night. They looked out into the darkness, and called upon their charge by her name. The night raven screamed from the old oak tree, the fox howled on the hill, the hoarse waterfall replied with its echoes – but there was no human answer. The terrified women did not dare to make further search till morning should appear, for the sudden disappearance of a creature so frail as Elspat, together with the wild tenor of her history, intimidated them from stirring from the hut. They remained, therefore, in dreadful terror, sometimes thinking they heard her voice without, and at other times that sounds of a different description were mingled with the mournful sigh of the night breeze, or the dash of the cascade. Sometimes, too, the latch rattled, as if some frail and impotent hand were in vain attempting to lift it, and ever and anon they expected the entrance of their terrible patient, animated by supernatural strength, and in the company, perhaps, of some being more dreadful than herself. Morning came at length. They sought brake, rock and thicket in vain. Two hours after daylight, the minister himself appeared, and, on the report of the watchers, caused the country to be alarmed, and a general and exact search to be made through the whole neighbourhood of the cottage and the oak tree. But it was all in vain. Elspat MacTavish was never found, whether dead or alive – nor could there ever be traced the slightest circumstance to indicate her fate.

The neighbourhood was divided concerning the cause of her disappearance. The credulous thought that the evil spirit under whose influence she seemed to have acted had carried her away in the body, and there are many who are still unwilling, at untimely hours, to pass the oak tree, beneath which, as they allege, she may still be seen seated according to her wont. Others less superstitious supposed that, had it been possible to search the gulf of the *corrie dhu*, the profound deeps of the lake or the whelming eddies of the river, the remains of Elspat MacTavish might have been discovered, as nothing was more natural, considering her state of body and mind, than that she should have fallen in by accident or precipitated herself intentionally into one or other of those places of sure destruction. The clergyman entertained an opinion of his own. He thought that, impatient of the watch which was placed over her, this unhappy woman's instinct had taught her, as it directs various domestic animals, to withdraw herself from the sight of her own race, that the death struggle might take place in some secret den, where, in all probability, her mortal relics would never meet the eyes of mortals. This species of instinctive feeling seemed to him of a tenor with the whole course of her unhappy life, and most likely to influence her when it drew to a conclusion.

The Two Drovers*

INTRODUCTORY

MR CROFTANGRY INTRODUCES ANOTHER TALE*

> Together both on the high lawns appeared.
> Under the opening eyelids of the morn
> They drove afield.
>
> ELEGY ON LYCIDAS*

I have sometimes wondered why all the favourite occupations and pastimes of mankind go to the disturbance of that happy state of tranquillity, that *otium*, as Horace terms it,* which he says is the object of all men's prayers, whether preferred from sea or land, and that the undisturbed repose of which we are so tenacious when duty or necessity compels us to abandon it is precisely what we long to exchange for a state of excitation, as soon as we may prolong it at our own pleasure. Briefly, you have only to say to a man "Remain at rest", and you instantly inspire the love of labour. The sportsman toils like his gamekeeper, the master of the pack takes as severe exercise as his whipper-in, the statesman or politician drudges more than the professional lawyer – and, to come to my own case, the volunteer author subjects himself to the risk of painful criticism and the assured certainty of mental and manual labour just as completely as his needy brother whose necessities compel him to assume the pen.

These reflections have been suggested by an annunciation, on the part of Janet, that the "little gillie-whitefoot"* was come from the printing office.

"Gillie-blackfoot you should call him, Janet," was my response, "for he is neither more nor less than an imp of the devil, come to torment me for 'copy', for so the printers call a supply of manuscript for the press."

"Now, Cot forgie Your Honour," said Janet, "for it is no like your ainsell to give such names to a faitherless bairn."

"I have got nothing else to give him, Janet – he must wait a little."

"Then I have got some breakfast to give the bit gillie," said Janet, "and he can wait by the fireside in the kitchen till Your Honour's ready, and cood enough for the like of him, if he was to wait Your Honour's pleasure all day."

"But, Janet," said I to my little active superintendent on her return to the parlour, after having made her hospitable arrangements, "I begin to find this writing our chronicles is rather more tiresome than I expected, for here comes this little fellow to ask for manuscript – that is, for something to print – and I have got none to give him."

"Your Honour can be at nae loss: I have seen you write fast and fast enough – and for subjects you have the whole Highlands to write about, and I am sure you know a hundred tales better than that about Hamish MacTavish, for it was but about a young cateran and an auld carline, when all's done, and if they had burnt the rudas quean for a witch, I am thinking, maybe, they would not have tyned their coals, and her to gar her neer-do-well son shoot a gentleman Cameron! I am third cousin to the Camerons mysell: my blood warms to them. And if you want to write about deserters, I am sure there were deserters enough on the top of Arthur's Seat when the MacRaas broke out, and on that woeful day beside Leith Pier* – ohonari!"

Here Janet began to weep and to wipe her eyes with her apron. For my part, the idea I wanted was supplied, but I hesitated to make use of it. Topics, like times, are apt to become common by frequent use. It is only an ass like Justice Shallow who would pitch upon "the overscutched tunes which the carmen whistled" and try to pass them off as his "fancies and his goodnights".* Now, the Highlands, though formerly a rich mine for original matter, are, as my friend Mrs Bethune Baliol warned me, in some degree worn out by the incessant labour of modern romancers and novelists, who, finding in those remote regions primitive habits and manners, have vainly imagined that the public can never tire of them, and so kilted Highlanders are to be found as frequently, and nearly of as genuine descent, on the shelves of a circulating library as at a Caledonian ball. Much might have been made at an earlier time out of the history of a Highland regiment and the singular revolution of ideas which must have taken place in the minds of those who composed it when exchanging their native hills for the battlefields of the Continent and their simple, and sometimes indolent, domestic habits for the regular exertions demanded by modern discipline. But the market is forestalled. There is Mrs Grant of Laggan has drawn the manners, customs and superstitions of the mountains in their natural, unsophisticated state,* and my friend General Stewart of

Garth,* in giving the real history of the Highland regiments, has rendered any attempt to fill up the sketch with fancy-colouring extremely rash and precarious. Yet I, too, have still a lingering fancy to add a stone to the cairn, and without calling in imagination to aid the impressions of juvenile recollection, I may just attempt to embody one or two scenes illustrative of the Highland character, and which belong peculiarly to the *Chronicles of the Canongate*, to the grey-headed eld of whom they are as familiar as to Chrystal Croftangry. Yet I will not go back to the days of clanship and claymores.* Have at you, gentle reader, with a tale of two drovers.* An oyster may be crossed in love, says the gentle Tilburnia,* and a drover may be touched on a point of honour, says the Chronicler of the Canongate.

CHAPTER I

It was the day after Doune Fair* when my story commences. It had been a brisk market: several dealers had attended from the northern and Midland counties in England, and English money had flown so merrily about as to gladden the hearts of the Highland farmers. Many large droves were about to set off for England, under the protection of their owners, or of the topsmen whom they employed in the tedious, laborious and responsible office of driving the cattle for many hundred miles from the market where they had been purchased to the fields or farmyards where they were to be fattened for the shambles.

The Highlanders in particular are masters of this difficult trade of driving, which seems to suit them as well as the trade of war. It affords exercise for all their habits of patient endurance and active exertion. They are required to know perfectly the drove roads, which lie over the wildest tracts of the country, and to avoid as much as possible the highways, which distress the feet of the bullocks, and the turnpikes, which annoy the spirit of the drover, whereas on the broad green or grey track which leads across the pathless moor the herd not only move at ease and without taxation, but, if they mind their business, may pick up a mouthful of food by the way. At night, the drovers usually sleep along with their cattle, let the weather be what it will, and many of these hardy men do not once rest under a roof during a journey on foot from Lochaber to Lincolnshire. They are paid very highly, for the trust reposed is of the last importance, as it depends on their prudence, vigilance and honesty whether the cattle reach the final market in good order and afford a profit to the grazier. But, as they maintain themselves at their own expense, they are especially economical in that particular. At the period we speak of, a Highland drover was victualled for his long and toilsome journey with a few handfuls of oatmeal and two or three onions, renewed from time to time, and a ram's horn filled with whisky, which he used regularly, but sparingly, every night and morning. His dirk, or *skene-dhu* (i.e. "black knife"), so worn as to be concealed beneath the arm or by the folds of the plaid, was his only weapon, excepting the cudgel with which he directed the movements of the cattle. A Highlander was never so happy as on these occasions. There was a variety in the whole journey which exercised the Celt's natural curiosity and love of motion; there were the constant change of place and scene, the petty adventures incidental to the traffic, and the intercourse with the various farmers, graziers and traders, intermingled with occasional merry-makings, not the less acceptable to Donald* that they were void of expense – and there was the consciousness of superior skill, for the Highlander, a child amongst flocks, is a prince amongst herds,* and his natural habits induce him to disdain the shepherd's slothful life, so that he feels himself nowhere more at home than when following a gallant drove of his country cattle in the character of their guardian.

Of the number who left Doune in the morning, and with the purpose we have described, not a *glunamie* of them all cocked his bonnet more briskly, or gartered his tartan hose under knee over a pair of more promising *spiogs* (legs), than did Robin Oig McCombich, called familiarly Robin Oig – that is, Young (or the Lesser) Robin. Though small of stature, as the epithet "Oig" implies, and not very strongly limbed, he was as light and alert as one of the deer of his mountains. He had an elasticity of step which, in the course of a long march, made many a stout fellow envy him, and the manner in which he busked his plaid and adjusted his bonnet argued a consciousness that so smart a John Highlandman as himself would not pass unnoticed among the Lowland lasses. The ruddy cheek, red lips and white teeth set off a countenance which had gained by exposure to the weather a healthful and hardy rather than a rugged hue. If Robin Oig did not laugh or even smile frequently, as indeed is not the practice among his countrymen, his bright eyes usually gleamed from under his bonnet with an expression of cheerfulness ready to be turned into mirth.

The departure of Robin Oig was an incident in the little town, in and near which he had many friends, male and female. He was a topping person in his way, transacted considerable business on his own behalf, and was entrusted by the best farmers in the Highlands, in preference to any other drover in that district. He might have increased his business to any extent, had he condescended to manage it by deputy, but, except a lad or two, sister's sons of his own, Robin rejected the idea of assistance, conscious perhaps how much his reputation depended upon his attending in person to the practical discharge of his duty in every instance. He remained, therefore, contented with the highest premium given to persons of his description, and comforted himself with the hopes that a few journeys to England might enable him to conduct business on his own account in a manner becoming his birth. For Robin Oig's father, Lachlan McCombich, or "son of my friend" (his actual clan surname being McGregor), had been so called by the celebrated Rob Roy,* because of the particular friendship which had subsisted between the grandsire of Robin and that renowned cateran. Some people even say that Robin Oig derived his Christian name from one as renowned in the wilds of Loch Lomond as ever was his namesake, Robin Hood, in the precincts of merry Sherwood. "Of such ancestry," as James Boswell says, "who would not be proud?"* Robin Oig was proud accordingly, but his frequent visits to England and to the Lowlands had given him tact enough to know that pretensions which still gave him a little right to distinction in his own lonely glen might be both obnoxious and ridiculous if preferred elsewhere. The pride of birth, therefore, was like the miser's treasure: the secret subject of his contemplation, but never exhibited to strangers as a subject of boasting.

Many were the words of gratulation and good luck which were bestowed on Robin Oig. The judges commended his drove, especially Robin's own property, which were the best of them. Some thrust out their snuff-mulls for the parting pinch; others tendered the *doch-an-dorroch*, or parting cup. All cried: "Good luck travel out with you and come home with you. Give you luck in the Saxon market – brave notes in the *leabhar-dhu*" (black pocketbook) "and plenty of English gold in the *sporran*" (pouch of goatskin).

The bonny lasses made their adieus more modestly, and more than one, it was said, would have given her best brooch to be certain that it was upon her that his eye last rested as he turned towards the road.

Robin Oig had just given the preliminary "Hoo – hoo!" to urge forward the loiterers of the drove when there was a cry behind him.

"Stay, Robin – bide a blink. Here is Janet of Tomahourich – auld Janet, your father's sister."

"Plague on her, for an auld Highland witch and spaewife," said a farmer from the Carse of Stirling. "She'll cast some of her cantrips on the cattle."

"She canna do that," said another sapient of the same profession. "Robin Oig is not the lad to leave any of them without tying St Mungo's knot on their tails,* and that will put to her speed the best witch that ever flew over Dimayet* upon a broomstick."

It may not be indifferent to the reader to know that the Highland cattle are peculiarly liable to be "taken", or infected, by spells and witchcraft, which judicious people guard against by knitting knots of peculiar complexity on the tuft of hair which terminates the animal's tail.

But the old woman who was the object of the farmer's suspicion seemed only busied about the drover, without paying any attention to the drove. Robin, on the contrary, appeared rather impatient of her presence.

"What auld-world fancy," he said, "has brought you so early from the ingleside this morning, muhme? I am sure I bid you good even and had your Godspeed last night."

"And left me more siller than the useless old woman will use till you come back again, bird of my bosom," said the sibyl. "But it is little I would care for the food that nourishes me or the fire that warms me, or for God's blessed sun itself, if aught but weal should happen to the grandson of my father. So let me walk the *deasil* round you,* that you may go safe out into the far foreign land and come safe home."

Robin Oig stopped, half embarrassed, half laughing, and signing to those around that he only complied with the old woman to soothe her humour. In the mean time, she traced around him, with wavering steps, the propitiation which some have thought has been derived from the Druidical mythology.* It consists, as is well known, in the person who makes the *deasil* walking three times round the person who is the object of the ceremony, taking care to move according to the course of the sun. At once, however, she stopped short and exclaimed, in a voice of alarm and horror, "Grandson of my father, there is blood on your hand."

"Hush, for God's sake, Aunt," said Robin Oig. "You will bring more trouble on yourself with this *taishataragh*" (second sight) "than you will be able to get out of for many a day."

The old woman only repeated, with a ghastly look, "There is blood on your hand, and it is English blood. The blood of the Gael is richer and redder. Let us see – let us…"

Ere Robin Oig could prevent her – which, indeed, could only have been by positive violence, so hasty and peremptory were her proceedings – she had drawn from his side the dirk which lodged in the folds of his plaid and held it up, exclaiming, although the weapon gleamed clear and bright in the sun, "Blood, blood – Saxon blood again. Robin Oig McCombich, go not this day to England!"

"Prutt, trutt," answered Robin Oig, "that will never do neither – it would be next thing to running the country.* For shame, muhme, give me the dirk. You cannot tell by the colour the difference betwixt the blood of a black bullock and a white one, and you speak of knowing Saxon from Gaelic blood. All men have their blood from Adam, muhme. Give me my *skene-dhu*, and let me go on my road. I should have been halfway to Stirling brig by this time. Give me my dirk and let me go."

"Never will I give it to you," said the old woman. "Never will I quit my hold on your plaid, unless you promise me not to wear that unhappy weapon."

The women around him urged him also, saying few of his aunt's words fell to the ground,* and as the Lowland farmers continued to look moodily on the scene, Robin Oig determined to close it at any sacrifice.

"Well, then," said the young drover, giving the scabbard of the weapon to Hugh Morrison, "you Lowlanders care nothing for these freats. Keep my dirk for me. I cannot give it you, because it was my father's, but your drove follows ours, and I am content it should be in your keeping, not in mine. Will this do, muhme?"

"It must," said the old woman, "that is, if the Lowlander is mad enough to carry the knife."

The strong westlandman laughed aloud.

"Goodwife," said he, "I am Hugh Morrison from Glenae,* come of the Manly Morrisons of auld lang syne, that never took short weapon against a man in their lives. And neither needed they: they had their broadswords, and I have this bit supple" – showing a formidable cudgel. "For dirking ower the board,* I leave that to John Highlandman. Ye needna snort, none of you Highlanders, and you in especial, Robin. I'll keep the bit knife, if you are feared for the auld spaewife's tale, and give it back to you whenever you want it."

Robin was not particularly pleased with some part of Hugh Morrison's speech, but he had learnt in his travels more patience than belonged to his Highland constitution originally, and he accepted the service of the descendant of the Manly Morrisons without finding fault with the rather depreciating manner in which it was offered.

"If he had not had his morning in his head, and been but a Dumfriesshire hog into the boot, he would have spoken more like a gentleman. But you cannot have more of a sow than a grumph.* It's shame my father's knife should ever slash a haggis for the like of him."

Thus saying, but saying it in Gaelic, Robin drove on his cattle and waved farewell to all behind him. He was in the greater haste because he expected to join at Falkirk a comrade and brother in profession, with whom he proposed to travel in company.

Robin Oig's chosen friend was a young Englishman, Harry Wakefield by name, well known at every northern market, and in his way as much famed and honoured as our Highland driver of bullocks. He was nearly six feet high, gallantly formed to keep the rounds at Smithfield or maintain the ring at a wrestling match, and although he might have been overmatched, perhaps, among the regular professors of the fancy,* yet, as a yokel or rustic, or a chance customer, he was able to give a bellyful to any amateur of the pugilistic art. Doncaster races* saw him in his glory, betting his guinea, and generally successfully, nor was there a main fought in Yorkshire, the feeders being persons of celebrity, at which he was not to be seen, if business permitted. But though a "sprack" lad, and fond of pleasure and its haunts, Harry Wakefield was steady, and not the cautious Robin Oig McCombich himself was more attentive to the main chance.* His holidays were holidays indeed, but his days of work were dedicated to steady and persevering labour. In countenance and temper, Wakefield was the model of Old England's merry yeomen, whose clothyard shafts,* in so many hundred battles, asserted her superiority over the nations, and whose good sabres, in our own time, are her cheapest and most assured defence. His mirth was readily excited, for, strong in limb and constitution, and fortunate in circumstances, he was disposed to be pleased with everything about him, and such difficulties as he might occasionally encounter were, to a man of his energy, rather matter of amusement than serious annoyance. With all the merits of a sanguine temper, our young English drover was not without his defects. He was irascible, sometimes to the verge of being quarrelsome, and perhaps not the less inclined to bring his disputes to a pugilistic decision because he found few antagonists able to stand up to him in the boxing ring.

It is difficult to say how Harry Wakefield and Robin Oig first became intimates, but it is certain a close acquaintance had taken place betwixt them, although they had apparently few common subjects of conversation or of interest, so soon as their talk ceased to be of bullocks. Robin Oig, indeed, spoke the English language rather imperfectly upon any other topics but stots and kyloes, and Harry Wakefield could never bring his broad Yorkshire tongue to utter a single word of Gaelic. It was in vain Robin spent a whole morning, during a walk over Minch Moor, in attempting to teach his companion to utter, with true precision, the shibboleth* *llhu*, which is the Gaelic for a calf. From Traquair to Murder Cairn, the hill rang with the discordant attempts of the Saxon upon the unmanageable monosyllable, and the heartfelt laugh which followed every failure. They had, however, better modes of awakening the echoes, for Wakefield could sing many a ditty to the praise of Moll, Susan and Cicely, and Robin Oig had a particular gift at whistling interminable pibrochs through all their involutions – and, what was more agreeable to his companion's southern ear, knew many of the northern airs, both lively and pathetic, to which Wakefield learnt to pipe a bass. Thus, though Robin could hardly have comprehended his companion's stories about horse racing and cockfighting or fox hunting, and although his own legends of clan fights and creaghs, varied with talk of Highland goblins and fairy folk, would have been caviar to his companion,* they contrived, nevertheless, to find a degree of pleasure in each other's company, which had for three years back induced them to join company and travel together, when the direction of their journey permitted. Each, indeed, found his advantage in this companionship, for where could the Englishman have found a guide through the Western Highlands like Robin Oig McCombich? And when they were on what Harry called the *right* side of the Border, his patronage, which was extensive, and his purse, which was heavy, were at all times at the service of his Highland friend, and on many occasions his liberality did him genuine yeoman's service.*

CHAPTER II

> Were ever two such loving friends!
>   How could they disagree?
> Oh thus it was, he loved him dear,
>   And thought how to requite him,
> And having no friend left but he,
>   He did resolve to fight him.
>
> DUKE UPON DUKE*

The pair of friends had traversed with their usual cordiality the grassy wilds of Liddesdale, and crossed the opposite part of Cumberland, emphatically called "the Waste". In these solitary regions the cattle under the charge of our drovers derived their subsistence chiefly by picking their food as they went along the drove road, or sometimes by the tempting opportunity of a "start and owerloup", or invasion of the neighbouring pasture, where an occasion presented itself. But now the scene changed before them: they were descending towards a fertile and enclosed country, where no such liberties would be taken with impunity, or without a previous arrangement and bargain with the possessors of the ground. This was more especially the case as a great northern fair was upon the eve of taking place, where both the Scotch and English drover expected to dispose of a part of their cattle, which it was desirable to produce in the market rested and in good order. Fields were therefore difficult to be obtained, and only upon high terms. This necessity occasioned a temporary separation betwixt the two friends, who went to bargain, each as he could, for the separate accommodation of his herd. Unhappily it chanced that both of them, unknown to each other, thought of bargaining for the ground they wanted on the property of a country gentleman of some fortune whose estate lay in the neighbourhood. The English drover applied to the bailiff on the property, who was known to him. It chanced that the Cumbrian squire, who had entertained some suspicions of his manager's honesty, was taking occasional measures to ascertain how far they were well founded, and had desired that any enquiries about his enclosures, with a view to occupy them for a temporary purpose, should be referred to himself. As, however, Mr Ireby had gone the day before upon a journey of some miles' distance to the northward, the bailiff chose to consider the check upon his full powers as for the time removed, and concluded that he should best consult his master's interest, and perhaps his own, in making an agreement with Harry Wakefield.

Meanwhile, ignorant of what his comrade was doing, Robin Oig, on his side, chanced to be overtaken by a good-looking, smart little man upon a pony, most knowingly hogged and cropped, as was then the fashion, the rider wearing tight leather breeches and long-necked bright spurs. This cavalier asked one or two pertinent questions about markets and the price of stock. So Robin, seeing him a well-judging, civil gentleman, took the freedom to ask him whether he could let him know if there was any grassland to be let in the neighbourhood, for the temporary accommodation of his drove. He could not have put the question to more willing ears. The gentleman of the buckskins was the proprietor with whose bailiff Harry Wakefield had dealt, or was in the act of dealing.

"Thou art in good luck, my canny Scot," said Mr Ireby, "to have spoken to me, for I see thy cattle have done their day's work, and I have at my disposal the only field within three miles that is to be let in these parts."

"The drove can pe gang two, three, four miles very pratty weel indeed," said the cautious Highlander. "Put what would His Honour pe axing for the peasts pe the head, if she was to tak the park* for twa or three days?"

"We won't differ, Sawney,* if you let me have six stots for winterers, in the way of reason."

"And which peasts wad Your Honour pe for having?"

"Why, let me see... the two black... the dun one... yon doddy... him with the twisted horn... the brockit. How much by the head?"

"Ah," said Robin, "Your Honour is a shudge – a real shudge: I couldna have set off the pest six peasts petter mysell, me that ken them as if they were my pairns, puir things."

"Well, how much per head, Sawney?" continued Mr Ireby.

"It was high markets at Doune and Falkirk," answered Robin.

And thus the conversation proceeded, until they had agreed on the *prix juste* for the bullocks, the squire throwing in the temporary accommodation of the enclosure for the cattle into the boot, and Robin making, as he thought, a very good bargain, provided the grass was but tolerable. The squire walked his pony alongside of the drove, partly to show him the way, and see him put into possession of the field, and partly to learn the latest news of the northern markets.

They arrived at the field, and the pasture seemed excellent. But what was their surprise when they saw the bailiff quietly inducting the cattle of Harry Wakefield into the grassy Goshen* which had just been assigned to those of Robin Oig McCombich by the proprietor himself! Squire Ireby set spurs to his horse, dashed up to his servant and, learning what had passed between the parties, briefly informed the English drover that his bailiff had let the ground without his authority, and that he might seek grass for his cattle wherever he would, since he was to get none there. At the same time he rebuked his servant severely for having transgressed his commands, and ordered him instantly to assist in ejecting the hungry and weary cattle of Harry Wakefield, which were just beginning to enjoy a meal of unusual plenty, and to introduce those of his comrade, whom the English drover now began to consider as a rival.

The feelings which arose in Wakefield's mind would have induced him to resist Mr Ireby's decision, but every Englishman has a tolerably accurate sense of law and justice, and John Fleecebumpkin, the bailiff, having acknowledged that he had exceeded his commission, Wakefield saw nothing else for it than to collect his hungry and disappointed charge, and drive them on to seek quarters elsewhere. Robin Oig saw what had happened with regret, and hastened to offer to his English friend to share with him the disputed possession. But Wakefield's pride was severely hurt, and he answered disdainfully: "Take it all, man, take it all – never make two bites of a cherry. Thou canst talk over the gentry and blear a plain man's eye. Out upon you, man – I would not kiss any man's dirty latchets for leave to bake in his oven."*

Robin Oig, sorry but not surprised at his comrade's displeasure, hastened to entreat his friend to wait but an hour till he had gone to the squire's house to receive payment for the cattle he had sold, and he would come back and help him to drive the cattle into some convenient place of rest, and explain to him the whole mistake they had both of them fallen into.

But the Englishman continued indignant. "Thou hast been selling, hast thou? Ay, ay – thou is a cunning lad for kenning the hours of bargaining. Go to the Devil with thyself, for I will ne'er see thy fause loon's visage again – thou should be ashamed to look me in the face."

"I am ashamed to look no man in the face," said Robin Oig, something moved, "and, moreover, I will look you in the face this blessed day, if you will bide at the clachan down yonder."

"Mayhap you had as well keep away," said his comrade, and, turning his back on his former friend, he collected his unwilling associates, assisted by the bailiff, who took some real and some affected interest in seeing Wakefield accommodated.

After spending some time in negotiating with more than one of the neighbouring farmers, who could not or would not afford the accommodation desired, Henry Wakefield at last, and in his necessity, accomplished his point by means of the landlord of the alehouse at which Robin Oig and he had agreed to pass the night, when they first separated from each other. Mine host was content to let him turn his cattle on a piece of barren moor, at a price little less than the bailiff had asked for the disputed enclosure, and the wretchedness of the pasture, as well as the price paid for it, were set down as exaggerations of the breach of faith and friendship of his Scottish crony. This turn of Wakefield's passions was encouraged by the bailiff, who had his own reasons for being offended against poor Robin, as having been the unwitting cause of his falling into disgrace with his master, as well as by the innkeeper and two or three chance guests, who stimulated the drover in his resentment against his quondam associate – some from the ancient grudge against the Scots, which, when it exists anywhere, is to be found lurking in the Border counties, and some from the general love of mischief which characterizes mankind in all ranks of life, to the honour of Adam's children be it spoken. Good John Barleycorn* also, who always heightens and exaggerates the prevailing passions, be they angry or kindly, was not wanting in his offices on this occasion, and confusion to false friends and hard masters was pledged in more than one tankard.

In the mean while, Mr Ireby found some amusement in detaining the northern drover at his ancient hall. He caused a cold round of beef to be placed before the Scot in the butler's pantry, together with a foaming tankard of home-brewed, and took pleasure in seeing the hearty appetite with which these unwonted edibles were discussed by Robin Oig McCombich. The squire himself, lighting his pipe, compounded between his patrician dignity and his love of agricultural gossip by walking up and down while he conversed with his guest.

"I passed another drove," said the squire, "with one of your countrymen behind them: they were something less beasts than your drove, doddies most of them; a big man was with them – none of your kilts though, but a decent pair of breeches. D'ye know who he may be?"

"Hout ay, that might, could and would be Hughie Morrison – I didna think he could hae peen sae weel up. He has made a day on us, but his Argyllshires will have wearied shanks. How far was he pehind?"

"I think about six or seven miles," answered the squire, "for I passed them at the Christenbury Crag, and I overtook you at the Hollan Bush. If his beasts be leg-weary, he will be maybe selling bargains."

"Na, na – Hughie Morrison is no the man for pargains; ye maun come to some Highland body like Robin Oig hersell* for the like of these. Put I maun pe wishing you gootnight, and twenty of them let alane ane, and I maun down to the clachan to see if the lad Harry Waakfelt is out of his humdudgeons yet."

The party at the alehouse were still in full talk, and the treachery of Robin Oig still the theme of conversation, when the supposed culprit entered the apartment. His arrival, as usually happens in such a case, put an instant stop to the discussion of which he had furnished the subject, and he was received by the company assembled with that chilling silence which, more than a thousand exclamations, tells an intruder that he is unwelcome. Surprised and offended, but not appalled, by the reception which he experienced, Robin entered with an undaunted and even a haughty air, attempted no greeting, as he saw he was received with none, and placed himself by the side of the fire, a little apart from a table at which Harry Wakefield, the bailiff and two or three other persons were seated. The ample Cumbrian kitchen would have afforded plenty of room, even for a larger separation.

Robin, thus seated, proceeded to light his pipe and call for a pint of twopenny.

"We have no twopence ale," answered Ralph Heskett, the landlord, "but, as thou fin'st thy own tobacco, it's like thou mayst find thy own liquor too – it's the wont of thy country, I wot."

"Shame, goodman," said the landlady, a blithe, bustling housewife, hastening herself to supply the guest with liquor. "Thou knowest well enow what the strange man wants, and it's thy trade to be civil, man. Thou shouldst know that if the Scot likes a small pot, he pays a sure penny."

Without taking any notice of this nuptial dialogue, the Highlander took the flagon in his hand and, addressing the company generally, drank the interesting toast of "Good markets" to the party assembled.

"The better that the wind blew fewer dealers from the north," said one of the farmers, "and fewer Highland runts to eat up the English meadows."

"Saul of my pody, put you are wrang there, my friend," answered Robin with composure. "It is your fat Englishmen that eat up our Scots cattle, puir things."

"I wish there was a summat to eat up their drovers," said another. "A plain Englishman canna make bread within a kenning of them."

"Or an honest servant keep his master's favour, but they will come sliding in between him and the sunshine,"* said the bailiff.

"If these pe jokes," said Robin Oig with the same composure, "there is ower mony jokes upon one man."

"It is no joke, but downright earnest," said the bailiff. "Harkye, Mr Robin Ogg, or whatever is your name, it's right we should tell you that we are all of one opinion – and that is that you, Mr Robin Ogg, have behaved to our friend, Mr Harry Wakefield here, like a raff and a blackguard."

"Nae doubt – nae doubt," answered Robin with great composure, "and you are a set of very pretty judges, for whose prains or pehaviour I wad not gie a pinch of sneeshing. If Mr Harry Waakfelt kens where he is wranged, he kens where he may be righted."

"He speaks truth," said Wakefield, who had listened to what passed, divided between the offence which he had taken at Robin's late behaviour and the revival of his habitual feelings of regard.

He now rose and went towards Robin, who got up from his seat as he approached, and held out his hand.

"That's right, Harry... go it... serve him out," resounded on all sides. "Tip him the nailer – show him the mill."*

"Hold your peace all of you, and be ——," said Wakefield, and then, addressing his comrade, he took him by the extended hand, with something alike of respect and defiance. "Robin," he said, "thou hast used me ill enough this day, but if you mean, like a frank fellow, to shake hands and take a tussle for love on the sod, why, I'll forgie thee, man, and we shall be better friends than ever."

"And would it not pe petter to pe cood friends without more of the matter?" said Robin. "We will be much petter friendships with our panes hale than proken."

Harry Wakefield dropped the hand of his friend, or rather threw it from him.

"I did not think I had been keeping company for three years with a coward."

"Coward pelongs to none of my name," said Robin, whose eyes began to kindle, but keeping the command of his temper. "It was no coward's legs or hands, Harry Waakfelt, that drew you out of the fords of Frew* when you was drifting ower the plack rock, and every eel in the river expected his share of you."

"And that is true enough, too," said the Englishman, struck by the appeal.

"Adzooks!" exclaimed the bailiff. "Sure Harry Wakefield, the nattiest lad at Whitson Tryste, Wooler Fair, Carlisle Sands or Stagshaw Bank,* is not going to show white feather? Ah, this comes of living so long with kilts and bonnets – men forget the use of their daddles."

"I may teach you, Master Fleecebumpkin, that I have not lost the use of mine," said Wakefield, and then went on: "This will never do, Robin. We must have a turn-up, or we shall be the talk of the countryside. I'll be d——d if I hurt thee. I'll put on the gloves gin thou like. Come, stand forward like a man."

"To be peaten like a dog," said Robin. "Is there any reason in that? If you think I have done you wrong, I'll go before your shudge, though I neither know his law nor his language."

A general cry of "No, no – no law, no lawyer! A bellyful and be friends!" was echoed by the bystanders.

"But," continued Robin, "if I am to fight, I have no skill to fight like a jackanapes, with hands and nails."

"How would you fight, then?" said his antagonist. "Though I am thinking it would be hard to bring you to the scratch* anyhow."

"I would fight with proadswords, and sink point on the first plood drawn,* like a gentlemans."

A loud shout of laughter followed the proposal, which indeed had rather escaped from poor Robin's swelling heart than been the dictate of his sober judgement.

"Gentleman, quotha!" was echoed on all sides, with a shout of unextinguishable laughter. "A very pretty gentleman, God wot. Canst get two swords for the gentleman to fight with, Ralph Heskett?"

"No, but I can send to the armoury at Carlisle, and lend them two forks, to be making shift with in the mean time."

"Tush, man," said another, "the bonny Scots come into the world with the blue bonnet on their heads, and dirk and pistol at their belt."

"Best send post," said Mr Fleecebumpkin, "to the squire of Corby Castle, to come and stand second to the *gentleman*."

In the midst of this torrent of general ridicule, the Highlander instinctively griped beneath the folds of his plaid.

"But it's better not," he said in his own language. "A hundred curses on the swine-eaters,* who know neither decency nor civility!"

"Make room, the pack of you," he said, advancing to the door.

But his former friend interposed his sturdy bulk and opposed his leaving the house, and when Robin Oig attempted to make his way by force, he hit him down on the floor, with as much ease as a boy bowls down a ninepin.

"A ring – a ring!" was now shouted, until the dark rafters and the hams that hung on them trembled again, and the very platters on the "bink" clattered against each other. "Well done, Harry" – "Give it him home, Harry" – "Take care of him now… he sees his own blood!"*

Such were the exclamations while the Highlander, starting from the ground, all his coldness and caution lost in frantic rage, sprung at his antagonist with the fury, the activity and the vindictive purpose of an incensed tiger cat. But when could rage encounter science and temper? Robin Oig again went down in the unequal contest, and as the blow was necessarily a severe one, he lay motionless on the floor of the kitchen.

The landlady ran to offer some aid, but Mr Fleecebumpkin would not permit her to approach.

"Let him alone," he said. "He will come to within time, and come up to the scratch again. He has not got half his broth* yet."

"He has got all I mean to give him, though," said his antagonist, whose heart began to relent towards his old associate, "and I would rather by half give the rest to yourself, Mr Fleecebumpkin, for you pretend to know a thing or two, and Robin had not art enough even to peel before setting to, but fought with his plaid dangling about him. Stand up, Robin, my man, all friends now, and let me hear the man that will speak a word against you, or your country, for your sake."

Robin Oig was still under the dominion of his passion and eager to renew the onset, but being withheld on the one side by the peacemaking Dame Heskett and on the other aware that Wakefield no longer meant to renew the combat, his fury sank into gloomy sullenness.

"Come, come – never grudge so much at it, man," said the brave-spirited Englishman with the placability of his country. "Shake hands, and we will be better friends than ever."

"Friends!" exclaimed Robin Oig with strong emphasis. "Friends! Never. Look to yourself, Harry Waakfelt."

"Then the curse of Cromwell on your proud Scots stomach, as the man says in the play,* and you may do your worst, and be d——d, for one man can say nothing more to another after a tussle than that he is sorry for it."

On these terms the friends parted. Robin Oig drew out, in silence, a piece of money, threw it on the table and then left the alehouse. But, turning at the door, he shook his hand at Wakefield, pointing with his forefinger upwards, in a manner which might imply either a threat or a caution. He then disappeared in the moonlight.

Some words passed after his departure between the bailiff, who piqued himself on being a little of a bully, and Harry Wakefield, who, with generous inconsistency, was now not indisposed to begin a new combat in defence of Robin Oig's reputation, although he could not use his daddles like an Englishman, as it did not come natural to him.

But Dame Heskett prevented this second quarrel from coming to a head by her peremptory interference. There should be no more fighting in her house, she said. There had been too much already. "And you, Mr Wakefield, may live to learn," she added, "what it is to make a deadly enemy out of a good friend."

"Pshaw, dame! Robin Oig is an honest fellow, and will never keep malice."

"Do not trust to that – you do not know the dour temper of the Scots, though you have dealt with them so often. I have a right to know them, my mother being a Scot."

"And so is well seen on her daughter," said Ralph Heskett.

This nuptial sarcasm gave the discourse another turn; fresh customers entered the taproom or kitchen, and others left it. The conversation turned on the expected markets and the report of prices from different parts both of Scotland and England; treaties were commenced, and Harry Wakefield was lucky enough to find a chap for a part of his drove, and at a very considerable profit – an event of consequence more than sufficient to blot out all remembrances of the unpleasant scuffle in the earlier part of the day.

But there remained one party from whose mind that recollection could not have been wiped away by the possession of every head of cattle betwixt Esk and Eden. This was Robin Oig McCombich. "That I should have had no weapon," he said, "and for the first time in my life! Blighted be the tongue that bids the Highlander part with the dirk. The dirk – ha! The English blood! My muhme's word – when did her word fall to the ground?"

The recollection of the fatal prophecy confirmed the deadly intention which instantly sprang up in his mind.

"Ha! Morrison cannot be many miles behind – and if it were an hundred, what then?"

His impetuous spirit had now a fixed purpose and motive of action, and he turned the light foot of his country towards the wilds, through which he knew, by Mr Ireby's report, that Morrison was advancing. His mind was wholly engrossed by the sense of injury – injury sustained from a friend – and by the desire of vengeance on one whom he now accounted his most bitter enemy. The treasured ideas of self-importance and self-opinion – of ideal birth and quality – had become more precious to him, like the hoard to the miser, because he could only enjoy them in secret. But that hoard was pillaged – the idols which he had secretly worshipped had been desecrated and profaned. Insulted, abused and beaten, he was no longer worthy, in his own opinion, of the name he bore or the lineage which he belonged to: nothing was left to him – nothing but revenge, and, as the reflection added a galling spur to every step, he determined it should be as sudden and signal as the offence.

When Robin Oig left the door of the alehouse, seven or eight English miles* at least lay betwixt Morrison and him. The advance of the former was slow, limited by the sluggish pace of his cattle; the last left behind him stubble field and hedgerow, crag and dark heath, all glittering with frost rime in the broad November moonlight, at the rate of six miles an hour. And now the distant lowing of Morrison's cattle is heard, and now they are seen creeping like moles in size and slowness of motion on the broad face of the moor, and now he meets them, passes them and stops their conductor.

"May good betide us," said the Southlander. "Is this you, Robin McCombich, or your wraith?"

"It is Robin Oig McCombich," answered the Highlander, "and it is not. But never mind that, put pe giving me the *skene-dhu*."

"What? You are for back to the Highlands. The devil! Have you selt all off before the fair? This beats all for quick markets."

"I have not sold – I am not going north. Maype I will never go north again. Give me pack my dirk, Hugh Morrison, or there will pe words petween us."

"Indeed, Robin, I'll be better advised before I gie it back to you – it is a wanchancy weapon in a Highlandman's hand, and I am thinking you will be about some barns-breaking."

"Prutt, trutt! Let me have my weapon," said Robin Oig impatiently.

"Hooly and fairly," said his well-meaning friend. "I'll tell you what will do better than these dirking doings. Ye ken Highlander and Lowlander and Bordermen are a' ae man's bairns when you are over the Scots' Dyke.* See, the Eskdale callants, and fighting Charlie of Liddesdale, and the Lockerby lads, and the four Dandies of Lustruther, and a wheen mair grey plaids are coming up behind, and if you are wranged, there is the hand of a Manly Morrison – we'll see you righted, if Carlisle and Stanwix* baith took up the feud."

"To tell you the truth," said Robin Oig, desirous of eluding the suspicions of his friend, "I have enlisted with a party of the Black Watch,* and must march off tomorrow morning."

"Enlisted! Were you mad or drunk? You must buy yourself off. I can lend you twenty notes, and twenty to that, if the drove sell."

"I thank you – thank ye, Hughie, but I go with good will the gate that I am going, so the dirk – the dirk!"

"There it is for you, then, since less wunna serve. But think on what I was saying. Wae's me, it will be sair news in the braes of Balquidder* that Robin Oig McCombich should have run an ill gate, and ta'en on."

"Ill news in Balquidder, indeed!" echoed poor Robin. "But Cot speed you, Hughie, and send you good marcats. Ye winna meet with Robin Oig again, either at tryste or fair."

So saying, he shook hastily the hand of his acquaintance and set out in the direction from which he had advanced, with the spirit of his former pace.

"There is something wrang with the lad," muttered the Morrison to himself, "but we will maybe see better into it the morn's morning."

But long ere the morning dawned, the catastrophe of our tale had taken place. It was two hours after the affray had happened, and it was totally forgotten by almost everyone, when Robin Oig returned to Heskett's inn. The place was filled at once by various sorts of men and with noises corresponding to their character. There were the grave low sounds of men engaged in busy traffic, with the laugh, the song and the riotous jest of those who had nothing to do but to enjoy themselves. Among the last was Harry Wakefield, who, amidst a grinning group of smock-frocks, hobnailed shoes and jolly English physiognomies, was trolling forth the old ditty:

> What though my name be Roger,
> Who drives the plough and cart?...*

when he was interrupted by a well-known voice saying in a high and stern voice, marked by the sharp Highland accent, "Harry Waakfelt, if you be a man, stand up!"

"What is the matter? What is it?" the guests demanded of each other.

"It is only a d——d Scotsman," said Fleecebumpkin, who was by this time very drunk, "whom Harry Wakefield helped to his broth today, who is now come to have his cauld kail het again."

"Harry Waakfelt," repeated the same ominous summons, "stand up, if you be a man!"

There is something in the tone of deep and concentrated passion which attracts attention and imposes awe, even by the very sound. The guests shrank back on every side and gazed at the Highlander as he stood in the middle of them, his brows bent and his features rigid with resolution.

"I will stand up with all my heart, Robin, my boy, but it shall be to shake hands with you and drink down all unkindness.* It is not the fault of your heart, man, that you don't know how to clench your hands."

By this time he stood opposite to his antagonist, his open and unsuspecting look strangely contrasted with the stern purpose which gleamed wild, dark and vindictive in the eyes of the Highlander.

"'Tis not thy fault, man, that, not having the luck to be an Englishman, thou canst not fight more than a schoolgirl."

"I *can* fight," answered Robin Oig, sternly but calmly, "and you shall know it. You, Harry Waakfelt, showed me today how the Saxon churls fight – I show you now how the Highland *dunniewassel* fights."

He seconded the word with the action, and plunged the dagger, which he suddenly displayed, into the broad breast of the English yeoman, with such fatal certainty and force that the hilt made a hollow sound against the breastbone and the double-edged point split the very heart of his victim. Harry Wakefield fell and expired with a single groan. His assassin next seized the bailiff by the collar and offered the bloody poniard to his throat, whilst dread and surprise rendered the man incapable of defence.

"It were very just to lay you beside him," he said, "but the blood of a base pickthank shall never mix on my father's dirk with that of a brave man."

As he spoke, he cast the man from him with so much force that he fell on the floor, while Robin, with his other hand, threw the fatal weapon into the blazing turf fire.

"There," he said, "take me who likes, and let fire cleanse blood, if it can."

The pause of astonishment still continuing, Robin Oig asked for a peace officer – and, a constable having stepped out, he surrendered himself to his custody.

"A bloody night's work you have made of it," said the constable.

"Your own fault," said the Highlander. "Had you kept his hands off me twa hours since, he would have been now as well and merry as he was twa minutes since."

"It must be sorely answered," said the peace officer.

"Never you mind that. Death pays all debts – it will pay that too."

The horror of the bystanders began now to give way to indignation, and the sight of a favourite companion murdered in the midst of them, the provocation being, in their opinion, so utterly inadequate to the excess of vengeance, might have induced them to kill the perpetrator of the deed even upon the very spot. The constable, however, did his duty on this occasion, and, with the assistance of some of the more reasonable persons present, procured horses to guard the prisoner to Carlisle, to abide his doom at the next assizes. While the escort was preparing, the prisoner neither expressed the least interest nor attempted the slightest reply. Only, before he was carried from the fatal apartment, he desired to look at the dead body, which, raised from the floor, had been deposited upon the large table (at the head of which Harry Wakefield had presided but a few minutes before, full of life, vigour and animation), until the surgeons should examine the mortal wound. The face of the corpse was decently covered with a napkin. To the surprise and horror of the bystanders, which displayed itself in a general "Ah!" drawn through clenched teeth and half-shut lips, Robin Oig removed the cloth and gazed with a mournful but steady eye on the lifeless visage, which had been so lately animated that the smile of good-humoured confidence in his own strength, of conciliation at once and contempt towards his enemy, still curled his lip. While those present expected that the wound, which had so lately flooded the apartment with gore, would send forth fresh streams at the touch of the homicide,* Robin Oig replaced the covering with the brief exclamation "He was a pretty man!"

My story is nearly ended. The unfortunate Highlander stood his trial at Carlisle. I was myself present, and as a young Scottish lawyer, or barrister at least, and reputed a man of some quality, the politeness of the sheriff of Cumberland offered me a place on the bench. The facts of the case were proved in the manner I have related them, and whatever might be at first the prejudice of the audience against a crime so un-English as that of assassination from revenge, yet when the rooted national prejudices of the prisoner had been explained, which made him consider himself as stained with indelible dishonour when subjected to personal violence, when his previous patience, moderation and endurance were considered, the generosity of the English audience was inclined to regard his crime as the wayward aberration of a false idea of honour rather than as flowing from a heart naturally savage or perverted by habitual vice. I shall never forget the charge of the venerable judge to the jury, although not at that time liable to be much affected either by that which was eloquent or pathetic.

"We have had," he said, "in the previous part of our duty" (alluding to some former trials), "to discuss crimes which infer disgust and abhorrence, while they call down the well-merited vengeance of the law. It is now our still more melancholy task to apply its salutary though severe enactments to a case of a very singular character, in which the crime (for a crime it is, and a deep one) arose less out of the malevolence of the heart than the error of the understanding – less from any idea of committing wrong than from an unhappily perverted notion of that which is right. Here we have two men (highly esteemed, it has been stated, in their rank of life, and attached, it seems, to each other as friends), one of whose lives has been already sacrificed to a punctilio, and the other is about to prove the vengeance of the offended laws – and yet both may claim our commiseration at least as men acting in ignorance of each other's national prejudices, and unhappily misguided rather than voluntarily erring from the path of right conduct.

"In the original cause of the misunderstanding, we must in justice give the right to the prisoner at the bar. He had acquired possession of the enclosure, which was the object of competition, by a legal contract with the proprietor, Mr Ireby, and yet, when accosted with reproaches undeserved in themselves, and galling doubtless to a temper at least sufficiently susceptible of passion, he offered notwithstanding to yield up half his acquisition for

THE TWO DROVERS

the sake of peace and good neighbourhood, and his amicable proposal was rejected with scorn. Then follows the scene at Mr Heskett the publican's, and you will observe how the stranger was treated by the deceased, and, I am sorry to observe, by those around, who seem to have urged him in a manner which was aggravating in the highest degree. While he asked for peace and for composition, and offered submission to a magistrate, or to a mutual arbiter, the prisoner was insulted by a whole company, who seem on this occasion to have forgotten the national maxim of 'fair play', and while attempting to escape from the place in peace he was intercepted, struck down and beaten to the effusion of his blood.

"Gentlemen of the jury, it was with some impatience that I heard my learned brother, who opened the case for the Crown, give an unfavourable turn to the prisoner's conduct on this occasion. He said the prisoner was afraid to encounter his antagonist in fair fight, or to submit to the laws of the ring,* and that, therefore, like a cowardly Italian, he had recourse to his fatal stiletto to murder the man whom he dared not meet in manly encounter. I observed the prisoner shrink from this part of the accusation with the abhorrence natural to a brave man, and as I would wish to make my words impressive when I point his real crime, I must secure his opinion of my impartiality by rebutting everything that seems to me a false accusation. There can be no doubt that the prisoner is a man of resolution – too much resolution. I wish to Heaven that he had less, or rather that he had had a better education to regulate it.

"Gentlemen, as to the laws my brother talks of, they may be known in the bullring or the bear garden, or the cockpit, but they are not known here. Or, if they should be so far admitted as furnishing a species of proof that no malice was intended in this sort of combat, from which fatal accidents do sometimes arise, it can only be so admitted when both parties are *in pari casu*,* equally acquainted with and equally willing to refer themselves to that species of arbitrament. But will it be contended that a man of superior rank and education is to be subjected, or is obliged to subject himself, to this coarse and brutal strife, perhaps in opposition to a younger, stronger or more skilful opponent? Certainly even the pugilistic code, if founded upon the fair play of Merry Old England, as my brother alleges it to be, can contain nothing so preposterous. And, gentlemen of the jury, if the laws would support an English gentleman wearing, we will suppose, his sword in defending himself by force against a violent personal aggression of the nature afforded to this prisoner, they will not less protect a foreigner and a stranger involved in the same unpleasing circumstances. If, therefore, gentlemen of the jury, when thus pressed by a *vis major*,* the object of obloquy to a whole company and of direct violence from one at least, and, as he might reasonably apprehend, from more, the panel had produced the weapon which his countrymen, as we are informed, generally carry about their persons, and the same unhappy circumstance had ensued which you have heard detailed in evidence, I could not in my conscience have asked from you a verdict of murder. The prisoner's personal defence might indeed, even in that case, have gone more or less beyond the *moderamen inculpatæ tutelæ** spoken of by lawyers, but the punishment incurred would have been that of manslaughter, not of murder. I beg leave to add that I should have thought this milder species of charge was demanded in the case supposed, notwithstanding the statute of James I cap. 8, which takes the case of slaughter by stabbing with a short weapon, even without malice prepense, out of the benefit of clergy.* For this statute of stabbing, as it is termed, arose out of a temporary cause, and as the real guilt is the same whether the slaughter be committed by the dagger or by sword or pistol, the benignity of the modern law places them all on the same (or nearly the same) footing.

"But, gentlemen of the jury, the pinch of the case lies in the interval of two hours interposed betwixt the reception of the injury and the fatal retaliation. In the heat of affray and *chaude mêlée*,* law, compassionating the infirmities of humanity, makes allowance for the passions which rule such a stormy moment – for the sense of present pain, for the apprehension of further injury, for the difficulty of ascertaining with due accuracy the precise degree of violence which is necessary to protect the person of the individual without annoying or injuring the assailant more than is absolutely necessary. But the time necessary to walk twelve miles, however speedily performed, was an interval sufficient for the prisoner to have recollected himself, and the violence with which he carried his purpose into effect, with so many circumstances of deliberate determination, could neither be induced by the passion of anger nor that of fear. It was the purpose and the act of predetermined revenge, for which law neither can, will nor ought to have sympathy or allowance.

"It is true, we may repeat to ourselves, in alleviation of this poor man's unhappy action, that his case is a very peculiar one. The country which he inhabits was, in the days of many now alive, inaccessible to the laws not only of England, which have not even yet penetrated thither, but to those to which our neighbours of Scotland are subjected, and which must be supposed to be, and no doubt actually are, founded upon the general principles of justice and equity which pervade every civilized country. Amongst their mountains, as among the North American Indians, the various tribes were wont to make war upon each other, so that each man was obliged to go armed for his own protection. These men, from the ideas which they entertained of their own descent and of their own consequence, regarded themselves as so many cavaliers or men-at-arms, rather than as the peasantry of a peaceful country. Those laws of the ring, as my brother terms them, were unknown to the race of warlike mountaineers – that decision of quarrels by no other weapons than those which nature has given every man must to them have seemed as vulgar and as preposterous as to the *noblesse* of France. Revenge, on the other hand, must have been as familiar to their habits of society as to those of the Cherokees or Mohawks. It is indeed, as described by Bacon, at bottom, a kind of wild, untutored justice,* for the fear of retaliation must withhold the hands of the oppressor where there is no regular law to check daring violence. But though all this may be granted, and though we may allow that, such having been the case of the Highlands in the days of the prisoner's fathers, many of the opinions and sentiments must still continue to influence the present generation, it cannot, and ought not, even in this most painful case, to alter the administration of the law, either in your hands, gentlemen of the jury, or in mine. The first object of civilization is to place the general protection of the law, equally administered, in the room of that wild justice which every man cut and carved for himself, according to the length of his sword and the strength of his arm. The law says to the subjects, with a voice only inferior to that of the Deity, "Vengeance is mine."* The instant that there is time for passion to cool and reason to interpose, an injured party must become aware that the law assumes the exclusive cognizance of the right and wrong betwixt the parties, and opposes her inviolable buckler to every attempt of the private party to right himself. I repeat that this unhappy man ought personally to be the object rather of our pity than our abhorrence, for he failed in his ignorance and from mistaken notions of honour. But his crime is not the less that of murder, gentlemen, and, in your high and important office, it is your duty so to find. Englishmen have their angry passions as well as Scots, and should this man's action remain unpunished, you may unsheath, under various pretences, a thousand daggers betwixt the Land's End and the Orkneys."*

The venerable judge thus ended what, to judge by his apparent emotion and by the tears which filled his eyes, was really a painful task. The jury, according to his instructions, brought in a verdict of guilty, and Robin Oig McCombich, alias McGregor, was sentenced to death, and left for execution, which took place accordingly. He met his fate with great firmness, and acknowledged the justice of his sentence. But he repelled indignantly the observations of those who accused him of attacking an unarmed man. "I give a life for the life I took," he said, "and what can I do more?"*

My Aunt Margaret's Mirror*

INTRODUCTION

The species of publication which has come to be generally known by the title of "annual", being a miscellany of prose and verse equipped with numerous engravings and put forth every year about Christmas, had flourished for a long while in Germany before it was imitated in this country by an enterprising bookseller, a German by birth, Mr Ackermann.* The rapid success of his work, as is the custom of the time, gave birth to a host of rivals, and, among others, to an annual styled *The Keepsake*,* the first volume of which appeared in 1828, and attracted much notice, chiefly in consequence of the very uncommon splendour of its illustrative accompaniments. The expenditure which the spirited proprietors lavished on this magnificent volume is understood to have been not less than from ten to twelve thousand pounds sterling.

Various gentlemen of such literary reputation that anyone might think it an honour to be associated with them had been announced as contributors to this annual before application was made to me to assist in it,* and I accordingly placed with much pleasure at the editor's disposal a few fragments originally designed to have been worked into the *Chronicles of the Canongate*, besides a MS drama, the long-neglected performance of my youthful days: *The House of Aspen*.*

The Keepsake for 1828 included, however, only three of these little prose tales, of which the first in order was that entitled 'My Aunt Margaret's Mirror'. By way of introduction to this, when now included in a general collection of my lucubrations,* I have only to say that it is a mere transcript, or at least with very little embellishment, of a story that I remembered being struck with in my childhood, when told at the fireside by a lady of eminent virtues and no inconsiderable share of talent, one of the ancient and honourable house of Swinton.* She was a kind relation of my own, and met her death in a manner so shocking, being killed in a fit of insanity by a female attendant who had been attached to her person for half a lifetime, that I cannot now recall her memory, child as I was when the catastrophe occurred, without a painful reawakening of perhaps the first images of horror that the scenes of real life stamped on my mind.

This good spinster had in her composition a strong vein of the superstitious, and was pleased, among other fancies, to read alone in her chamber by a taper fixed in a candlestick which she had had formed out of a human skull. One night this strange piece of furniture acquired suddenly the power of locomotion, and, after performing some odd circles on her chimney piece, fairly leapt on the floor and continued to roll about the apartment. Mrs Swinton calmly proceeded to the adjoining room for another light, and had the satisfaction to penetrate the mystery on the spot. Rats abounded in the ancient building she inhabited, and one of these had managed to ensconce itself within her favourite memento mori.* Though thus endowed with a more than feminine share of nerve, she entertained largely that belief in supernaturals which in those times was not considered as sitting ungracefully on the grave and aged of her condition, and the story of the magic mirror was one for which she vouched with particular confidence, alleging, indeed, that one of her own family had been an eyewitness of the incidents recorded in it.

I tell the tale as it was told to me.*

Stories enow of much the same cast will present themselves to the recollection of such of my readers as have ever dabbled in a species of lore to which I certainly gave more hours, at one period of my life, than I should gain any credit by confessing.

AUGUST 1831

MY AUNT MARGARET'S MIRROR

> There are times
> When fancy plays her gambols, in despite
> Even of our watchful senses, when in sooth
> Substance seems shadow, shadow substance seems,
> When the broad, palpable and marked partition
> 'Twixt that which is and is not seems dissolved,
> As if the mental eye gained power to gaze
> Beyond the limits of the existing world.
> Such hours of shadowy dreams I better love
> Than all the gross realities of life.
>
> ANONYMOUS*

My Aunt Margaret was one of that respected sisterhood upon whom devolve all the trouble and solicitude incidental to the possession of children, excepting only that which attends their entrance into the world. We were a large family, of very different dispositions and constitutions. Some were dull and peevish – they were sent to Aunt Margaret to be amused; some were rude, romping and boisterous – they were sent to Aunt Margaret to be kept quiet, or rather, that their noise might be removed out of hearing; those who were indisposed were sent with the prospect of being nursed, those who were stubborn with the hope of their being subdued by the kindness of Aunt Margaret's discipline; in short, she had all the various duties of a mother without the credit and dignity of the maternal character. The busy scene of her various cares is now over: of the invalid and the robust, the kind and the rough, the peevish and pleased children, who thronged her little parlour from morning to night, not one now remains alive but myself, who, afflicted by early infirmity, was one of the most delicate of her nurslings – yet, nevertheless, have outlived them all.

It is still my custom, and shall be so while I have the use of my limbs, to visit my respected relation at least three times a week. Her abode is about half a mile from the suburbs of the town in which I reside, and is accessible not only by the high road, from which it stands at some distance, but by means of a greensward footpath leading through some pretty meadows. I have so little left to torment me in life that it is one of my greatest vexations to know that several of these sequestered fields have been devoted as sites for building. In that which is nearest the town, wheelbarrows have been at work for several weeks in such numbers that, I verily believe, its whole surface, to the depth of at least eighteen inches, was mounted in these monotrochs at the same moment, and in the act of being transported from one place to another. Huge triangular piles of planks are also reared in different parts of the devoted messuage, and a little group of trees that still grace the eastern end, which rises in a gentle ascent, have just received notice to quit, expressed by a daub of white paint, and are to give place to a curious grove of chimneys.

It would, perhaps, hurt others in my situation to reflect that this little range of pasturage once belonged to my father, whose family was of some consideration in the world, and was sold by patches to remedy distresses in which he involved himself in an attempt by commercial adventure to redeem his diminished fortune. While the building scheme was in full operation, this circumstance was often pointed out to me by the class of friends who are anxious that no part of your misfortunes should escape your observation. "Such pasture ground! Lying at the very town's end – in turnips and potatoes, the parks would bring £20 per acre, and if leased for building... Oh, it was a gold mine! And all sold for an old song out of the ancient possessor's hands!" My comforters cannot bring me to repine much on this subject. If I could be allowed to look back on the past without interruption, I could willingly give up the enjoyment of present income and the hope of future profit to those who have purchased what my father sold. I regret the alteration of the ground only because it destroys associations, and I would more willingly, I think, see the Earl's Closes in the hands of strangers, retaining their silvan appearance, than know them for my own, if torn up by agriculture or covered with buildings. Mine are the sensations of poor Logan:

> The horrid plough has razed the green
>   Where yet a child I strayed;
> The axe has felled the hawthorn screen,
>   The schoolboy's summer shade.*

I hope, however, the threatened devastation will not be consummated in my day. Although the adventurous spirit of times short while since passed gave rise to the undertaking, I have been encouraged to think that the subsequent changes have so far damped the spirit of speculation that the rest of the woodland footpath leading to Aunt Margaret's retreat will be left undisturbed for her time and mine. I am interested in this, for every step of the way, after I have passed through the green already mentioned, has for me something of early remembrance. There is the stile at which I can recollect a cross child's maid upbraiding me with my infirmity as she lifted me coarsely and carelessly over the flinty steps which my brothers traversed with shout and bound. I remember the suppressed bitterness of the moment and, conscious of my own inferiority, the feeling of envy with which I regarded the easy movements and elastic steps of my more happily formed brethren. Alas! These goodly barks have all perished on life's wide ocean, and only that which seemed so little seaworthy, as the naval phrase goes, has reached the port when the tempest is over. Then there is the pool, where, manoeuvring our little navy constructed out of the broad water flags,* my elder brother fell in, and was scarce saved from the watery element to die under Nelson's banner.* There is the hazel copse also, in which my brother Henry used to gather nuts, thinking little that he was to die in an Indian jungle in quest of rupees.

There is so much more of remembrance about the little walk that, as I stop, rest on my crutch-headed cane and look round with that species of comparison between the thing I was and that which I now am, it almost induces me to doubt my own identity, until I find myself in face of the honeysuckle porch of Aunt Margaret's dwelling, with its irregularity of front and its odd projecting latticed windows, where the workmen seem to have made a study that no one of them should resemble another in form, size or in the old-fashioned stone entablature and labels which adorn them. This tenement, once the manor house of Earl's Closes, we still retain a slight hold upon – for, in some family arrangements, it had been settled upon Aunt Margaret during the term of her life. Upon this frail tenure depends, in a great measure, the last shadow of the family of Bothwell of Earl's Closes and their last slight connection with their paternal inheritance. The only representative will then be an infirm old man moving not unwillingly to the grave, which has devoured all that were dear to his affections.

When I have indulged such thoughts for a minute or two, I enter the mansion, which is said to have been the gatehouse only of the original building, and find one being on whom time seems to have made little impression – for the Aunt Margaret of today bears the same proportional age to the Aunt Margaret of my early youth that the boy of ten years old does to the man of – by'r Lady! – some fifty-six years. The old lady's invariable costume has doubtless some share in confirming one in the opinion that time has stood still with Aunt Margaret.

The brown or chocolate-coloured silk gown, with ruffles of the same stuff at the elbow, within which are others of Mechlin lace,* the black silk gloves, or mitts, the white hair combed back upon a roll and the cap of spotless cambric, which closes around the venerable countenance, as they were not the costume of 1780, so neither were they that of 1826 – they are altogether a style peculiar to the individual Aunt Margaret. There she still sits, as she sat thirty years since, with her wheel or the stocking, which she works by the fire in winter and by the window in summer, or perhaps venturing as far as the porch in an unusually fine summer evening. Her frame, like some well-constructed piece of mechanics, still performs the operations for which it had seemed destined, going its round with an activity which is gradually diminished, yet indicating no probability that it will soon come to a period.

The solicitude and affection which had made Aunt Margaret the willing slave to the inflictions of a whole nursery have now for their object the health and comfort of one old and infirm man, the last remaining relative of her family, and the only one who can still find interest in the traditional stores which she hoards, as some miser hides the gold which he desires that no one should enjoy after his death.

My conversation with Aunt Margaret generally relates little either to the present or to the future: for the passing day we possess as much as we require, and we neither of us wish for more, and for that which is to follow we have on this side of the grave neither hopes, nor fears, nor anxiety. We therefore naturally look back to the past and forget the present fallen fortunes and declined importance of our family, in recalling the hours when it was wealthy and prosperous.

With this slight introduction, the reader will know as much of Aunt Margaret and her nephew as is necessary to comprehend the following conversation and narrative.

Last week, when, late in a summer evening, I went to call on the old lady to whom my reader is now introduced, I was received by her with all her usual affection and benignity, while, at the same time, she seemed abstracted and disposed to silence. I asked her the reason. "They have been clearing out the old chapel," she said, "John Clayhudgeons having, it seems, discovered that the stuff within – being, I suppose, the remains of our ancestors – was excellent for top-dressing the meadows."

Here I started up with more alacrity than I have displayed for some years, but sat down while my aunt added, laying her hand upon my sleeve, "The chapel has been long considered as common ground, my dear, and used for a penfold – and what objection can we have to the man for employing what is his own to his own profit? Besides, I did speak to him, and he very readily and civilly promised that, if he found bones or monuments, they should be carefully respected and reinstated – and what more could I ask? So, the first stone they found bore the name of Margaret Bothwell, 1585, and I have caused it to be laid carefully aside, as I think it betokens death, and having served my namesake two hundred years, it has just been cast up in time to do me the same good turn. My house has been long put in order, as far as the small earthly concerns require it, but who shall say that their account with Heaven is sufficiently revised?"

"After what you have said, Aunt," I replied, "perhaps I ought to take my hat and go away, and so I should, but that there is on this occasion a little alloy mingled with your devotion. To think of death at all times is a duty; to suppose it nearer from the finding an old gravestone is superstition – and you, with your strong, useful common sense, which was so long the prop of a fallen family, are the last person whom I have should have suspected of such weakness."

"Neither would I deserve your suspicions, kinsman," answered Aunt Margaret, "if we were speaking of any incident occurring in the actual business of human life. But for all this, I have a sense of superstition about me which I do not wish to part with. It is a feeling which separates me from this age and links me with that to which I am hastening, and even when it seems, as now, to lead me to the brink of the grave and bids me gaze on it, I do not love that it should be dispelled. It soothes my imagination, without influencing my reason or conduct."

"I profess, my good lady," replied I, "that had anyone but you made such a declaration, I should have thought it as capricious as that of the clergyman who, without vindicating his false reading, preferred, from habit's sake, his old *mumpsimus* to the modern *sumpsimus*."*

"Well," answered my aunt, "I must explain my inconsistency in this particular by comparing it to another. I am, as you know, a piece of that old-fashioned thing called a Jacobite, but I am so in sentiment and feeling only, for a more loyal subject never joined in prayers for the health and wealth of George IV, whom God long preserve! But I dare say that kind-hearted sovereign would not deem that an old woman did him much injury if she leant back in her armchair, just in such a twilight as this, and thought of the high-mettled men whose sense of duty called them to arms against his grandfather* – and how, in a cause which they deemed that of their rightful prince and country,

"They fought till their hand to the broadsword was glued;
They fought against fortune with hearts unsubdued.*

"Do not come at such a moment when my head is full of plaids, pibrochs and claymores, and ask my reason to admit what, I am afraid, it cannot deny: I mean that the public advantage peremptorily demanded that these things should cease to exist. I cannot, indeed, refuse to allow the justice of your reasoning, but yet, being convinced against my will, you will gain little by your motion. You might as well read to an infatuated lover the catalogue of his mistress's imperfections, for, when he has been compelled to listen to the summary, you will only get for answer that he 'lo'es her a' the better'."

I was not sorry to have changed the gloomy train of Aunt Margaret's thoughts, and replied in the same tone, "Well, I can't help being persuaded that our good king is the more sure of Mrs Bothwell's loyal affection that he has the Stuart right of birth, as well as the Act of Succession, in his favour."*

"Perhaps my attachment, were its source of consequence, might be found warmer for the union of the rights you mention," said Aunt Margaret, "but, upon my word, it would be as sincere if the king's right were founded only on the will of the nation, as declared at the Revolution. I am none of your *jure divino* folks."*

"And a Jacobite notwithstanding."

"And a Jacobite notwithstanding – or rather, I will give you leave to call me one of the party which, in Queen Anne's time, were called 'Whimsicals', because they were sometimes operated upon by feelings, sometimes by principle.* After all, it is very hard that you will not allow an old woman to be as inconsistent in her political sentiments as mankind in general show themselves in all the various courses of life, since you cannot point out one of them in which the passions and prejudices of those who pursue it are not perpetually carrying us away from the path which our reason points out."

"True, Aunt, but you are a wilful wanderer, who should be forced back into the right path."

"Spare me, I entreat you," replied Aunt Margaret. "You remember the Gaelic song, though I dare say I mispronounce the words:

"*Hatil mohatil, na dowski mi.**
(I am asleep, do not waken me.)

"I tell you, kinsman, that the sort of waking dreams which my imagination spins out, in what your favourite Wordsworth calls 'moods of my own mind',* are worth all the rest of my more active days. Then, instead of looking forward, as I did in youth, and forming for myself fairy palaces, upon the verge of the grave I turn my eyes backward upon the days and manners of my better time, and the sad, yet soothing, recollections come so close and interesting that I almost think it sacrilege to be wiser or more rational, or less prejudiced, than those to whom I looked up in my younger years."

"I think I now understand what you mean," I answered, "and can comprehend why you should occasionally prefer the twilight of illusion to the steady light of reason."

"Where there is no task," she rejoined, "to be performed, we may sit in the dark if we like it – if we go to work, we must ring for candles."

"And amidst such shadowy and doubtful light," continued I, "imagination frames her enchanted and enchanting visions, and sometimes passes them upon the senses for reality."

"Yes," said Aunt Margaret, who is a well-read woman, "to those who resemble the translator of Tasso:

"Prevailing poet, whose undoubting mind
Believed the magic wonders which he sung.*

"It is not required for this purpose that you should be sensible of the painful horrors which an actual belief in such prodigies inflicts: such a belief, nowadays, belongs only to fools and children. It is not necessary that your ears should tingle and your complexion change, like that of Theodore, at the approach of the spectral huntsman.* All that is indispensable for the enjoyment of the milder feeling of supernatural awe is that you should be susceptible of the slight shuddering which creeps over you when you hear a tale of terror – that well-vouched tale which the narrator, having first expressed his general disbelief of all such legendary lore, selects and produces as having something in it which he has been always obliged to give up as inexplicable. Another symptom is a momentary hesitation to look round you when the interest of the narrative is at the highest, and the third a desire to avoid looking into a mirror when you are alone in your chamber for the evening. I mean such are signs which indicate the crisis when a female imagination is in due temperature to enjoy a ghost story. I do not pretend to describe those which express the same disposition in a gentleman."

"That last symptom, dear Aunt, of shunning the mirror, seems likely to be a rare occurrence amongst the fair sex."

"You are a novice in toilet fashions, my dear cousin. All women consult the looking glass with anxiety before they go into company, but when they return home, the mirror has not the same charm. The die has been cast: the party has been successful or unsuccessful, in the impression which she desired to make. But, without going deeper into the mysteries of the dressing table, I will tell you that I myself, like many other honest folks, do not like to see the blank front of a large mirror in a room dimly lighted, and where the reflection of the candle seems rather to lose itself in the deep obscurity of the glass than to be reflected back again into the apartment. That space of inky darkness seems to be a field for fancy to play her revels in. She may call up other features to meet us, instead of the reflection of our own, or, as in the spells of Hallowe'en, which we learnt in childhood, some unknown form may be seen peeping over our shoulder. In short, when I am in a ghost-seeing humour, I make my handmaiden draw the green curtains over the mirror before I go into the room, so that she may have the first shock of the apparition, if there be any to be seen. But, to tell you the truth, this dislike to look into a mirror in particular times and places has, I believe, its original foundation in a story which came to me by tradition from my grandmother, who was a party concerned in the scene of which I will now tell you."

CHAPTER I

You are fond (said my aunt) of sketches of the society which has passed away. I wish I could describe to you Sir Philip Forester, the "chartered libertine" of Scottish good company, about the end of the last century. I never saw him indeed, but my mother's traditions were full of his wit, gallantry and dissipation. This gay knight flourished about the end of the seventeenth and beginning of the eighteenth century. He was the Sir Charles Easy and the Lovelace* of his day and country, renowned for the number of duels he had fought and the successful intrigues which he had carried on. The supremacy which he had attained in the fashionable world was absolute, and when we combine it with one or two anecdotes, for which, "if laws were made for every degree",* he ought certainly to have been hanged, the popularity of such a person really serves to show either that the present times are much more decent, if not more virtuous, than they formerly were, or that high-breeding then was of more difficult attainment than that which is now so called, and, consequently, entitled the successful professor to a proportional degree of plenary indulgences and privileges. No beau of this day could have borne out so ugly a story as that of Pretty Peggy Grindstone, the miller's daughter at Sillermills – it had well-nigh made work for the Lord Advocate.* But it hurt Sir Philip Forester no more than the hail hurts the hearthstone. He was as well received in society as ever, and dined with the Duke of A—— the day the poor girl was buried. She died of heartbreak. But that has nothing to do with my story.

Now, you must listen to a single word upon kith, kin and ally – I promise you I will not be prolix. But it is necessary to the authenticity of my legend that you should know that Sir Philip Forester, with his handsome person, elegant accomplishments and fashionable manners, married the younger Miss Falconer of King's-Copland. The elder sister of this lady had previously become the wife of my grandfather, Sir Geoffrey Bothwell, and brought into our family a good fortune. Miss Jemima, or Miss Jemmie Falconer, as she was usually called, had also about ten thousand pounds sterling, then thought a very handsome portion indeed.

The two sisters were extremely different, though each had their admirers while they remained single. Lady Bothwell had some touch of the old King's-Copland blood about her. She was bold (though not to the degree of audacity), ambitious and desirous to raise her house and family, and was, as has been said, a considerable spur to my grandfather, who was otherwise an indolent man, but whom, unless he has been slandered, his lady's influence involved in some political matters which had been more wisely let alone. She was a woman of high principles, however, and masculine good sense, as some of her letters testify, which are still in my wainscot cabinet.

Jemmie Falconer was the reverse of her sister in every respect. Her understanding did not reach above the ordinary pitch – if, indeed, she could be said to have attained it. Her beauty, while it lasted, consisted, in a great measure, of delicacy of complexion and regularity of features, without any peculiar force of expression. Even these charms faded under the sufferings attendant on an ill-sorted match. She was passionately attached to her husband, by whom she was treated with a callous, yet polite, indifference, which, to one whose heart was as tender as her judgement was weak, was more painful perhaps than absolute ill-usage. Sir Philip was a voluptuary – that is, a completely selfish egotist – whose disposition and character resembled the rapier he wore: polished, keen and brilliant, but inflexible and unpitying. As he observed carefully all the usual forms towards his lady, he had the art to deprive her even of the compassion of the world, and useless and unavailing as that may be while actually possessed by the sufferer, it is, to a mind like Lady Forester's, most painful to know she has it not.

The tattle of society did its best to place the peccant husband above the suffering wife. Some called her a poor spiritless thing, and declared that, with a little of her sister's spirit, she might have brought to reason any Sir Philip whatsoever, were it the termagant Falconbridge* himself. But the greater part of their acquaintance affected candour, and saw faults on both sides, though, in fact, there only existed the oppressor and the oppressed. The tone of such critics was: "To be sure, no one will justify Sir Philip Forester, but then we all know Sir Philip, and Jemmie Falconer might have known what she had to expect from the beginning. What made her set her cap at Sir Philip? He would never have looked at her if she had not thrown herself at his head, with her poor ten thousand pounds. I am sure, if it is money he wanted, she spoilt his market. I know where Sir Philip could have done much better. And then, if she *would* have the man, could not she try to make him more comfortable at home, and have his friends oftener, and not plague him with the squalling children, and take care all was handsome and in good style about the house? I declare I think Sir Philip would have made a very domestic man, with a woman who knew how to manage him."

Now, these fair critics, in raising their profound edifice of domestic felicity, did not recollect that the cornerstone was wanting, and that, to receive good company with good cheer, the means of the banquet ought to have been furnished by Sir Philip, whose income, dilapidated as it was, was not equal to the display of the hospitality required, and at the same time to the supply of the good knight's *menus plaisirs*.* So, in spite of all that was so sagely suggested by female friends, Sir Philip carried his good humour everywhere abroad, and left at home a solitary mansion and a pining spouse.

At length, inconvenienced in his money affairs, and tired even of the short time which he spent in his own dull house, Sir Philip Forester determined to take a trip to the Continent, in the capacity of a volunteer. It was then common for men of fashion to do so, and our knight perhaps was of opinion that a touch of the military character, just enough to exalt, but not render pedantic, his qualities as a *beau garçon*,* was necessary to maintain possession of the elevated situation which he held in the ranks of fashion.

Sir Philip's resolution threw his wife into agonies of terror, by which the worthy baronet was so much annoyed that, contrary to his wont, he took some trouble to soothe her apprehensions, and once more brought her to shed tears in which sorrow was not altogether unmingled with pleasure. Lady Bothwell asked, as a favour, Sir Philip's permission to receive her sister and her family into her own house during his absence on the Continent. Sir Philip readily assented to a proposition which saved expense, silenced the foolish people who might have talked of a deserted wife and family, and gratified Lady Bothwell, for whom he felt some respect, as for one who often spoke to him, always with freedom and sometimes with severity, without being deterred either by his raillery or the prestige of his reputation.

A day or two before Sir Philip's departure, Lady Bothwell took the liberty of asking him, in her sister's presence, the direct question which his timid wife had often desired but never ventured to put to him.

"Pray, Sir Philip, what route do you take when you reach the Continent?"

"I go from Leith to Helvoet by a packet with advices."*

"That I comprehend perfectly," said Lady Bothwell drily, "but you do not mean to remain long at Helvoet, I presume, and I should like to know what is your next object?"

"You ask me, my dear lady," answered Sir Philip, "a question which I have not dared to ask myself. The answer depends on the fate of war. I shall, of course, go to headquarters, wherever they may happen to be for the time, deliver my letters of introduction, learn as much of the noble art of war as may suffice a poor interloping amateur, and then take a glance at the sort of thing of which we read so much in the *Gazette*."*

"And I trust, Sir Philip," said Lady Bothwell, "that you will remember that you are a husband and a father, and that, though you think fit to indulge this military fancy, you will not let it hurry you into dangers which it is certainly unnecessary for any save professional persons to encounter?"

"Lady Bothwell does me too much honour," replied the adventurous knight, "in regarding such a circumstance with the slightest interest. But to soothe your flattering anxiety, I trust Your Ladyship will recollect that I cannot expose to hazard the venerable and paternal character which you so obligingly recommend to my protection without putting in some peril an honest fellow called Philip Forester, with whom I have kept company for thirty years, and with whom, though some folks consider him a coxcomb, I have not the least desire to part."

"Well, Sir Philip, you are the best judge of your own affairs; I have little right to interfere – you are not my husband."

"God forbid!" said Sir Philip hastily, instantly adding, however: "God forbid that I should deprive my friend Sir Geoffrey of so inestimable a treasure."

"But you are my sister's husband," replied the lady, "and I suppose you are aware of her present distress of mind…"

"If hearing of nothing else from morning to night can make me aware of it," said Sir Philip, "I should know something of the matter."

"I do not pretend to reply to your wit, Sir Philip," answered Lady Bothwell, "but you must be sensible that all this distress is on account of apprehensions for your personal safety."

"In that case, I am surprised that Lady Bothwell, at least, should give herself so much trouble upon so insignificant a subject."

"My sister's interest may account for my being anxious to learn something of Sir Philip Forester's motions – about which, otherwise, I know, he would not wish me to concern myself. I have a brother's safety, too, to be anxious for."

"You mean Major Falconer, your brother by the mother's side. What can he possibly have to do with our present agreeable conversation?"

"You have had words together, Sir Philip," said Lady Bothwell.

"Naturally – we are connections," replied Sir Philip, "and as such have always had the usual intercourse."

"That is an evasion of the subject," answered the lady. "By 'words' I mean angry words, on the subject of your usage of your wife."

"If," replied Sir Philip Forester, "you suppose Major Falconer simple enough to intrude his advice upon me, Lady Bothwell, in my domestic matters, you are indeed warranted in believing that I might possibly be so far displeased with the interference as to request him to reserve his advice till it was asked."

"And being on these terms, you are going to join the very army in which my brother Falconer is now serving?"

"No man knows the path of honour better than Major Falconer," said Sir Philip. "An aspirant after fame, like me, cannot choose a better guide than his footsteps."

Lady Bothwell rose and went to the window, the tears gushing from her eyes.

"And this heartless raillery," she said, "is all the consideration that is to be given to our apprehensions of a quarrel which may bring on the most terrible consequences? Good God, of what can men's hearts be made, who can thus dally with the agony of others?"

Sir Philip Forester was moved: he laid aside the mocking tone in which he had hitherto spoken.

"Dear Lady Bothwell," he said, taking her reluctant hand, "we are both wrong: you are too deeply serious; I, perhaps, too little so. The dispute I had with Major Falconer was of no earthly consequence. Had anything occurred betwixt us that ought to have been settled *par voie du fait*,* as we say in France, neither of us are persons that are likely to postpone such a meeting. Permit me to say that were it generally known that you or my Lady Forester are apprehensive of such a catastrophe, it might be the very means of bringing about what would not otherwise be likely to happen. I know your good sense, Lady Bothwell, and that you will understand me when I say that really my affairs require my absence for some months. This Jemima cannot understand – it is a perpetual recurrence of questions: why can you not do this or that, or the third thing – and when you have proved to her that her expedients are totally ineffectual, you have just to begin the whole round again. Now, do you tell her, dear Lady Bothwell, that *you* are satisfied. She is, you must confess, one of those persons with whom authority goes further than reasoning. Do but repose a little confidence in me, and you shall see how amply I will repay it."

Lady Bothwell shook her head, as one but half satisfied. "How difficult it is to extend confidence when the basis on which it ought to rest has been so much shaken! But I will do my best to make Jemima easy – and further, I can only say that for keeping your present purpose I hold you responsible both to God and man."

"Do not fear that I will deceive you," said Sir Philip. "The safest conveyance to me will be through the general post office, Helvoetsluys, where I will take care to leave orders for forwarding my letters. As for Falconer, our only encounter will be over a bottle of burgundy – so make yourself perfectly easy on his score."

Lady Bothwell could *not* make herself easy, yet she was sensible that her sister hurt her own cause by "taking on", as the maidservants call it, too vehemently, and by showing before every stranger, by manner and sometimes by words also, a dissatisfaction with her husband's journey that was sure to come to his ears, and equally certain to displease him. But there was no help for this domestic dissension, which ended only with the day of separation.

I am sorry I cannot tell, with precision, the year in which Sir Philip Forester went over to Flanders, but it was one of those in which the campaign opened with extraordinary fury, and many bloody, though indecisive, skirmishes were fought between the French on the one side and the Allies on the other.* In all our modern improvements, there are none, perhaps, greater than in the accuracy and speed with which intelligence is transmitted from any scene of action to those in this country whom it may concern. During Marlborough's* campaigns, the sufferings of the many who had relations in, or along with, the army were greatly augmented by the suspense in which they were detained for weeks, after they had heard of bloody battles in which, in all probability, those for whom their bosoms throbbed with anxiety had been personally engaged. Amongst those who were most agonized by this state of uncertainty was the... I had almost said "deserted"... wife of the gay Sir Philip Forester. A single letter had informed her of his arrival on the Continent – no others were received. One notice occurred in the newspapers, in which Volunteer Sir Philip Forester was mentioned as having been entrusted with a dangerous reconnaissance, which he had executed with the greatest courage, dexterity and intelligence, and received the thanks of the commanding officer. The sense of his having acquired distinction brought a momentary glow into the lady's pale cheek, but it was instantly lost in ashen whiteness at the recollection of his danger. After this they had no news whatever, neither from Sir Philip nor even from their brother Falconer. The case of Lady Forester was not indeed different from that of hundreds in the same situation, but a feeble mind is necessarily an irritable one, and the suspense which some bear with constitutional indifference or philosophical resignation, and some with a disposition to believe and hope the best, was intolerable to Lady Forester, at once solitary and sensitive, low-spirited and devoid of strength of mind, whether natural or acquired.

CHAPTER II

As she received no further news of Sir Philip, whether directly or indirectly, his unfortunate lady began now to feel a sort of consolation even in those careless habits which had so often given her pain. "He is so thoughtless," she repeated a hundred times a day to her sister, "he never writes when things are going on smoothly – it is his way: had anything happened, he would have informed us."

Lady Bothwell listened to her sister without attempting to console her. Probably she might be of opinion that even the worst intelligence which could be received from Flanders might not be without some touch of consolation, and that the Dowager Lady Forester, if so she was doomed to be called, might have a source of happiness unknown to the wife of the gayest and finest gentleman in Scotland. This conviction became stronger as they learnt from enquiries made at headquarters that Sir Philip was no longer with the army, though whether he had been taken or slain in some of those skirmishes which were perpetually occurring, and in which he loved to distinguish himself, or whether he had, for some unknown reason or capricious change of mind, voluntarily left the service, none of his countrymen in the camp of the Allies could form even a conjecture. Meantime, his creditors at home became clamorous, entered into possession of his property and threatened his person, should he be rash enough to return to Scotland. These additional disadvantages aggravated Lady Bothwell's displeasure against the fugitive husband, while her sister saw nothing in any of them save what tended to increase her grief for the absence of him whom her imagination now represented, as it had before marriage, gallant, gay and affectionate.

About this period there appeared in Edinburgh a man of singular appearance and pretensions. He was commonly called the Paduan Doctor, from having received his education at that famous university. He was supposed to possess some rare receipts* in medicine, with which, it was affirmed, he had wrought remarkable cures. But though, on the one hand, the physicians of Edinburgh termed him an empiric,* there were many persons, and among them some of the clergy, who, while they admitted the truth of the cures and the force of his remedies, alleged that Doctor Baptista Damiotti made use of charms and unlawful arts in order to obtain success in his practice. The resorting to him was even solemnly preached against as a seeking of health from idols and a trusting to the help which was to come from Egypt.* But the protection which the Paduan Doctor received from some friends of interest and consequence enabled him to set these imputations at defiance, and to assume, even in the city of Edinburgh, famed as it was for abhorrence of witches and necromancers, the dangerous character of an expounder of futurity. It was at length rumoured that, for a certain gratification, which of course was not an inconsiderable one, Doctor Baptista Damiotti could tell the fate of the absent and even show his visitors the personal form of their absent friends, and the action in which they were engaged at the moment. This rumour came to the ears of Lady Forester, who had reached that pitch of mental agony in which the sufferer will do anything, or endure anything, that suspense may be converted into certainty.

Gentle and timid in most cases, her state of mind made her equally obstinate and reckless, and it was with no small surprise and alarm that her sister, Lady Bothwell, heard her express a resolution to visit this man of art and learn from him the fate of her husband. Lady Bothwell remonstrated on the improbability that such pretensions as those of this foreigner could be founded in anything but imposture.

"I care not," said the deserted wife, "what degree of ridicule I may incur – if there be any one chance out of a hundred that I may obtain some certainty of my husband's fate, I would not miss that chance for whatever else the world can offer me."

Lady Bothwell next urged the unlawfulness of resorting to such sources of forbidden knowledge.

"Sister," replied the sufferer, "he who is dying of thirst cannot refrain from drinking even poisoned water. She who suffers under suspense must seek information, even were the powers which offer it unhallowed and infernal. I go to learn my fate alone, and this very evening will I know it – the sun that rises tomorrow shall find me, if not more happy, at least more resigned."

"Sister," said Lady Bothwell, "if you are determined upon this wild step, you shall not go alone. If this man be an impostor, you may be too much agitated by your feelings to detect his villainy. If, which I cannot believe, there be any truth in what he pretends, you shall not be exposed alone to a communication of so extraordinary a nature. I will go with you, if indeed you determine to go. But yet reconsider your project, and renounce enquiries which cannot be prosecuted without guilt, and perhaps without danger."

Lady Forester threw herself into her sister's arms, and, clasping her to her bosom, thanked her a hundred times for the offer of her company, while she declined with a melancholy gesture the friendly advice with which it was accompanied.

When the hour of twilight arrived, which was the period when the Paduan Doctor was understood to receive the visits of those who came to consult with him, the two ladies left their apartments in the Canongate of Edinburgh, having their dress arranged like that of women of an inferior description and their plaids disposed around their faces as they were worn by the same class, for, in those days of aristocracy, the quality of the wearer was generally indicated by the manner in which her plaid was disposed, as well as by the fineness of its texture. It was Lady Bothwell who had suggested this species of disguise, partly to avoid observation as they should go to the conjuror's house, and partly in order to make trial of his penetration by appearing before him in a feigned character. Lady

Forester's servant, of tried fidelity, had been employed by her to propitiate the doctor by a suitable fee, and a story intimating that a soldier's wife desired to know the fate of her husband – a subject upon which, in all probability, the sage was very frequently consulted.

To the last moment, when the palace clock struck eight, Lady Bothwell earnestly watched her sister, in hopes that she might retreat from her rash undertaking, but as mildness, and even timidity, is capable at times of vehement and fixed purposes, she found Lady Forester resolutely unmoved and determined when the moment of departure arrived. Ill-satisfied with the expedition, but determined not to leave her sister at such a crisis, Lady Bothwell accompanied Lady Forester through more than one obscure street and lane, the servant walking before and acting as their guide. At length he suddenly turned into a narrow court, and knocked at an arched door, which seemed to belong to a building of some antiquity. It opened, though no one appeared to act as porter, and the servant, stepping aside from the entrance, motioned the ladies to enter. They had no sooner done so than it shut, and excluded their guide. The two ladies found themselves in a small vestibule, illuminated by a dim lamp, and having, when the door was closed, no communication with the external light or air. The door of an inner apartment, partly open, was at the farther side of the vestibule.

"We must not hesitate now, Jemima," said Lady Bothwell, and walked forwards into the inner room, where, surrounded by books, maps, philosophical utensils and other implements of peculiar shape and appearance, they found the man of art.

There was nothing very peculiar in the Italian's appearance. He had the dark complexion and marked features of his country, seemed about fifty years old and was handsomely but plainly dressed in a full suit of black clothes, which was then the universal costume of the medical profession. Large wax lights, in silver sconces, illuminated the apartment, which was reasonably furnished. He rose as the ladies entered, and, notwithstanding the inferiority of their dress, received them with the marked respect due to their quality, and which foreigners are usually punctilious in rendering to those to whom such honours are due.

Lady Bothwell endeavoured to maintain her proposed incognito, and, as the doctor ushered them to the upper end of the room, made a motion declining his courtesy, as unfitted for their condition. "We are poor people, sir," she said. "Only my sister's distress has brought us to consult your worship whether—"

He smiled as he interrupted her. "I am aware, madam, of your sister's distress and its cause; I am aware, also, that I am honoured with a visit from two ladies of the highest consideration – Lady Bothwell and Lady Forester. If I could not distinguish them from the class of society which their present dress would indicate, there would be small possibility of my being able to gratify them by giving the information which they came to seek."

"I can easily understand—" said Lady Bothwell.

"Pardon my boldness to interrupt you, milady," cried the Italian. "Your Ladyship was about to say that you could easily understand that I had got possession of your names by means of your domestic. But, in thinking so, you do injustice to the fidelity of your servant and, I may add, to the skill of one who is also not less your humble servant – Baptista Damiotti."

"I have no intention to do either, sir," said Lady Bothwell, maintaining a tone of composure, though somewhat surprised, "but the situation is something new to me. If you know who we are, you also know, sir, what brought us here."

"Curiosity to know the fate of a Scottish gentleman of rank, now or lately, upon the Continent," answered the seer. "His name is *il cavaliero* Filippo Forester – a gentleman who has the honour to be husband to this lady, and, with Your Ladyship's permission for using plain language, the misfortune not to value as it deserves that inestimable advantage."

Lady Forester sighed deeply, and Lady Bothwell replied:

"Since you know our object without our telling it, the only question that remains is whether you have the power to relieve my sister's anxiety."

"I have, madam," answered the Paduan scholar, "but there is still a previous enquiry. Have you the courage to behold with your own eyes what the Cavaliero Filippo Forester is now doing, or will you take it on my report?"

"That question my sister must answer for herself," said Lady Bothwell.

"With my own eyes will I endure to see whatever you have power to show me," said Lady Forester, with the same determined spirit which had stimulated her since her resolution was taken upon this subject.

"There may be danger in it."

"If gold can compensate the risk…" said Lady Forester, taking out her purse.

"I do not such things for the purpose of gain," answered the foreigner. "I dare not turn my art to such a purpose. If I take the gold of the wealthy, it is but to bestow it on the poor – nor do I ever accept more than the sum I have already received from your servant. Put up your purse, madam – an adept needs not your gold."

Lady Bothwell, considering this rejection of her sister's offer as a mere trick of an empiric to induce her to press a larger sum upon him, and willing that the scene should be commenced and ended, offered some gold in turn, observing that it was only to enlarge the sphere of his charity.

"Let Lady Bothwell enlarge the sphere of her own charity," said the Paduan, "not merely in giving of alms, in which I know she is not deficient, but in judging the character of others, and let her oblige Baptista Damiotti by believing him honest till she shall discover him to be a knave. Do not be surprised, madam, if I speak in answer to your thoughts rather than your expressions, and tell me once more whether you have courage to look on what I am prepared to show."

"I own, sir," said Lady Bothwell, "that your words strike me with some sense of fear, but whatever my sister desires to witness, I will not shrink from witnessing along with her."

"Nay, the danger only consists in the risk of your resolution failing you. The sight can only last for the space of seven minutes, and should you interrupt the vision by speaking a single word, not only would the charm be broken, but some danger might result to the spectators. But if you can remain steadily silent for the seven minutes, your curiosity will be gratified without the slightest risk, and for this I will engage my honour."

Internally Lady Bothwell thought the security was but an indifferent one, but she suppressed the suspicion, as if she had believed that the adept, whose dark features wore a half-formed smile, could in reality read even her most secret reflections. A solemn pause then ensued, until Lady Forester gathered courage enough to reply to the physician, as he termed himself, that she would abide with firmness and silence the sight which he had promised to exhibit to them. Upon this, he made them a low obeisance and, saying he went to prepare matters to meet their wish, left the apartment. The two sisters, hand in hand, as if seeking by that close union to divert any danger which might threaten them, sat down on two seats in immediate contact with each other – Jemima seeking support in the manly and habitual courage of Lady Bothwell, and she, on the other hand, more agitated than she had expected, endeavouring to fortify herself by the desperate resolution which circumstances had forced her sister to assume. The one perhaps said to herself that her sister never feared anything, and the other might reflect that what so feeble-minded a woman as Jemima did not fear could not properly be a subject of apprehension to a person of firmness and resolution like her own.

In a few moments the thoughts of both were diverted from their own situation by a strain of music so singularly sweet and solemn that, while it seemed calculated to avert or dispel any feeling unconnected with its harmony, increased, at the same time, the solemn excitation which the preceding interview was calculated to produce. The music was that of some instrument with which they were unacquainted, but circumstances afterwards led my ancestress to believe that it was that of the harmonica, which she heard at a much later period in life.

When these heaven-born sounds had ceased, a door opened in the upper end of the apartment, and they saw Damiotti, standing at the head of two or three steps, sign to them to advance. His dress was so different from that which he had worn a few minutes before that they could hardly recognize him, and the deadly paleness of his countenance and a certain stern rigidity of muscles, like that of one whose mind is made up to some strange and daring action, had totally changed the somewhat sarcastic expression with which he had previously regarded them both, and particularly Lady Bothwell. He was barefooted, excepting a species of sandals in the antique fashion; his legs were naked beneath the knees; above them he wore hose, and a doublet of dark-crimson silk close to his body; and over that a flowing loose robe, something resembling a surplice, of snow-white linen; his throat and neck were uncovered; and his long, straight, black hair was carefully combed down at full length.

As the ladies approached at his bidding, he showed no gesture of that ceremonious courtesy of which he had been formerly lavish. On the contrary, he made the signal of advance with an air of command – and when, arm in arm and with insecure steps, the sisters approached the spot where he stood, it was with a warning frown that he pressed his finger to his lips, as if reiterating his condition of absolute silence, while, stalking before them, he led the way into the next apartment.

This was a large room, hung with black, as if for a funeral. At the upper end was a table, or rather a species of altar, covered with the same lugubrious colour, on which lay divers objects resembling the usual implements of sorcery. These objects were not indeed visible as they advanced into the apartment, for the light which displayed them, being only that of two expiring lamps, was extremely faint. The master – to use the Italian phrase for persons of this description – approached the upper end of the room, with a genuflection like that of a Catholic to the crucifix, and at the same time crossed himself. The ladies followed in silence, and arm in arm. Two or three low broad steps led to a platform in front of the altar, or what resembled such. Here the sage took his stand and placed the ladies beside him, once more earnestly repeating by signs his injunctions of silence. The Italian then, extending his bare arm from under his linen vestment, pointed with his forefinger to five large flambeaux, or torches, placed on each side of the altar. They took fire successively at the approach of his hand, or rather of his finger, and spread a strong light through the room. By this the visitors could discern that on the seeming altar were disposed two naked swords laid crosswise, a large open book, which they conceived to be a copy of the Holy Scriptures, but in a language to them unknown, and besides this mysterious volume was placed a human skull. But what struck the sisters most was a very tall and broad mirror, which occupied all the space behind the altar and, illumined by the lighted torches, reflected the mysterious articles which were laid upon it.

The master then placed himself between the two ladies, and, pointing to the mirror, took each by the hand, but without speaking a syllable. They gazed intently on the polished and sable space to which he had directed their attention. Suddenly the surface assumed a new and singular appearance. It no longer simply reflected the objects placed before it, but, as if it had self-contained scenery of its own, objects began to appear within it, at first in a disorderly, indistinct and miscellaneous manner, like form arranging itself out of chaos, at length in distinct and defined shape and symmetry. It was thus that, after some shifting of light and darkness over the face of the wonderful glass, a long perspective of arches and columns began to arrange itself on its sides, and a vaulted roof on the upper part of it, till, after many oscillations, the whole vision gained a fixed and stationary appearance, representing the interior of a foreign church. The pillars were stately and hung with scutcheons; the arches were lofty and magnificent; the floor was lettered with funeral inscriptions. But there were no separate shrines, no images, no display of chalice or crucifix on the altar. It was, therefore, a Protestant church upon the Continent. A clergyman dressed in the Geneva gown and band* stood by the Communion table, and, with the Bible opened before him and his clerk awaiting in the background, seemed prepared to perform some service of the Church to which he belonged.

At length, there entered the middle aisle of the building a numerous party, which appeared to be a bridal one, as a lady and gentleman walked first, hand in hand, followed by a large concourse of persons of both sexes, gaily – nay, richly attired. The bride, whose features they could distinctly see, seemed not more than sixteen years old, and extremely beautiful. The bridegroom, for some seconds, moved rather with his shoulder towards them and his face averted, but his elegance of form and step struck the sisters at once with the same apprehension. As he turned his face suddenly, it was frightfully realized, and they saw, in the gay bridegroom before them, Sir Philip Forester. His wife uttered an imperfect exclamation, at the sound of which the whole scene stirred and seemed to separate.

"I could compare it to nothing," said Lady Bothwell, while recounting the wonderful tale, "but to the dispersion of the reflection offered by a deep and calm pool when a stone is suddenly cast into it, and the shadows become dissipated and broken."

The master pressed both the ladies' hands severely, as if to remind them of their promise, and of the danger which they incurred. The exclamation died away on Lady Forester's tongue without attaining perfect utterance, and the scene in the glass, after the fluctuation of a minute, again resumed to the eye its former appearance of a real scene, existing within the mirror as if represented in a picture, save that the figures were movable instead of being stationary.

The representation of Sir Philip Forester, now distinctly visible in form and feature, was seen to lead on towards the clergyman that beautiful girl, who advanced at once with diffidence and with a species of affectionate pride. In the mean time, and just as the clergyman had arranged the bridal company before him and seemed about to commence the service, another group of persons, of whom two or three were officers, entered the church. They moved, at first, forward, as though they came to witness the bridal ceremony, but suddenly one of the officers, whose back was towards the spectators, detached himself from his companions and rushed hastily towards the marriage party, when the whole of them turned towards him, as if attracted by some exclamation which had accompanied his advance. Suddenly the intruder drew his sword; the bridegroom unsheathed his own and made towards him; swords were also drawn by other individuals, both of the marriage party and of those who had last entered. They fell into a sort of confusion, the clergyman and some elder and graver persons labouring apparently to keep the peace, while the hotter spirits on both sides brandished their weapons. But now the period of the brief space during which the soothsayer, as he pretended, was permitted to exhibit his art was arrived. The fumes again mixed together, and dissolved gradually from observation; the vaults and columns of the church rolled asunder and disappeared, and the front of the mirror reflected nothing save the blazing torches and the melancholy apparatus placed on the altar or table before it.

The doctor led the ladies, who greatly required his support, into the apartment from whence they came, where wine, essences and other means of restoring suspended animation had been provided during his absence. He motioned them to chairs, which they occupied in silence, Lady Forester, in particular, wringing her hands and casting her eyes up to heaven, but without speaking a word, as if the spell had been still before her eyes.

"And what we have seen is even now acting?" said Lady Bothwell, collecting herself with difficulty.

"That," answered Baptista Damiotti, "I cannot justly, or with certainty, say. But it is either now acting or has been acted during a short space before this. It is the last remarkable transaction in which the Cavalier Forester has been engaged."

Lady Bothwell then expressed anxiety concerning her sister, whose altered countenance and apparent unconsciousness of what passed around her excited her apprehensions how it might be possible to convey her home.

"I have prepared for that," answered the adept. "I have directed the servant to bring your equipage as near to this place as the narrowness of the street will permit. Fear not for your sister, but give her, when you return home, this composing draught, and she will be better tomorrow morning. Few," he added in a melancholy tone, "leave this house as well in health as they entered it. Such being the consequence of seeing knowledge by mysterious means, I leave you to judge the condition of those who have the power of gratifying such irregular curiosity. Farewell, and forget not the potion."

"I will give her nothing that comes from you," said Lady Bothwell. "I have seen enough of your art already. Perhaps you would poison us both to conceal your own necromancy. But we are persons who want neither the means of making our wrongs known nor the assistance of friends to right them."

"You have had no wrongs from me, madam," said the adept. "You sought one who is little grateful for such honour. He seeks no one, and only gives responses to those who invite and call upon him. After all, you have but learnt a little sooner the evil which you must still be doomed to endure. I hear your servant's step at the door, and will detain Your Ladyship and Lady Forester no longer. The next packet from the Continent will explain what you have already partly witnessed. Let it not, if I may advise, pass too suddenly into your sister's hands."

So saying, he bid Lady Bothwell goodnight. She went, lighted by the adept, to the vestibule, where he hastily threw a black cloak over his singular dress, and, opening the door, entrusted his visitors to the care of the servant. It was with difficulty that Lady Bothwell sustained her sister to the carriage, though it was only twenty steps distant.

When they arrived home, Lady Forester required medical assistance. The physician of the family attended, and shook his head on feeling her pulse.

"Here has been," he said, "a violent and sudden shock on the nerves. I must know how it has happened."

Lady Bothwell admitted they had visited the conjuror, and that Lady Forester had received some bad news respecting her husband, Sir Philip.

"That rascally quack would make my fortune were he to stay in Edinburgh," said the graduate.* "This is the seventh nervous case I have heard of his making for me, and all by effect of terror." He next examined the composing draught which Lady Bothwell had unconsciously brought in her hand, tasted it and pronounced it very germane to the matter, and what would save an application to the apothecary. He then paused, and, looking at Lady Bothwell very significantly, at length added, "I suppose I must not ask Your Ladyship anything about this Italian warlock's proceedings?"

"Indeed, doctor," answered Lady Bothwell, "I consider what passed as confidential, and though the man may be a rogue, yet, as we were fools enough to consult him, we should, I think, be honest enough to keep his counsel."

"*May* be a knave! Come," said the doctor, "I am glad to hear Your Ladyship allows such a possibility in anything that comes from Italy."

"What comes from Italy may be as good as what comes from Hanover, doctor. But you and I will remain good friends – and that it may be so, we will say nothing of Whig and Tory."*

"Not I," said the doctor, receiving his fee and taking his hat. "A Carolus serves my purpose as well as a Willielmus.* But I should like to know why old Lady St Ringan's, and all that set, go about wasting their decayed lungs in puffing this foreign fellow."

"Ay, you had best 'set him down a Jesuit', as Scrub says."* On these terms they parted.

The poor patient, whose nerves, from an extraordinary state of tension, had at length become relaxed in as extraordinary a degree, continued to struggle with a sort of imbecility, the growth of superstitious terror, when the shocking tidings were brought from Holland which fulfilled even her worst expectations.

They were sent by the celebrated Earl of Stair, and contained the melancholy event of a duel betwixt Sir Philip Forester and his wife's half-brother,

Captain Falconer, of the Scotch Dutch, as they were then called, in which the latter had been killed. The cause of quarrel rendered the incident still more shocking. It seemed that Sir Philip had left the army suddenly, in consequence of being unable to pay a very considerable sum which he had lost to another volunteer at play. He had changed his name and taken up his residence at Rotterdam, where he had insinuated himself into the good graces of an ancient and rich burgomaster, and, by his handsome person and graceful manners, captivated the affection of his only child, a very young person of great beauty, and the heiress of much wealth. Delighted with the specious attractions of his proposed son-in-law, the wealthy merchant, whose idea of the British character was too high to admit of his taking any precaution to acquire evidence of his condition and circumstances, gave his consent to the marriage. It was about to be celebrated in the principal church of the city when it was interrupted by a singular occurrence.

Captain Falconer having been detached to Rotterdam to bring up a part of the brigade of Scottish auxiliaries who were in quarters there, a person of consideration in the town, to whom he had been formerly known, proposed to him for amusement to go to the high church to see a countryman of his own married to the daughter of a wealthy burgomaster. Captain Falconer went accordingly, accompanied by his Dutch acquaintance, with a party of his friends and two or three officers of the Scotch brigade. His astonishment may be conceived when he saw his own brother-in-law, a married man, on the point of leading to the altar the innocent and beautiful creature, upon whom he was about to practise a base and unmanly deceit. He proclaimed his villainy on the spot, and the marriage was interrupted, of course. But against the opinion of more thinking men, who considered Sir Philip Forester as having thrown himself out of the rank of men of honour, Captain Falconer admitted him to the privilege of such, accepted a challenge from him, and in the rencounter received a mortal wound. Such are the ways of Heaven, mysterious in our eyes.

Lady Forester never recovered the shock of this dismal intelligence.

"And did this tragedy," said I, "take place exactly at the time when the scene in the mirror was exhibited?"

"It is hard to be obliged to maim one's story," answered my aunt, "but to speak the truth, it happened some days sooner than the apparition was exhibited."

"And so there remained a possibility," said I, "that by some secret and speedy communication the artist might have received early intelligence of that incident."

"The incredulous pretended so," replied my aunt.

"What became of the adept?" demanded I.

"Why, a warrant came down shortly afterwards to arrest him for high treason as an agent of the Chevalier St George,* and Lady Bothwell, recollecting the hints which had escaped the doctor, an ardent friend of the Protestant succession, did then call to remembrance that this man was chiefly *prôné* among the ancient patrons of her own political persuasion. It certainly seemed probable that intelligence from the Continent, which could easily have been transmitted by an active and powerful agent, might have enabled him to prepare such a scene of phantasmagoria as she had herself witnessed. Yet there were so many difficulties in assigning a natural explanation that, to the day of her death, she remained in great doubt on the subject, and much disposed to cut the Gordian knot* by admitting the existence of supernatural agency."

"But, my dear aunt," said I, "what became of the man of skill?"

"Oh, he was too good a fortune-teller not to be able to foresee that his own destiny would be tragical if he waited the arrival of the man with the silver greyhound upon his sleeve.* He made, as we say, a moonlight flitting, and was nowhere to be seen or heard of. Some noise there was about papers or letters found in the house, but it died away, and Doctor Baptista Damiotti was soon as little talked of as Galen or Hippocrates."*

"And Sir Philip Forester," said I, "did he too vanish for ever from the public scene?"

"No," replied my kind informer. "He was heard of once more, and it was upon a remarkable occasion. It is said that we Scots, when there was such a nation in existence, have, among our full peck of virtues, one or two little barleycorns of vice. In particular, it is alleged that we rarely forgive, and never forget, any injuries received, that we used to make an idol of our resentment, as poor Lady Constance did of her grief,* and are addicted, as Burns says, to 'nursing our wrath to keep it warm'.* Lady Bothwell was not without this feeling, and, I believe, nothing whatever, scarce the restoration of the Stuart line, could have happened so delicious to her feelings as an opportunity of being revenged on Sir Philip Forester for the deep and double injury which had deprived her of a sister and of a brother. But nothing of him was heard or known till many a year had passed away.

"At length – it was on a Fastern's E'en (Shrovetide)* assembly, at which the whole fashion of Edinburgh attended, full and frequent, and when Lady Bothwell had a seat amongst the lady patronesses, that one of the attendants on the company whispered into her ear that a gentleman wished to speak with her in private.

"'In private, and in an assembly room! He must be mad – tell him to call upon me tomorrow morning.'"

"'I said so, my lady,' answered the man, 'but he desired me to give you this paper.'

"She undid the billet, which was curiously folded and sealed. It only bore the words 'On business of life and death', written in a hand which she had never seen before. Suddenly it occurred to her that it might concern the safety of some of her political friends – she therefore followed the messenger to a small apartment where the refreshments were prepared, and from which the general company was excluded. She found an old man, who at her approach rose up and bowed profoundly. His appearance indicated a broken constitution, and his dress, though sedulously rendered conforming to the etiquette of a ballroom, was worn and tarnished, and hung in folds about his emaciated person. Lady Bothwell was about to feel for her purse, expecting to get rid of the supplicant at the expense of a little money, but some fear of a mistake arrested her purpose. She therefore gave the man leisure to explain himself.

"'I have the honour to speak with the Lady Bothwell?'

"'I am Lady Bothwell – allow me to say that this is no time or place for long explanations. What are your commands with me?'

"'Your Ladyship,' said the old man, 'had once a sister.'

"'True – whom I loved as my own soul.'

"'And a brother.'

"'The bravest, the kindest, the most affectionate,' said Lady Bothwell.

"'Both these beloved relatives you lost by the fault of an unfortunate man,' continued the stranger.

"'By the crime of an unnatural, bloody-minded murderer,' said the lady.

"'I am answered,' replied the old man, bowing as if to withdraw.

"'Stop, sir, I command you,' said Lady Bothwell. 'Who are you that, at such a place and time, come to recall these horrible recollections? I insist upon knowing.'

"'I am one who means Lady Bothwell no injury, but, on the contrary, to offer her the means of doing a deed of Christian charity which the world would wonder at, and which Heaven would reward, but I find her in no temper for such a sacrifice as I was prepared to ask.'

"'Speak out, sir – what is your meaning?' said Lady Bothwell.

"'The wretch that has wronged you so deeply,' rejoined the stranger, 'is now on his deathbed. His days have been days of misery, his nights have been sleepless hours of anguish, yet he cannot die without your forgiveness. His life has been an unremitting penance, yet he dares not part from his burden while your curses load his soul.'

"'Tell him,' said Lady Bothwell sternly, 'to ask pardon of that Being whom he has so greatly offended, not of an erring mortal like himself. What could my forgiveness avail him?'

"'Much,' answered the old man. 'It will be an earnest of that which he may then venture to ask from his Creator, lady, and from yours. Remember, Lady Bothwell, you too have a deathbed to look forward to: your soul may – all human souls must – feel the awe of facing the judgement seat, with the wounds of an untented conscience raw and rankling: what thought would it be then that should whisper, "I have given no mercy, how then shall I ask it?"'

"'Man, whosoever thou mayst be,' replied Lady Bothwell, 'urge me not so cruelly. It would be but blasphemous hypocrisy to utter with my lips the words which every throb of my heart protests against. They would open the earth and give to light the wasted form of my sister, the bloody form of my murdered brother. Forgive him! Never – never.'

"'Great God,' cried the old man, holding up his hands, 'is it thus the worms which thou hast called out of dust obey the commands of their Maker? Farewell, proud and unforgiving woman. Exult that thou hast added to a death in want and pain the agonies of religious despair, but never again mock Heaven by petitioning for the pardon which thou hast refused to grant.'

"He was turning from her.

"'Stop,' she exclaimed. 'I will try – yes, I will try to pardon him.'

"'Gracious lady,' said the old man, 'you will relieve the overburdened soul which dare not sever itself from its sinful companion of earth without being at peace with you. What do I know? Your forgiveness may perhaps preserve for penitence the dregs of a wretched life.'

"'Ha!' said the lady, as a sudden light broke on her. 'It is the villain himself.' And grasping Sir Philip Forester (for it was he and no other) by the collar, she raised a cry of 'Murder – murder! Seize the murderer!'

"At an exclamation so singular, in such a place, the company thronged into the apartment, but Sir Philip Forester was no longer there. He had forcibly extricated himself from Lady Bothwell's hold and had run out of the apartment, which opened on the landing place of the stair. There seemed no escape in that direction, for there were several persons coming up the steps, and others descending. But the unfortunate man was desperate. He threw himself over the balustrade, and alighted safely in the lobby, though a leap of fifteen feet at least, then dashed into the street, and was lost in darkness. Some of the Bothwell family made pursuit, and had they come up with the fugitive they might have perhaps slain him, for in those days men's blood ran warm in their veins. But the police did not interfere, the matter most criminal having happened long since, and in a foreign land. Indeed, it was always thought that this extraordinary scene originated in a hypocritical experiment by which Sir Philip desired to ascertain whether he might return to his native country in safety from the resentment of a family which he had injured so deeply. As the result fell out so contrary to his wishes, he is believed to have returned to the Continent, and there died in exile."

So closed the tale of the mysterious mirror.

The Tapestried Chamber
or
The Lady in the Sacque*

INTRODUCTION

This is another little story from *The Keepsake* of 1828. It was told to me many years ago by the late Miss Anna Seward,* who, among other accomplishments that rendered her an amusing inmate in a country house, had that of recounting narratives of this sort with very considerable effect – much greater, indeed, than anyone would be apt to guess from the style of her written performances. There are hours and moods when most people are not displeased to listen to such things, and I have heard some of the greatest and wisest of my contemporaries take their share in telling them.

AUGUST 1831

THE TAPESTRIED CHAMBER

OR

THE LADY IN THE SACQUE

The following narrative is given from the pen, so far as memory permits, in the same character in which it was presented to the author's ear, nor has he claim to further praise, or to be more deeply censured, than in proportion to the good or bad judgement which he has employed in selecting his materials, as he has studiously avoided any attempt at ornament which might interfere with the simplicity of the tale.

At the same time, it must be admitted that the particular class of stories which turns on the marvellous possesses a stronger influence when told than when committed to print. The volume taken up at noonday, though rehearsing the same incidents, conveys a much more feeble impression than is achieved by the voice of the speaker on a circle of fireside auditors, who hang upon the narrative as the narrator details the minute incidents which serve to give it authenticity, and lowers his voice with an affectation of mystery while he approaches the fearful and wonderful part. It was with such advantages that the present writer heard the following events related, more than twenty years since, by the celebrated Miss Seward of Lichfield, who to her numerous accomplishments added, in a remarkable degree, the power of narrative in private conversation. In its present form the tale must necessarily lose all the interest which was attached to it by the flexible voice and intelligent features of the gifted narrator. Yet still, read aloud to an undoubting audience by the doubtful light of the closing evening, or in silence by a decaying taper and amidst the solitude of a half-lighted apartment, it may redeem its character as a good ghost story. Miss Seward always affirmed that she had derived her information from an authentic source, although she suppressed the names of the two persons chiefly concerned. I will not avail myself of any particulars I may have since received concerning the localities of the detail, but suffer them to rest under the same general description in which they were first related to me – and, for the same reason, I will not add to or diminish the narrative by any circumstance, whether more or less material, but simply rehearse, as I heard it, a story of supernatural terror.

About the end of the American war, when the officers of Lord Cornwallis's army which surrendered at Yorktown* and others who had been made prisoners during the impolitic and ill-fated controversy were returning to their own country to relate their adventures and repose themselves after their fatigues, there was amongst them a general officer to whom Miss S. gave the name of Browne – but merely, as I understood, to save the inconvenience of introducing a nameless agent in the narrative. He was an officer of merit, as well as a gentleman of high consideration for family and attainments.

Some business had carried General Browne upon a tour through the western counties, when, in the conclusion of a morning stage,* he found himself in the vicinity of a small country town which presented a scene of uncommon beauty, and of a character peculiarly English.

The little town, with its stately old church, whose tower bore testimony to the devotion of ages long past, lay amidst pastures and cornfields of small extent, but bounded and divided with hedgerow timber of great age and size. There were few marks of modern improvement. The environs of the place intimated neither the solitude of decay nor the bustle of novelty; the houses were old, but in good repair, and the beautiful little river murmured freely on its way to the left of the town, neither restrained by a dam nor bordered by a towing path.

THE TAPESTRIED CHAMBER

Upon a gentle eminence, nearly a mile to the southward of the town, were seen, amongst many venerable oaks and tangled thickets, the turrets of a castle, as old as the wars of York and Lancaster,* but which seemed to have received important alterations during the age of Elizabeth and her successor.* It had not been a place of great size, but whatever accommodation it formerly afforded was, it must be supposed, still to be obtained within its walls – at least, such was the inference which General Browne drew from observing the smoke arise merrily from several of the ancient wreathed and carved chimney stalks. The wall of the park ran alongside of the highway for two or three hundred yards, and through the different points by which the eye found glimpses into the woodland scenery it seemed to be well stocked. Other points of view opened in succession – now a full one of the front of the old castle and now a side glimpse at its particular towers, the former rich in all the bizarrerie of the Elizabethan school, while the simple and solid strength of other parts of the building seemed to show that they had been raised more for defence than ostentation.

Delighted with the partial glimpses which he obtained of the castle through the woods and glades by which this ancient feudal fortress was surrounded, our military traveller was determined to enquire whether it might not deserve a nearer view, and whether it contained family pictures or other objects of curiosity worthy of a stranger's visit, when, leaving the vicinity of the park, he rolled through a clean and well-paved street, and stopped at the door of a well-frequented inn.

Before ordering horses to proceed on his journey, General Browne made enquiries concerning the proprietor of the chateau which had so attracted his admiration, and was equally surprised and pleased at hearing in reply a nobleman named whom we shall call Lord Woodville. How fortunate! Much of Browne's early recollections, both at school and at college, had been connected with young Woodville, whom, by a few questions, he now ascertained to be the same with the owner of this fair domain. He had been raised to the peerage by the decease of his father a few months before, and, as the general learnt from the landlord, the term of mourning being ended, was now taking possession of his paternal estate, in the jovial season of merry autumn, accompanied by a select party of friends, to enjoy the sports of a country famous for game.

This was delightful news to our traveller. Frank Woodville had been Richard Browne's fag at Eton, and his chosen intimate at Christ Church:* their pleasures and their tasks had been the same, and the honest soldier's heart warmed to find his early friend in possession of so delightful a residence, and of an estate, as the landlord assured him with a nod and a wink, fully adequate to maintain and add to his dignity. Nothing was more natural than that the traveller should suspend a journey which there was nothing to render hurried to pay a visit to an old friend under such agreeable circumstances.

The fresh horses, therefore, had only the brief task of conveying the general's travelling carriage to Woodville Castle. A porter admitted them at a modern Gothic lodge, built in that style to correspond with the castle itself, and at the same time rang a bell to give warning of the approach of visitors. Apparently the sound of the bell had suspended the separation of the company, bent on the various amusements of the morning, for, on entering the court of the chateau, several young men were lounging about in their sporting dresses, looking at and criticizing the dogs, which the keepers held in readiness to attend their pastime. As General Browne alighted, the young lord came to the gate of the hall, and for an instant gazed, as at a stranger, upon the countenance of his friend, on which war, with its fatigues and its wounds, had made a great alteration. But the uncertainty lasted no longer than till the visitor had spoken, and the hearty greeting which followed was such as can only be exchanged betwixt those who have passed together the merry days of careless boyhood or early youth.

"If I could have formed a wish, my dear Browne," said Lord Woodville, "it would have been to have you here, of all men, upon this occasion, which my friends are good enough to hold as a sort of holiday. Do not think you have been unwatched during the years you have been absent from us. I have traced you through your dangers, your triumphs, your misfortunes, and was delighted to see that, whether in victory or defeat, the name of my old friend was always distinguished with applause."

The general made a suitable reply, and congratulated his friend on his new dignities, and the possession of a place and domain so beautiful.

"Nay, you have seen nothing of it as yet," said Lord Woodville, "and I trust you do not mean to leave us till you are better acquainted with it. It is true, I confess, that my present party is pretty large, and the old house, like other places of the kind, does not possess so much accommodation as the extent of the outward walls appears to promise. But we can give you a comfortable old-fashioned room, and I venture to suppose that your campaigns have taught you to be glad of worse quarters."

The general shrugged his shoulders and laughed. "I presume," he said, "the worst apartment in your chateau is considerably superior to the old tobacco cask in which I was fain to take up my night's lodging when I was in the bush, as the Virginians call it, with the light corps. There I lay, like Diogenes himself,* so delighted with my covering from the elements that I made a vain attempt to have it rolled on to my next quarters, but my commander for the time would give way to no such luxurious provision, and I took farewell of my beloved cask with tears in my eyes."

"Well, then, since you do not fear your quarters," said Lord Woodville, "you will stay with me a week at least. Of guns, dogs, fishing rods, flies and means of sport by sea and land, we have enough and to spare: you cannot pitch on an amusement but we will find the means of pursuing it. But if you prefer the gun and pointers, I will go with you myself, and see whether you have mended your shooting since you have been amongst the Indians of the back settlements."

The general gladly accepted his friendly host's proposal in all its points. After a morning of manly exercise, the company met at dinner, where it was the delight of Lord Woodville to conduce to the display of the high properties of his recovered friend, so as to recommend him to his guests, most of whom were persons of distinction. He led General Browne to speak of the scenes he had witnessed, and as every word marked alike the brave officer and the sensible man, who retained possession of his cool judgement under the most imminent dangers, the company looked upon the soldier with general respect, as on one who had proved himself possessed of an uncommon portion of personal courage – that attribute, of all others, of which everybody desires to be thought possessed.

The day at Woodville Castle ended as usual in such mansions. The hospitality stopped within the limits of good order; music, in which the young lord was a proficient, succeeded to the circulation of the bottle; cards and billiards, for those who preferred such amusements, were in readiness; but the exercise of the morning required early hours, and not long after eleven o'clock the guests began to retire to their several apartments.

The young lord himself conducted his friend, General Browne, to the chamber destined for him, which answered the description he had given of it, being comfortable but old-fashioned. The bed was of the massive form, used in the end of the seventeenth century, and the curtains of faded silk, heavily trimmed with tarnished gold. But then the sheets, pillows and blankets looked delightful to the campaigner when he thought of his mansion, "the cask". There was an air of gloom in the tapestry hangings which, with their worn-out graces, curtained the walls of the little chamber and gently undulated as the autumnal breeze found its way through the ancient lattice window, which pattered and whistled as the air gained entrance. The toilet too, with its mirror, turbaned, after the manner of the beginning of the century, with a coiffure of murrey-coloured silk, and its hundred strange-shaped boxes, providing for arrangements which had been obsolete for more than fifty years, had an antique, and in so far a melancholy, aspect. But nothing could blaze more brightly and cheerfully than the two large wax candles – or, if aught could rival them, it was the flaming, bickering faggots in the chimney, that sent at once their gleam and their warmth through the snug apartment, which, notwithstanding the general antiquity of its appearance, was not wanting in the least convenience that modern habits rendered either necessary or desirable.

"This is an old-fashioned sleeping apartment, general, said the young lord, "but I hope you find nothing that makes you envy your old tobacco cask."

"I am not particular respecting my lodgings," replied the general, "yet were I to make any choice, I would prefer this chamber by many degrees to the gayer and more modern rooms of your family mansion. Believe me that when I unite its modern air of comfort with its venerable antiquity, and recollect that it is Your Lordship's property, I shall feel in better quarters here than if I were in the best hotel London could afford."

"I trust – I have no doubt – that you will find yourself as comfortable as I wish you, my dear general," said the young nobleman, and, once more bidding his guest goodnight, he shook him by the hand and withdrew.

The general once more looked round him, and, internally congratulating himself on his return to peaceful life, the comforts of which were endeared by the recollection of the hardships and dangers he had lately sustained, undressed himself and prepared for a luxurious night's rest.

Here, contrary to the custom of this species of tale, we leave the general in possession of his apartment until the next morning.

The company assembled for breakfast at an early hour, but without the appearance of General Browne, who seemed the guest that Lord Woodville was desirous of honouring above all whom his hospitality had assembled around him. He more than once expressed surprise at the general's absence, and at length sent a servant to make enquiry after him. The man brought back information that General Browne had been walking abroad since an early hour of the morning, in defiance of the weather, which was misty and ungenial.

"The custom of a soldier," said the young nobleman to his friends. "Many of them acquire habitual vigilance, and cannot sleep after the early hour at which their duty usually commands them to be alert."

Yet the explanation which Lord Woodville thus offered to the company seemed hardly satisfactory to his own mind, and it was in a fit of silence and abstraction that he awaited the return of the general. It took place near an hour after the breakfast bell had rung. He looked fatigued and feverish. His hair, the powdering and arrangement of which was at this time one of the most important occupations of a man's whole day, and marked his fashion as much as in the present time the tying of a cravat or the want of one, was dishevelled, uncurled, void of powder and dank with dew. His clothes were huddled on with a careless negligence remarkable in a military man, whose real or supposed duties are usually held to include some attention to the toilet, and his looks were haggard and ghastly in a peculiar degree.

"So you have stolen a march upon us this morning, my dear general," said Lord Woodville. "Or you have not found your bed so much to your mind as I had hoped and you seemed to expect. How did you rest last night?"

"Oh, excellently well... remarkably well – never better in my life!" said General Browne rapidly, and yet with an air of embarrassment which was obvious to his friend. He then hastily swallowed a cup of tea and, neglecting or refusing whatever else was offered, seemed to fall into a fit of abstraction.

"You will take the gun today, general?" said his friend and host, but had to repeat the question twice ere he received the abrupt answer: "No, my lord – I am sorry I cannot have the honour of spending another day with Your Lordship: my post-horses are ordered, and will be here directly."

All who were present showed surprise, and Lord Woodville immediately replied: "Post-horses, my good friend! What can you possibly want with them, when you promised to stay with me quietly for at least a week?"

"I believe," said the general, obviously much embarrassed, "that I might, in the pleasure of my first meeting with Your Lordship, have said something about stopping here a few days, but I have since found it altogether impossible."

"That is very extraordinary," answered the young nobleman. "You seemed quite disengaged yesterday, and you cannot have had a summons today, for our post has not come up from the town, and therefore you cannot have received any letters."

General Browne, without giving any further explanation, muttered something of indispensable business, and insisted on the absolute necessity of his departure in a manner which silenced all opposition on the part of his host, who saw that his resolution was taken, and forbore all further importunity.

"At least, however," he said, "permit me, my dear Browne, since go you will or must, to show you the view from the terrace, which the mist, that is now rising, will soon display."

He threw open a sash window and stepped down upon the terrace as he spoke. The general followed him mechanically, but seemed little to attend to what his host was saying as, looking across an extended and rich prospect, he pointed out the different objects worthy of observation. Thus they moved on till Lord Woodville had attained his purpose of drawing his guest entirely apart from the rest of the company, when, turning round upon him with an air of great solemnity, he addressed him thus:

"Richard Browne, my old and very dear friend, we are now alone. Let me conjure you to answer me upon the word of a friend and the honour of a soldier. How did you in reality rest during last night?"

"Most wretchedly indeed, my lord," answered the general in the same tone of solemnity. "So miserably that I would not run the risk of such a second night, not only for all the lands belonging to this castle, but for all the country which I see from this elevated point of view."

"This is most extraordinary," said the young lord, as if speaking to himself. "Then there must be something in the reports concerning that apartment." Again turning to the general, he said, "For God's sake, my dear friend, be candid with me, and let me know the disagreeable particular which have befallen you under a roof where, with consent of the owner, you should have met nothing save comfort."

The general seemed distressed by this appeal, and paused a moment before he replied. "My dear lord," he at length said, "what happened to me last night is of a nature so peculiar and so unpleasant that I could hardly bring myself to detail it even to Your Lordship, were it not that, independent of my wish to gratify any request of yours, I think that sincerity on my part may lead to some explanation about a circumstance equally painful and mysterious. To others, the communication I am about to make might place me in the light of a weak-minded, superstitious fool who suffered his own imagination to delude and bewilder him, but you have known me in childhood and youth, and will not suspect me of having adopted in manhood the feelings and frailties from which my early years were free."

Here he paused, and his friend replied:

"Do not doubt my perfect confidence in the truth of your communication, however strange it may be," replied Lord Woodville. "I know you firmness of disposition too well to suspect you could be made the object of imposition, and am aware that Your Honour and your friendship will equally deter you from exaggerating whatever you may have witnessed."

"Well, then," said the general, "I will proceed with my story as well as I can, relying upon your candour, and yet distinctly feeling that I would rather face a battery than recall to my mind the odious recollections of last night."

He paused a second time, and then, perceiving that Lord Woodville remained silent and in an attitude of attention, he commenced, though not without obvious reluctance, the history of his night adventures in the Tapestried Chamber.

"I undressed and went to bed, so soon as Your Lordship left me yesterday evening, but the wood in the chimney, which nearly fronted my bed, blazed brightly and cheerfully, and, aided by a hundred exciting recollections of my childhood and youth, which had been recalled by the unexpected pleasure of meeting Your Lordship, prevented me from falling immediately asleep. I ought, however, to say that these reflections were all of a pleasant and agreeable kind, grounded on a sense of having for a time exchanged the labour, fatigues and dangers of my profession for the enjoyments of a peaceful life and the reunion of those friendly and affectionate ties which I had torn asunder at the rude summons of war.

"While such pleasing reflections were stealing over my mind and gradually lulling me to slumber, I was suddenly aroused by a sound like that of the rustling of a silken gown and the tapping of a pair of high-heeled shoes, as if a woman were walking in the apartment. Ere I could draw the curtain to see what the matter was, the figure of a little woman passed between the bed and the fire. The back of this form was turned to me, and I could observe, from the shoulders and neck, it was that of an old woman, whose dress was an old-fashioned gown, which, I think, ladies call a sacque – that is, a sort of robe completely loose in the body, but gathered into broad plaits upon the neck and shoulders, which fall down to the ground and terminate in a species of train.

"I thought the intrusion singular enough, but never harboured for a moment the idea that what I saw was anything more than the mortal form of some old woman about the establishment who had a fancy to dress like her grandmother, and who, having perhaps (as Your Lordship mentioned that you were rather straitened for room) been dislodged from her chamber for my accommodation, had forgotten the circumstance and returned by twelve to her old haunt. Under this persuasion I moved myself in bed and coughed a little, to make the intruder sensible of my being in possession of the premises. She turned slowly round, but – gracious Heaven! – my lord, what a countenance did she display to me! There was no longer any question what she was, or any thought of her being a living being. Upon a face which wore the fixed features of a corpse were imprinted the traces of the vilest and most hideous passions which had animated her while she lived. The body of some atrocious criminal seemed to have been given up from the grave, and the soul restored from the penal fire, in order to form, for a space, a union with the ancient accomplice of its guilt. I started up in bed and sat upright, supporting myself on my palms, as I gazed on this horrible spectre. The hag made, as it seemed, a single and swift stride to the bed where I lay, and squatted herself down upon it, in precisely the same attitude which I had assumed in the extremity of horror, advancing her diabolical countenance within half a yard of mine, with a grin which seemed to intimate the malice and the derision of an incarnate fiend."

Here General Browne stopped and wiped from his brow the cold perspiration with which the recollection of his horrible vision had covered it.

"My lord," he said, "I am no coward. I have been in all the mortal dangers incidental to my profession, and I may truly boast that no man ever knew Richard Browne dishonour the sword he wears, but in these horrible circumstances, under the eyes and, as it seemed, almost in the grasp of an incarnation of an evil spirit, all firmness forsook me, all manhood melted from me like wax in the furnace, and I felt my hair individually bristle. The current of my lifeblood ceased to flow, and I sank back in a swoon, as very a victim to panic terror as ever was a village girl or child of ten years old. How long I lay in this condition I cannot pretend to guess.

"But I was roused by the castle clock striking one, so loud that it seemed as if it were in the very room. It was some time before I dared open my eyes, lest they should again encounter the horrible spectacle. When, however, I summoned courage to look up, she was no longer visible. My first idea was to pull my bell, wake the servants and remove to a garret or a hayloft, to be ensured against a second visitation. Nay, I will confess the truth: that my resolution was altered not by the shame of exposing myself, but by the fear that, as the bell cord hung by the chimney, I might, in making my way to it, be again crossed by the fiendish hag, who, I figured to myself, might be still lurking about some corner of the apartment.

"I will not pretend to describe what hot and cold fever fits tormented me for the rest of the night, through broken sleep, weary vigils and that dubious state which forms the neutral ground between them. A hundred terrible objects appeared to haunt me, but there was the great difference betwixt the vision which I have described and those which followed: that I knew the last to be deceptions of my own fancy and overexcited nerves.

"Day at last appeared, and I rose from my bed ill in health and humiliated in mind. I was ashamed of myself as a man and a soldier, and still more so at feeling my own extreme desire to escape from the haunted apartment, which, however, conquered all other considerations, so that, huddling on my clothes with the most careless haste, I made my escape from Your Lordship's mansion, to seek in the open air some relief to my nervous system, shaken as it was by this horrible rencounter with a visitant, for such I must believe her, from the other world. Your Lordship has now heard the cause of my discomposure, and of my sudden desire to leave your hospitable castle. In other places I trust we may often meet, but God protect me from ever spending a second night under that roof!"

Strange as the general's tale was, he spoke with such a deep air of conviction that it cut short all the usual commentaries which are made on such stories. Lord Woodville never once asked him if he was sure he did not dream of the apparition, or suggested any of the possibilities by which it is fashionable to explain supernatural appearances as wild vagaries of the fancy or deceptions of the optic nerves. On the contrary, he seemed deeply impressed with the truth and reality of what he had heard, and, after a considerable pause, regretted, with much appearance of sincerity, that his early friend should in his house have suffered so severely.

"I am the more sorry for your pain, my dear Browne," he continued, "that it is the unhappy, though most unexpected result of an experiment of my own. You must know that, for my father and grandfather's time, at least, the apartment which was assigned to you last night had been shut on account of reports that it was disturbed by supernatural sights and noises. When I came, a few weeks since, into possession of the estate, I thought the accommodation which the castle afforded for my friends was not extensive enough to permit the inhabitants of the invisible world to retain possession of a comfortable sleeping apartment. I therefore caused the Tapestried Chamber, as we call it, to be opened, and, without destroying its air of antiquity, I had such new articles of furniture placed in it as became the modern times. Yet, as the opinion that the room was haunted very strongly prevailed among the domestics, and was also known in the neighbourhood and to many of my friends, I feared some prejudice might be entertained by the first occupant of the Tapestried Chamber, which might tend to revive the evil report which it had laboured under and so disappoint my purpose of rendering it a useful part of the house. I must confess, my dear Browne, that your arrival yesterday, agreeable to me for a thousand reasons besides, seemed the most favourable opportunity of removing the unpleasant rumours which attached to the room, since your courage was indubitable, and your mind free of any preoccupation on the subject. I could not, therefore, have chosen a more fitting subject for my experiment."

"Upon my life," said General Browne, somewhat hastily, "I am infinitely obliged to Your Lordship – very particularly indebted indeed. I am likely to remember for some time the consequences of the experiment, as Your Lordship is pleased to call it."

"Nay, now you are unjust, my dear friend," said Lord Woodville. "You have only to reflect for a single moment in order to be convinced that I could not augur the possibility of the pain to which you have been so unhappily exposed. I was yesterday morning a complete sceptic on the subject of supernatural appearances. Nay, I am sure that, had I told you what was said about that room, those very reports would have induced you, by your own choice, to select it for your accommodation. It was my misfortune, perhaps my error, but really cannot be termed my fault, that you have been afflicted so strangely."

"Strangely indeed!" said the general, resuming his good temper. "And I acknowledge that I have no right to be offended with Your Lordship for treating me like what I used to think myself, a man of some firmness and courage. But I see my post-horses are arrived, and I must not detain Your Lordship from your amusement."

"Nay, my old friend," said Lord Woodville, "since you cannot stay with us another day – which, indeed, I can no longer urge – give me at least half an hour more. You used to love pictures, and I have a gallery of portraits, some of them by Van Dyck,* representing ancestry to whom this property and castle formerly belonged. I think that several of them will strike you as possessing merit."

General Browne accepted the invitation, though somewhat unwillingly. It was evident he was not to breathe freely or at ease till he left Woodville Castle far behind him. He could not refuse his friend's invitation, however, and the less so that he was a little ashamed of the peevishness which he had displayed towards his well-meaning entertainer.

The general, therefore, followed Lord Woodville through several rooms, into a long gallery hung with pictures, which the latter pointed out to his guest, telling the names and giving some account of the personages whose portraits presented themselves in progression. General Browne was but little interested in the details which these accounts conveyed to him. They were, indeed, of the kind which are usually found in an old family gallery. Here was a Cavalier who had ruined the estate in the royal cause, there a fine lady who had reinstated it by contracting a match with a wealthy Roundhead.* There hung a gallant who had been in danger for corresponding with the exiled court at St Germain's, here one who had taken arms for William at the Revolution, and there a third that had thrown his weight alternately into the scale of Whig and Tory.*

While Lord Woodville was cramming these words into his guest's ear, "against the stomach of his sense",* they gained the middle of the gallery, when he beheld General Browne suddenly start and assume an attitude of the utmost surprise, not unmixed with fear, as his eyes were caught and suddenly riveted by a portrait of an old lady in a sacque, the fashionable dress of the end of the seventeenth century.

"There she is!" he exclaimed. "There she is, in form and features, though inferior in demoniac expression to the accursed hag who visited me last night."

"If that be the case," said the young nobleman, "there can remain no longer any doubt of the horrible reality of your apparition. That is the picture of a wretched ancestress of mine, of whose crimes a black and fearful catalogue is recorded in a family history in my charter chest. The recital of them would be too horrible: it is enough to say that in yon fatal apartment incest and unnatural murder were committed. I will restore it to the solitude to which the better judgement of those who preceded me had consigned it, and never shall anyone, so long as I can prevent it, be exposed to a repetition of the supernatural horrors which could shake such courage as yours."

Thus the friends, who had met with such glee, parted in a very different mood – Lord Woodville to command the Tapestried Chamber to be unmantled and the door built up, and General Browne to seek in some less beautiful country, and with some less dignified friend, forgetfulness of the painful night which he had passed in Woodville Castle.

Donnerhugel's Narrative*

> These be the adept's doctrines – every element
> Is peopled with its separate race of spirits.
> The airy sylphs on the blue ether float;
> Deep in the earthy cavern skulks the gnome;
> The sea-green naiad skims the ocean billow,
> And the fierce fire is yet a friendly home
> To its peculiar sprite – the salamander.
>
> ANONYMOUS*

I told you (said Rudolph)* that the Lords of Arnheim, though from father to son they were notoriously addicted to secret studies, were, nevertheless, like the other German nobles, followers of war and the chase. This was peculiarly the case with Anne's maternal grandfather, Herman of Arnheim, who prided himself on possessing a splendid stud of horses, and one steed in particular, the noblest ever known in these circles of Germany. I should make wild work were I to attempt a description of such an animal, so I will content myself with saying his colour was jet black, without a hair of white either on his face or feet. For this reason, and the wildness of his disposition, his master had termed him Apollyon,* a circumstance which was secretly considered as tending to sanction the evil reports which touched the house of Arnheim, being, it was said, the naming of a favourite animal after a foul fiend.

It chanced, one November day, that the baron had been hunting in the forest, and did not reach home till nightfall. There were no guests with him, for, as I hinted to you before, the castle of Arnheim seldom received any other than those from whom its inhabitants hoped to gain augmentation of knowledge. The baron was seated alone in his hall, illuminated with cressets and torches. His one hand held a volume covered with characters unintelligible to all save himself. The other rested on the marble table, on which was placed a flask of Tokay wine.* A page stood in respectful attendance near the bottom of the large and dim apartment, and no sound was heard save that of the night wind, when it sighed mournfully through the rusty coats of mail and waved the tattered banners which were the tapestry of the feudal hall. At once the footstep of a person was heard ascending the stairs in haste and trepidation; the door of the hall was thrown violently open, and, terrified to a degree of ecstasy, Caspar, the head of the baron's stable, or his master of horse, stumbled up almost to the foot of the table at which his lord was seated, with the exclamation in his mouth:

"My lord, my lord, a fiend is in the stable!"

"What means this folly?" said the baron, arising, surprised and displeased at an interruption so unusual.

"Let me endure your displeasure," said Caspar, "if I speak not truth! Apollyon..."

Here he paused.

"Speak out, thou frightened fool," said the baron. "Is my horse sick, or injured?"

The master of the stalls again gasped forth the word "Apollyon!"

"Say on," said the baron. "Were Apollyon in presence personally, it were nothing to shake a brave man's mind."

"The Devil," answered the master of the horse, "is in Apollyon's stall!"

"Fool!" exclaimed the nobleman, snatching a torch from the wall. "What is it that could have turned thy brain in such silly fashion? Things like thee, that are born to serve us, should hold their brains on a firmer tenure, for our sakes, if not for that of their worthless selves."

As he spoke, he descended to the court of the castle to visit the stately range of stables which occupied all the lower part of the quadrangle on one side. He entered where fifty gallant steeds stood in rows, on each side of the ample hall. At the side of each stall hung the weapons of offence and defence of a man-at-arms, as bright as constant attention could make them, together with the buff coat which formed the trooper's undergarment. The baron, followed by one or two of the domestics, who had assembled full of astonishment at the unusual alarm, hastened up to the head of the stable, betwixt the rows of steeds. As he approached the stall of his favourite horse, which was the uppermost of the right-hand row, the gallant steed neither neighed nor shook his head, nor stamped with his foot, nor gave the usual signs of joy at his lord's approach – a faint moaning, as if he implored assistance, was the only acknowledgement he gave of the baron's presence.

Sir Herman held up the torch, and discovered that there was indeed a tall dark figure standing in the stall, resting his hand on the horse's shoulder. "Who art thou," said the baron, "and what dost thou here?"

"I seek refuge and hospitality," replied the stranger, "and I conjure thee to grant it me, by the shoulder of thy horse, and by the edge of thy sword, and so as they may never fail thee when thy need is at the utmost!"

"Thou art, then, a brother of the Sacred Fire,"* said Baron Herman of Arnheim, "and I may not refuse thee the refuge which thou requirest of me, after the ritual of the Persian Magi. From whom, and for what length of time, dost thou crave my protection?"

"From those," replied the stranger, "who shall arrive in quest of me before the morning cock shall crow, and for the full space of a year and a day from this period."

"I may not refuse thee," said the baron, "consistently with my oath and my honour. For a year and a day I will be thy pledge, and thou shalt share with me roof and chamber, wine and food. But thou too must obey the law of Zoroaster, which, as it says, 'Let the stronger protect the weaker brother,' says also, 'Let the wiser instruct the brother who hath less knowledge.' I am the stronger, and thou shalt be safe under my protection, but thou art the wiser, and must instruct me in the more secret mysteries."

"You mock your servant," said the strange visitor, "but if aught is known to Dannischemend which can avail Herman, his instructions shall be as those of a father to a son."

"Come forth, then, from thy place of refuge," said the Baron of Arnheim. "I swear to thee by the sacred fire which lives without terrestrial fuel, and by the fraternity which is betwixt us, and by the shoulder of my horse and the edge of my good sword, I will be thy warrand for a year and a day, if so far my power shall extend."

The stranger came forth accordingly, and those who saw the singularity of his appearance scarce wondered at the fears of Caspar, the stall master, when he found such a person in the stable, by what mode of entrance he was unable to conceive. When he reached the lighted hall to which the baron conducted him, as he would have done a welcome and honoured guest, the stranger appeared to be very tall and of a dignified aspect. His dress was Asiatic, being a long black kaftan, or gown, like that worn by Armenians, and a lofty square cap, covered with the wool of astrakhan lambs.* Every article of the dress was black, which gave relief to the long white beard that flowed down over his bosom. His gown was fastened by a sash of black silk network, in which, instead of a poniard or sword, was stuck a silver case, containing writing materials and a roll of parchment. The only ornament of his apparel consisted in a large ruby of uncommon brilliancy, which, when he approached the light, seemed to glow with such liveliness as if the gem itself had emitted the rays which it only reflected back. To the offer of refreshment the stranger replied, "Bread I may not eat, water shall not moisten my lips, until the avenger shall have passed by the threshold."

The baron commanded the lamps to be trimmed and fresh torches to be lighted, and, sending his whole household to rest, remained seated in the hall along with the stranger, his suppliant. At the dead hour of midnight, the gates of the castle were shaken as by a whirlwind, and a voice, as of a herald, was heard to demand a herald's lawful prisoner, Dannischemend, the son of Hali. The warder then heard a lower window of the hall thrown open, and could distinguish his master's voice addressing the person who had thus summoned the castle. But the night was so dark that he might not see the speakers, and the language which they used was either entirely foreign or so largely interspersed with strange words that he could not understand a syllable which they said. Scarce five minutes had elapsed when he who was without again elevated his voice as before, and said in German, "For a year and a day, then, I forbear my forfeiture – but coming for it when that time shall elapse, I come for my right, and will no longer be withstood."

From that period, Dannischemend, the Persian, was a constant guest at the castle of Arnheim, and, indeed, never for any visible purpose crossed the drawbridge. His amusements, or studies, seemed centred in the library of the castle, and in the laboratory, where the baron sometimes toiled in conjunction with him for many hours together. The inhabitants of the castle could find no fault in the magus,* or Persian, excepting his apparently dispensing with the ordinances of religion, since he neither went to Mass nor confession, nor attended upon other religious ceremonies. The chaplain did indeed profess himself satisfied with the state of the stranger's conscience, but it had been long suspected that the worthy ecclesiastic held his easy office on the very reasonable condition of approving the principles and asserting the orthodoxy of all guests whom the baron invited to share his hospitality.

It was observed that Dannischemend was rigid in paying his devotions by prostrating himself in the first rays of the rising sun, and that he constructed a silver lamp of the most beautiful proportions, which he placed on a pedestal, representing a truncated column of marble, having its base sculptured with hieroglyphical imagery. With what essences he fed this flame was unknown to all, unless perhaps to the baron, but the flame was more steady, pure and lustrous than any which was ever seen, excepting the sun of heaven itself, and it was generally believed that the Magian* made it an object of worship in the absence of that blessed luminary. Nothing else was observed of him, unless that his morals seemed severe, his gravity extreme, his general mode of life very temperate, and his fasts and vigils of frequent recurrence. Except on particular occasions, he spoke to no one of the castle but the baron, but, as he had money and was liberal, he was regarded by the domestics with awe indeed, but without fear or dislike.

Winter was succeeded by spring, summer brought her flowers, and autumn her fruits, which ripened and were fading, when a foot page, who sometimes attended them in the laboratory to render manual assistance when required, heard the Persian say to the baron of Arnheim, "You will do well, my son, to mark my words, for my lessons to you are drawing to an end, and there is no power on earth which can longer postpone my fate."

"Alas, my master!" said the baron. "And must I then lose the benefit of your direction, just when your guiding hand becomes necessary to place me on the very pinnacle of the temple of wisdom?"

"Be not discouraged, my son," answered the sage. "I will bequeath the task of perfecting you in your studies to my daughter, who will come hither on purpose. But remember, if you value the permanence of your family, look not upon her as aught else than a helpmate in your studies, for if you forget the instructress in the beauty of the maiden, you will be buried with your sword and your shield as the last male of your house, and further evil, believe me, will arise, for such alliances never come to a happy issue, of which my own is an example. But hush, we are observed."

The household of the castle of Arnheim, having but few things to interest them, were the more eager observers of those which came under their notice, and when the termination of the period when the Persian was to receive shelter in the castle began to approach, some of the inmates, under various pretexts, but which resolved into very terror, absconded, while others held themselves in expectation of some striking and terrible catastrophe. None such, however, took place, and on the expected anniversary, long ere the witching hour of midnight, Dannischemend terminated his visit in the castle of Arnheim by riding away from the gate in the guise of an ordinary traveller. The baron had meantime taken leave of his tutor with many marks of regret, and some which amounted even to sorrow. The sage Persian comforted him by a long whisper, of which the last part only was heard: "By the first beam of sunshine she will be with you. Be kind to her, but not overkind." He then departed, and was never again seen or heard of in the vicinity of Arnheim.

The baron was observed during all the day after the departure of the stranger to be particularly melancholy. He remained, contrary to his custom, in the great hall, and neither visited the library nor the laboratory, where he could no longer enjoy the company of his departed instructor. At dawn of the ensuing morning, Sir Herman summoned his page, and, contrary to his habits, which used to be rather careless in respect of apparel, he dressed himself with great accuracy, and as he was in the prime of life and of a noble figure, he had reason to be satisfied with his appearance. Having performed his toilet, he waited till the sun had just appeared above the horizon, and, taking from the table the key of the laboratory, which the page believed must have lain there all night, he walked thither, followed by his attendant. At the door the baron made a pause, and seemed at one time to doubt whether he should not send away the page, at another to hesitate whether he should open the door, as one might do who expected some strange sight within. He pulled up resolution, however, turned the key, threw the door open and entered. The page followed close behind his master, and was astonished to the point of extreme terror at what he beheld, although the sight, however extraordinary, had in it nothing save what was agreeable and lovely.

The silver lamp was extinguished, or removed from its pedestal, where stood in place of it a most beautiful female figure in the Persian costume, in which the colour of pink predominated. But she wore no turban or headdress of any kind, saving a blue ribbon drawn through her auburn hair and secured by a gold clasp, the outer side of which was ornamented by a superb opal, which, amid the changing lights peculiar to that gem, displayed internally a slight tinge of red like a spark of fire.

The figure of this young person was rather under the middle size, but perfectly well formed: the Eastern dress, with the wide trousers gathered round the ankles, made visible the smallest and most beautiful feet which had ever been seen, while hands and arms of the most perfect symmetry were partly seen from under the folds of the robe. The little lady's countenance was of a lively and expressive character, in which spirit and wit seemed to predominate, and the quick dark eye, with its beautifully formed eyebrow, seemed to presage the arch remark to which the rosy and half-smiling lip appeared ready to give utterance.

The pedestal on which she stood, or rather was perched, would have appeared unsafe had any figure heavier than her own been placed there. But, however she had been transported thither, she seemed to rest on it as lightly and safely as a linnet when it has dropped from the sky on the tendril of a rosebud. The first beam of the rising sun, falling through a window directly opposite to the pedestal, increased the effect of this beautiful figure, which remained as motionless as if it had been carved in marble. She only expressed her sense of the Baron of Arnheim's presence by something of a quicker respiration and a deep blush, accompanied by a slight smile.

Whatever reason the Baron of Arnheim might have for expecting to see some such object as now exhibited its actual presence, the degree of beauty which it presented was so much beyond his expectation that for an instant he stood without breath or motion. At once, however, he seemed to recollect that it was his duty to welcome the fair stranger to his castle and to relieve her from her precarious situation. He stepped forward accordingly with the words of welcome on his tongue, and was extending his arms to lift her from the pedestal, which was nearly six feet high, but the light and active stranger merely accepted the support of his hand and descended on the floor as light and as safe as if she had been formed of gossamer. It was, indeed, only by the momentary pressure of her little hand that the Baron of Arnheim was finally made sensible that he had to do with a being of flesh and blood.

"I am come as I have been commanded," she said, looking around her. "You must expect a strict and diligent mistress, and I hope for the credit of an attentive pupil."

After the arrival of this singular and interesting being in the castle of Arnheim, various alterations took place within the interior of the household. A lady of high rank and small fortune, the respectable widow of a count of the empire,* who was the baron's blood relation, received and accepted an invitation to preside over her kinsman's domestic affairs, and remove, by her countenance, any suspicions which might arise from the presence of Hermione, as the beautiful Persian was generally called.

The Countess Waldstetten carried her complaisance so far as to be present on almost all occasions, whether in the laboratory or library, when the Baron of Arnheim received lessons from, or pursued studies with, the young and lovely tutor who had been thus strangely substituted for the aged magus. If this lady's report was to be trusted, their pursuits were of a most extraordinary nature, and the results which she sometimes witnessed were such as to create fear as well as surprise. But she strongly vindicated them from practising unlawful arts, or overstepping the boundaries of natural science.

A better judge of such matters, the Bishop of Bamberg himself, made a visit to Arnheim, on purpose to witness the wisdom of which so much was reported through the whole Rhine country. He conversed with Hermione, and found her deeply impressed with the truths of religion, and so perfectly acquainted with its doctrines that he compared her to a doctor of theology in the dress of an Eastern dancing girl. When asked regarding her knowledge of languages and science, he answered that he had been attracted to Arnheim by the most extravagant reports on these points, but that he must return confessing the half thereof had not been told unto him.

In consequence of this indisputable testimony, the sinister reports which had been occasioned by the singular appearance of the fair stranger were in a great measure lulled to sleep, especially as her amiable manners won the involuntary goodwill of everyone that approached her.

Meantime, a marked alteration began to take place in the interviews between the lovely tutor and her pupil. These were conducted with the same caution as before, and never, so far as could be observed, took place without the presence of the Countess of Waldstetten or some other third person of respectability. But the scenes of these meetings were no longer the scholar's library or the chemist's laboratory – the gardens, the groves, were resorted to for amusement, and parties of hunting and fishing, with evenings spent in the dance, seemed to announce that the studies of wisdom were for a time abandoned for the pursuits of pleasure. It was not difficult to guess the meaning of this: the Baron of Arnheim and his fair guest, speaking a language different from all others, could enjoy their private conversation even amid all the tumult of gaiety around them, and no one was surprised to hear it formally announced, after a few weeks of gaiety, that the fair Persian was to be wedded to the Baron of Arnheim.

The manners of this fascinating young person were so pleasing, her conversation so animated, her wit so keen, yet so well tempered with good nature and modesty, that, notwithstanding her unknown origin, her high fortune attracted less envy than might have been expected in a case so singular. Above all, her generosity amazed and won the hearts of all the young persons who approached her. Her wealth seemed to be measureless, for the many rich jewels which she distributed among her fair friends would otherwise have left her without ornaments for herself. These good qualities, her liberality above all, together with a simplicity of thought and character which formed a beautiful contrast to the depth of acquired knowledge which she was well known to possess – these, and her total want of ostentation, made her superiority be pardoned among her companions. Still there was notice taken of some peculiarities, exaggerated perhaps by envy, which seemed to draw a mystical distinction between the beautiful Hermione and the mere mortals with whom she lived and conversed.

In the merry dance she was so unrivalled in lightness and agility that her performance seemed that of an aerial being. She could, without suffering from her exertion, continue the pleasure till she had tired out the most active revellers, and even the young Duke of Hochspringen, who was reckoned the most indefatigable at that exercise in Germany, having been her partner for half an hour, was compelled to break off the dance and throw himself, totally exhausted, on a couch, exclaiming he had been dancing not with a woman, but with an ignis fatuus.*

Other whispers averred that while she played with her young companions in the labyrinth and mazes of the castle gardens at hide-and-seek, or similar games of activity, she became animated with the same supernatural alertness which was supposed to inspire her in the dance. She appeared amongst her companions, and vanished from them, with a degree of rapidity which was inconceivable, and hedges, treillage or suchlike obstructions were surmounted by her in a manner which the most vigilant eye could not detect, for, after being observed on the side of the barrier at one instant, in another she was beheld close beside the spectator.

In such moments, when her eyes sparkled, her cheeks reddened and her whole frame became animated, it was pretended that the opal clasp amid her tresses, the ornament which she never laid aside, shot forth the little spark, or tongue of flame, which it always displayed with an increased vivacity. In the same manner, if in the half-darkened hall the conversation of Hermione became unusually animated, it was believed that the jewel became brilliant, and even displayed a twinkling and flashing gleam which seemed to be emitted by the gem itself, and not produced in the usual manner by the reflection of some external light. Her maidens were also heard to surmise that when their mistress was agitated by any hasty or brief resentment (the only weakness of temper which she was sometimes observed to display), they could observe dark-red sparks flash from the mystic brooch, as if it sympathized with the wearer's emotions. The women who attended on her toilet further reported that this gem was never removed but for a few minutes, when the baroness's hair was combed out – that she was unusually pensive and silent during the time it was laid aside, and particularly apprehensive when any liquid was brought near it. Even in the use of holy water at the door of the church she was observed to omit the sign of the cross on the forehead, for fear, it was supposed, of the water touching the valued jewel.

These singular reports did not prevent the marriage of the Baron of Arnheim from proceeding as had been arranged. It was celebrated in the usual form, and with the utmost splendour, and the young couple seemed to commence a life of happiness rarely to be found on earth. In the course of twelve months, the lovely baroness presented her husband with a daughter, which was to be christened Sibylla, after the count's mother. As the health of the child was excellent, the ceremony was postponed till the recovery of the mother from her confinement. Many were invited to be present on the occasion, and the castle was thronged with company.

It happened that amongst the guests was an old lady, notorious for playing in private society the part of a malicious fairy in a minstrel's tale. This was the Baroness of Steinfeldt, famous in the neighbourhood for her insatiable curiosity and overweening pride. She had not been many days in the castle ere, by the aid of a female attendant, who acted as an intelligencer, she had made herself mistress of all that was heard, said or suspected concerning the peculiarities of the Baroness Hermione. It was on the morning of the day appointed for the christening, while the whole company were assembled in the hall and waiting till the baroness should appear to pass with them to the chapel, that there arose between the censorious and haughty dame whom we have just mentioned and the Countess Waldstetten a violent discussion concerning some point of disputed precedence. It was referred to the Baron von Arnheim, who decided in favour of the countess. Madame de Steinfeldt instantly ordered her palfrey to be prepared and her attendants to mount.

"I leave this place," she said, "which a good Christian ought never to have entered – I leave a house of which the master is a sorcerer, the mistress a demon who dares not cross her brow with holy water, and their trencher companion one who, for a wretched pittance, is willing to act as matchmaker between a wizard and an incarnate fiend!"

She then departed, with rage in her countenance and spite in her heart.

The Baron of Arnheim then stepped forward and demanded of the knights and gentlemen around if there were any among them who would dare to make good with his sword the infamous falsehoods thrown upon himself, his spouse and his kinswoman.

There was a general answer, utterly refusing to defend the Baroness of Steinfeldt's words in so bad a cause, and universally testifying the belief of the company that she spoke in the spirit of calumny and falsehood.

"Then let that lie fall to the ground which no man of courage will hold up," said the Baron of Arnheim. "Only, all who are here this morning shall be satisfied whether the Baroness Hermione doth or doth not share the rites of Christianity."

The Countess of Waldstetten made anxious signs to him while he spoke thus, and when the crowd permitted her to approach near him, she was heard to whisper, "Oh, be not rash! Try no experiment! There is something mysterious about that opal talisman – be prudent, and let the matter pass by."

The baron, who was in a more towering passion than well became the wisdom to which he made pretence – although it will be perhaps allowed that an affront so public, and in such a time and place, was enough to shake the prudence of the most staid and the philosophy of the most wise – answered sternly and briefly "Are you too such a fool?" and retained his purpose.

The Baroness of Arnheim at this moment entered the hall, looking just so pale from her late confinement as to render her lovely countenance more interesting, if less animated, than usual. Having paid her compliments to the assembled company with the most graceful and condescending attention, she was beginning to enquire why Madame de Steinfeldt was not present when her husband made the signal for the company to move forward to the chapel, and lent the baroness his arm to bring up the rear. The chapel was nearly filled by the splendid company, and all eyes were bent on their host and hostess as they entered the place of devotion immediately after four young ladies, who supported the infant babe in a light and beautiful litter.

As they passed the threshold, the baron dipped his finger in the font stone and offered holy water to his lady, who accepted it, as usual, by touching his finger with her own. But then, as if to confute the calumnies of the malevolent lady of Steinfeldt, with an air of sportive familiarity which was rather unwarranted by the time and place, he flirted on her beautiful forehead a drop or two of the moisture which remained on his own hand. The opal, on which one of these drops had lighted, shot out a brilliant spark like a falling star, and became the instant afterwards lightless and colourless as a common pebble, while the beautiful baroness sank on the floor of the chapel with a deep sigh of pain. All crowded around her in dismay. The unfortunate Hermione was raised from the ground and conveyed to her chamber, and so much did her countenance and pulse alter, within the short time necessary to do this, that those who looked upon her pronounced her a dying woman. She was no sooner in her own apartment than she requested to be left alone with her husband. He remained an hour in the room, and when he came out he locked and double-locked the door behind him. He then betook himself to the chapel and remained there for an hour or more, prostrated before the altar.

In the mean time, most of the guests had dispersed in dismay, though some abode out of courtesy or curiosity. There was a general sense of impropriety in suffering the door of the sick lady's apartment to remain locked, but, alarmed at the whole circumstances of her illness, it was some time ere anyone dared disturb the devotions of the baron.

At length medical aid arrived, and the Countess of Waldstetten took upon her to demand the key. She spoke more than once to a man, who seemed incapable of hearing, at least of understanding, what she said. At length he gave her the key, and added sternly, as he did so, that all aid was unavailing, and that it was his pleasure that all strangers should leave the castle. There were few who inclined to stay, when, upon opening the door of the chamber in which the baroness had been deposited little more than two hours before, no traces of her could be discovered, unless that there was about a handful of light-grey ashes, like such as might have been produced by burning fine paper, found on the bed where she had been laid. A solemn funeral was nevertheless performed, with masses, and all other spiritual rites, for the soul of the high and noble Lady Hermione of Arnheim, and it was exactly on that same day three years that the baron himself was laid in the grave of the same chapel of Arnheim, with sword, shield and helmet, as the last male of his family.

Here the Swiss paused, for they were approaching the bridge of the castle of Graffs-lust.

The Bridal of Janet Dalrymple*

Miss Janet Dalrymple, daughter of the first Lord Stair and Dame Margaret Ross, had engaged herself without the knowledge of her parents to the Lord Rutherford,* who was not acceptable to them either on account of his political principles or his want of fortune. The young couple broke a piece of gold together, and pledged their troth in the most solemn manner, and it is said the young lady imprecated dreadful evils on herself should she break her plighted faith. Shortly after, a suitor who was favoured by Lord Stair, and still more so by his lady, paid his addresses to Miss Dalrymple. The young lady refused the proposal, and, being pressed on the subject, confessed her secret engagement. Lady Stair, a woman accustomed to universal submission (for even her husband did not dare to contradict her), treated this objection as a trifle, and insisted upon her daughter yielding her consent to marry the new suitor, David Dunbar, son and heir to David Dunbar of Baldoon,* in Wigtonshire. The first lover, a man of very high spirit, then interfered by letter, and insisted on the right he had acquired by his troth plighted with the young lady. Lady Stair sent him for answer that her daughter, sensible of her undutiful behaviour in entering into a contract unsanctioned by her parents, had retracted her unlawful vow, and now refused to fulfil her engagement with him.

The lover, in return, declined positively to receive such an answer from anyone but his mistress in person, and as she had to deal with a man who was both of a most determined character and of too high condition to be trifled with, Lady Stair was obliged to consent to an interview between Lord Rutherford and her daughter. But she took care to be present in person, and argued the point with the disappointed and incensed lover with pertinacity equal to his own. She particularly insisted on the Levitical law, which declares that a woman shall be free of a vow which her parents dissent from. This is the passage of Scripture she founded on:

> If a man vow a vow unto the Lord, or swear an oath to bind his soul with a bond, he shall not break his word, he shall do according to all that proceedeth out of his mouth.

> If a woman also vow a vow unto the Lord, and bind *herself* by a bond, *being* in her father's house in her youth,
>
> And her father hear her vow, and her bond wherewith she hath bound her soul, and her father shall hold his peace at her, then all her vows shall stand, and every bond wherewith she hath bound her soul shall stand.
>
> But if her father disallow her in the day that he heareth, not any of her vows, or of her bonds wherewith she hath bound her soul, shall stand, and the Lord shall forgive her, because her father disallowed her.*

While the mother insisted on these topics, the lover in vain conjured the daughter to declare her own opinion and feelings. She remained totally overwhelmed, as it seemed – mute, pale and motionless as a statue. Only at her mother's command, sternly uttered, she summoned strength enough to restore to her plighted suitor the piece of broken gold which was the emblem of her troth. On this he burst forth into a tremendous passion, took leave of the mother with maledictions and, as he left the apartment, turned back to say to his weak, if not fickle mistress, "For you, madam, you will be a world's wonder" – a phrase by which some remarkable degree of calamity is usually implied. He went abroad, and returned not again. If the last Lord Rutherford was the unfortunate party, he must have been the third who bore that title, and who died in 1685.

The marriage betwixt Janet Dalrymple and David Dunbar of Baldoon now went forward, the bride showing no repugnance, but being absolutely passive in every thing her mother commanded or advised. On the day of the marriage – which, as was then usual, was celebrated by a great assemblage of friends and relations – she was the same: sad, silent and resigned, as it seemed, to her destiny. A lady, very nearly connected with the family,* told the author that she had conversed on the subject with one of the brothers of the bride, a mere lad at the time, who had ridden before his sister to church. He said her hand, which lay on his as she held her arm round his waist, was as cold and damp as marble. But, full of his new dress and the part he acted in the procession, the circumstance, which he long afterwards remembered with bitter sorrow and compunction, made no impression on him at the time.

The bridal feast was followed by dancing; the bride and bridegroom retired as usual, when of a sudden the most wild and piercing cries were heard from the nuptial chamber. It was then the custom, to prevent any coarse pleasantry which old times perhaps admitted, that the key of the nuptial chamber should be entrusted to the brideman.* He was called upon, but refused at first to give it up, till the shrieks became so hideous that he was compelled to hasten with others to learn the cause. On opening the door, they found the bridegroom lying across the threshold, dreadfully wounded and streaming with blood. The bride was then sought for: she was found in the corner of the large chimney, having no covering save her shift, and that dabbled in gore. There she sat grinning at them, mopping and mowing, as I heard the expression used – in a word, absolutely insane. The only words she spoke were, "Tak up your bonny bridegroom." She survived this horrible scene little more than a fortnight, having been married on 24th August, and dying on 12th September 1669.

The unfortunate Baldoon recovered from his wounds, but sternly prohibited all enquiries respecting the manner in which he had received them. If a lady, he said, asked him any question upon the subject, he would neither answer her nor speak to her again while he lived; if a gentleman, he would consider it as a mortal affront, and demand satisfaction as having received such. He did not very long survive the dreadful catastrophe, having met with a fatal injury by a fall from his horse as he rode between Leith and Holyroodhouse,* of which he died the next day, 28th March 1682. Thus a few years removed all the principal actors in this frightful tragedy.

Various reports went abroad on this mysterious affair, many of them very inaccurate, though they could hardly be said to be exaggerated. It was difficult at that time to become acquainted with the history of a Scottish family above the lower rank, and strange things sometimes took place there, into which even the law did not scrupulously inquire.

The credulous Mr Law says, generally, that the Lord President Stair had a daughter who, "being married, the night she was *bride in* [that is, bedded bride], was taken from her bridegroom and *harled* [dragged] through the house [by spirits, we are given to understand], and soon afterwards died. Another daughter," he says, "was possessed by an evil spirit."*

My friend Mr Sharpe gives another edition of the tale. According to his information, it was the bridegroom who wounded the bride. The marriage, according to this account, had been against her mother's inclination, who had given her consent in these ominous words: "You may marry him, but soon shall you repent it."

I find still another account darkly insinuated in some highly scurrilous and abusive verses, of which I have an original copy. They are docketed as being written "Upon the late Viscount Stair and his family, by Sir William Hamilton of Whitelaw. The marginals by William Dunlop, writer in Edinburgh, a son of the Laird of Househill, and nephew to the said Sir

William Hamilton." There was a bitter and personal quarrel and rivalry betwixt the author of this libel, a name which it richly deserves, and Lord President Stair,* and the lampoon, which is written with much more malice than art, bears the following motto:

> Stair's neck, mind, wife, sons, grandson and the rest,
> Are wry, false, witch, pests, parricide, possessed.

This malignant satirist, who calls up all the misfortunes of the family, does not forget the fatal bridal of Baldoon. He seems, though his verses are as obscure as unpoetical, to intimate that the violence done to the bridegroom was by the intervention of the foul fiend, to whom the young lady had resigned herself in case she should break her contract with her first lover. His hypothesis is inconsistent with the account given in the note upon Law's *Memorials*, but easily reconcilable to the family tradition.

> In al Stair's offspring we no difference know,
> They doe the females as the males bestow;
> So he of's daughter's marriage gave the ward,
> Like a true vassal, to Glenluce's laird;
> He knew what she did to her suitor plight,
> If she her faith to Rutherfurd should slight,
> Which, like his own, for greed he broke outright.
> Nick did Baldoon's posterior right deride,
> And, as first substitute, did seize the bride;
> Whate'er he to his mistress did or said,
> He threw the bridegroom from the nuptial bed,
> Into the chimney did so his rival maul,
> His bruised bones ne'er were cured but by the fall.*

One of the marginal notes ascribed to William Dunlop applies to the above lines: "She had betrothed herself to Lord Rutherfoord under horrid imprecations, and afterwards married Baldoon, his nevoy, and her mother was the cause of her breach of faith."

The same tragedy is alluded to in the following couplet and note:

> What train of curses that base brood pursues,
> When the young nephew weds old uncle's spouse.

The note on the word *uncle* explains it as meaning "Rutherfoord, who should have married the Lady Baldoon, was Baldoon's uncle". The poetry of this satire on Lord Stair and his family was, as already noticed, written by Sir William Hamilton of Whitelaw, a rival of Lord Stair for the situation of president of the Court of Session, a person much inferior to that great lawyer in talents, and equally ill-treated by the calumny or just satire of his contemporaries as an unjust and partial judge. Some of the notes are by that curious and laborious antiquary Robert Mylne, who, as a virulent Jacobite, willingly lent a hand to blacken the family of Stair.*

Another poet of the period, with a very different purpose, has left an elegy in which he darkly hints at and bemoans the fate of the ill-starred young person, whose very uncommon calamity Whitelaw, Dunlop and Mylne thought a fitting subject for buffoonery and ribaldry. This bard of milder mood was Andrew Symson,* before the Revolution minister of Kirkinner, in Galloway, and, after his expulsion as an Episcopalian, following the humble occupation of a printer in Edinburgh. He furnished the family of Baldoon, with which he appears to have been intimate, with an elegy on the tragic event in their family. In this piece he treats the mournful occasion of the bride's death with mysterious solemnity.

The verses bear this title: 'On the Unexpected Death of the Virtuous Lady, Mrs Janet Dalrymple, Lady Baldone, Younger', and afford us the precise dates of the catastrophe, which could not otherwise have been easily ascertained: "Nupta August 12. Domum Ducta August 24. Obiit September 12. Sepult. September 30, 1669."* The form of the elegy is a dialogue betwixt a passenger and a domestic servant. The first, recollecting that he had passed that way lately, and seen all around enlivened by the appearances of mirth and festivity, is desirous to know what had changed so gay a scene into mourning. We preserve the reply of the servant as a specimen of Mr Symson's verses, which are not of the first quality:

> Sir, 'tis truth you've told,
> We did enjoy great mirth; but now, ah me!
> Our joyful song's turn'd to an elegie.
> A virtuous lady, not long since a bride,
> Was to a hopeful plant by marriage tied,
> And brought home hither. We did all rejoice,
> Even for her sake. But presently our voice
> Was turn'd to mourning for that little time
> That she'd enjoy: she wanèd in her prime,

For Atropos, with her impartial knife,
Soon cut her thread, and therewithal her life;
And for the time we may it well remember,
It being in unfortunate September;
Where we must leave her till the resurrection:
'Tis then the saints enjoy their full perfection.*

LETTERS ON DEMONOLOGY AND WITCHCRAFT*

...But something remains to be said upon another species of superstition, so general that it may be called proper to mankind in every climate, so deeply rooted also in human belief that it is found to survive in states of society during which all other fictions of the same order are entirely dismissed from influence. Mr Crabbe, with his usual felicity, has called the belief in ghosts "the last lingering fiction of the brain".*

Nothing appears more simple at the first view of the subject than that human memory should recall and bring back to the eye of the imagination, in perfect similitude, even the very form and features of a person with whom we have been long conversant, or which have been imprinted in our minds with indelible strength by some striking circumstances touching our meeting in life. The son does not easily forget the aspect of an affectionate father, and, for reasons opposite but equally powerful, the countenance of a murdered person is engraved upon the recollection of his slayer. A thousand additional circumstances, far too obvious to require recapitulation, render the supposed apparition of the dead the most ordinary spectral phenomenon which is ever believed to occur among the living. All that we have formerly said respecting supernatural appearances in general applies with peculiar force to the belief of ghosts, for whether the cause of delusion exists in an excited imagination or a disordered organic system, it is in this way that it commonly exhibits itself. Hence Lucretius himself, the most absolute of sceptics, considers the existence of ghosts, and their frequent apparition, as facts so undeniable that he endeavours to account for them at the expense of assenting to a class of phenomena very irreconcilable to his general system. As he will not allow of the existence of the human soul, and at the same time cannot venture to question the phenomena supposed to haunt the repositories of the dead, he is obliged to adopt the belief that the body consists of several coats like those of an onion, and that the outmost and thinnest, being detached by death, continues to wander near the place of sepulture, in the exact resemblance of the person while alive.*

We have said there are many ghost stories which we do not feel at liberty to challenge as impostures, because we are confident that those who relate them on their own authority actually believe what they assert, and may have good reason for doing so, though there is no real phantom after all. We are far, therefore, from averring that such tales are necessarily false. It is easy to suppose the visionary has been imposed upon by a lively dream, a waking reverie, the excitation of a powerful imagination or the misrepresentation of a diseased organ of sight, and in one or other of these causes, to say nothing of a system of deception which may in many instances be probable, we apprehend a solution will be found for all cases of what are called real ghost stories.

In truth, the evidence with respect to such apparitions is very seldom accurately or distinctly questioned. A supernatural tale is in most cases received as an agreeable mode of amusing society, and he would be rather accounted a sturdy moralist than an entertaining companion who should employ himself in assailing its credibility. It would indeed be a solecism in manners, something like that of impeaching the genuine value of the antiquities exhibited by a good-natured collector for the gratification of his guests. This difficulty will appear greater should a company have the rare good fortune to meet the person who himself witnessed the wonders which he tells: a well-bred or prudent man will, under such circumstances, abstain from using the rules of cross-examination practised in a court of justice, and if in any case he presumes to do so, he is in danger of receiving answers, even from the most candid and honourable persons, which are rather fitted to support the credit of the story which they stand committed to maintain than to the pure service of unadorned truth. The narrator is asked, for example, some unimportant question with respect to the apparition; he answers it on the hasty suggestion of his own imagination, tinged as it is with belief of the general fact, and by doing so often gives a feature of minute evidence which was before wanting, and this with perfect unconsciousness on his own part. It is a rare occurrence, indeed, to find an opportunity of dealing with an actual ghost-seer – such instances, however, I have certainly myself met with, and that in the case of able, wise, candid and resolute persons, of whose veracity I had every reason to be confident. But in such instances shades of mental aberration have afterwards occurred which sufficiently accounted for the supposed apparitions, and will incline me always to feel alarmed in behalf of the continued health of a friend who should conceive himself to have witnessed such a visitation.

The nearest approximation which can be generally made to exact evidence in this case is the word of some individual who has had the story, it may be, from the person to whom it has happened, but most likely from his family, or some friend of the family. Far more commonly the narrator possesses no better means of knowledge than that of dwelling in the country where the thing happened, or being well acquainted with the outside of the mansion in the inside of which the ghost appeared.

In every point the evidence of such a second-hand retailer of the mystic story must fall under the adjudged case in an English court. The judge stopped a witness who was about to give an account of the murder upon trial, as it was narrated to him by the ghost of the murdered person. "Hold, sir," said His Lordship. "The ghost is an excellent witness, and his evidence the best possible, but he cannot be heard by proxy in this court. Summon him hither, and I'll hear him in person, but your communication is mere hearsay, which my office compels me to reject." Yet it is upon the credit of one man, who pledges it upon that of three or four persons who have told it successively to each other, that we are often expected to believe an incident inconsistent with the laws of Nature, however agreeable to our love of the wonderful and the horrible.

In estimating the truth or falsehood of such stories, it is evident we can derive no proofs from that period of society when men affirmed boldly, and believed stoutly, all the wonders which could be coined or fancied. That such stories are believed and told by grave historians only shows that the wisest men cannot rise in all things above the general ignorance of their age. Upon the evidence of such historians we might as well believe the portents of ancient or the miracles of modern Rome. For example, we read in Clarendon of the apparition of the ghost of Sir George Villiers to an ancient dependant.* This is no doubt a story told by a grave author, at a time when such stories were believed by all the world, but does it follow that our reason must acquiesce in a statement so positively contradicted by the voice of Nature through all her works? The miracle of raising a dead man was positively refused by our Saviour to the Jews, who demanded it as a proof of his mission, because they had already sufficient grounds of conviction, and, as they believed them not, it was irresistibly argued by the Divine Person whom they tempted that neither would they believe if one arose from the dead. Shall we suppose that a miracle refused for the conversion of God's chosen people was sent on a vain errand to save the life of a profligate spendthrift? I lay aside, you observe, entirely the not unreasonable supposition that Towers, or whatever was the ghost-seer's name, desirous to make an impression upon Buckingham, as an old servant of his house, might be tempted to give him his advice, of which we are not told the import, in the character of his father's spirit, and authenticate the tale by the mention of some token known to him as a former retainer of the family. The duke was superstitious, and the ready dupe of astrologers and soothsayers. The manner in which he had provoked the fury of the people must have warned every reflecting person of his approaching fate, and, the age considered, it was not unnatural that a faithful friend should take this mode of calling his attention to his perilous situation. Or, if we suppose that the incident was not a mere pretext to obtain access to the duke's ear, the messenger may have been impressed upon by an idle dream – in a word, numberless conjectures might be formed for accounting for the event in a natural way, the most extravagant of which is more probable than that the laws of Nature were broken through in order to give a vain and fruitless warning to an ambitious minion.

It is the same with all those that are called "accredited ghost stories",* usually told at the fireside. They want evidence. It is true that the general wish to believe, rather than power of believing, has given some such stories a certain currency in society. I may mention, as one of the class of tales I mean, that of the late Earl St Vincent, who watched, with a friend, it is said, a whole night, in order to detect the cause of certain nocturnal disturbances which took place in a certain mansion. The house was under lease to Mrs Ricketts, his sister.* The result of His Lordship's vigil is said to have been that he heard the noises without being able to detect the causes, and insisted on his sister giving up the house. This is told as a real story, with a thousand different circumstances. But who has heard or seen an authentic account from Earl St Vincent, or from his "companion of the watch", or from His Lordship's sister? And as in any other case such sure species of direct evidence would be necessary to prove the facts, it seems unreasonable to believe such a story on slighter terms. When the particulars are precisely fixed and known, it might be time to enquire whether Lord St Vincent, amid the other eminent qualities of a first-rate seaman, might not be in some degree tinged with their tendency to superstition, and still further whether, having ascertained the existence of disturbances not immediately or easily detected, His Lordship might not advise his sister rather to remove than to remain in a house so haunted, though he might believe that poachers or smugglers were the worst ghosts by whom it was disturbed.

The story of two highly respectable officers in the British army who are supposed to have seen the spectre of the brother of one of them in a hut, or barrack, in America* is also one of those accredited ghost tales which attain a sort of brevet rank* as true from the mention of respectable names as the parties who witnessed the vision. But we are left without a glimpse when, how and in what terms this story obtained its currency, as also by whom and in what manner it was first circulated – and among the numbers by whom it has been quoted, although all agree in the general event, scarcely two, even of those who pretend to the best information, tell the story in the same way.

Another such story, in which the name of a lady of condition is made use of as having seen an apparition in a country seat in France,* is so far better borne out than those I have mentioned that I have seen a narrative of the circumstances attested by the party principally concerned. That the house was disturbed seems to be certain, but the circumstances (though very remarkable) did not, in my mind, by any means exclude the probability that the disturbance and appearances were occasioned by the dextrous management of some mischievously disposed persons.

The remarkable circumstance of Thomas, the second Lord Lyttelton, prophesying his own death within a few minutes upon the information of an apparition,* has been always quoted as a true story. But of late it has been said and published that the unfortunate nobleman had previously determined to take poison, and of course had it in his own power to ascertain the execution of the prediction. It was no doubt singular that a man who meditated his exit from the world should have chosen to play such a trick on his friends. But it is still more credible that a whimsical man should do so wild a thing than that a messenger should be sent from the dead to tell a libertine at what precise hour he should expire.

To this list other stories of the same class might be added. But it is sufficient to show that such stories as these, having gained a certain degree of currency in the world, and bearing creditable names on their front, walk through society unchallenged, like bills through a bank when they bear respectable indorsations, although, it may be, the signatures are forged after all. There is, indeed, an unwillingness very closely to examine such subjects, for the secret fund of superstition in every man's bosom is gratified by believing them to be true, or at least induces him to abstain from challenging them as false. And no doubt it must happen that the transpiring of incidents in which men have actually seen, or conceived that they saw, apparitions which were invisible to others contributes to the increase of such stories – which do accordingly sometimes meet us in a shape of veracity difficult to question.

The following story was narrated to me by my friend, Mr William Clerk, chief clerk to the Jury Court, Edinburgh, when he first learnt it, now nearly thirty years ago, from a passenger in the mail coach. With Mr Clerk's consent, I gave the story at that time to poor Matt Lewis, who

published it with a ghost ballad which he adjusted on the same theme.*
From the minuteness of the original detail, however, the narrative is better
calculated for prose than verse, and more especially as the friend to whom
it was originally communicated is one of the most accurate, intelligent and
acute persons whom I have known in the course of my life, I am willing
to preserve the precise story in this place.

It was about the eventful year 1800, when the Emperor Paul laid his
ill-judged embargo on British trade,* that my friend Mr William Clerk,
on a journey to London, found himself in company, in the mail coach,
with a seafaring man of middle age and respectable appearance, who
announced himself as master of a vessel in the Baltic trade, and a sufferer by the embargo. In the course of the desultory conversation which
takes place on such occasions, the seaman observed, in compliance with
a common superstition, "I wish we may have good luck on our journey
– there is a magpie." "And why should that be unlucky?" said my friend.
"I cannot tell you that," replied the sailor, "but all the world agrees that
one magpie bodes bad luck – two are not so bad, but three are the devil.
I never saw three magpies but twice, and once I had near lost my vessel,
and the second I fell from a horse, and was hurt." This conversation led
Mr Clerk to observe that he supposed he believed also in ghosts, since he
credited such auguries. "And if I do," said the sailor, "I may have my own
reasons for doing so" – and he spoke this in a deep and serious manner,
implying that he felt deeply what he was saying. On being further urged,
he confessed that, if he could believe his own eyes, there was one ghost at
least which he had seen repeatedly. He then told his story as I now relate it.

Our mariner had in his youth gone mate of a slave vessel from Liverpool,
of which town he seemed to be a native. The captain of the vessel was a
man of a variable temper, sometimes kind and courteous to his men, but
subject to fits of humour, dislike and passion, during which he was very
violent, tyrannical and cruel. He took a particular dislike at one sailor
aboard, an elderly man called Bill Jones, or some such name. He seldom
spoke to this person without threats and abuse, which the old man, with
the licence which sailors take on merchant vessels, was very apt to return.
On one occasion Bill Jones appeared slow in getting out on the yard to
hand a sail.* The captain, according to custom, abused the seaman as a
lubberly rascal who got fat by leaving his duty to other people. The man
made a saucy answer, almost amounting to mutiny, on which, in a towering
passion, the captain ran down to his cabin and returned with a blunder-
buss loaded with slugs, with which he took deliberate aim at the supposed

mutineer, fired and mortally wounded him. The man was handed down from the yard and stretched on the deck, evidently dying. He fixed his eyes on the captain, and said, "Sir, you have done for me, but *I will never leave you*." The captain, in return, swore at him for a fat lubber, and said he would have him thrown into the slave kettle, where they made food for the Negroes, and see how much fat he had got. The man died. His body was actually thrown into the slave kettle, and the narrator observed, with a naivety which confirmed the extent of his own belief in the truth of what he told, "There was not much fat about him after all."

The captain told the crew they must keep absolute silence on the subject of what had passed, and as the mate was not willing to give an explicit and absolute promise, he ordered him to be confined below. After a day or two, he came to the mate and demanded if he had an intention to deliver him up for trial when the vessel got home. The mate, who was tired of close confinement in that sultry climate, spoke his commander fair, and obtained his liberty. When he mingled among the crew once more, he found them impressed with the idea, not unnatural in their situation, that the ghost of the dead man appeared among them when they had a spell of duty, especially if a sail was to be handed, on which occasion the spectre was sure to be out upon the yard before any of the crew. The narrator had seen this apparition himself repeatedly – he believed the captain saw it also, but he took no notice of it for some time, and the crew, terrified at the violent temper of the man, dared not call his attention to it. Thus they held on their course homeward with great fear and anxiety.

At length the captain invited the mate, who was now in a sort of favour, to go down to the cabin and take a glass of grog with him. In this interview he assumed a very grave and anxious aspect. "I need not tell you, Jack," he said, "what sort of hand we have got on board with us. He told me he would never leave me, and he has kept his word. You only see him now and then, but he is always by my side, and never out of my sight. At this very moment I see him – I am determined to bear it no longer, and I have resolved to leave you."

The mate replied that his leaving the vessel while out of the sight of any land was impossible. He advised that if the captain apprehended any bad consequences from what had happened, he should run for the west of France or Ireland, and there go ashore, and leave him, the mate, to carry the vessel into Liverpool. The captain only shook his head gloomily, and reiterated his determination to leave the ship. At this moment the mate was called to the deck for some purpose or other, and the instant he got up the companion ladder he heard a splash in the water, and, looking over the ship's side, saw that the captain had thrown himself into the sea from the quarter gallery, and was running astern at the rate of six knots an hour. When just about to sink, he seemed to make a last exertion, sprung half out of the water and clasped his hands towards the mate, calling, "By ——, Bill is with me now!" – and then sank, to be seen no more.

After hearing this singular story, Mr Clerk asked some questions about the captain, and whether his companion considered him as at all times rational. The sailor seemed struck with the question, and answered, after a moment's delay, that in general *he conversationed well enough*.

It would have been desirable to have been able to ascertain how far this extraordinary tale was founded on fact, but want of time and other circumstances prevented Mr Clerk from learning the names and dates that might to a certain degree have verified the events. Granting the murder to have taken place, and the tale to have been truly told, there was nothing more likely to arise among the ship's company than the belief in the apparition: as the captain was a man of a passionate and irritable disposition, it was nowise improbable that he, the victim of remorse, should participate in the horrible visions of those less concerned, especially as he was compelled to avoid communicating his sentiments with anyone else – and the catastrophe would in such a case be but the natural consequence of that superstitious remorse which has conducted so many criminals to suicide or the gallows. If the fellow traveller of Mr Clerk be not allowed this degree of credit, he must at least be admitted to have displayed a singular talent for the composition of the horrible in fiction. The tale, properly detailed, might have made the fortune of a romancer.

I cannot forbear giving you, as congenial to this story, another instance of a guilt-formed phantom,* which made considerable noise about twenty years ago or more. I am, I think, tolerably correct in the details, though I have lost the account of the trial. Jarvis Matcham – such, if I am not mistaken, was the name of my hero – was pay sergeant in a regiment, where he was so highly esteemed as a steady and accurate man that he was permitted opportunity to embezzle a considerable part of the money lodged in his hands for pay of soldiers, bounty of recruits (then a large sum) and other charges which fell within his duty. He was summoned to join his regiment from a town where he had been on the recruiting service, and this perhaps under some shade of suspicion. Matcham perceived discovery was at hand, and would have deserted had it not been for the presence of a little drummer lad, who was the only one of his party appointed to attend him. In the desperation of his crime he resolved to murder the poor boy and avail himself of some balance of money to make his escape. He meditated this wickedness the more readily that the drummer, he thought, had been put as a spy on him. He perpetrated his crime, and, changing his dress after the deed was done, made a long walk across the country to an inn on the Portsmouth road, where he halted and went to bed, desiring to be called when the first Portsmouth coach came. The waiter summoned him accordingly, but long after remembered that, when he shook the guest by the shoulder, his first words as he awoke were: "My God! I did not kill him."

Matcham went to the seaport by the coach, and instantly entered as an able-bodied landsman or marine, I know not which. His sobriety and attention to duty gained him the same good opinion of the officers in his new service which he had enjoyed in the army. He was afloat for several years, and behaved remarkably well in some actions. At length the vessel came into Plymouth, was paid off, and some of the crew, amongst whom was Jarvis Matcham, were dismissed as too old for service. He and another seaman resolved to walk to town, and took the route by Salisbury. It was when within two or three miles of this celebrated city that they were overtaken by a tempest so sudden, and accompanied with such vivid lightning and thunder so dreadfully loud, that the obdurate conscience of the old sinner began to be awakened. He expressed more terror than seemed natural for one who was familiar with the war of elements, and began to look and talk so wildly that his companion became aware that something more than usual was the matter. At length Matcham complained to his companion that the stones rose from the road and flew after him. He desired the man to walk on the other side of the highway to see if they would follow him when he was alone. The sailor complied, and Jarvis Matcham complained that the stones still flew after him and did not pursue the other. "But what is worse," he added, coming up to his companion and whispering with a tone of mystery and fear, "who is that little drummer boy, and what business has he to follow us so closely?" "I can see no one," answered the seaman, infected by the superstition of his associate. "What! Not see that little boy with the bloody pantaloons!" exclaimed the secret murderer, so much to the terror of his comrade that he conjured him, if he had anything on his mind, to make a clear conscience as far as confession could do it. The criminal fetched a deep groan and declared that he was unable longer to endure the life which he had led for years. He then confessed the murder of the drummer, and added that, as a considerable reward had been offered, he wished his comrade to deliver him up to the magistrates of Salisbury, as he would desire a shipmate to profit by his fate, which he was now convinced was inevitable. Having overcome his friend's objections to this mode of proceeding, Jarvis Matcham was surrendered to justice accordingly, and made a full confession of his guilt. But before the trial the love of life returned. The prisoner denied his confession, and pleaded not guilty. By this time, however, full evidence had been procured from other quarters. Witnesses appeared from his former regiment to prove his identity with the murderer and deserter, and the waiter remembered the ominous words which he had spoken when he awoke him to join the Portsmouth coach. Jarvis Matcham was found guilty and executed. When his last chance of life was over, he returned to his confession, and with his dying breath averred – and truly, as he thought – the truth of the vision on Salisbury Plain. Similar stories might be produced, showing plainly that, under the direction of Heaven, the influence of superstitious fear may be the appointed means of bringing the criminal to repentance for his own sake, and to punishment for the advantage of society.

Cases of this kind are numerous and easily imagined, so I shall dwell on them no further, but rather advert to at least an equally abundant class of ghost stories in which the apparition is pleased not to torment the actual murderer, but proceeds in a very circuitous manner, acquainting some stranger or ignorant old woman with the particulars of his fate, who, though perhaps unacquainted with all the parties, is directed by a phantom to lay the facts before a magistrate. In this respect we must certainly allow that ghosts have, as we are informed by the facetious Captain Grose, forms and customs peculiar to themselves.*

There would be no edification and little amusement in treating of clumsy deceptions of this kind, where the grossness of the imposture detects itself. But occasionally cases occur like the following, with respect to which it is more difficult, to use James Boswell's phrase, "to know what to think".*

Upon 10th June 1754, Duncan Terig, alias Clark, and Alexander Bain MacDonald, two Highlanders, were tried before the Court of Justiciary, Edinburgh, for the murder of Arthur Davis, sergeant in Guise's regiment, on 28th September 1749.* The accident happened not long after the civil war, the embers of which were still reeking, so there existed too many reasons on account of which an English soldier, straggling far from assistance, might be privately cut off by the inhabitants of these wilds. It appears that Sergeant Davis was missing for years, without any certainty as to his fate. At length, an account of the murder appeared from the evidence of one Alexander MacPherson (a Highlander, speaking no language but Gaelic, and sworn by an interpreter), who gave the following extraordinary account of his cause of knowledge: he was, he said, in bed in his cottage, when an apparition came to his bedside and commanded him to rise and follow him out of doors. Believing his visitor to be one Farquharson, a neighbour and friend, the witness did as he was bid, and when they were without the cottage, the appearance told the witness he was the ghost of Sergeant Davis, and requested him to go and bury his mortal remains, which lay concealed in a place he pointed out in a moorland tract called the Hill of Christie. He desired him to take Farquharson with him as an assistant. Next day the witness went to the place specified, and there found the bones of a human body much decayed. The witness did not at that time bury the bones so found, in consequence of which negligence the sergeant's ghost again appeared to him, upbraiding him with his breach of promise. On this occasion the witness asked the ghost who were the murderers, and received for answer that he had been slain by the prisoners at the bar. The witness, after this second visitation, called the assistance of Farquharson, and buried the body.

Farquharson was brought in evidence to prove that the preceding witness, MacPherson, had called him to the burial of the bones, and told him the same story which he repeated in court. Isabel MacHardie, a person who slept in one of the beds which run along the wall in an ordinary Highland hut, declared that upon the night when MacPherson said he saw the ghost, she saw a naked man enter the house and go towards MacPherson's bed.

Yet though the supernatural incident was thus fortified, and although there were other strong presumptions against the prisoners, the story of the apparition threw an air of ridicule on the whole evidence for the prosecution. It was followed up by the counsel for the prisoners asking, in the cross-examination of MacPherson, "What language did the ghost speak in?" The witness, who was himself ignorant of English, replied, "As good Gaelic as I ever heard in Lochaber." "Pretty well for the ghost of an English sergeant," answered the counsel. The inference was rather smart and plausible than sound, for, the apparition of the ghost being admitted, we know too little of the other world to judge whether all languages may not be alike familiar to those who belonged to it. It imposed, however, on the jury, who found the accused parties not guilty, although their counsel and solicitor and most of the court were satisfied of their having committed the murder. In this case the interference of the ghost seems to have rather impeded the vengeance which it was doubtless the murdered sergeant's desire to obtain. Yet there may be various modes of explaining this mysterious story, of which the following conjecture may pass for one.

The reader may suppose that MacPherson was privy to the fact of the murder, perhaps as an accomplice or otherwise, and may also suppose that, from motives of remorse for the action, or of enmity to those who had committed it, he entertained a wish to bring them to justice. But through the whole Highlands there is no character more detestable than that of an informer, or one who takes what is called tascal money, or reward for discovery of crimes. To have informed against Terig and MacDonald might have cost MacPherson his life, and it is far from being impossible that he had recourse to the story of the ghost, knowing well that his superstitious countrymen would pardon his communicating the commission entrusted to him by a being from the other world, although he might probably have been murdered if his delation of the crime had been supposed voluntary. This explanation, in exact conformity with the sentiments of the Highlanders on such subjects, would reduce the whole story to a stroke of address on the part of the witness.

It is therefore of the last consequence, in considering the truth of stories of ghosts and apparitions, to consider the possibility of wilful deception, whether on the part of those who are agents in the supposed disturbances or the author of the legend. We shall separately notice an instance or two of either kind.

The most celebrated instance in which human agency was used to copy the disturbances imputed to supernatural beings refers to the ancient palace of Woodstock, when the commissioners of the Long Parliament came down to dispark what had been lately a royal residence.* The commissioners arrived at Woodstock, 13th October 1649, determined to wipe away the memory of all that connected itself with the recollection of monarchy in England. But in the course of their progress they were encountered by obstacles which apparently came from the next world. Their bedchambers were infested with visits of a thing resembling a dog, but which came and passed as mere earthly dogs cannot do. Logs of wood, the remains of a very large tree called the King's Oak, which they had splintered into billets for burning, were tossed through the house, and the chairs displaced and shuffled about. While they were in bed, the feet of their couches were lifted higher than their heads, and then dropped with violence. Trenchers "without a wish" flew at their heads of free will. Thunder and lightning came next, which were set down to the same cause. Spectres made their appearance, as they thought, in different shapes, and one of the party saw the apparition of a hoof, which kicked a candlestick and lighted candle into the middle of the room, and then politely scratched on the red snuff to extinguish it. Other and worse tricks were practised on the astonished commissioners, who, considering that all the fiends of hell were let loose upon them, retreated from Woodstock without completing an errand which was, in their opinion, impeded by infernal powers, though the opposition offered was rather of a playful and malicious than of a dangerous cast.

The whole matter was, after the Restoration, discovered to be the trick of one of their own party, who had attended the commissioners as a clerk, under the name of Giles Sharp. This man, whose real name was Joseph Collins of Oxford, called "Funny Joe",* was a concealed loyalist, and well acquainted with the old mansion of Woodstock, where he had been brought up before the civil war. Being a bold, active, spirited man, Joe availed himself of his local knowledge of trapdoors and private passages so as to favour the tricks which he played off upon his masters by aid of his fellow domestics. The commissioners' personal reliance on him made his task the more easy, and it was all along remarked that trusty Giles Sharp saw the most extraordinary sights and visions among the whole party. The unearthly terrors experienced by the commissioners are detailed with due gravity by Sinclair, and also, I think, by Dr Plot. But although the detection or explanation of the real history of the Woodstock demons has also been published, and I have myself seen it, I have at this time forgotten whether it exists in a separate collection, or where it is to be looked for.

Similar disturbances have been often experienced while it was the custom to believe in and dread such frolics of the invisible world, and under circumstances which induce us to wonder both at the extreme trouble taken by the agents in these impostures and the slight motives from which they have been induced to do much wanton mischief. Still greater is our modern surprise at the apparently simple means by which terror has been excited to so general an extent that even the wisest and most prudent have not escaped its contagious influence.

On the first point I am afraid there can be no better reason assigned than the conscious pride of superiority, which induces the human being in all cases to enjoy and practise every means of employing an influence over his fellow mortals, to which we may safely add that general love of tormenting, as common to our race as to that noble mimic of humanity, the monkey. To this is owing the delight with which every schoolboy anticipates the effects of throwing a stone into a glass shop, and to this we must also ascribe the otherwise unaccountable pleasure which individuals have taken in practising the tricksy pranks of a goblin, and filling a household or neighbourhood with anxiety and dismay, with little gratification to themselves besides the consciousness of dexterity if they remain undiscovered, and with the risk of loss of character and punishment should the imposture be found out.

In the year 1772, a train of transactions, commencing upon Twelfth Day,* threw the utmost consternation into the village of Stockwell,* near London, and impressed upon some of its inhabitants the inevitable belief that they were produced by invisible agents. The plates, dishes, china and glassware, and small movables of every kind, contained in the house of Mrs Golding, an elderly lady, seemed suddenly to become animated, shifted their places, flew through the room, and were broken to pieces. The particulars of this commotion were as curious as the loss and damage occasioned in this extraordinary manner were alarming and intolerable. Amidst this combustion, a young woman, Mrs Golding's maid, named Anne Robinson, was walking backwards and forwards, nor could she be prevailed on to sit down for a moment excepting while the family were at prayers, during which time no disturbance happened. This Anne Robinson had been but a few days in the old lady's service, and it was remarkable that she endured with great composure the extraordinary display which others beheld with terror, and coolly advised her mistress not to be alarmed or uneasy, as these things could not be helped. This excited an idea that she had some reason for being so composed, not inconsistent with a degree of connection with what was going forward. The afflicted Mrs Golding, as she might be well termed, considering such a commotion and demolition among her goods and chattels, invited neighbours to stay in her house, but they soon became unable to bear the sight of these supernatural proceedings, which went so far that not above two cups and saucers remained out of a valuable set of china. She next abandoned her dwelling and took refuge with a neighbour, but, finding his movables were seized with the same sort of St Vitus's dance,* her landlord reluctantly refused to shelter any longer a woman who seemed to be persecuted by so strange a subject of vexation. Mrs Golding's suspicions against Anne Robinson now gaining ground, she dismissed her maid, and the hubbub among her movables ceased at once and for ever.

This circumstance of itself indicates that Anne Robinson was the cause of these extraordinary disturbances, as has been since more completely ascertained by a Mr Brayfield, who persuaded Anne, long after the events had happened, to make him her confidant. There was a love story connected with the case, in which the only magic was the dexterity of Anne Robinson and the simplicity of the spectators. She had fixed long horse hairs to some of the crockery, and placed wires under others, by which she could throw them down without touching them. Other things she dextrously threw about, which the spectators, who did not watch her motions, imputed to invisible agency. At times, when the family were absent, she loosened the hold of the strings by which the hams, bacon and similar articles were suspended, so that they fell on the slightest motion. She employed some simple chemical secrets, and, delighted with the success of her pranks, pushed them further than she at first intended. Such was the solution of the whole mystery, which, known by the name of the Stockwell ghost, terrified many well-meaning persons, and had been nearly as famous as that of Cock Lane,* which may be hinted at as another imposture of the same kind. So many and wonderful are the appearances described that when I first met with the original publication I was strongly impressed with the belief that the narrative was like some of Swift's advertisements, a jocular experiment upon the credulity of the public. But it was certainly published bona fide, and Mr Hone, on the authority of Mr Brayfield, has since fully explained the wonder.*

Many such impositions have been detected, and many others have been successfully concealed, but to know what has been discovered in many instances gives us the assurance of the ruling cause in all. I remember a scene of the kind attempted to be got up near Edinburgh, but detected at once by a sheriff's officer, a sort of persons whose habits of incredulity and suspicious observation render them very dangerous spectators on such occasions. The late excellent Mr Walker, minister at Dunnottar, in the Mearns,* gave me a curious account of an imposture of this kind, practised by a young country girl, who was surprisingly quick at throwing stones, turf and other missiles, with such dexterity that it was for a long time impossible to ascertain her agency in the disturbances of which she was the sole cause.

The belief of the spectators that such scenes of disturbance arise from invisible beings will appear less surprising if we consider the common feats of jugglers, or professors of legerdemain, and recollect that it is only the frequent exhibition of such powers which reconciles us to them as matters of course, although they are wonders at which in our fathers' time men would have cried out either sorcery or miracles. The spectator also, who has been himself duped, makes no very respectable appearance when convicted of his error, and thence, if too candid to add to the evidence of supernatural agency, is yet unwilling to stand convicted by cross-examination of having been imposed on, and unconsciously becomes disposed rather to colour more highly than the truth than acquiesce in an explanation resting on his having been too hasty a believer. Very often, too, the detection depends upon the combination of certain circumstances which, apprehended, necessarily explain the whole story.

For example, I once heard a sensible and intelligent friend in company express himself convinced of the truth of a wonderful story, told him by an intelligent and bold man, about an apparition. The scene lay in an ancient castle on the coast of Morven or the Isle of Mull, where the ghost-seer chanced to be resident. He was given to understand by the family, when betaking himself to rest, that the chamber in which he slept was occasionally disquieted by supernatural appearances. Being at that time no believer in such stories, he attended little to this hint, until the witching hour of night, when he was awakened from a dead sleep by the pressure of a human hand on his body. He looked up at the figure of a tall Highlander, in the antique and picturesque dress of his country, only that his brows were bound with a bloody bandage. Struck with sudden and extreme fear, he was willing to have sprung from bed, but the spectre stood before him in the bright moonlight, its one arm extended so as to master him if he attempted to rise, the other hand held up in a warning and grave posture, as menacing the Lowlander if he should attempt to quit his recumbent position. Thus he lay in mortal agony for more than an hour, after which it pleased the spectre of ancient days to leave him to more sound repose. So singular a story had on its side the usual number of votes from the company, till, upon cross-examination, it was explained that the principal person concerned was an exciseman. After which *éclaircissement* the same explanation struck all present, viz., the Highlanders of the mansion had chosen to detain the exciseman by the apparition of an ancient heroic ghost in order to disguise from his vigilance the removal of certain modern enough spirits, which his duty might have called upon him to seize. Here a single circumstance explained the whole ghost story.

At other times it happens that the meanness and trifling nature of a cause not very obvious to observation has occasioned it to be entirely overlooked, even on account of that very meanness, since no one is willing to acknowledge that he has been alarmed by a cause of little consequence, and which he would be ashamed of mentioning. An incident of this sort happened to a gentleman of birth and distinction who is well known in the political world, and was detected by the precision of his observation.

Shortly after he succeeded to his estate and title, there was a rumour among his servants concerning a strange noise heard in the family mansion at night, the cause of which they had found it impossible to trace. The gentleman resolved to watch himself, with a domestic who had grown old in the family and who had begun to murmur strange things concerning the knocking having followed so close upon the death of his old master. They watched until the noise was heard, which they listened to with that strange uncertainty attending midnight sounds which prevents the hearers from immediately tracing them to the spot where they arise, while the silence of the night generally occasions the imputing to them more than the due importance which they would receive if mingled with the usual noises of daylight. At length the gentleman and his servant traced the sounds which they had repeatedly heard to a small storeroom used as a place for keeping provisions of various kinds for the family, of which the old butler had the key. They entered this place, and remained there for some time without hearing the noises which they had traced thither; at length the sound was heard, but much lower than it had formerly seemed to be, while acted upon at a distance by the imagination of the hearers. The cause was immediately discovered. A rat caught in an old-fashioned trap had occasioned this tumult by its efforts to escape, in which it was able to raise the trapdoor of its prison to a certain height, but was then obliged to drop it. The noise of the fall, resounding through the house, had occasioned the disturbance which, but for the cool investigation of the proprietor, might easily have established an accredited ghost story. The circumstance was told me by the gentleman to whom it happened.

There are other occasions in which the ghost story is rendered credible by some remarkable combination of circumstances very unlikely to have happened, and which no one could have supposed unless some particular fortune occasioned a discovery.

An apparition which took place at Plymouth is well known,* but it has been differently related, and, having some reason to think the following edition correct, it is an incident so much to my purpose that you must pardon its insertion.

A club of persons connected with science and literature was formed at the great sea town I have named. During the summer months, the society met in a cave by the seashore; during those of autumn and winter, they convened within the premises of a tavern, but, for the sake of privacy, had their meetings in a summer house situated in the garden, at a distance from the main building. Some of the members to whom the position of their own dwellings rendered this convenient had a pass key to the garden door, by which they could enter the garden and reach the summer house without the publicity or trouble of passing through the open tavern. It was the rule of this club that its members presided alternately. On one occasion, in the winter, the president of the evening chanced to be very ill – indeed, was reported to be on his deathbed. The club met as usual, and, from a sentiment of respect, left vacant the chair which ought to have been occupied by him if in his usual health; for the same reason, the conversation turned upon the absent gentleman's talents, and the loss expected to the society by his death. While they were upon this melancholy theme, the door suddenly opened, and the appearance of the president entered the room. He wore a white wrapper, a nightcap round his brow, the appearance of which was that of death itself. He stalked into the room with unusual gravity, took the vacant place of ceremony, lifted the empty glass which stood before him, bowed around and put it to his lips, then replaced it on the table and stalked out of the room as silent as he had entered it. The company remained deeply appalled; at length, after many observations on the strangeness of what they had seen, they resolved to dispatch two of their number as ambassadors, to see how it fared with the president, who had thus strangely appeared among them. They went, and returned with the frightful intelligence that the friend after whom they had enquired was that evening deceased.

The astonished party then resolved that they would remain absolutely silent respecting the wonderful sight which they had seen. Their habits were too philosophical to permit them to believe that they had actually seen the ghost of their deceased brother, and at the same time they were too wise men to wish to confirm the superstition of the vulgar by what might seem indubitable evidence of a ghost. The affair was therefore kept a strict secret, although, as usual, some dubious rumours of the tale found their way to the public. Several years afterwards, an old woman who had long filled the place of a sick nurse was taken very ill, and on her deathbed was attended by a medical member of the philosophical club. To him, with many expressions of regret, she acknowledged that she had long before attended Mr ———, naming the president whose appearance had surprised the club so strangely, and that she felt distress of conscience on account of the manner in which he died. She said that as his malady was attended by light-headedness, she had been directed to keep a close watch upon him during his illness. Unhappily she slept, and during her sleep the patient had awaked and left the apartment. When, on her own awaking, she found the bed empty and the patient gone, she forthwith hurried out of the house to seek him, and met him in the act of returning. She got him, she said, replaced in bed, but it was only to die there. She added, to convince her hearer of the truth of what she said, that immediately after the poor gentleman expired, a deputation of two members from the club came to enquire after their president's health, and received for answer that he was already dead. This confession explained the whole matter. The delirious patient had very naturally taken the road to the club, from some recollections of his duty of the night. In approaching and retiring from the apartment he had used one of the pass keys already mentioned, which made his way shorter. On the other hand, the gentlemen sent to enquire after his health had reached his lodging by a more circuitous road, and thus there had been time for him to return to what proved his deathbed long before they reached his chamber. The philosophical witnesses of this strange scene were now as anxious to spread the story as they had formerly been to conceal it, since it showed in what a remarkable manner men's eyes might turn traitors to them, and impress them with ideas far different from the truth.

Another occurrence of the same kind, although scarcely so striking in its circumstances, was yet one which, had it remained unexplained, might have passed as an indubitable instance of a supernatural apparition.

A Teviotdale farmer was riding from a fair, at which he had indulged himself with John Barleycorn, but not to that extent of defying goblins which it inspired into the gallant Tam o' Shanter.* He was pondering with some anxiety upon the dangers of travelling alone on a solitary road which passed the corner of a churchyard, now near at hand, when he saw before him in the moonlight a pale female form standing upon the very wall which surrounded the cemetery. The road was very narrow, with no opportunity of giving the apparent phantom what seamen call "a wide berth". It was, however, the only path which led to the rider's home, who therefore resolved, at all risks, to pass the apparition. He accordingly approached, as slowly as possible, the spot where the spectre stood, while the figure remained, now perfectly still and silent, now brandishing its arms and gibbering to the moon. When the farmer came close to the spot, he dashed in the spurs and set the horse off upon a gallop, but the spectre did not miss its opportunity. As he passed the corner where she was perched, she contrived to drop behind the horseman and seize him round the waist, a manoeuvre which greatly increased the speed of the horse and the terror of the rider, for the hand of her who sat behind him, when pressed upon his, felt as cold as that of a corpse. At his own house at length he arrived, and bid the servants who came to attend him, "Tak aff the ghaist!" They took off accordingly a female in white, and the poor farmer himself was conveyed to bed, where he lay struggling for weeks with a strong nervous fever. The female was found to be a maniac who had been left a widow very suddenly by an affectionate husband, and the nature and cause of her malady induced her, when she could make her escape, to wander to the churchyard, where she sometimes wildly wept over his grave, and sometimes, standing on the corner of the churchyard wall, looked out, and mistook every stranger on horseback for the husband she had lost. If this woman, which was very possible, had dropped from the horse unobserved by him whom she had made her involuntary companion, it would have been very hard to have convinced the honest farmer that he had not actually performed part of his journey with a ghost behind him.

There is also a large class of stories of this sort, where various secrets of chemistry, of acoustics, ventriloquism or other arts have been either employed to dupe the spectators or have tended to do so through mere accident and coincidence. Of these it is scarce necessary to quote instances, but the following may be told as a tale recounted by a foreign nobleman known to me nearly thirty years ago, whose life, lost in the service of his sovereign, proved too short for his friends and his native land.

At a certain old castle on the confines of Hungary, the lord to whom it belonged had determined upon giving an entertainment worthy of his own rank and of the magnificence of the antique mansion which he inhabited. The guests of course were numerous, and among them was a veteran officer of hussars, remarkable for his bravery. When the arrangements for the night were made, this officer was informed that there would be difficulty in accommodating the company in the castle, large as it was, unless someone would take the risk of sleeping in a room supposed to be haunted, and that, as he was known to be above such prejudices, the apartment was in the first place proposed for his occupation, as the person least likely to suffer a bad night's rest from such a cause. The major thankfully accepted the preference, and, having shared the festivity of the evening, retired after midnight, having denounced vengeance against anyone who should presume by any trick to disturb his repose – a threat which his habits would, it was supposed, render him sufficiently ready to execute. Somewhat contrary to the custom in these cases, the major went to bed, having left his candle burning and laid his trusty pistols, carefully loaded, on the table by his bedside.

He had not slept an hour when he was awakened by a solemn strain of music. He looked out. Three ladies, fantastically dressed in green, were seen in the lower end of the apartment, who sung a solemn requiem. The major listened for some time with delight; at length he tired. "Ladies," he said, "this is very well, but somewhat monotonous – will you be so kind as to change the tune?" The ladies continued singing; he expostulated, but the music was not interrupted. The major began to grow angry. "Ladies," he said, "I must consider this as a trick for the purpose of terrifying me, and as I regard it as an impertinence, I shall take a rough mode of stopping it." With that he began to handle his pistols. The ladies sang on. He then got seriously angry. "I will but wait five minutes," he said, "and then fire without hesitation." The song was uninterrupted – the five minutes were expired. "I still give you law,* ladies," he said, "while I count twenty." This produced as little effect as his former threats. He counted one, two, three accordingly, but on approaching the end of the number, and repeating more than once his determination to fire, the last numbers – seventeen... eighteen... nineteen... – were pronounced with considerable pauses between, and an assurance that the pistols were cocked. The ladies sang on. As he pronounced the word "twenty" he fired both pistols against the musical damsels – but the ladies sang on! The major was overcome by the unexpected inefficacy of his violence, and had an illness which lasted more than three weeks. The trick put upon him may be shortly described by the fact that the female choristers were placed in an adjoining room, and that he only fired at their reflection thrown forward into that in which he slept by the effect of a concave mirror.

Other stories of the same kind are numerous and well known. The apparition of the Brocken mountain,* after having occasioned great admiration and some fear, is now ascertained by philosophers to be a gigantic reflection, which makes the traveller's shadow, represented upon the misty clouds, appear a colossal figure of almost immeasurable size. By a similar deception men have been induced, in Westmoreland and other mountainous countries, to imagine they saw troops of horse and armies marching and countermarching, which were in fact only the reflection of horses pasturing upon an opposite height, or of the forms of peaceful travellers.

A very curious case of this kind was communicated to me by the son of the lady principally concerned, and tends to show out of what mean materials a venerable apparition may be sometimes formed. In youth this lady resided with her father, a man of sense and resolution. Their house was situated in the principal street of a town of some size. The back part of the house ran at right angles to an Anabaptist* chapel, divided from it by a small cabbage garden. The young lady used sometimes to indulge the romantic love of solitude by sitting in her own apartment in the evening till twilight, and even darkness, was approaching. One evening, while she was thus placed, she was surprised to see a gleamy figure, as of some aerial being, hovering, as it were, against the arched window in the end of the Anabaptist chapel. Its head was surrounded by that halo which painters give to the Catholic saints, and while the young lady's attention was fixed on an object so extraordinary, the figure bent gracefully towards her more than once, as if intimating a sense of her presence, and then disappeared. The seer of this striking vision descended to her family, so much discomposed as to call her father's attention. He obtained an account of the cause of her disturbance, and expressed his intention to watch in the apartment next night. He sat accordingly in his daughter's chamber, where she also attended him. Twilight came, and nothing appeared, but as the grey light faded into darkness, the same female figure was seen hovering on the window: the same shadowy form, the same pale light around the head, the same inclinations as the evening before. "What do you think of this?" said the daughter to the astonished father. "Anything, my dear," said the father, "rather than allow that we look upon what is supernatural." A strict research established a natural cause for the appearance on the window. It was the custom of an old woman, to whom the garden beneath was rented, to go out at night to gather cabbages. The lantern she carried in her hand threw up the refracted reflection of her form on the chapel window. As she stooped to gather her cabbages, the reflection appeared to bend forward, and that was the whole matter.

Another species of deception, affecting the credit of such supernatural communications, arises from the dexterity and skill of the authors who have made it their business to present such stories in the shape most likely to attract belief. Defoe – whose power in rendering credible that which was in itself very much the reverse was so peculiarly distinguished – has not failed to show his superiority in this species of composition. A bookseller of his acquaintance had, in the trade phrase, rather overprinted an edition of Drelincourt on Death, and complained to Defoe of the loss which was likely to ensue. The experienced bookmaker, with the purpose of recommending the edition, advised his friend to prefix the celebrated narrative of Mrs Veal's ghost,* which he wrote for the occasion, with such an air of truth that although in fact it does not afford a single tittle of evidence properly so called, it nevertheless was swallowed so eagerly by the people that Drelincourt's work on death, which the supposed spirit recommended to the perusal of her friend Mrs Bargrave, instead of sleeping on the editor's shelf, moved off by thousands at once; the story, incredible in itself, and unsupported as it was by evidence or inquiry, was received as true merely from the cunning of the narrator and the addition of a number of adventitious circumstances which no man alive could have conceived as having occurred to the mind of a person composing a fiction.

It did not require the talents of Defoe, though in that species of composition he must stand unrivalled, to fix the public attention on a ghost story. John Dunton, a man of scribbling celebrity at the time, succeeded to a great degree in imposing upon the public a tale which he calls the 'Apparition Evidence'.* The beginning of it, at least (for it is of great length), has something in it a little new. At Minehead, in Somersetshire, lived an ancient gentlewoman named Mrs Leckie, whose only son and daughter resided in family with her. The son traded to Ireland, and was supposed to be worth eight or ten thousand pounds. They had a child about five or six years old. This family was generally respected in Minehead, and especially Mrs Leckie, the old lady, was so pleasant in society that her friends used to say to her, and to each other, that it was a thousand pities such an excellent, good-humoured gentlewoman must, from her age, be soon lost to her friends. To which Mrs Leckie often made the somewhat startling reply: "Forasmuch as you now seem to like me, I am afraid you will but little care to see or speak with me after my death, though I believe you may have that satisfaction." Die, however, she did, and after her funeral was repeatedly seen in her personal likeness, at home and abroad, by night and by noonday.

One story is told of a doctor of physic walking into the fields, who in his return met with this spectre, whom he at first accosted civilly, and paid her the courtesy of handing her over a stile. Observing, however, that she did not move her lips in speaking, or her eyes in looking round, he became suspicious of the condition of his companion, and showed some desire to be rid of her society. Offended at this, the hag at next stile planted herself upon it and obstructed his passage. He got through at length with some difficulty, and not without a sound kick and an admonition to pay more attention to the next aged gentlewoman whom he met. "But this," says John Dunton,

was a petty and inconsiderable prank to what she played in her son's house and elsewhere. She would at noonday appear upon the quay of Minehead and cry, "A boat, a boat, ho! A boat, a boat, ho!" If any boatmen or seamen were in sight and did not come, they were sure to be cast away, and if they did come, 'twas all one: they were cast away. It was equally dangerous to please and displease her. Her son had several ships sailing between Ireland and England: no sooner did they make land and come in sight of England but this ghost would appear in the same garb and likeness as when she was alive, and, standing at the mainmast, would blow with a whistle – and though it were never so great a calm, yet immediately there would arise a most dreadful storm, that would break, wreck and drown the ship and goods; only the seamen would escape with their lives – the Devil had no permission from God to take them away. Yet at this rate, by her frequent apparitions and disturbances, she had made a poor merchant of her son, for his fair estate was all buried in the sea, and he that was once worth thousands was reduced to a very poor and low condition in the world, for whether the ship were his own or hired, or he had but goods on board it to the value of twenty shillings, this troublesome ghost would come as before, whistle in a calm at the mainmast at noonday, when they had descried land, and then ship and goods went all out of hand to wreck, insomuch that he could at last get no ships wherein to stow his goods, nor any mariner to sail in them – for knowing what an uncomfortable, fatal and losing voyage they should make of it, they did all decline his service. In her son's house she hath her constant haunts by day and night, but whether he did not, or would not own if he did, see her, he always professed he never saw her. Sometimes, when in bed with his wife, she would cry out, "Husband, look, there's your mother!" And when he would turn to the right side, then was she gone to the left, and when to the left side of the bed, then was she gone to the right; only one evening their only child, a girl of about five or six years old, lying in a truckle bed under them, cries out, "Oh, help me, Father! Help me, Mother! For Grandmother will choke me!" – and, before they could get to their child's assistance, she had murdered it, they finding the poor girl dead, her throat having been pinched by two fingers, which stopped her breath and strangled her. This was the sorest of all their afflictions: their estate is gone, and now their child is gone also – you may guess at their grief and great sorrow. One morning after the child's funeral, her husband being abroad, about eleven in the forenoon, Mrs Leckie the younger goes up into her chamber to dress her head, and as she was looking into the glass she spies her mother-in-law, the old beldam, looking over her shoulder. This cast her into a great horror, but, recollecting her affrighted spirits and recovering the exercise of her reason, faith and hope, having cast up a short and silent prayer to God, she turns about and bespeaks her: "In the name of God, Mother, why do you trouble me?" "Peace," says the spectrum. "I will do thee no hurt." "What will you have of me?" says the daughter," etc.*

Dunton, the narrator and probably the contriver of the story, proceeds to inform us at length of a commission which the wife of Mr Leckie receives from the ghost to deliver to Atherton, Bishop of Waterford, a guilty and unfortunate man, who afterwards died by the hands of the executioner, but that part of the subject is too disagreeable and tedious to enter upon.

So deep was the impression made by the story on the inhabitants of Minehead that it is said the tradition of Mrs Leckie still remains in that port, and that mariners belonging to it often, amid tempestuous weather, conceive they hear the whistle call of the implacable hag who was the source of so much mischief to her own family. However, already too desultory and too long, it would become intolerably tedious were I to insist further on the peculiar sort of genius by which stories of this kind may be embodied and prolonged.

I may, however, add that the charm of the tale depends much upon the age of the person to whom it is addressed, and that the vivacity of fancy which engages us in youth to pass over much that is absurd, in order to enjoy some single trait of imagination, dies within us when we obtain the age of manhood and the sadder and graver regions which lie beyond it. I am the more conscious of this because I have been myself at two periods of my life, distant from each other, engaged in scenes favourable to that degree of superstitious awe which my countrymen expressively call being *eerie*.

On the first of these occasions I was only nineteen or twenty years old, when I happened to pass a night in the magnificent old baronial castle of Glamis, the hereditary seat of the Earls of Strathmore. The hoary pile contains much in its appearance, and in the traditions connected with it, impressive to the imagination. It was the scene of the murder of a Scottish king of great antiquity – not indeed the gracious Duncan, with whom the name naturally associates itself, but Malcolm II.* It contains also a curious monument of the peril of feudal times, being a secret chamber, the entrance of which, by the law or custom of the family, must only be known to three persons at once, viz., the Earl of Strathmore, his heir apparent and any third person whom they may take into their confidence. The extreme antiquity of the building is vouched by the immense thickness of the walls and the wild and straggling arrangement of the accommodation within doors.

As the late Earl of Strathmore seldom resided in that ancient mansion, it was, when I was there, but half furnished, and that with movables of great antiquity, which, with the pieces of chivalric armour hanging upon the walls, greatly contributed to the general effect of the whole. After a very hospitable reception from the late Peter Proctor, Esq., then seneschal of the castle, in Lord Strathmore's absence, I was conducted to my apartment in a distant corner of the building. I must own that as I heard door after door shut, after my conductor had retired, I began to consider myself too far from the living and somewhat too near the dead. We had passed through what is called "the King's Room", a vaulted apartment garnished with stags' antlers and similar trophies of the chase, and said by tradition to be the spot of Malcolm's murder, and I had an idea of the vicinity of the castle chapel.

In spite of the truth of history, the whole night scene in Macbeth's castle rushed at once upon my mind, and struck my imagination more forcibly than even when I have seen its terrors represented by the late John Kemble and his inimitable sister.* In a word, I experienced sensations which, though not remarkable either for timidity or superstition, did not fail to affect me to the point of being disagreeable, while they were mingled at the same time with a strange and indescribable kind of pleasure, the recollection of which affords me gratification at this moment.

In the year 1814 accident placed me, then past middle life, in a situation somewhat similar to that which I have described.

I had been on a pleasure voyage with some friends around the north coast of Scotland, and in that course had arrived in the saltwater lake under the castle of Dunvegan,* whose turrets, situated upon a frowning rock, rise immediately above the waves of the loch. As most of the party, and I myself in particular, chanced to be well known to the Laird of MacLeod, we were welcomed to the castle with Highland hospitality, and glad to find ourselves in polished society, after a cruise of some duration. The most modern part of the castle was founded in the days of James VI; the more ancient is referred to a period "whose birth tradition notes not".* Until the present MacLeod connected by a drawbridge the site of the castle with the mainland of Skye, the access must have been extremely difficult. Indeed, so much greater was the regard paid to security than to convenience that in former times the only access to the mansion arose through a vaulted cavern in a rock, up which a staircase ascended from the seashore, like the buildings we read of in the romances of Mrs Radcliffe.*

Such a castle, in the extremity of the Highlands, was of course furnished with many a tale of tradition and many a superstitious legend to fill occasional intervals in the music and song, as proper to the halls of Dunvegan as when Johnson commemorated them. We reviewed the arms and ancient valuables of this distinguished family – saw the dirk and broadsword of Rorie Mhor, and his horn, which would drench three chiefs of these degenerate days. The solemn drinking cup of the Kings of Man must not be forgotten, nor the fairy banner given to MacLeod by the Queen of Fairies: that magic flag which has been victorious in two pitched fields, and will still float in the third, the bloodiest and the last, when the elfin sovereign shall, after the fight is ended, recall her banner and carry off the standard-bearer.*

Amid such tales of ancient tradition I had from MacLeod and his lady the courteous offer of the haunted apartment of the castle, about which, as a stranger, I might be supposed interested. Accordingly, I took possession of it about the witching hour. Except perhaps some tapestry hangings and the extreme thickness of the walls, which argued great antiquity, nothing could have been more comfortable than the interior of the apartment, but if you looked from the windows, the view was such as to correspond with the highest tone of superstition. An autumnal blast, sometimes driving mist before it, swept along the troubled billows of the lake, which it occasionally concealed and by fits disclosed. The waves rushed in wild disorder on the shore, and covered with foam the steep piles of rock, which, rising from the sea in forms something resembling the human figure, have obtained the name of MacLeod's Maidens, and in such a night seemed no bad representatives of the Norwegian goddesses called Choosers of the Slain, or Riders of the Storm.* There was something of the dignity of danger in the scene, for on a platform beneath the windows lay an ancient battery of cannon, which had sometimes been used against privateers even of late years. The distant scene was a view of that part of the Quillan mountains* which are called, from their form, MacLeod's Dining Tables. The voice of an angry cascade, termed the Nurse of Rorie Mhor, because that chief slept best in its vicinity, was heard from time to time mingling its notes with those of wind and wave. Such was the haunted room at Dunvegan, and as such it well deserved a less sleepy inhabitant. In the language of Dr Johnson, who has stamped his memory on this remote place, "I looked around me, and wondered that I was not more affected, but the mind is not at all times equally ready to be moved."* In a word, it is necessary to confess that, of all I heard or saw, the most engaging spectacle was the comfortable bed, in which I hoped to make amends for some rough nights on shipboard, and where I slept accordingly without thinking of ghost or goblin till I was called by my servant in the morning.

From this I am taught to infer that tales of ghosts and demonology are out of date at forty years and upwards – that it is only in the morning of life that this feeling of superstition "comes o'er us like a summer cloud",* affecting us with fear which is solemn and awful rather than painful – and I am tempted to think that, if I were to write on the subject at all, it should have been during a period of life when I could have treated it with more interesting vivacity, and might have been at least amusing, if I could not be instructive. Even the present fashion of the world seems to be ill suited for studies of this fantastic nature, and the most ordinary mechanic has learning sufficient to laugh at the figments which in former times were believed by persons far advanced in the deepest knowledge of the age.

I cannot, however, in conscience carry my opinion of my countrymen's good sense so far as to exculpate them entirely from the charge of credulity. Those who are disposed to look for them may, without much trouble, see such manifest signs, both of superstition and the disposition to believe in its doctrines, as may render it no useless occupation to compare the follies of our fathers with our own. The sailors have a proverb that every man in his lifetime must eat a peck of impurity, and it seems yet more clear that every generation of the human race must swallow a certain measure of nonsense. There remains hope, however, that the grosser faults of our ancestors are now out of date, and that whatever follies the present race may be guilty of, the sense of humanity is too universally spread to permit them to think of tormenting wretches till they confess what is impossible, and then burning them for their pains.

Note on the Texts

For details of the original publication of the tales in this collection, as well as of the sources from which the texts are taken (if different), see the first note for each story. With the exceptions of 'Phantasmagoria' and 'Letters on Demonology and Witchcraft', all of them represent the revised versions produced for the "Magnum Opus edition" of Scott's works, the forty-eight-volume series published in Edinburgh by Cadell & Co. between 1829 and 1833, also known as the "Waverley Novels" series. Spelling and punctuation have been standardized, modernized and made consistent throughout.

Notes

p. 3, *The Fortunes of Martin Waldeck*: Originally included in Chapter 18 of *The Antiquary*, one of the Waverley novels, published in three volumes in Edinburgh by Archibald Constable & Co. on 4th May 1816, and in London by Longman, Hurst, Rees, Orme & Brown on 8th May 1816. The text in this volume is from the edition published in Toronto by Copp, Clark and in London by Adam & Charles Black in 1897, which is itself based on the revised version of the novel that constituted the fifth and sixth volumes – published in October and November 1829, respectively – of the "Magnum Opus" edition.

p. 3, *the Harz forest in Germany*: The outline of this story is taken from the German, though the author is at present unable to say in which of the various collections of the popular legends in that language the original is to be found [SCOTT'S NOTE].

p. 3, *optical deception*: The shadow of the person who sees the phantom, being reflected upon a cloud of mist, like the image of the magic lantern upon a white sheet, is supposed to have formed the apparition [SCOTT'S NOTE]. The seemingly unearthly phenomenon here described is known as a "Brocken spectre", since it was first observed on the Brocken, the highest peak in the Harz mountain range in northern Germany, and the setting for this story.

p. 3, *Capuchin*: A friar belonging to Friars Minor Capuchin, an offshoot of the Franciscan order, founded in 1525 by Matteo da Bascio (*c.*1495–1552).

p. 4, *The doctrines of Luther... Charles V*: The German priest Martin Luther (1483–1546) was the spearhead of the Protestant Reformation with his attacks on Roman Catholic doctrine and on corrupt practices such as the selling of papal indulgences. Charles V is Charles I of Spain (1500–58), who was also the Holy Roman Emperor, as Charles V, from 1519 to 1556.

p. 4, *Baal-peor... Tophet*: Baal-peor, Ashtaroth and Beelzebub are prominent beings in Christian demonology. Baal-peor is a deity mentioned in the Old Testament who was associated with the mountain Peor in the land of Moab, to the east of the Dead Sea, and worshipped by the ancient Moabites. (See Numbers 25:3, 5, 18.) Ashtaroth, or Astarte, was a Phoenician goddess of fertility and sexual love. In the Old Testament, she was worshipped by the sinful King Solomon (1 Kings 11:5). Beelzebub is the name given in the Old Testament to the god of the Philistine city of Ekron (2 Kings 1:1–18); in Christian theology, "Beelzebub" is another name for Satan. According to Jeremiah 19:4–6, Tophet was a place in the Valley of Hinnom outside Jerusalem where child sacrifices were carried out to the god Baal. "Tophet" thus became a name for hell.

p. 4, *the Electorate*: The Electorate of Hanover, a former state in northern Germany.

p. 6, *the verse of the Psalmist, "All good angels, praise the Lord!"*: See Psalm 148:2.

p. 8, *the wedding of Hermes with the Black Dragon*: Hermes is Hermes Trismegistus, a legendary figure from the Hellenistic period (323–30 BC) who combined the Greek god Hermes and the Egyptian god Thoth. He is regarded as the author of a collection of alchemical and esoteric writings dating from the first to the third century AD. The Black Dragon is presumably Satan.

p. 9, *As deep calls unto deep*: "Deep calleth unto deep at the noise of thy waterspouts: all thy waves and thy billows are gone over me" (Psalm 42:7).

p. 10, *to enter the lists*: That is, to enter the contest. The lists are the palisades (fences) surrounding an area for a tournament.

p. 11, *hollow way*: Otherwise known as a "sunken lane", a hollow way is a road or path at a significantly lower level than the land on either side.

p. 13, *Phantasmagoria*: Originally published in *Blackwood's Edinburgh Magazine*, vol. 3, No. 14 (May 1818), from which the text in this volume is taken.

p. 13, *"Come like shadows – so depart"*: The words of the three witches, also known as the Weird Sisters, in Shakespeare's *Macbeth* (Act IV, Sc. 1, l. 126).

NOTES

p. 13, *the black silk gown... denomination*: The description closely matches one given by Scott of the "Lady Dowager Don" in his diary entry for 17th January 1826: "a venerable lady who always wore a haunch-hoop, silk *négligé* and triple ruffles at the elbow". The suggestion is that the source of the tale is a highly distinguished elderly widow.

p. 14, *These companies... the Black Watch*: In the aftermath of the Jacobite rising of 1715 – a failed attempt to restore the Catholic House of Stuart to the British throne led by James Francis Edward Stuart (1688–1766), known as the "Old Pretender", the son of the deposed James II of England and James VII of Scotland (1633–1701) – the British government was, through lack of manpower, compelled to recruit men from local clans to keep order in the Highlands, where most people were sympathetic to the Jacobite cause. In 1725, General George Wade (1673–1748) raised a militia consisting of several "Independent Highland Companies", who were collectively referred to as the "Black Watch", a name of uncertain origin, although it is often believed to be a reference to the dark-coloured tartans worn by the soldiers, as suggested by Scott himself in *Waverley* (1814): "They call them *sidier dhu* because they wear the tartans" (Chapter 18). In 1739, the ten "Black Watch" companies became the "43rd Highland Regiment of Foot", before being renumbered (as the 42nd) in 1748. The name "Black Watch" became part of the regiment's official title in 1861. The terms *sidier dhu* and *sidier roy* are Gaelic. Soldiers of the British army were known as "redcoats" due to the colour of their uniforms.

p. 14, *only liable to do duty in their native country*: The Black Watch served in numerous campaigns abroad, including at the Battle of Fontenoy in Flanders in May 1745, during the War of the Austrian Succession (1740–48), and in North America during the French and Indian War (1754–63) – part of the wider Seven Years War (1756–63) – in which the colonies belonging to the British Empire fought those belonging to the French. They were also involved in the American War of Independence, notably in the defeat of George Washington (1732–99) at the Battle of Long Island in August 1776.

p. 14, *the Brunswick government*: That is, the government headed nominally by George II (1683–1760), King of Great Britain and Ireland, who also bore the title of Duke of Brunswick–Lüneburg, a former name of the German state of Hanover. George was the grandson of Princess Sophia, Electress of Hanover (1630–1714), to whom, according to the terms of the Act of Settlement of 1701, the British throne was to pass on the death of Anne (1665–1714) in order to guarantee a Protestant succession. In the event, however, Sophia died shortly before Anne, and therefore her son George became king, as George I (1660–1727). He in turn was succeeded by his own son, George II.

p. 16, *the Father of the fatherless and Husband of the widow*: See Psalm 68:5: "A father of the fatherless, and a judge of the widows, is God in his holy habitation."

p. 19, *Wandering Willie's Tale*: Originally included in 'Letter Eleventh' in *Redgauntlet*, one of the Waverley novels, published in three volumes in Edinburgh by Archibald Constable & Co. on 14th June 1824, and in London by Hurst, Robinson & Co. on 29th June 1824. The text in this volume is from the edition published in New York by John Wurtele Lovell in 1881, which is itself based on the revised version of the novel that constituted the thirty-fifth and thirty-sixth volumes of Cadell's "Magnum Opus", which appeared in April and May 1832, respectively. The narrator is the blind fiddler Willie Steenson, who relates his tale in broad Scots to the novel's hero, Darsie Latimer.

p. 19, *Sir Robert Redgauntlet*: The character of Sir Robert Redgauntlet is based on the Scottish nobleman Sir Robert Grierson, 1st Baronet of Lag (1655–1733), a notorious persecutor of the Covenanters, militant adherents of Scottish Presbyterianism, a branch of Protestantism that believes in government of the Church by representative assemblies of elders, as opposed to bishops. The Scots' abolition of episcopacy (government by bishops) following the signing of the National Covenant (1638) led to the Bishops' Wars of 1639–40, during which Charles I (1600–49) sought to enforce Anglican observances in the Scottish Church. This represented the beginning of the wider Wars of the Three Kingdoms (1639–53), during which a second covenant, the Solemn League and Covenant (1643), was signed, and in which the Covenanters would side at different times with both Royalists and Parliamentarians. Following the Restoration of the monarchy under Charles II (1630–85) in 1660, the Scottish parliament passed the Rescissory Act 1661, which at a stroke annulled all legislation passed since 1633, thereby re-establishing episcopacy in the Scottish Church. Then, in 1662, an Abjuration Act formally rejected the National Covenant and the Solemn League and Covenant. The Covenanters were the targets of brutal persecution for the next twenty-five years, during which a number of rebellions were violently suppressed. Grierson, who sat in the Scottish parliament for Dumfriesshire in the south-west of the country from 1678 to 1686, is remembered for his role in what is known as "the Killing Time", an especially bloody period lasting from 1679 to 1688, and in particular as the presiding officer at the court that, in May 1685, condemned two women, Margaret Wilson and Margaret McLachlan, known as the "Wigtown Martyrs", who were tied to stakes and drowned by the rising tide. Following the "Glorious Revolution" of 1688–89, in which the Catholic monarch James II was deposed and the Protestant Dutch prince William of Orange (1650–1702) – husband of James's Protestant daughter

Mary (1662–94) – was invited by the political establishment to replace him as king of England, Scotland and Ireland, Presbyterian Church government was re-established in Scotland, and persecution of the Covenanters ceased.

p. 19, *dear years*: That is, years of dearth, when the prices of staples such as wheat were high, perhaps due to poor harvests.

p. 19, *He was out... saxteen hundred and fifty-twa*: Initially a Covenanter himself, the Scottish general James Graham, 1st Marquess of Montrose (1612–50), known as the "Great Montrose", switched allegiances during the English Civil War (1642–49), leading a Royalist army consisting of Highlanders and Irish troops to several victories against the Covenanters, who were then allied with the English Parliamentarians, in 1644–45, before being routed at the Battle of Philiphaugh in September 1645. Following the defeat of the Scots in the Anglo-Scottish War (1650–52) and the subsequent absorption of Scotland into the Commonwealth that, led by Oliver Cromwell (1599–1658), had been created following the abolition of the monarchy in 1649, the Scottish nobleman and Royalist William Cunningham, 9th Earl of Glencairn (1610–64), was placed in charge of the Royalist forces in Scotland by Charles II, and went on to lead a rebellion in the Highlands in 1653–54. Though initially successful, it was ultimately suppressed at the Battle of Dalnaspidal in July 1654.

p. 19, *the Whigs*: In this context, the terms "Whig" and "Covenanter" are essentially interchangeable. "Whig" is a shortening of "Whiggamore", which refers to the "Whiggamore Raid" of September 1648, when Covenanters from the south-west of Scotland – who were known as "Whiggamores", a term perhaps derived from "Whiggam", a Scots cry uttered to encourage horses – marched on Edinburgh in opposition to the then-dominant "Engager" faction, who had recently been defeated by Cromwell's New Model Army at the Battle of Preston (17th–19th August 1648). The term was later extended to refer to all Covenanters. Later still, during the "Exclusion Crisis" of 1679–81, the term came to refer to supporters of the party that unsuccessfully opposed the succession of the Catholic heir presumptive, James, Duke of York – the future James II of England and James VII of Scotland – to the throne. In early-eighteenth-century Scotland, the "Whigs" were therefore those who supported the Glorious Revolution of 1688–89 (in which James II was deposed) and the resulting restoration of Presbyterianism. The opposing party, the Tories, supported James's succession, and hence came to be associated with Jacobitism.

p. 19, *Claverhouse's or Tam Dalyell's*: John Graham of Claverhouse, 1st Viscount of Dundee (1649–89), was, from September 1678, the commander of a company of Highlanders charged with policing the militantly Presbyterian south-west of Scotland and suppressing illicit Covenanter conventicles. On 1st June 1679 he was defeated by a force of armed Covenanters at the Battle of Drumclog in South Lanarkshire, although he was victorious against the same group at the Battle of Bothwell Bridge later that month. The zeal with which he executed his role earned him the nickname of "Bluidy Clavers". The Scottish Royalist general Sir Thomas Dalyell of the Binns (1615–85) was commander-in-chief in Scotland from July 1666, having been appointed by Charles II with instructions to crush the Covenanters. In November of the same year he suppressed a Covenanter rebellion at the Battle of Rullion Green near the Pentland Hills in Midlothian. He later became known as "Bluidy Tam", due to his brutal treatment of the vanquished dissenters.

p. 19, *hill folk*: The Covenanters, who hid in the hills during the persecution.

p. 19, *Will ye tak the test?*: A reference to the Test Act passed by the Scottish parliament in 1681 at the behest of James, Duke of York, the brother of Charles II and the king's viceroy in Scotland, which required anyone seeking public office to swear an oath acknowledging royal supremacy, something inconceivable for Covenanters.

p. 19, *buff coat*: A coat made from buff, a heavy yellow leather with a velvety surface, typically worn by soldiers.

p. 19, *turn a hare*: That is, outrun a hare and cause it to change direction.

p. 19, *Carrifra-gawns*: A precipitous side of a mountain in Moffatdale [SCOTT'S NOTE].

p. 19, *killing times*: See second note to p. 19.

p. 20, *'Hoopers and Girders'... 'Jockie Lattin'*: 'Hoopers and Girders', also known as 'Hoop Her and Gird Her', is a traditional jig whose name refers to barrel-making: to "gird" meant to fasten a metal band around a barrel. 'Jockie Lattin' is a traditional Irish tune that became popular in the Scottish Borders based on the legendary story of Jack Lattin from Kildare, who, in the early eighteenth century, danced from Morristown (in Kildare) to Dublin.

p. 20, *a Tory... Jacobites*: See fifth note to p. 19.

p. 20, *the Revolution*: The Glorious Revolution of 1688–89. See second note to p. 19.

p. 20, *So Parliament... just the man he was*: The caution and moderation of King William III, and his principles of unlimited toleration, deprived the Cameronians of the opportunity they ardently desired to retaliate the injuries which they had received during the reign of prelacy, and purify the land, as they called it, from the pollution of blood. They esteemed the Revolution, therefore, only a half-measure, which neither comprehended the rebuilding the Kirk in its full splendour, nor the revenge of the death of the saints on their persecutors [SCOTT'S NOTE]. King William III is William of Orange – see second note to

NOTES

p. 19. The Cameronians were the most radical faction of the Covenanters. They were named after the Covenanter martyr Richard Cameron (c.1648–80), who was killed in a clash with royal troops at Airds Moss in Ayrshire in June 1680. "The Kirk" is the Church of Scotland.

p. 20, *he lacked... larder and cellar*: In other words, he could no longer rely on the financial penalties that were exacted from Covenanters during the period following the Restoration as a source of income.

p. 20, *Martinmas*: St Martin's Day, 11th November.

p. 21, *He was a professor... at a bytime*: In other words, he was a professed Presbyterian, but also appreciated the worldly pleasure of music.

p. 21, *Major Weir, after the warlock that was burnt*: A celebrated wizard, executed at Edinburgh for sorcery and other crimes [SCOTT'S NOTE]. On falling ill in 1670, the Scottish soldier and Covenanter Thomas Weir (1599–1670) confessed to, among other things, witchcraft, bestiality and incest, and was consequently executed along with his sister, Jean Weir.

p. 21, *gravel*: A disease characterized by crystals formed in the kidneys, passed along the urinary tract and expelled with urine.

p. 21, *like a sheep's head between a pair of tangs*: A proverbial expression.

p. 23, *the Union*: Although the kingdoms of England and Scotland had been united with the accession of James VI of Scotland (1566–1625) to the throne of England as James I in 1603, full political union did not occur until 1707 with the passage of the Act of Union, which created the United Kingdom of Great Britain.

p. 23, *Davie Lindsay*: The Scottish knight and "makar" (poet) Sir David Lyndsay of the Mount (c.1486–c.1555).

p. 24, *In fact, Alan*: This interjection from Darsie Latimer (see first note to p. 19) is addressed to his friend and correspondent, Alan Fairford.

p. 24, *Domesday Book*: The name given to a comprehensive survey of the land in England completed in 1086 by order of William the Conqueror (c.1027–87), whose invading Norman army had defeated the Anglo-Saxons under Harold II at the Battle of Hastings twenty years earlier.

p. 25, *talis qualis evidence*: The Latin phrase *talis qualis* means "such as it is" – in other words, out of goodwill Sir John is willing to accept any evidence that Stephen can provide, even if it does not represent absolute proof.

p. 26, *the bailie and the baron officer*: Respectively, a municipal magistrate equivalent to an English alderman and an estate official.

p. 27, *they suld hae caa'd her*: That is, "I believe that she was called".

p. 28, *my father*: The narrator means, of course, his grandfather.

p. 29, *There was the fierce Middleton... silver bullet had made*: The personages here mentioned are most of them characters of historical fame, but those less known and remembered may be found in the tract entitled *The Judgement and Justice of God Exemplified, or, a Brief Historical Account of Some of the Wicked Lives and Miserable Deaths of Some of the Most Remarkable Apostates and Bloody Persecutors from the Reformation till after the Revolution.* This constitutes a sort of postscript or appendix to John Howie of Lochgoin's *Account of the Lives of the Most Eminent Scots Worthies.* The author has, with considerable ingenuity, reversed his reasoning upon the inference to be drawn from the prosperity or misfortunes which befall individuals in this world, either in the course of their lives or in the hour of death. In the account of the martyrs' sufferings, such inflictions are mentioned only as trials permitted by Providence, for the better and brighter display of their faith and constancy of principle. But when similar afflictions befell the opposite party, they are imputed to the direct vengeance of Heaven upon their impiety. If, indeed, the life of any person obnoxious to the historian's censures happened to have passed in unusual prosperity, the mere fact of its being finally concluded by death is assumed as an undeniable token of the judgement of Heaven, and, to render the conclusion inevitable, his last scene is generally garnished with some singular circumstances. Thus the Duke of Lauderdale is said, through old age but immense corpulence, to have become so sunk in spirits "that his heart was not the bigness of a walnut" [SCOTT'S NOTE]. John Middleton, 1st Earl of Middleton (*c.*1608–74), fought on the side of the Parliamentarians and Covenanters during the Bishops' Wars and the earlier stages of the Wars of the Three Kingdoms before switching allegiances in 1648. At the Restoration of 1660 he was made commander-in-chief of the troops in Scotland. John Leslie, 1st Duke of Rothes (*c.*1630–81), was Lord High Treasurer of Scotland after the Restoration and an enthusiastic persecutor of the Covenanters. John Maitland, 1st Duke of Lauderdale (1616–82), was an ardent Covenanter who supported the Parliamentarians in their rebellion against Charles I, but became a Royalist in 1647 following the king's promise (known as the "Engagement") to impose Presbyterianism on England in exchange for military support. He later became Secretary of State for Scotland and a ruthless suppressor of the Covenanters. For Dalyell, see sixth note to p. 19. Sir Andrew Bruce of Earlshall commanded the government troops at Airds Moss in June 1680, where the leading Covenanter Richard Cameron was killed (see fourth note to p. 20). James Irvine of Bonshaw was the leader of a company of dragoons who captured the Covenanter Donald Cargill (1619–81), a close associate of Richard Cameron, on 12th July 1681. Cargill was subsequently executed in Edinburgh on 27th July 1681. "Dunbarton Douglas" is George Douglas, 1st Earl of Dumbarton (1635–92). According to *A Cloud of Witnesses,* a work of Covenanter martyrology published in 1714, he – along with Claverhouse (see sixth note to p. 19) and others – caused a group of Covenanters "to be put to death upon a gibbet, without legal trial or sentence, suffering them neither to have a Bible, nor to pray before they died, at Mauchlein [Mauchline], 1685". The Scottish lawyer Sir George Mackenzie (1636–91) was known as "Bloody Mackenzie" as a result of his zealous pursuit of the Covenanters in his capacity as Lord Advocate, a position to which he was appointed by Charles II in 1677. Claverhouse (see sixth note to p. 19) was killed by a stray bullet at the Battle of Killiecrankie, fought on 27th July 1689, part of the Scottish Jacobite rising that occurred during that year in an attempt to restore the Catholic James II of England (James VII of Scotland) to the throne, and at which Claverhouse's outnumbered Jacobites were victorious. According to legend, he was impervious to lead as a result of a diabolical pact, and thus the bullet that struck him was made of silver. In his note Scott refers to *Biographia Scoticana* – first published in 1775, also known as *The Scots Worthies*, a work of Presbyterian martyrology by the Scottish biographer John Howie (1735–93) – according to which, Claverhouse's "own waiting man, taking a resolution to rid this world of this truculent bloody monster, and knowing he had proof of lead, shot him with a silver button he had before taken off his own coat for that purpose".

p. 29, *the Lang Lad of the Nethertown… Highland Amorites*: Archibald Campbell, 9th Earl of Argyll (1629–85), participated in the unsuccessful Protestant rebellion led by James Scott, 1st Duke of Monmouth (1649–85), illegitimate son of Charles II, against his father's brother and successor, the Catholic James II, in 1685. Captured at Inchinnan in Renfrewshire, he was beheaded in Edinburgh on 30th June 1685. According to *Biographia Scoticana* (see previous note), the "long lad of the Nethertoun" was a man from Hamilton in Lanarkshire who "got his leg broken, which no physician could cure, and so corrupted that scarce any person for the stink could come near him". The "bishop's summoner, that they called the Deil's Rattle-Bag" is David Mason, a Covenanter turned informer. He is referred to in *Biographia Scoticana*, in the section describing the life of the leading Covenanter Alexander Peden (1626–86): "About this time as he was preaching in the daytime, in the parish of Girvin, and being in the fields, one David Mason, then a professor, came in haste trampling upon the people, to be near him. At which he said, 'There comes the devil's rattle-bag – we do not want him here.' After this, the said David became officer and informer in that bounds, running through rattling and summoning the people to their unhappy courts for nonconformity, at which he and his got the name of 'the devil's rattle-bag'. Since the revolution, he complained to his minister that he and his family got that name. The minister said, 'Ye weel deserved it, and he was an honest man that gave you it; you and yours must enjoy it; there is no help for that.'" A "rattle-bag" is a bag containing pellets or the like, used as a rattle to attract deer when hunting. The "wicked guardsmen" are His Majesty's Regiment of Horse, created in 1682, of which Claverhouse (see sixth note to p. 19) was the first commander. The "Highland Amorites" are the "Highland Host", a 5,000-strong militia of Highlanders assembled in 1678 to crack down on illegal conventicles in south-western Scotland. They are referred to as the "Highland Amorites" in the anonymous poem 'Fight at Bothwel Bridge' (1766): "Montrose did come and Athol both, / And with them many more, / And all the Highland Amorites / That had been here before." The Amorites are an ancient nation referred to frequently in the Old Testament. Their name was often thought to be derived from the Hebrew for "highlanders" or "mountaineers".

p. 29, *'Weel Hoddled, Luckie'*: To "hoddle" is to waddle, or hobble. "Luckie" is a form of address to an elderly woman.

p. 30, *Donald of the Isles*: Donald of Islay, Lord of the Isles (1350–1423), ruler of the Western Isles.

p. 30, *the very words... Threave Castle*: The reader is referred for particulars to Pitscottie's *History of Scotland* [SCOTT'S NOTE]. When the royalist Patrick MacLellan of Bombie (d. *c*.1452), sheriff of Galloway and head of Clan MacLellan, turned down an invitation by William Douglas, 8th Earl of Douglas (1425–52), then the most powerful nobleman in the country, to join an alliance against James II of Scotland (1430–60), the earl laid siege to Raeberry Castle, MacLellan's home, and then imprisoned him at Threave Castle. A relative of MacLellan's, Sir Patrick Gray, later travelled to Threave with a letter from the king requesting his release. Douglas refused to read the communication until his guest had eaten a meal, after which he presented Gray with MacLellan's headless corpse in the courtyard. The story is told in *The Historie and Chronicles of Scotland, 1436–1565* by Robert Lindsay of Pitscottie (*c*.1532–80), the first history of Scotland to be written in Scots.

p. 34, *charged for a warlock*: For the "Magnum Opus" edition of *Redgauntlet*, Scott here inserted a lengthy note in which he first acknowledged that the blind fiddler's tale was influenced by one he had heard in his youth concerning Sir Robert Grierson of Lag (see second note to p. 19), and then went on to relate a truncated version of the story published in 1818 as 'Phantasmagoria' (included in this collection) as an example of a tale in which "the excessive lamentation over the loss of friends disturbed the repose of the dead".

NOTES

p. 35, *The Highland Widow*: Originally included in the first series of *Chronicles of the Canongate*, published in two volumes in Edinburgh by Cadell & Co. on 30th October 1827 and in London by Simpkin & Marshall on 5th November 1827, and comprising the introductory 'Chrystal Croftangry's Narrative', the short stories 'The Highland Widow' and 'The Two Drovers', and the novella *The Surgeon's Daughter* (not included in this collection). The texts of 'The Highland Widow' and 'The Two Drovers' in the present volume are from the identically titled *Chronicles of the Canongate*, published by Collins' Clear-Type Press in London in around 1910. Though it shares the name of the 1827 edition referred to above, this volume in fact contains only the first three elements, namely 'Chrystal Croftangry's Narrative', 'The Highland Widow' and 'The Two Drovers', which are followed by three short stories that were originally published in the 1829 number of the literary annual *The Keepsake*, which appeared in late 1828: 'My Aunt Margaret's Mirror', 'The Tapestried Chamber, or, The Lady in the Sacque' and 'Death of the Laird's Jock', the first two of which are also included in this collection. (Scott explains in his introduction to 'My Aunt Margaret's Mirror' that these three "fragments" were "originally designed to have been worked into the *Chronicles of the Canongate*" – see p. 117.) These six pieces ('Chrystal Croftangry's Narrative', the first two of the *Chronicles* and the three *Keepsake* tales) first appeared together in October 1832, under the title *The Highland Widow*, as the forty-first volume of Cadell's "Magnum Opus". The title 'The Highland Widow' is a reference to the song 'The Highland Widow's Lament' (1796) by the Scottish poet Robert Burns (1759–96), written from the perspective of a woman who has lost her Jacobite husband at Culloden (see fourth note to p. 35).

p. 35, *It wound as near... Coleridge*: From *Christabel* (I, ll. 39–42) by the English Romantic poet Samuel Taylor Coleridge (1772–1834), a narrative poem in the Gothic mode in which the titular character, while praying by an oak tree, hears a strange sound that proves to emanate from a beautiful young woman, Geraldine, who may be of supernatural origin.

p. 35, *Mrs Bethune Baliol's memorandum begins thus*: The framing narrative that introduces this story in *Chronicles of the Canongate* is by Chrystal Croftangry, a bankrupt who, having returned from abroad to find his family estate of Glentanner in ruins, has moved back to Edinburgh's Canongate and decided to turn his hand to literature. Writing in 1826, he introduces his first story as being taken from the Highland journal of his friend, Mrs Martha Bethune Baliol, whom Scott based on his friend Anne Murray Keith (1736–1818). In his introduction to the "Magnum Opus" edition Scott explains that 'The Highland Widow' is "very much as the excellent old lady used to tell the story".

SUPERNATURAL SHORT STORIES

p. 35, *It is five-and-thirty, or perhaps nearer forty, years ago*: The story is set some years after the Jacobite rising of 1745–46, in which the son of James Francis Edward Stuart, the "Old Pretender" (see first note to p. 14), Charles Edward Stuart (1720–88), known as the "Young Pretender" or "Bonnie Prince Charlie", embarked on a new rebellion, one supported by many of the Highland clans, which came to its climax at the Battle of Culloden in April 1746, at which the Jacobites were comprehensively defeated. There followed a period of brutal repression of the rebellious Highlanders – in which anyone found in arms was shot, thousands were taken prisoner and the estates of clan chiefs who had participated in the rising were confiscated – and an attempt by the British government to integrate the Highlands into the rest of the kingdom more fully in the hope of preventing further revolts. Notably, the Abolition of Heritable Jurisdictions (Scotland) Act of 1747 stripped clan chiefs of the judicial and military powers they had retained following the Act of Union of 1707. Furthermore, the Highland Dress Proscription Act of 1746 famously banned the wearing of tartans and Highland dress. (It was repealed in 1782.) The reference to "the French in America" in Chapter IV places the main events of the story in around 1756, when the "Black Watch" were sent to North America (see the first two notes to p. 14). The reference to "King George" later in the paragraph is therefore to George III (1738–1820), who reigned 1760–1820, the successor to and grandson of George II (1683–1760), who reigned 1727–60, during the 1745–46 rebellion.

p. 35, *the military roads*: From 1725, an extensive road-building operation was undertaken in order to promote the integration of the Highlands into the rest of Great Britain following the Jacobite rising of 1715. The operation was led by General Wade, who was also responsible for the formation of the new "Independent Highland Companies", whose movements the new roads were designed to facilitate (see first note to p. 14).

p. 35, *Greatheart in the Pilgrim's Progress*: In the second part of *The Pilgrim's Progress* (1684), a religious allegory by the English writer and preacher John Bunyan (1628–88), Christian (the titular pilgrim) is led on his journey to the Celestial City by a guide named Greatheart.

p. 35, *postilion*: A postilion, or post boy, rides the leading nearside horse drawing a coach or carriage.

p. 36, *a wheaten loaf... the Land of Cakes*: A reference to the fact that loaves made from wheat, as opposed to barley or oatmeal (bannocks), were scarce in the Highlands. Scotland's famous bannocks earned it the nickname "the Land of Cakes".

p. 36, *could tell to an inch... decidedly dangerous*: This is, or was, at least, a necessary accomplishment. In one of the most beautiful districts of the

NOTES

Highlands was, not many years since, a bridge bearing this startling caution: "Keep to the right side, the left being dangerous" [SCOTT'S NOTE].

p. 36, *piques himself on being a maize-eater*: That is, he proudly asserts his poverty. Maize was a staple food of the poor.

p. 37, *Gil Blas or Don Quixote*: The picaresque novel *Gil Blas* by the French writer Alain-René Lesage (1668–1747), published between 1715 and 1735, about the adventures and journey of upward social mobility of a young man born in poverty, and the satirical novel *Don Quixote* by the Spanish writer Miguel de Cervantes (1547–1616), published between 1605 and 1615, about a confused old man who, fixated with stories of romance, comes to believe he is a knight on a heroic quest.

p. 37, *Falkirk or Preston*: Jacobite victories during the rising of 1745–46: the Battle of Prestonpans, fought at Prestonpans just east of Edinburgh on 21st September 1745, and the Battle of Falkirk Muir, which took place near Falkirk in central Scotland on 17th January 1746.

p. 37, *mountain dew*: Whisky.

p. 37, *like Gideon's fleece, moist with the noble element*: "Behold, I will put a fleece of wool in the floor, and if the dew be on the fleece only, and it be dry upon all the earth beside, then shall I know that thou wilt save Israel by mine hand, as thou hast said" (Judges 6:37).

p. 38, *baiting place*: A stopping place at which travellers take refreshments.

p. 38, *the excellent clergyman who was then incumbent at Glenorquhy*: This venerable and hospitable gentleman's name was MacIntyre [SCOTT'S NOTE].

p. 38, *the stern chiefs of Loch Awe*: For the "Magnum Opus" edition of *Chronicles of the Canongate*, Scott here inserted a lengthy note consisting of a geographical description of Loch Awe in Argyll in western Scotland taken from the notes to *The Bridal of Caolchairn*, an 1822 poem by the Scottish poet John Allen (1798–1872). The "stern chiefs" are Clan Campbell, who were granted possession of Loch Awe following the victory of Robert I (1274–1329), known as Robert the Bruce, over Clan MacDougall at the Battle of the Pass of Brander in 1308. The Campbells went on to become the most powerful clan in Argyll, taking control of Glen Orchy, some twenty miles to the north-east, in the early fifteenth century, under the clan chief Duncan Campbell, 1st Lord Campbell (d. 1453). "Duncan with the thrum bonnet", mentioned in the same sentence, is apparently one of the clan chiefs. A "thrum bonnet" is one made from waste thread.

p. 38, *Kilchurn*: A castle at the north-eastern end of Loch Awe, once the Campbells' base.

p. 38, *Cruachan Ben*: Ben Cruachan, the highest mountain in Argyll.

p. 38, *the warlike clan... Robert Bruce*: See third note to p. 38.

p. 38, *Wellington*: Arthur Wellesley, 1st Duke of Wellington (1769–1852), who led the British forces to victory at Waterloo (1815), thereby ending the Napoleonic Wars, fought against the French under Napoleon Bonaparte, or Napoleon I (1769–1821).

p. 38, *even a Baliol must admit that*: Robert the Bruce was the grandson of Robert V de Brus, 5th Lord of Annandale (c.1215–95), known as "Robert the Competitor", who had vied for the Scottish throne in the "Great Cause" of 1290–92, when it became vacant on the death of the seven-year-old Queen Margaret (1283–90). The victor was John Balliol (c.1249–1314), who reigned as king of Scotland between 1292 and 1296.

p. 39, *defence and protection*: For the "Magnum Opus" edition of *Chronicles of the Canongate*, Scott here inserted a lengthy note consisting of an account of the Battle of the Pass of Brander taken from a biography of Robert the Bruce by the Scottish historian Patrick Fraser Tytler (1791–1849), part of the same author's series *Lives of Scottish Worthies* (1831–33).

p. 39, *like the Irish lady... long enough a-gone*: This is a line from a very pathetic ballad which I heard sung by one of the young ladies of Edgeworthstown in 1825. I do not know that it has been printed [SCOTT'S NOTE]. The young lady in question was Sophia Edgeworth (1803–37), stepsister of the Irish novelist Maria Edgeworth (1768–1849), from Edgeworthstown, County Longford, Ireland, who performed the song during the Edgeworths' stay at Abbotsford, Scott's home near Galashiels in the Scottish Borders.

p. 39, *the old Roman engineers*: A reference to the road-building that took place during the invasion of Caledonia attempted by the Romans under Septimius Severus (145–211 AD), emperor from 193 to 211, in 209.

p. 39, *Had you but seen... General Wade*: Attributed to the British army officer William Caulfeild (d. 1767), Wade's successor as coordinator of the road-building programme in the Highlands (see fifth note to p. 35).

p. 39, *his road over the Simplon*: Between 1801 and 1805 a mountain pass, known as the Simplon Pass, was constructed between the Pennine Alps and the Lepontine Alps in Switzerland, during the country's occupation by the French under Napoleon Bonaparte.

p. 39, *the iron foundries at the Bunawe*: An iron furnace was established at Bunawe, a small settlement on the southern shore of Loch Etive, close to the mouth of the Awe, in 1753. It was supplied by wood from the forests in the area.

p. 41, *as Judah... palm tree*: A reference to coins bearing the legend "Judaea Capta" that were issued by the emperor Vespasian (9–79 AD) to commemorate the Roman conquest of Judaea in 70 AD. On the reverse of many of the coins was the image of a woman, an allegorical representative of Judaea, sitting in an attitude of mourning beneath a palm tree.

p. 42, *the Furies*: Three goddesses of vengeance and punishment in Greek mythology.

p. 42, *Orestes and Oedipus*: Figures from Greek mythology. The hero Orestes avenges the murder of his father, Agamemnon, by his mother, Clytemnestra, by killing her and her lover, Aegisthus, and is then pursued by the Furies. The story is best known from the sequence of three tragedies by the ancient Greek dramatist Aeschylus (c.525–c.456 BC) known as the *Oresteia*. Oedipus is a king of Thebes who fulfils a prophecy by unwittingly killing his father and marrying his mother, and then, consumed by grief, gouges out his own eyes. The story is famously told in *Oedipus Rex*, the first of the three "Theban plays" by the tragedian Sophocles (c.496–406 BC).

p. 43, *John Home... my brave!*: Words addressed by the grieving Lady Randolph to her dead son in the 1756 play *Douglas* (Act V, Sc. 1) by the Scottish minister and dramatist John Home (1722–1808).

p. 44, *Oh, I'm come to the Low Country... Old Song*: 'The Highland Widow's Lament', ll. 1–4, 17–20 (see first note to p. 35).

p. 44, *MacTavish Mhor*: That is, "MacTavish the Great", from the Gaelic *mór*. MacTavish Mhor is modelled on the Scottish Jacobite outlaw Robert Roy MacGregor (1671–1734), known as "Rob Roy", often described as a Scottish Robin Hood, whose status as a folk hero was consolidated by his depiction in Scott's eponymous novel of 1818, in which his exploits were romanticized. Like MacTavish Mhor, Rob Roy was a cattle thief and ran a protection racket in which he guaranteed the safety of herds belonging to Lowland gentry in return for money.

p. 44, *the Lowland line*: The historical distinction between the Gaelic-speaking "Highlands" in the north and west and the Scots-speaking "Lowlands" in the south and east was formalized by the Wash Act of 1784, which, as a means of stimulating legal whisky distilling in the Highlands and reducing illicit production of the spirit, divided the country along a diagonal line between the Firth of Clyde in the west and the Firth of Tay in the east, with different custom duties and provisions applying on either side.

p. 44, *the Highland Watch*: The Black Watch. See first note to p. 14.

p. 45, *My sword, my spear... have is mine*: From 'The Cretan Warrior' (ll. 7–12), a translation by the Scottish poet and orientalist John Leyden (1775–1811) of the 'Spear Song' by the Cretan mercenary and poet Hybrias (*fl.* sixth century BC).

p. 45, *the expedition of Prince Charles Edward*: The Jacobite rising of 1745–46. See fourth note to p. 35.

p. 45, *sidier roy*: The red soldier [SCOTT'S NOTE]. See first note to p. 14.

p. 46, *"the stormy sons of the sword"*: A phrase taken from Book I of the epic *Fingal* (1762), one of several supposed translations in prose by the Scottish poet James Macpherson (1736–96) of a cycle of tales about the hero and bard Finn MacCool, claimed to have been written in Gaelic in the third century by Ossian, a legendary Irish warrior-poet. In fact, although Macpherson based his "translations" on authentic Gaelic ballads – "Ossian" is derived from Oisín, a warrior-poet in Irish legend; Finn MacCool is the hero Fionn mac Cumhaill, father of Oisín – in reality the works were largely Macpherson's invention. Opinion was divided as to the authenticity of the translations in the eighteenth century; the fraud was eventually exposed in the late nineteenth century.

p. 47, *the long-skirted Lowland coat... romantic garb*: See fourth note to p. 35.

p. 49, *Taymouth Castle*: In fact Balloch Castle, built in 1552 on the south bank of the River Tay, north-east of the village of Kenmore in the Grampians. Balloch was the seat of Clan Campbell, who rebuilt it as Taymouth Castle in the early nineteenth century.

p. 50, *of whom the bard... thrush's song*: Not a quotation from a particular bardic poem, but rather Scott's evocation of the language of such poetry, influenced by the "translations" of Macpherson (see note to p. 46).

p. 51, *barbarous... Battle of Culloden*: See fourth note to p. 35.

p. 51, *combined government*: That is, the governments of Scotland and England, unified since 1707. See first note to p. 23.

p. 52, *the emphatic language of Scripture... and was refreshed*: "Then David arose from the earth, and washed, and anointed himself, and changed his apparel, and came into the house of the Lord, and worshipped; then he came to his own house, and when he required, they set bread before him, and he did eat" (2 Samuel 12:20).

p. 52, *the Feast of the Tabernacles*: Otherwise known as Succoth, a Jewish festival held in the autumn that commemorates the Israelites' years of wandering in the wilderness after the Exodus from Egypt, during which time they lived in movable huts, or tents (tabernacles).

p. 53, *sidier dhu*: See first note to p. 14.

p. 54, *Hope deferred... heart sick*: "Hope deferred maketh the heart sick; but when the desire cometh, it is a tree of life" (Proverbs 13:12). The "royal sage" is Solomon, king of ancient Israel c.970–c.930 BC, traditionally considered the author of the biblical Book of Proverbs. His association with wisdom derives from the famous story known as the Judgement of Solomon (1 Kings 3:16–28), in which he adjudicates on a dispute between two women who each claim ownership of a baby. The infant's real mother is revealed by her reaction when he proposes cutting the baby in two.

NOTES

p. 54, *sporran mollach*: The goatskin pouch worn by the Highlanders round their waist [SCOTT'S NOTE].

p. 54, *breacan*: That which is variegated, i.e. the tartan [SCOTT'S NOTE].

p. 54, *Fort Augustus*: A barracks built by Wade in the aftermath of the 1715 Jacobite rising (see first note to p. 14), at the settlement known as Kiliwhimin at the south-west end of Loch Ness in the Highlands. It was named after the second son of George II, Prince William Augustus, Duke of Cumberland (1721–65), the figure associated more than any other with the brutal repression of the Jacobites in the aftermath of Culloden (see fourth note to p. 35).

p. 55, *Breadalbane and broad Lorn*: Two of the traditional provinces of the Highlands, both controlled by Clan Campbell.

p. 55, *the impenetrable deserts of Y Mac Y Mhor*: That is, the territories of Clan Mackay in Sutherland, in the far north of the Highlands.

p. 55, *the Sound of Mull, the Isles of Treshornish and the rough rocks of Harris*: In order, the sound between the Inner Hebridean island of Mull and mainland Scotland, an archipelago west of Mull and the southern third of the island of Lewis and Harris in the Outer Hebrides.

p. 56, *one of the new regiments... French in America*: Several new regiments of the Black Watch were raised in order to serve against the French in the Seven Years War – see second note to p. 14.

p. 56, *MacAllan Mhor*: The chief of Clan MacDonald of Clanranald.

p. 56, *Caberfae*: Caberfae – anglice, "the Stag's Head", the Celtic designation for the arms of the family of the high chief of Seaforth [SCOTT'S NOTE]. The Earl of Seaforth was the chief of Clan Mackenzie.

p. 56, *Glengarry, Lochiel, Perth, Lord Lewis*: Prominent Jacobites. Aeneas MacDonell, known as "Young Glengarry", commanded the Highland regiment of his father, John MacDonell, 2nd Lord MacDonell, 12th Chief of Glengarry (d. 1754), during the 1745–46 rising, and was accidentally killed at the Battle of Falkirk Muir (see second note to p. 37). Donald Cameron of Lochiel (*c*.1695–1748), hereditary chief of Clan Cameron, was a key ally of Charles Edward Stuart. After the defeat at Culloden he fled to France. James Drummond, 3rd Duke of Perth (1713–46), was the joint commander of the Jacobite forces in 1745–46, alongside Lord George Murray (1694–1760). He escaped on a French ship after the defeat, but died at sea. Lord Lewis Gordon (1724–54) was appointed Lord Lieutenant of Aberdeenshire and Banffshire by Charles Edward Stuart during the rebellion. He escaped to France after Culloden.

p. 56, *Drummossie Muir*: An area of moorland south-east of Inverness that encompasses the site of the Battle of Culloden.

p. 57, *him of Hanover's*: George II's. See third note to p. 14.

p. 58, *one of the race of Dermid... Glencoe!*: The "race of Dermid" is Clan Campbell, whose founder was believed to be Diarmuid Ua Duibhne, a hero and demigod in Irish mythology. On 13th February 1692, more than thirty members of the Jacobite Clan MacDonald of Glencoe were killed by soldiers from the regiment of Archibald Campbell, 10th Earl of Argyll (1658–1703), for having missed the deadline (1st January) for swearing an oath of allegiance to the new Protestant monarchs, William III and Mary II, who came to the throne in the Glorious Revolution of 1688–89 (see second note to p. 19), even though the chief of the clan, MacIain, had in fact taken the oath on 6th January at Inveraray, having been unable to do so at Fort William due to the unavailability of a magistrate. The 120 men from the Earl of Argyll's regiment, who were led by Captain Robert Campbell of Glenlyon (1630–96), arrived in Glencoe in late January and were peaceably quartered on the MacDonalds' estate for two weeks before receiving the order to attack them – hence Elspat's subsequent reference to their being "received in friendship".

p. 58, *screams and murder!*: For the "Magnum Opus" edition of *Chronicles of the Canongate*, Scott here inserted a lengthy note consisting of an account of the Glencoe massacre (see previous note) taken from the article 'Britain' from the *Encyclopaedia Britannica*, beginning: "In the beginning of the year 1692, an action of unexampled barbarity disgraced the government of King William III in Scotland."

p. 58, *the unhappy house of Glenlyon*: That is, the house of Robert Campbell of Glenlyon. See first note to p. 58.

p. 59, *Dumbarton*: Dumbarton Castle, built upon Dumbarton Rock, a volcanic plug on the north bank of the River Clyde, north-west of Glasgow, had been a fortress since Roman times, and was used as a garrison for government troops during the Jacobite uprisings of 1689, 1715 and 1745.

p. 62, *But for your son... Coriolanus*: The words of the exiled general Coriolanus to his mother, Volumnia, after she has succeeded in persuading him not to attack Rome in Shakespeare's *Coriolanus* (Act V, Sc. 3, ll. 210–12).

p. 63, *white cockade*: A cockade is a rosette or plume worn in the hat as part of a military uniform. White cockades were worn by Jacobites.

p. 66, *the great and wise... successive administration*: Although he did not become prime minister until 1766 – at which time he was created Earl of Chatham – William Pitt (1708–78) was the de facto head of the government in 1756–61, during the Seven Years War, for which new regiments of the Black Watch were created – see the first two notes to p. 14.

NOTES

p. 66, *bred in the German wars*: The War of the Austrian Succession (1740–48), a group of related conflicts involving most of the European powers that was provoked by the death of the Holy Roman Emperor Charles VI (1685–1740) and the accession of his daughter Maria Theresa (1717–80) as ruler of the Habsburg monarchy (which included Austria, Hungary, Croatia and Bohemia, among others). Maria Theresa's succession was contested by Charles Albert of Bavaria (1697–1745), who rejected Charles's Pragmatic Sanction of 1713 – four years before the birth of Maria Theresa – which decreed that all Habsburg kingdoms and lands were to be passed on after his death as a single unit, without partition, and that they could be inherited by a daughter in the absence of a son. The principal belligerents in the war were, on one side, France, Prussia and Bavaria, and, on the other, the Pragmatic Army, a coalition of British, Hanoverian and Austrian forces led by the Duke of Cumberland (for whom see fourth note to p. 54).

p. 66, *brought to the halberds*: A reference to a method of corporal punishment in which a soldier was tied to a post made from halberds and flogged. A halberd is a weapon combining a spear and battleaxe.

p. 67, *within the general's power*: For the "Magnum Opus" edition of *Chronicles of the Canongate*, Scott here inserted a lengthy note consisting of two quotations from the two-volume *Sketches of the Character, Manners and Present State of the Highlanders of Scotland, with Details of the Military Services of the Highland Regiments* (1822) by David Stewart of Garth (1772–1829), who had himself served in the Black Watch between 1787 and 1804. The extracts illustrated, in Scott's words, "the strong, undeviating attachment of the Highlanders to the person, and their deference to the will or commands of their chiefs and superiors, their rigid adherence to duty and principle, and their chivalrous acts of self-devotion to these in the face of danger and death", representing instances of valour that "might not inaptly supply parallels to the deeds of the Romans themselves, at the era when Rome was in her glory".

p. 67, *the double summit of the ancient dun*: Dumbarton Castle on Dumbarton Rock, which is formed of two peaks. See note to p. 59.

p. 70, *the salt lakes of Kintail*: A reference to the sea inlet of Loch Alsh between the Isle of Skye in the Inner Hebrides and the north-west Highlands, which, 7.5 miles inland, diverges into Loch Duich to the south-east and the smaller Loch Long to the north-east. The surrounding mountainous region is known as Kintail.

p. 70, *the children of Kenneth*: Clan Mackenzie, a name that means, literally, "son of Kenneth". Kenneth was a powerful landowner in Kintail in the second half of the thirteenth century.

p. 70, *Skooroora*: Sgùrr Fhuaran, one of the Five Sisters, a mountain range in Kintail.

p. 71, *the enchanted... oil to the lamp*: The seals are considered by the Highlanders as enchanted princes [SCOTT'S NOTE].

p. 72, *the stern sound sleep... interval of their torments*: Although written after Scott's time, evidence of this notion is found in *Principles of Mental Physiology* (1874) by the English physician William Benjamin Carpenter (1813–85): "Even natural sleep, when following upon extreme fatigue, may be so intensified as almost to resemble coma... The North American Indian at the stake of torture will go to sleep on the least remission of agony, and will slumber until the fire is applied to awaken him" (Chapter 15).

p. 72, *greishogh*: *Greishogh*, a glowing ember [SCOTT'S NOTE].

p. 74, *Fionn*: Fionn mac Cumhaill – see note to p. 46.

p. 78, *MacDhonuil Dhu*: The chief of Clan Cameron is known as Mac Dhòmhnaill Dubh after its first chief, Donald Dubh Cameron (*fl.* 1411).

p. 79, *wolf-burd*: Wolf-brood, i.e. wolf-cub [SCOTT'S NOTE].

p. 83, *the civil wars*: The Jacobite rising of 1745–46.

p. 86, *clachan*: The village, literally the stones [SCOTT'S NOTE].

p. 87, *the sacring bell*: The bell rung at the moment of the consecration of the Eucharist in the Catholic Mass.

p. 87, *the Black Abbot of Inchaffray*: The head of the community of Augustinian canons at Inchaffray Abbey in southern Perthshire, founded in 1200. The Augustinians are the followers of a rule derived from the works of the Church Father St Augustine of Hippo (354–430). They were known as the "Black Canons" due to the colour of their habits.

p. 91, *The Two Drovers*: For details of the first publication of this story and of the edition from which the text is taken, see first note to p. 35. In his introduction to the "Magnum Opus", edition Scott explains that 'The Two Drovers' is based on an account of the trial and execution in Carlisle of a Highland cattle-drover who was accused of the murder of a fellow drover, an Englishman, which Scott heard from a friend of his father, George Constable (1719–1803), the model for Jonathan Oldbuck in *The Antiquary* (1816).

p. 91, *Mr Croftangry Introduces Another Tale*: For Chrystal Croftangry, see third note to p. 35.

p. 91, *Together both... Elegy on Lycidas*: From *Lycidas* (1637) by John Milton (1608–74), an elegy about a recently deceased friend of the poet (ll. 25–27).

p. 91, *that otium, as Horace terms it*: The Latin term *otium* means "leisure". Scott here refers to one of the *Odes* by the Roman poet Quintus Horatius Flaccus, known as Horace (65–8 BC), addressed to a wealthy Sicilian named

Grosphus: "*Otium divos rogat in patenti / prensus Aegaeo, simul atra nubes / condidit lunam neque certa fulgent / sidera nautis; / otium bello furiosa Thrace, / otium Medi pharetra decori, / Grosphe, non gemmis neque purpura ve- / nale neque auro*" (II, 16, ll. 1–8), translated by Christopher Smart (1756) as follows: "O Grosphus, he that is caught in the wide Aegean Sea, when a black tempest has obscured the moon, and not a star appears with steady light for the mariners, supplicates the gods for repose: for repose, Thrace furious in war, the quiver-graced Medes, for repose neither purchasable by jewels, nor by purple, nor by gold."

p. 91, *gillie-whitefoot*: Literally, a gillie whose duty it was to carry his master over streams. The term is translated from the Gaelic *gillie-casfliuch*, meaning "lad with wet feet". It was also used contemptuously to refer to the servant of a Highland chief.

p. 92, *top of Arthur's Seat… Leith Pier*: Respectively, "the affair of the wild Macraes", in which, in 1778, soldiers of the 78th Highland Regiment, known as the Seaforth Highlanders, including many men of Clan Macrae, staged a mutiny in response to a rumour that they were being shipped to India without their consent, occupying Arthur's Seat, an extinct volcano in Edinburgh, and an incident in April 1779 in which a number of soldiers belonging to the 42nd and 71st Highland regiments, having heard reports that they were to be transferred to a Lowland regiment and would therefore lose the right to wear a kilt, refused to board the ship that was to take them from Leith (a port north of Edinburgh) to America, resulting in a violent quarrel with the troops who were dispatched to take them prisoner.

p. 92, *an ass like Justice Shallow… his goodnights*: A misquotation of the words of Sir John Falstaff, the debauched companion of the young Prince Hal, the future Henry V, in Shakespeare's *Henry IV, Part 2*, forming part of a ribald description of the Justice of the Peace Robert Shallow: "He came ever in the rearward of the fashion, and sung those tunes to the overscutched huswives that he heard the carmen whistle, and swore they were his fancies or his goodnights" (Act III, Sc. 2, ll. 326–30). "Overscutched huswives" means, literally, "over-whipped prostitutes"; Croftangry rearranges the terms so that it is the carmen's tunes rather than the "huswives" that are "overscutched", that is, overfamiliar.

p. 92, *Mrs Grant of Laggan… unsophisticated state*: *Letters from the Mountains*, 3 vols; *Essays on the Superstitions of the Highlanders*; *The Highlanders and Other Poems*, etc. [SCOTT'S NOTE]. The Scottish writer Anne Grant (1755–1838), known as Mrs Anne Grant of Laggan, was the author of a number of largely autobiographical works about life in the Highlands, including *Letters from the Mountains* (1806) and *Essays on the Superstitions of the Highlanders* (1811). Her long poem 'The Highlanders' was published in the collection *Poems on Various Subjects* (1803).

p. 93, *General Stewart of Garth*: The gallant and amiable author of the *History of the Highland Regiments*, in whose glorious services his own share had been great, went out governor of St Lucia in 1828, and died in that island on 18th December 1829 – no man more regretted, or perhaps by a wider circle of friends and acquaintance [SCOTT'S NOTE]. For David Stewart of Garth, see first note to p. 67.

p. 93, *the days of clanship and claymores*: That is, the era preceding the Jacobite rising of 1745–46.

p. 93, *drovers*: Cattle-drovers. In the eighteenth and nineteenth centuries, Scottish drovers would escort their Highland-bred herds into England, typically to East Anglia and Lincolnshire, where they would be fattened before being taken to market at London's Smithfield, the site of a livestock market since the tenth century. Such a trade was necessitated by the demographic expansion that was a consequence of the industrial revolution.

p. 93, *An oyster... gentle Tilburnia*: In Acts II and III of the satirical burlesque *The Critic* (1779) by the Irish playwright Richard Brinsley Sheridan (1751–1816), the critics Dangle and Sneer attend rehearsals for the historical play *The Spanish Armada* by the literary charlatan Mr Puff, which includes a nonsensical speech from the "mad" Tilburnia: "An oyster may be crossed in love! / Who says 'A whale's a bird?' / Ha! Did you call, my love? / He's here! He's there! / He's everywhere! / Ah me! He's nowhere!" (Act III, Sc. 1).

p. 93, *Doune Fair*: That is, the cattle fair (or "tryste") at Doune in Perthshire in central Scotland, where drovers would bring their livestock from the Isle of Skye and the Highlands, and from where cattle would be driven south into England. From Doune Robin Oig and Harry Wakefield travel south-east, first to Stirling, then to Falkirk, Traquair (a village in Peeblesshire in the Scottish Borders), Minch Moor (an elevated area south of Traquair) and Liddesdale, and then over the border into the English county of Cumberland, where they first pass through "the Waste" (presumably an area of uncultivated land) and then reach Christenbury Crag, or Christianbury Crag, an area consisting of small tors of sandstone near the hamlet of Bewcastle, a few miles south of the border, and "Hollan Bush", or Holynbush, a hamlet on the north bank of the River Eden in Cumberland.

p. 94, *Donald*: That is, a Highlander.

p. 94, *a child amongst flocks, is a prince amongst herds*: Sheep-farming was not widespread in the Highlands until the late eighteenth century.

NOTES

p. 95, *Rob Roy*: See second note to p. 44.

p. 95, *"Of such ancestry"... "who would not be proud?"*: From a footnote to the entry for 15th August 1773 in *The Journal of a Tour to the Hebrides* (1785), a travelogue describing a journey made by the English lexicographer, writer and critic Samuel Johnson (1709–84), the dominant literary figure of his day, through the Highlands and Western Isles of Scotland in 1773 by his Scottish biographer, James Boswell (1740–95): "My great-grandfather, the husband of Countess Veronica, was Alexander, Earl of Kincardine, that eminent Royalist... From him the blood of Bruce flows in my veins. Of such ancestry who would not be proud?" "Bruce" is Robert the Bruce – see third and eighth notes to p. 38.

p. 96, *tying St Mungo's knot on their tails*: The Christian missionary Mungo, or Kentigern (d. *c*.612 AD), is considered the first bishop of Glasgow and is the patron saint of the city. Tying decorative knots in the tails of cattle to protect against witchcraft is a traditional Highland practice.

p. 96, *Dimayet*: Dumyat, a hill north of Stirling, at the western end of the Ochil range in central Scotland.

p. 96, *walk the deasil round you*: "Walking the *deasil*" was the custom of walking around a person following the direction of the sun in order to prevent ill fortune.

p. 96, *the Druidical mythology*: The Druids were the priestly class among the ancient Celts of pre-Roman Britain.

p. 97, *running the country*: That is, fleeing the country.

p. 97, *few of his aunt's words fell to the ground*: That is, few of her predictions failed to be realized.

p. 97, *Glenae*: In Dumfriesshire, in south-west Scotland. Hence he is a "westlandman".

p. 97, *dirking ower the board*: Stabbing over the table.

p. 97, *you cannot have more of a sow than a grumph*: That is, you cannot expect more from a pig than a grunt.

p. 98, *keep the rounds... professors of the fancy*: That is, he is able to conduct himself in the rounds of a boxing match at London's Smithfield (see third note to p. 93) or in a wrestling match. Smithfield was the site of St Bartholomew Fair, at which boxing booths were a popular attraction. "Professors of the fancy" are professional boxers. "The fancy" is a name for the art of pugilism.

p. 98, *Doncaster races*: The Yorkshire town of Doncaster has been a centre for horse racing since the sixteenth century.

p. 98, *the main chance*: The most advantageous course of action; one's best interests.

p. 98, *clothyard shafts*: The arrows of the longbow, which were the length of a "clothyard", a measure slightly longer than a standard yard. Many famous English victories against the French during the Hundred Years War (1337–1453) – such as at the Battle of Crécy in 1346 and the Battle of Agincourt in 1415 – are traditionally attributed to the use by English archers of the longbow.

p. 99, *shibboleth*: A word or sound that non-natives have difficulty pronouncing, and that is therefore used as a way of detecting foreigners. In the Old Testament the word "shibboleth" is used by the judge Jephthah to distinguish the fleeing Ephraimites, who could not pronounce it, from his own Gileadites (Judges 12:6).

p. 99, *caviar to his companion*: In other words, something fine that he would have been incapable of appreciating.

p. 99, *yeoman's service*: That is, good service as provided by a faithful servant. See *Hamlet*, Act v, Sc. 2, l. 37: "It did me yeoman's service."

p. 99, *Were ever two such loving friends!... Duke upon Duke*: Originally published anonymously, but generally attributed today to Alexander Pope (1688–1744), *Duke upon Duke: An Excellent New Ballad to the Tune of Chevy Chase* (1720) is a satirical poem about a quarrel between the Members of Parliament Sir John Guise, 3rd Baronet (c.1677–1732), and Nicholas Lechmere, 1st Baron Lechmere (1675–1727). The extract here is a close paraphrase of stanza XI. ('The Ballad of Chevy Chase' is a medieval English ballad about a hunting expedition on an area of unenclosed land reserved for that purpose – a "chase" – in the Cheviot Hills on the border of Scotland and England.)

p. 101, *if she was to tak the park*: "She" was sometimes used for "I" in representations of Highland speech, although this is not an authentic Highland usage.

p. 101, *Sawney*: A Scots diminutive of Alexander, a common Scottish name, and therefore a generic name for a Scotsman.

p. 101, *Goshen*: The pastoral land in Egypt given to Jacob and his descendants by the king of Egypt, and where they dwelt until the Exodus. See especially Genesis 45:9–10.

p. 102, *I would not... his oven*: In other words, he would not grovel at anyone's feet for permission to make a living.

p. 103, *John Barleycorn*: The anthropomorphized embodiment of malt whisky, made from barley.

p. 103, *Robin Oig hersell*: The use of "hersell" to mean "myself" – or, as here, "himself" – was another inauthentic convention used in representations of Highland speech.

p. 104, *come sliding in between him and the sunshine*: That is, they are an obstacle to his prosperity.

p. 104, *go it... show him the mill*: "Go it" means, essentially, "go for it". To "serve out" is boxing slang meaning to punish or take revenge on. A "nailer" is a slang term for a knock-out punch. "Mill" or "mell" was a Scottish or northern-English term for a kind of heavy hammer or mallet, as well as for a blow from such an implement. The term was also used to refer to a hammer that was presented to the loser as a booby prize in a horse race or other competition.

p. 105, *fords of Frew*: A crossing on the River Forth west of Stirling.

p. 105, *Whitson Tryste... Stagshaw Bank*: Cattle markets, many of which were held on Whitsun. The places named are, respectively, the town of Wooler in Northumberland, the island in the river Eden at Carlisle known as the Sands, and Stagshaw Bank, a common south of Hadrian's Wall in Northumberland.

p. 105, *bring you to the scratch*: A boxing term. The "scratch" is a line or mark drawn across the ring, to which boxers are brought before a match can begin.

p. 105, *sink point on the first plood drawn*: That is, end the fight as soon as one of the combatants draws blood.

p. 106, *swine-eaters*: Historically, Highlanders had an aversion to the eating of pork. In a footnote to his novel *The Fortunes of Nigel* (1822), Scott wrote: "The Scots, till within the last generation, disliked swine's flesh as an article of food as much as the Highlanders do at present" (Chapter 27).

p. 106, *he sees his own blood*: The notion that "a Scot will not fight until he sees his own blood" was proverbial.

p. 106, *his broth*: His deserts.

p. 107, *the curse of Cromwell... in the play*: The reference here is to the words of the poor Irishman Teague in the comedy *The Committee, or The Faithful Irishman* (1665) by the English Royalist playwright Sir Robert Howard (1626–98): "And now, my curse, and the curse of Cromwell, light upon you all, you thieves, you" (Act II). The "curse of Cromwell" was proverbial in Ireland as a consequence of the invasion of that country by Oliver Cromwell's New Model Army in 1649–53. Cromwell's name was similarly abominated in Scotland, which was invaded in 1650 in order to suppress support for Charles II. Scotland became part of the new Commonwealth of England in February 1652. For Cromwell and the Anglo-Scottish War (1650–52), see fourth note to p. 19.

p. 108, *English miles*: Until 1824, a Scottish mile was defined as the length of the Royal Mile in Edinburgh (1,984 yards), which was roughly 10 per cent longer than an English mile (1,760 yards).

p. 109, *Highlander... Scots' Dyke*: That is, all Scotsmen are brothers when they are in England. Scots' Dyke is a 3.5-mile earthwork marking the border between England and Scotland in the so-called "Debatable Lands", which extended from the Solway Firth near Carlisle to Langholm in Dumfries and Galloway. It was constructed in 1552.

p. 109, *Stanwix*: A settlement outside Carlisle.

p. 109, *Black Watch*: See first note to p. 14.

p. 109, *Balquidder*: A village in Perthshire, and the birthplace of Rob Roy (see second note to p. 44).

p. 110, *What though... plough and cart*: From the ballad 'Hodge of the Mill and Buxom Nell' (ll. 35–36), published in *The Tea-Table Miscellany: A Collection of Choice Songs, Scots and English* (1723–37), compiled by the Scottish poet Allan Ramsay (1686–1758).

p. 110, *drink down all unkindness*: The words of Ann Page in Shakespeare's *The Merry Wives of Windsor*: "Come, gentlemen, I hope we shall drink down all unkindness" (Act 1, Sc. 1).

p. 112, *fresh streams at the touch of the homicide*: It was traditionally believed that a corpse would bleed in the presence of the murderer. The supposed phenomenon was known as "cruentation".

p. 113, *the laws of the ring*: The rules of boxing were first codified by the English bare-knuckle fighter John "Jack" Broughton (c.1703–89) in August 1743. They remained in effect until 1838, when they were superseded by the "London Prize Ring Rules".

p. 113, *in pari casu*: "In a similar position" (Latin).

p. 114, *vis major*: "Superior force" (Latin).

p. 114, *moderamen inculpatæ tutelæ*: "*Moderamen inculpatæ tutelæ* are the terms used in the Roman law to express that degree of self-defence which a person may safely use, although it should occasion the death of the aggressor, without incurring the guilt of murder, or even of culpable homicide" – Robert Bell, *A Dictionary of the Law of Scotland* (1815).

p. 114, *James I cap. 8... benefit of clergy*: A reference to an Act of Parliament enacted in 1604, during the reign of James I of England (James VI of Scotland), known as the "statute of stabbing", which provided that a person who stabbed another "that hath not any weapon drawn or that hath not then first stricken the party", and whose action resulted in the death of the victim within six months, would be "excluded from the benefit of his... clergy, and suffer death as in case of wilful murder" – that is, they would be tried in the secular courts rather than their ecclesiastical counterparts, which did not have the power to sentence a defendant to death. "Benefit of clergy" was an extension of the medieval principle of clerical immunity from trial or punishment in the secular courts, latterly applied to anyone who was literate. According to the English lawyer and legal writer Joseph Chitty (1776–1841) in *A Practical Treatise on the Criminal Law* (1819), the legislation was "enacted at a critical period, and intended to remedy an immediate evil. It is said to have been directed against a number of persons who adopted a method of deadly revenge by wearing short daggers under their clothes, which they were prepared to use on slight provocations, and those frequently sought for by themselves" – hence, it "arose out of a temporary cause", as the judge goes on to say. "Malice prepense" is malice aforethought, that is, premeditation.

p. 114, *chaude mêlée*: "Hot affray" (French).

p. 115, *as described by Bacon... untutored justice*: The essay 'Of Revenge' by the English statesman and philosopher Francis Bacon (1561–1626) begins: "Revenge is a kind of wild justice which the more man's nature runs to, the more ought law to weed it out."

p. 115, *Vengeance is mine*: "Dearly beloved, avenge not yourselves, but rather give place unto wrath, for it is written, 'Vengeance is mine; I will repay,' saith the Lord" (Romans 12:19).

p. 115, *betwixt the Land's End and the Orkneys*: Land's End, a promontory in south-western Cornwall, is the southernmost tip of the island of Great Britain. The Orkneys are a group of islands off the north-eastern tip of Scotland.

p. 116, *and what can I do more?*: For the "Magnum Opus" edition of *Chronicles of the Canongate*, Scott here inserted a note consisting principally of English translations of two songs by the illiterate Scottish Gaelic "drover poet" Rob Donn (1714–78) – meaning "Brown-Haired Rob" – whose real name was probably Robert Mackay, which were published in the *Quarterly Review* No. 90 (July 1831). Scott introduces the quotations thus: "The picture which that paper gives of the habits and feelings of a class of persons with which the general reader would be apt to associate no ideas but those of wild superstition and rude manners is in the highest degree interesting." The lyrics quoted are 'Easy Is My Bed, It Is Easy' and 'Heavy to Me Is the Shieling and the Hum That Is in It'. The note concludes with the verdict of the *Quarterly Review*: "Rude and bald as these things appear in a verbal translation, and rough as they might possibly appear even were the originals intelligible, we confess we are disposed to think they would of themselves justify Dr Mackay (their editor) in placing this herdsman-lover among the true sons of song."

p. 117, *My Aunt Margaret's Mirror*: For details of the first publication of this story and of the edition from which the text is taken, see first note to p. 35.

p. 117, *Mr Ackermann*: The German-born London-based publisher Rudolph Ackermann (1764–1834) introduced the literary annual – based on Continental literary almanacs such as the French *L'Almanach des Muses* (1765–1833) or the German *Musen-Almanach* (1796–1800) – to England in the form of

Forget-Me-Not, published in 1823. An annual, also known as a gift book or keepsake, was typically a lavishly illustrated collection of essays, short fiction and poetry, and usually appeared in the autumn in order that it might be purchased as a Christmas gift.

p. 117, *an annual styled The Keepsake*: See first note to p. 35.

p. 117, *Various gentlemen... assist in it*: The 1829 edition of *The Keepsake* included two stories by Mary Shelley (1797–1851), 'The Sisters of Albano' and 'Ferdinando Eboli', several poems by William Wordsworth (1770–1850), including 'The Country Girl', 'The Triad' and 'The Wishing Gate', and several more by Samuel Taylor Coleridge (1772–1834), including 'The Garden of Boccaccio', as well as contributions by the Irish poet Thomas Moore (1779–1852), the Anglo-Welsh poet Felicia Hemans (1793–1835), the English poet and novelist Letitia Elizabeth Landon (1802–38), known as "L.E.L.", and the English poet Robert Southey (1774–1843).

p. 117, *The House of Aspen*: A five-act Gothic drama written in 1799 for the London stage but rejected by the actor-manager John Philip Kemble (1757–1823) of the Theatre Royal, Drury Lane, and never performed. It was eventually published in 1829. Its subtitle was 'A Drama of Chivalry Founded upon a German Story'.

p. 117, *a general collection of my lucubrations*: The "Magnum Opus" edition. See Note on the Text.

p. 117, *a lady of eminent virtues... house of Swinton*: Scott's great-aunt Margaret Swinton (d. 1780), from whom, along with his mother, Anne Rutherford (c.1739–1819), he also heard the story that inspired the novel *The Bride of Lammermoor* (1819).

p. 118, *memento mori*: "Remember that you must die" (Latin), a phrase used in English as a noun meaning an object retained as a reminder of the inevitability of death, such as a skull.

p. 118, *I tell the tale as it was told to me*: The standard English rendering of the Latin proverb *relata refero*.

p. 119, *There are times... anonymous*: Untraced, possibly Scott's own composition.

p. 120, *The horrid plough... summer shade*: The seventy-eighth stanza of 'The Tale' by the Scottish poet John Logan (1748–88).

p. 121, *water flags*: The yellow iris, which has flag-shaped petals.

p. 121, *die under Nelson's banner*: That is, die while serving in the Royal Navy under the leadership of the English admiral and national hero Horatio Nelson (1758–1805) during the Napoleonic Wars. Nelson himself was mortally wounded on board his flagship HMS *Victory* during the Battle of Trafalgar (1805), a famous British victory. Scott's own elder brother, Robert (1767–87), was a naval officer who, according to the author's memoirs, "was in most of" the battles fought by Admiral George Brydges Rodney (1718–92), best known for his leadership during the American War of Independence. Scott's 'Memoir of the Early Life of Sir Walter Scott, Written by Himself' was published posthumously in 1837 as the first chapter of the seven-volume *Memoirs of the Life of Sir Walter Scott, Bart* (1837–38) by Scott's son-in-law J.G. Lockhart (1794–1854).

p. 122, *Mechlin lace*: Lace made at Mechelen in Belgium.

p. 123, *his old mumpsimus to the modern sumpsimus*: A reference to an apocryphal story originally told in a letter by the Dutch Renaissance humanist Desiderius Erasmus (*c.*1469–1536), about an illiterate priest who, through ignorance, habitually substituted the meaningless word *mumpsimus* in place of the Latin *sumpsimus* in the phrase *Quod ore sumpsimus, Domine* ("What has passed our lips, O Lord"), part of the prayer said after Holy Communion. The term *mumpsimus* subsequently came to refer to any custom that continues to be observed even after it has been shown to be nonsensical.

p. 123, *George IV... his grandfather*: George IV (1762–1830) reigned from 1820 until his death, after serving as regent from 1811 due to the mental illness of his father, George III. "His grandfather" refers to George II, the reigning monarch at the time of the Jacobite rebellion of 1745–46 – although in fact George IV was the *great*-grandson of George II, who, following the premature death of his eldest son, Frederick, Prince of Wales (1707–51), was succeeded by his grandson, George III, son of Frederick.

p. 124, *They fought... hearts unsubdued*: Scott's composition.

p. 124, *the Stuart right of birth... in his favour*: The narrator's point is that George IV is related by blood both to the deposed House of Stuart and to the House of Hanover that replaced it. The king's great-great grandmother, Princess Sophia, Electress of Hanover (1630–1714) – see third note to p. 14 – was the granddaughter of the Stuart monarch James I. The "Act of Succession" here refers to the Act of Settlement of 1701, by which the British throne passed to the House of Hanover in order to ensure a Protestant succession – see ibid. In preparation for George IV's visit to Scotland in August 1822, the first visit of a reigning monarch to the country in nearly two centuries, Scott, who had been a close friend of the king since 1815, when the then regent had invited the author to dine with him after admiring his novel *Waverley* (1814), and who was instrumental in stage-managing what became known as the "King's Jaunt", succeeded in persuading the king of his Jacobite credentials, and that he could be presented to the people of Edinburgh in that capacity. Thus an elaborate and spectacular pageant was devised, in which the king appeared in Highland dress, and which many Highland clans and their chiefs attended in full regalia. The royal visit of

1822 allowed Scott to engineer a new national identity for Scotland modelled on the romanticized version of the country he presented in his fiction.

p. 124, *founded only... jure divino folks*: The Glorious Revolution of 1688–89 (see second note to p. 19) brought to an end the doctrine of the "divine right of kings", a form of absolutism in which monarchs were said to derive their authority from God and therefore were not accountable to any temporal authority, and of which the Stuarts – particularly James I – were noted proponents. *Jure divino* is the Latin for "by divine right".

p. 124, *one of the party... sometimes by principle*: In one of Scott's annotations to *Some Free Thoughts upon the Present State of Affairs* by the Irish cleric and satirist Jonathan Swift (1667–1745), which was written in 1714 but unpublished until 1741, he defined the "Whimsicals" as "Tories who deserted their party after peace was concluded" – a reference to the Peace of Utrecht (1713), a series of treaties that marked the end of the War of the Spanish Succession (1701–14), a Europe-wide conflict in which a "Grand Alliance" consisting of Britain, the Netherlands and the Holy Roman Empire sought to thwart French hegemony on the Continent.

p. 124, *Hatil mohatil, na dowski mi*: From a song by the late-seventeenth- and early-eighteenth-century Gaelic poet Silis Nighean Mhic Raonaill.

p. 125, *Wordsworth calls 'moods of my own mind'*: The works in Wordsworth's collection *Poems, in Two Volumes* (1807) are arranged into a number of sections, one of which, in the second volume, bears the heading 'Moods of My Own Mind'.

p. 125, *to those who resemble... which he sung*: Margaret's quotation is from 'An Ode on the Popular Superstitions of the Highlands of Scotland, Considered as the Subject of Poetry' (*c.*1750) by the English poet William Collins (1721–59), which is addressed to John Home (see note to p. 43) on his return to Scotland. In the poem's eleventh stanza, Collins urges Home that he should "in forceful sounds and colours bold / The native legends of thy land rehearse", and relate the fantastical tales "which, daring to depart / From sober truth, are still to nature true". He then cites as an example of this approach the epic poem *La Gerusalemme liberata* (*Jerusalem Delivered*, 1581) by the Italian poet Torquato Tasso (1544–95), about the First Crusade (1096–99), and specifically an episode in Canto 13 in which the Muslim sorcerer Ismen casts a spell over a forest in order to prevent the Christian knights, including the hero Tancredi, from felling the trees for their timber: "How have I trembled when, at Tancred's stroke, / Its gushing blood the gaping cypress poured; / When each live plant with mortal accents spoke, / And the wild blast up-heaved the vanished sword! / How have I sat, where piped the pensive wind, / To hear his harp, by British

Fairfax strung, / Prevailing poet, whose undoubting mind / Believed the magic wonders which he sung!" The "British Fairfax" is the English translator Edward Fairfax (c.1580–1635), whose rendering of *La Gerusalemme liberata* appeared in 1600, under the title *Godfrey of Bouillon*.

p. 125, *Theodore, at the approach of the spectral huntsman*: A reference to 'Theodore and Honoria', a free translation by the English poet John Dryden (1631–1700) of a story from the *Decameron* (1348–58) by the Italian writer Giovanni Boccaccio (1313–75) that was published in Dryden's *Fables, Ancient and Modern* (1700). The poem concerns a youth who, rejected by the woman he loves, encounters the ghost of one of his ancestors, who explains that he too was spurned by the object of his affection, and that he is doomed to spend eternity hunting her spirit on horseback. Before Theodore meets the spectre, "A sudden horror seized his giddy head, / And his ears tinkled, and his colour fled" (ll. 93–94).

p. 126, *Sir Charles Easy and the Lovelace*: Respectively, a womanizer in the comedy *The Careless Husband* (1704) by the English actor-manager and playwright Colley Cibber (1671–1757) and the libertine Robert Lovelace, tormentor of the virtuous Clarissa Harlowe in *Clarissa* (1747–48) by the English novelist Samuel Richardson (1689–1761).

p. 126, *if laws were made for every degree*: From a song that occurs in Act III, Sc. 13 of *The Beggar's Opera* (1728) by the English poet and playwright John Gay: "Since laws were made for ev'ry degree, / To curb vice in others, as well as me, / I wonder we han't better company, / Upon Tyburn tree!" Tyburn was a village outside London, where Marble Arch stands today, where public hangings took place.

p. 127, *Lord Advocate*: Scotland's principal public prosecutor.

p. 128, *the termagant Falconbridge*: The ebullient, irrepressible Philip Faulconbridge, known as "Philip the Bastard", the illegitimate son of Richard I (1157–99), as portrayed in Shakespeare's *King John*.

p. 128, *menus plaisirs*: "Small pleasures" (French).

p. 128, *beau garçon*: Literally, "handsome boy" (French) – a fop.

p. 129, *I go from Leith to Helvoet by a packet with advices*: That is, he is sailing from the Scottish port of Leith, north of Edinburgh, to Nieuw-Helvoet, a village west of Rotterdam in the Netherlands, part of the municipality of Hellevoetsluis (referred to later in the story as "Helvoetsluys"). A "packet with advices" is a mail boat.

p. 129, *the Gazette*: A publication produced by the British government since 1665 that lists military promotions, news of military campaigns and other official notices.

p. 131, *par voie du fait*: "By violence" (French).

p. 132, *the campaign... Allies on the other*: The reference is to the War of the Spanish Succession – see fourth note to p. 124.

p. 132, *Marlborough's*: The English general John Churchill, first Duke of Marlborough (1650–1722), commander of the British and Dutch forces during the War of the Spanish Succession.

p. 133, *receipts*: Recipes, in this case for medical preparations.

p. 133, *empiric*: A quack.

p. 133, *the help which was to come from Egypt*: That is, from Gypsies, who were popularly associated with witchcraft, sorcery and, especially, clairvoyance, and believed to have originated in Egypt.

p. 139, *Geneva gown and band*: Respectively, a black gown and a white cloth strip attached to the collar, vestments associated with Calvinist clergymen. The religious doctrines and practices of the French Protestant reformer John Calvin (1509–64) were first introduced in the Swiss city of Geneva in the mid-sixteenth century.

p. 142, *graduate*: "One who is advanced in any art, career, occupation or profession; a proficient" (*OED*).

p. 142, *we will say nothing of Whig and Tory*: For the political and religious differences between Whigs and Tories in the early eighteenth century, see fifth note to p. 19.

p. 142, *A Carolus serves my purpose as well as a Willielmus*: That is, the doctor is as happy to be paid in coins minted during the reign of the Stuart monarch Charles I as he is to be paid in those minted during the reign of the Protestant William III – in other words, he is uninterested in the political affiliations of his patients. The monarchs' Latin names normally appeared on coins.

p. 142, *'set him down a Jesuit', as Scrub says*: In the comedy *The Beaux' Stratagem* (1707) by the Irish dramatist George Farquhar (1677–1707), the character Scrub, a servant, says the following about the stranger Aimwell, in reality a beau who has fallen on hard times: "Why, some think he's a spy, some guess he's a mountebank, some say one thing, some another, but, for my own part, I believe he's a Jesuit" (Act III, Sc. 1).

p. 144, *Chevalier St George*: A nickname for James Francis Edward Stuart, the "Old Pretender" – see first note to p. 14.

p. 144, *Gordian knot*: An intractable problem. The name refers to the legend of an intricate knot tied by Gordius, founder of Gordium in Asia Minor, who prophesied that whoever untied it would become ruler of Asia. According to tradition, it was cut through by Alexander the Great in 333 BC.

p. 144, *the man with the silver greyhound upon his sleeve*: An arresting officer. The uniform of the Corps of King's Messengers was decorated with the image of a silver greyhound.

p. 144, *Galen or Hippocrates*: The Greek physicians Galen (129–99 AD) and Hippocrates (c.460–377 BC), two of the fathers of medicine.

p. 144, *an idol... of her grief*: A reference to Lady Constance's lamentation over the death of her son, Prince Arthur, in Shakespeare's *King John*. After stating that "grief fills the room up of my absent child", she asks herself the question: "Have I reason to be fond of grief?" (Act III, Sc. 4, ll. 95–100).

p. 144, *as Burns says... keep it warm*: In Burns's narrative poem 'Tam o' Shanter' (1790), the titular character makes merry in public houses while avoiding thoughts of the "lang Scots miles" between himself and home, "Whare sits our sulky, sullen dame, / Gathering her brows like gathering storm, / Nursing her wrath to keep it warm" (ll. 10–12).

p. 145, *Fastern's E'en (Shrovetide)*: "Fastern's E'en" – meaning "eve of the fast" – is a Scottish term for Shrove Tuesday, the Tuesday before Lent, a period of fasting and abstinence.

p. 149, *The Tapestried Chamber or The Lady in the Sacque*: For details of the first publication of this story and of the edition from which the text is taken, see first note to p. 35.

p. 149, *the late Miss Anna Seward*: The English Romantic poet Anna Seward (1742–1809), known as the "Swan of Lichfield", the Staffordshire town where she lived.

p. 150, *the end of the American war... Yorktown*: The Siege of Yorktown, fought at Yorktown, Virginia, between 28th September and 19th October 1781, was the last major land battle of the American War of Independence, in which the American Continental Army led by General George Washington, with support from the French, defeated the British army commanded by Lieutenant General Charles Cornwallis (1738–1805). The British surrender at Yorktown effectively brought the conflict to an end.

p. 150, *in the conclusion of a morning stage*: That is, at a stopping place on a journey by road conducted by post-horse.

p. 151, *the wars of York and Lancaster*: The thirty-year dynastic dispute known as the Wars of the Roses (1455–87), fought between supporters of the house of York and those of the house of Lancaster during the reigns of Henry VI (1421–71), Edward IV (1442–83) and Richard III (1452–85). It culminated in the Battle of Bosworth in 1485, at which the Yorkist king Richard III was defeated by the Lancastrian Henry Tudor, who went on to rule as Henry VII (1457–1509).

SUPERNATURAL SHORT STORIES

p. 151, *Elizabeth and her successor*: Elizabeth I (1533–1603) and James VI of Scotland (see first note to p. 23), who came to the throne of England as James I in 1603 when Elizabeth died without issue.

p. 151, *Richard Browne's fag… Christ Church*: That is, he had been a junior pupil responsible for performing minor chores for Richard Browne, a senior pupil, at Eton College, a public school on the banks of the Thames at Windsor. Christ Church is a college in Oxford.

p. 153, *like Diogenes himself*: The Greek philosopher Diogenes of Sinope (c.400–c.325 BC), the most celebrated of the Cynics – adherents of a school of philosophy that advocated extreme asceticism – who is believed to have slept in a tub in the open air in central Athens.

p. 160, *Van Dyck*: The Flemish painter Sir Anthony Van Dyck (1599–1641), famous for his portraits of members of the English court.

p. 161, *Here was a Cavalier… wealthy Roundhead*: The supporters of Charles I during the English Civil War (1642–49) were known as "Cavaliers". Their opponents, the Parliamentarians, were known as "Roundheads", a name alluding to the Puritan custom of wearing closely cropped hair.

p. 161, *There hung a gallant… Whig and Tory*: The first was a Jacobite and a Tory: St Germain's is Saint-Germain-en-Laye, west of Paris, where James II lived in exile from his deposition in 1688 until his death in 1701. The second was a supporter of William of Orange during the Glorious Revolution of 1688–89, and therefore a Whig. The third apparently fluctuated between the two camps. (For the origins of the Whigs and the Tories in the "Exclusion Crisis" of 1679–81, see fifth note to p. 19.)

p. 161, *"against the stomach of his sense"*: The words of Alonso in Shakespeare's *The Tempest*: "You cram these words into mine ears against / The stomach of my sense" (Act II, Sc. 1, ll. 112–13).

p. 163, *Donnerhugel's Narrative*: Originally Chapter 11 of *Anne of Geierstein*, one of the Waverley novels, published in three volumes in Edinburgh by Cadell & Co. on 20th May 1829, and in London by Simpkin & Marshall on 25th May 1829. The text in this volume is from the edition published in London by John C. Nimmo in 1894, which is itself based on the revised version of the novel that constituted the forty-fourth and forty-fifth volumes of Cadell's "Magnum Opus", which appeared in January and February 1833, respectively.

p. 163, *These be the adept's doctrines… anonymous*: Untraced, possibly Scott's own composition. The typology of supernatural beings is likely derived from Pope's mock-heroic *The Rape of the Lock* (1712), the source for which was the esoteric novel *Comte de Gabalis* by Henri de Montfaucon, known as the

Abbé de Villars (1638–73), as acknowledged in the dedicatory letter included by the poet in the second edition (1714).

p. 163, *Rudolph*: The narrator of the story is Rudolph Donnerhugel, a Swiss beau. He is addressing Arthur, the son of John Philipson, an Englishman (in reality the Earl of Oxford). At the outset of the novel, the Philipsons are travelling through Switzerland, disguised as merchants, with the intention of enlisting the support of Charles the Bold, Duke of Burgundy, for the House of Lancaster. (The story is set in the aftermath of the Battle of Tewkesbury, fought in 1471 during the Wars of the Roses – see first note to p. 151.) Along the way they encounter Arnold Biederman, a magistrate who was once the Count of Geierstein, and his niece, Anne, who saves Arthur's life during a storm. At Biederman's home they meet Rudolph Donnerhugel, a "young gallant". They resume their journey, accompanied by the Biederman family, since Biederman also has business with Charles the Bold. Later, as the party takes shelter in the ruins of a castle, Arthur has what seems to be a supernatural encounter with an apparition that is the exact likeness of Anne. When he relates his experience to Rudolph, the latter promises to share with him "the whole, or at least all that I know or apprehend, on the mysterious subject".

p. 163, *Apollyon*: A name for the Devil.

p. 163, *Tokay wine*: A rich, sweet and aromatic wine made near Tokay (or Tokaj) in Hungary.

p. 165, *a brother of the Sacred Fire*: That is, a Zoroastrian, an adherent of the religion founded by the Persian prophet Zoroaster (*c.*628–*c.*551 BC), in which fire was held to be sacred and considered the manifestation of the god Ahura Mazda.

p. 165, *astrakhan lambs*: That is, wool from fetal or newborn lambs of the Central Asian karakul breed.

p. 166, *magus*: A Zoroastrian priest.

p. 167, *Magian*: Another term for a magus.

p. 169, *the empire*: The Holy Roman Empire, established in 800 by Pope Leo III (d. 816) with the Frankish king Charlemagne as its first emperor (742–814). In the Middle Ages it covered much of Western and central Europe.

p. 171, *ignis fatuus*: A phosphorescent light glimpsed at night above marshy ground and caused by the spontaneous combustion of methane. Also known as a "will-o'-the-wisp", it is traditionally attributed to supernatural sources and considered a bad omen. "Ignis fatuus" is Latin for "foolish fire".

p. 175, *The Bridal of Janet Dalrymple*: Extracted from Scott's introduction to the revised edition of the novel *The Bride of Lammermoor* that made up part of the thirteenth and all of the fourteenth volumes of Cadell's "Magnum Opus", published in June and July 1830, respectively. (*The Bride of Lammermoor* was originally published alongside another work, *A Legend of Montrose*, in Edinburgh by Archibald Constable & Co. on 21st June 1819, and in London by Longman, Hurst, Rees, Orme & Brown on 26th June 1819.) The text in this volume is from the edition published in London by Macmillan in 1904. The novel concerns a young woman, Lucy Ashton, who, in love with the Master of Ravenswood but forced by her parents into a marriage with the Laird of Bucklaw, loses her mind and stabs her husband on their wedding night, before descending into madness and dying. In the three paragraphs that precede this extract, Scott explains that the "real source from which he drew the tragic subject of this history" is a legendary tale concerning the historical family of Dalrymple, headed by "one of the most eminent lawyers that ever lived", James Dalrymple, 1st Viscount Stair (1619–95), whose wife, Margaret Ross (d. 1692), coheiress of Balneil in Wigtownshire, was suspected of "necromancy". He states that, having been previously unwilling to divulge this information, which could be "unpleasing to the feelings of the descendants of the parties", he now feels himself at liberty to do so, having read accounts of the same circumstances by two other authors: first, the Scottish antiquary Charles Kirkpatrick Sharpe (*c*.1781–1851), a friend of Scott, in a footnote to his 1818 edition of *Memorials, or the Memorable Things That Fell Out within This Island of Britain from 1638 to 1684* by the Covenanting preacher Robert Law (d. *c*.1690), and, second, the Scottish judge and antiquary Thomas Maitland, Lord Dundrennan (1792–1851), in a footnote to the elegy 'On the Unexpected Death of the Virtuous Lady, Mrs Janet Dalrymple, Lady Baldone, Younger' by the Episcopalian minister Andrew Symson (*c*.1638–1712), appended to the same author's *A Large Description of Galloway*, written in 1684 but unpublished until 1823. The tale of the tragic events that befell the Stairs' eldest daughter, Janet, is related in the remainder of the introduction. Scott acknowledged elsewhere that he heard the story himself from his mother, Anne Rutherford, and his great-aunt Margaret Swinton (see seventh note to p. 117).

p. 175, *the Lord Rutherford*: Archibald Rutherfurd, 3rd Lord Rutherfurd (d. 1685).

p. 175, *David Dunbar... Baldoon*: Sir David Dunbar of Baldoon, 1st Baronet (1610–86).

p. 176, *If a man vow... disallowed her*: Numbers 30: 2–5 [SCOTT'S NOTE].

p. 176, *A lady, very nearly connected with the family*: Most likely Margaret Swinton – see seventh note to p. 117.

p. 176, *It was then the custom... the brideman*: "Coarse pleasantry" refers to an ancient custom whereby certain of the wedding guests would visit the bride and groom in their bedchamber after they had retired. A brideman was the bridegroom's attendant, responsible for certain ceremonial duties.

p. 177, *Holyroodhouse*: The Palace of Holyroodhouse in Edinburgh, the principal royal residence in Scotland.

p. 177, *The credulous Mr Law... possessed by an evil spirit*: From Law's *Memorials*. It is after this passage that Sharpe inserts his footnote containing an account of the Dalrymple legend, as referred to in Scott's introduction – see first note to p. 175. The next paragraph, beginning "My friend Mr Sharpe", refers to the same footnote.

p. 178, *I find still another account... Lord President Stair*: The poem in question is 'Satyre on the Familie of Stairs', found in *A Book of Scottish Pasquils, 1568–1715*, a collection consisting largely of the works of the Scottish satirist and antiquary Robert Mylne (c.1643–1747), and edited by the English-born Scottish antiquary James Maidment (1793–1879). A "pasquil" is a pasquinade, or lampoon. The "bitter and personal quarrel and rivalry" was caused by the competition between the Scottish lawyer Sir William Hamilton of Whitelaw (d. 1705), the author of the satire, and Sir Hew Dalrymple (1652–1737), the third son of James Dalrymple, 1st Viscount Stair, for the presidency of the Scottish Court of Session. According to Hew Dalrymple's entry in the *Dictionary of National Biography, 1885–1900* (1885): "On 17th March [1698] he was nominated by William III Lord President of the Court of Session, an office which had remained vacant since the death of Lord Stair in 1695. It appears that a commission had already been made out appointing Sir William Hamilton of Whitelaw to the post, but that it had been revoked at the last moment." Despite Hamilton's attempts to thwart the appointment, Dalrymple held the office of president until his death in 1737. The term "writer" ("writer in Edinburgh") means solicitor.

p. 178, *but by the fall*: The fall from his horse, by which he was killed [SCOTT'S NOTE].

p. 179, *Some of the notes... family of Stair*: I have compared the satire which occurs in the first volume of the curious little collection called *A Book of Scottish Pasquils*, 1827, with that which has a more full text and more extended notes, and which is in my own possession by gift of Thomas Thomson, Esq. Register-Depute. In the second *Book of Pasquils*, p. 72, is a most abusive epitaph on Sir James Hamilton of Whitelaw [SCOTT'S NOTE]. Scott was evidently in possession of another version of 'Satyre on the Familie of Stairs', one supplied to him by his friend, the Scottish advocate and antiquary Thomas Thomson (1768–1852). The "most abusive epitaph" is titled 'Epitaph on Whytlaw', and concludes with the following couplet: "In hell for ever, he ryves the claim of right, / And giv'st King William for his a—— to dight" – "ryves" means "tears apart"; "dight" means "clean". (Scott mistakenly calls Sir William Hamilton

"James" in this note.) For Robert Mylne, see first note to p. 178. The Jacobites were hostile to the Stairs due to their close friendship with William III.

p. 179, *Andrew Symson*: See first note to p. 175.

p. 179, *Nupta August 12... September 30, 1669*: That is, she was married on 12th August, was brought home on 24th August, died on 12th September and was buried on 30th September 1669.

p. 180, *Sir, 'tis truth... full perfection*: This elegy is reprinted in the appendix to a topographical work by the same author, entitled *A Large Description of Galloway, by Andrew Symson, Minister of Kirkinner*, 8vo, Taits, Edinburgh, 1823. The reverend gentleman's elegies are extremely rare, nor did the author ever see a copy but his own, which is bound up with the *Tripatriarchicon*, a religious poem from the biblical history, by the same author [SCOTT'S NOTE]. Symson's religious poem *Tripatriarchicon, or, The Lives of the Three Patriarchs Abraham, Isaac and Jacob, Digested into English Verse* was published in 1705. For Symson and *A Large Description of Galloway*, see first note to p. 175. Atropos is one of the three Fates in Greek mythology, who cuts the threads of mortals' lives.

p. 181, *Letters on Demonology and Witchcraft*: Extracted from the tenth of the *Letters on Demonology and Witchcraft Addressed to J.G. Lockhart, Esq.*, originally published in London by John Murray on 14th September 1830. The text in this volume is from the third edition, published in London by George Routledge & Sons in 1887. J.G. Lockhart was Scott's son-in-law, later the author of his biography (see second note to p. 121).

p. 183, *Mr Crabbe... fiction of the brain*: From 'The Library' by the English poet George Crabbe (1754–1832), in which the poet discusses the way in which "Reason" and "Time" have defeated fancy and superstition: "E'en the last lingering fiction of the brain, / The churchyard ghost, is now at rest again; / And all these wayward wanderings of my youth / Fly Reason's power, and shun the light of Truth" (ll. 579–82).

p. 183, *Hence Lucretius... the person while alive*: The philosophical poem *De rerum natura* (*On the Nature of Things*), by the Roman poet Titus Lucretius Carus (*c*.94–*c*.55 BC), is a dissertation in verse on the physical theories of the Greek philosopher Epicurus (341–270 AD), which argues, among other things, for an atomic theory of the universe and the mortality of the human soul. In its fourth book Lucretius posits that our visual perception is formed by a constant stream of infinitesimal particles, which travel at great speed from the surface of external objects into our eyes. Given that an astronomical number of such particles reach us from a variety of different sources at any one moment, what we perceive as ghosts can be explained as the chance resemblance of a random combination of particles to the image of a deceased loved one (IV, ll. 757–67).

NOTES

- p. 185, *we read in Clarendon... ancient dependant*: In *The History of the Rebellion and Civil Wars in England* (1702–4), a history of the English Civil War, the English statesman and historian Edward Hyde, Earl of Clarendon (1609–74), claimed that, six months before the assassination of the royal favourite and statesman George Villiers, Duke of Buckingham (1592–1628), the ghost of the duke's own father – also called Sir George Villiers (*c*.1544–1606) – appeared to a courtier at Windsor Castle and implored him to warn his son that "if he did not do somewhat to ingratiate himself to the people, or, at least, to abate the extreme malice they had against him, he would be suffered to live but a short time".

- p. 186, *accredited ghost stories*: The title of a volume of ghost stories collected by "T.M. Jarvis, Esq." published in 1823, containing accounts of many well-known supernatural happenings, including the story of Sir George Villiers, discussed by Scott above, as well as a number of others described in the letter.

- p. 186, *the late Earl St Vincent... his sister*: A reference to the apparent poltergeist activity experienced at the Tudor manor house of Hinton Ampner in Hampshire by Mary Ricketts, wife of the absent plantation owner William Henry Ricketts (1736–98), between 1765 and 1771. Mary kept written records of the happenings, in which she stated: "Soon after we were settled at Hinton I frequently heard noises in the night, as of people shutting, or rather slapping doors with vehemence." When her brother, the statesman and Royal Navy officer John Jervis, 1st Earl of St Vincent (1735–1823), accompanied by his friend and fellow seaman James Luttrell (*c*.1751–88), volunteered to investigate the mysterious phenomena, they could find no rational explanation, and, in Mary's words, "declared the disturbances of the preceding night were of such a nature that the house was an unfit residence for any human being". The story of the haunting circulated in society in the early nineteenth century. Mary's written account of the events at Hinton Ampner was eventually published under the title 'A Hampshire Ghost Story' in the *Gentleman's Magazine* in 1872.

- p. 186, *The story of two... in America*: An incident of October 1785 that is the subject of a chapter in *Accredited Ghost Stories* (see first note to p. 186). It concerns Sir John Coape Sherbrooke (1764–1830) and George West Wynyard (1762–1809), two British army officers stationed in Nova Scotia, who witnessed an apparition of "a tall youth, of about twenty years of age, whose appearance was that of extreme emaciation", which passed through the sitting room of their billet. When Sherbrooke, who saw the figure first, drew Wynyard's attention to it, the latter responded: "Great God! My brother!" Later it was revealed that Wynyard's brother "had died on the day and at the very hour on which the friends had seen his spirit pass so mysteriously through the apartment".

p. 186, *brevet rank*: A rank conferred on an officer as reward for outstanding service, but without the corresponding increase in pay.

p. 187, *Another such story... country seat in France*: Scott here alludes to the 'Apparition Seen by Lady Pennyman and Mrs Atkins', described in *Accredited Ghost Stories* (see first note to p. 186). The story concerns an English family, the Pennymans, who rented a house on Place du Lion d'Or in Lille, northern France, shortly before the French Revolution, and there experienced a number of ghostly phenomena, seemingly emanating from a top-floor room containing an iron cage, in which a young boy, a former proprietor of the house, was said to have once been imprisoned by his sadistic uncle as part of a programme of systematic cruelty, and in which the youth died.

p. 187, *The remarkable circumstance... of an apparition*: An episode referred to in *Accredited Ghost Stories* (see first note to p. 186) as the 'Apparition Seen by Lord Lyttelton'. According to the account contained in that book, the "witty and profligate" Thomas Lyttelton, 2nd Baron Lyttelton (1744–79), revealed to a Christmas gathering at his home, Pit Place, near Epsom in Surrey, that two nights earlier he had been visited in his bedchamber by the ghost of a woman he had "seduced and deserted", and who had subsequently committed suicide, and that this apparition had announced that "at that very hour, on the third day after the visitation, his life and his sins would be concluded, and nothing but their punishment remain, if he availed himself not of the warning to repentance which he had received". On the next night he was found in his chamber, "pale and lifeless, and his countenance terribly convulsed".

p. 188, *The following story... on the same theme*: The story was published in the form of a ballad as 'Bill Jones: A Tale of Wonder' in the fourth volume of *Romantic Tales* (1808) by the English writer Matthew Lewis (1775–1818), best known as the author of the Gothic novel *The Monk* (1796). The Edinburgh lawyer William Clerk (1771–1847) was a friend of Scott, and the model for Darsie Latimer in *Redgauntlet* (1824).

p. 188, *when the Emperor Paul... British trade*: A reference to the deterioration in relations between Britain and Russia, erstwhile allies in the struggle against Napoleon, in 1800. In September, in retaliation for the capture of a Danish frigate by the British in July, at a time when Paul I of Russia (1754–1801) was strengthening his relations with the Scandinavian countries, as well as for the British refusal to return the island of Malta, which they had captured from the French, to the Order of St John – a military religious order of which Paul was the grand master, and which had controlled Malta between 1530 and the French invasion of 1798 – the tsar responded by ordering that British vessels were to be barred from Russian ports, and that any vessels already in the country were to be seized and their crews imprisoned.

p. 188, *to hand a sail*: To take in or to furl a sail.

p. 190, *another instance of a guilt-formed phantom*: The story that follows later appeared in the form of a poem titled 'The Dead Drummer: A Legend of Salisbury Plain' in *The Ingoldsby Legends*, a popular collection of stories and poetry by the English clergyman Richard Harris Barham (1788–1845), but claiming to be by "Thomas Ingoldsby of Tappington Manor", first published in 1837. The following words appear before the poem: "The incidents recorded in the succeeding legend were communicated to a dear friend of our family by the late lamented Sir Walter Scott."

p. 192, *In this respect... peculiar to themselves*: In the section of his work *A Provincial Glossary, with a Collection of Local Proverbs, and Popular Superstitions* (1787) devoted to ghosts, the English antiquary and lexicographer Francis Grose (1731–91) writes: "It is somewhat remarkable that ghosts do not go about their business like persons of this world. In cases of murder, a ghost, instead of going to the next justice of the peace and laying its information, or to the nearest relation of the person murdered, appears to some poor labourer who knows none of the parties, draws the curtains of some decrepit nurse or almswoman, or hovers about the place where his body is deposited... But it is presumptuous to scrutinize too far into these matters: ghosts have undoubtedly forms and customs peculiar to themselves."

p. 192, *James Boswell's... what to think*: Perhaps a reference to the following anecdote from Boswell's *Life of Samuel Johnson* (1791), taken from the section dealing with the year 1768: "An essay, written by Mr Deane, a divine of the Church of England, maintaining the future life of brutes, by an explication of certain parts of the Scriptures, was mentioned, and the doctrine insisted on by a gentleman who seemed fond of curious speculation. Johnson, who did not like to hear of anything concerning a future state which was not authorized by the regular canons of orthodoxy, discouraged this talk, and being offended at its continuation, he watched an opportunity to give the gentleman a blow of reprehension. So, when the poor speculatist, with a serious metaphysical pensive face, addressed him 'But really, sir, when we see a very sensible dog, we don't know what to think of him', Johnson, rolling with joy at the thought, which beamed in his eye, turned quickly round and replied, 'True, sir – and when we see a very foolish fellow, we don't know what to think of him.' He then rose up, strided to the fire and stood for some time laughing and exulting." For Boswell and Johnson, see second note to p. 95.

p. 192, *Upon 10th June 1754... 28th September 1749*: A collection of documents relating to this case appeared in 1831 as *Trial of Duncan Terig Alias Clerk, and Alexander Bane MacDonald for the Murder of Arthur Davis, Sergeant in General Guise's Regiment of Foot*, with an introduction by Scott. It was published by the Bannatyne Club – of which Scott was the founder and president – a society dedicated to the publication of rare documents of Scottish interest, named in honour of George Bannatyne (1545–1608), famous for compiling a large collection of Scottish poems. "Guise's regiment" was the 6th Regiment of Foot, commanded between 1738 and 1765 by General John Guise (1682–1765). After the Jacobite defeat at Culloden in 1746 (see fourth note to p. 35), the regiment was involved in the pacification of the Highlands.

p. 194, *The most celebrated... royal residence*: The story of the so-called "Good Devil" of Woodstock Palace in Oxfordshire, where Blenheim Palace now stands, had previously featured in Scott's novel *Woodstock, or, The Cavalier: A Tale of the Year Sixteen Hundred and Fifty-One* (1826), set in the aftermath of the English Civil War, up to the return of Charles II to London in May 1660. His sources for the tale were *Satan's Invisible World Discovered* (c.1685) by the Scottish mathematician and demonologist George Sinclair (c.1630–96), and *Saducismus triumphatus* (1681), a work on witchcraft by the English philosopher and clergyman Joseph Glanvil (1636–80). As Scott states later, he was also aware of the version of the story that appeared in *The Natural History of Oxfordshire* (1677) by the English naturalist and antiquarian Robert Plot (1640–96). The "Long Parliament" sat from November 1640 to March 1653, throughout the English Civil War and into the interregnum that followed.

p. 195, *The whole matter... "Funny Joe"*: When *Woodstock* was republished as the thirty-ninth and fortieth volumes of the "Magnum Opus" edition (August and September 1832), Scott provided an introduction in which he said that he had come across the true explanation for the events at Woodstock in an article titled 'The Genuine History of the Good Devil of Woodstock', originally from the *British Magazine* of April 1747, but quoted at length in the second volume of *The Everyday Book or Everlasting Calendar of Popular Amusements* (1826) by the English writer William Hone (1780–1842). The author of this article claimed to have come into possession of some papers titled 'Authentic Memoirs of the Memorable Joseph Collins of Oxford, Commonly Known by the Name of Funny Joe, and Now Intended for the Press', in which the deception was revealed.

p. 196, *Twelfth Day*: Twelfth Night (6th January).

p. 196, *Stockwell*: Now a district in south London.

NOTES

p. 196, *St Vitus's dance*: St Vitus's dance, today known as Sydenham's chorea, is a medical condition whose main symptom is rapid and involuntary jerking movements in the limbs and the face.

p. 197, *that of Cock Lane*: A purported haunting of a lodging house in Cock Lane, an alley near London's Smithfield Market, that came to public attention in 1762. A commission set up in the same year to investigate the phenomenon exposed the goings-on as a hoax.

p. 197, *the original publication... explained the wonder*: See Hone's *Everyday Book*, p. 62 [SCOTT'S NOTE]. The story of the Stockwell haunting is found in the first volume of *The Everyday Book* (see note to p. 195), which Hone took from a tract titled *An Authentic, Candid and Circumstantial Narrative of the Astonishing Transactions at Stockwell, in the County of Surrey, on Monday and Tuesday, the 6th and 7th Days of January, 1772* – the "original publication" referred to by Scott. In his reference to "Swift's advertisements" Scott is perhaps thinking of the satirical pamphlet *A Modest Proposal* (1729), in which Swift argued that, to alleviate their poverty, the Irish poor should sell their children as food to wealthy English landlords. For Swift, see also fourth note to p. 124.

p. 197, *Mr Walker, minister at Dunnottar, in the Mearns*: James Walker (1751–1813), minister in the parish of Dunnottar in Kincardineshire, also known as "the Mearns", in north-east Scotland.

p. 199, *An apparition which took place at Plymouth is well known*: According to an article titled 'Plymouth: The Story of a Town' that appeared in *Fraser's Magazine* in February 1873, the following story concerns the English clergyman Zachariah Mudge (1694–1769).

p. 201, *that extent... Tam o' Shanter*: On his journey home on horseback, the drunken reveller in Burns's poem (see sixth note to p. 144) experiences a vision of "warlocks and witches in a dance" outside Alloway Kirk, and reflects on the emboldening effects of alcohol: "Inspiring bold John Barleycorn! / What dangers thou canst make us scorn! / Wi' tippeny, we fear nae evil; / Wi' usquabae, we'll face the Devil!" (ll. 105–8).

p. 203, *give you law*: A hunting term. To give one's quarry "law" is to give it a chance to save itself.

p. 203, *apparition of the Brocken mountain*: See third note to p. 3.

p. 204, *Anabaptist*: The Anabaptists were a radical Protestant sect who believed that baptism should be reserved for believing adults.

p. 204, *A bookseller of his acquaintance... Mrs Veal's ghost*: The fourth edition (1706) of the English translation of the *Consolations de l'âme fidèle contre les frayeurs de la mort* (1651) by the French Protestant Charles Drelincourt (1595–1669), titled *The Christian's Defence against the Fears of Death*, was prefaced by the pamphlet *A True Relation of the Apparition of One Mrs Veal, the Next Day after Her Death, to One Mrs Bargrave at Canterbury*, often described as the first modern ghost story. It is traditionally attributed to the English novelist and journalist Daniel Defoe (1660–1731).

p. 205, *John Dunton... Apparition Evidence*: The story that follows is taken from the article titled 'Apparition Evidence, or, A Miraculous Detection of the Unnatural Lewdness of Dr John Atherton (Formerly Bishop of Waterford in Ireland) by a Spectrum', which appeared in the first volume of *Athenianism* (1710), described on its title page as being "six hundred treaties" written by the English bookseller and writer John Dunton (1659–1733), although the author of the treaty in question has since been shown to have been the Nonconformist minister John Quick (1636–1706) – see Peter Marshall, *Mother Leakey and the Bishop: A Ghost Story* (Oxford: Oxford University Press, 2007). In the section that follows the long extract provided by Scott in his letter, the article relates how the apparition charged Elizabeth Leakey, the daughter-in-law of the dead woman, with the task of travelling to Ireland to warn her relation, John Atherton (1598–1640), the Anglican Bishop of Waterford and Lismore in Ireland, that he must "repent of the sin whereof he knows himself to be guilty" in order to avoid execution. Atherton was hanged for sodomy along with his lover and steward, John Childe, in 1640, and was posthumously accused of a number of other crimes, including "incest" with his sister-in-law and the murder of the child that was the product of the liaison. Scott had previously described the Leakey legend, and specifically Mrs Leakey's supposed ability to summon bad weather and cause shipwrecks, in a note to Canto II (stanza XI) of his epic poem *Rokeby* (1813).

p. 207, *"But this... says the daughter," etc.*: 'Apparition Evidence' [SCOTT'S NOTE].

p. 207, *castle of Glamis... Malcolm II*: Malcolm II (*c.*954–1034), king of Scotland from 1005 until his death, is believed to have been assassinated at the castle of Glamis in Angus as a result of his attempt to install his grandson, Duncan (*c.*1001–40), on the throne of the neighbouring kingdom of Strathclyde, following the death of his ally Owen the Bald (*fl.* 1018), its ruler. Duncan went on to rule Scotland as Duncan I from 1034; his reign was contested by the historical Macbeth (d. 1057), who himself became king when his forces defeated Duncan in battle in 1040 (unlike in the Shakespearean version, in which Duncan is murdered by Macbeth at Glamis – a castle in which the real Macbeth never resided).

p. 208, *the late John Kemble and his inimitable sister*: For the actor-manager John Philip Kemble, see fifth note to p. 117. His sister was the actor Sarah Siddons (1755–1831), whose most famous role was that of Lady Macbeth, which she first performed in February 1785.

NOTES

p. 208, *the castle of Dunvegan*: The ancestral home of the chiefs of Clan MacLeod, located on the Isle of Skye, off the west coast of Scotland. Scott stayed overnight at the castle on 23rd August 1814 as the guest of John Norman MacLeod (1788–1835), the twenty-fourth chief of the MacLeods, and later Member of Parliament for Sudbury (1828–30), and his wife Anne MacLeod (née Stephenson, d. 1861).

p. 208, *The most modern... "whose birth tradition notes not"*: Scott recorded in his diary for 23rd August 1814: "A part of Dunvegan is very old: 'its birth tradition notes not'. Another large tower was built by the same Alaster MacLeod whose burial place and monument we saw yesterday at Rowdill... Roderick More (knighted by James VI) erected a long edifice combining these two ancient towers." "Roderick More" is Sir Roderick MacLeod of MacLeod (*c.*1559–1626), whose Gaelic name was Ruairidh Mór, meaning "Rory the Great", the fifteenth chief of Clan MacLeod. The quotation "whose birth tradition notes not" is taken from the dramatic poem *Caractacus* (1759) by the English poet William Mason (1724–97). The words refer to the bardic song that, according to tradition, enabled the Celtic Britons to repel the attempted Roman invasion led by Julius Caesar (100–44 BC) in 55 BC: "Now is the dreadful hour, now will our torches / Glare with more livid horror, now our shrieks / And clanking arms will more appal the foe. / But heed, ye bards, that for the sign of onset / Ye sound the ancientest of all your rhymes, / Whose birth tradition notes not, nor who framed / Its lofty strains: the force of that high air / Did Julius feel when, fired by it, our fathers / First drove him recreant to his ships." The Roman conquest of Britain was eventually achieved under the emperor Claudius after 43 AD, despite the resistance of the Celtic chieftain Caractacus, the subject of Mason's tragedy.

p. 208, *Mrs Radcliffe*: The English novelist Ann Radcliffe (1764–1823) was the author of Gothic novels such as *The Mysteries of Udolpho* (1794) and *The Italian* (1797).

p. 209, *Such a castle... carry off the standard-bearer*: In his travelogue *A Journey to the Western Islands of Scotland* (1775), his own account of the 1773 expedition described by Boswell in *The Journal of a Tour to the Hebrides* (see second note to p. 95), Samuel Johnson described some of the "standing traditions" of Dunvegan, including the famous horn of Sir Roderick MacLeod: "In the house is kept an ox's horn, hollowed so as to hold perhaps two quarts, which the heir of MacLeod was expected to swallow at one draught, as a test of his manhood, before he was permitted to bear arms, or could claim a seat among the men." Other MacLeod heirlooms held at the castle include the Dunvegan Cup, a ceremonial drinking vessel made of wood with elaborate silver decorations, dating from 1493 – of which Scott provided a detailed description in a note to the second canto of his narrative poem *The Lord of the Isles* (1815) – and the supposedly enchanted "Fairy Flag", described in Scott's diary as "a pennon of silk, with something like round red rowan berries wrought upon it". According to the Welsh antiquarian Thomas Pennant (1726–98), in *A Tour in Scotland, and Voyage to the Hebrides* (1772), the flag was a gift to the MacLeods from Titania, wife of Oberon, king of the fairies, who "blessed it, at the same time, with powers of the first importance, which were to be exerted only on three occasions; but on the last, after the end was obtained, an invisible being is to arrive and carry off the standard and standard-bearer, never more to be seen".

p. 209, *the Norwegian goddesses... Riders of the Storm*: The Valkyries, the twelve handmaidens of Odin in Norse mythology, who lead fallen warriors from the battlefield to Valhalla, their resting place. "Valkyrie" means "choosers of the slain" in Old Norse.

p. 209, *the Quillan mountains*: The Cuillin, a mountain range on the Isle of Skye.

p. 209, *I looked around me... ready to be moved*: From a letter written from the Isle of Skye by Johnson to the Welsh author and socialite Hester Thrale (1740–1821) on 21st September 1773.

p. 210, *"comes o'er us like a summer cloud"*: From Macbeth's reaction to the sight of the ghost of his former ally Banquo, whom he has had murdered: "Can such things be / And overcome us like a summer's cloud, / Without our special wonder?" (Act III, Sc. 4, ll. 135–37).

Glossary

All terms are Scots unless otherwise specified.

Adzooks!	(Eng.) an oath: short for "gadzooks", that is, "God's hooks" (the nails of the cross)
ae	one
ain	own
ainsell	own self
an it like	(Eng.) if it please
ane	one
aneath	underneath
anes and aye	once and for all
aneugh	enough
antic	(Eng.) grotesque, bizarre
arles	money given to confirm a bargain, notably that given when a servant is hired
at a bytime	(Eng.) occasionally
auld lang syne	(literally) old long since; the old times
aweel	well
aye	always
back-ganging	in arrears
back-lill	the left-hand thumb hole at the back of a *chanter*
bailie	municipal magistrate, alderman
bane	bone
bannock	(from Gael.) unleavened loaf made from barley or oatmeal flour
barns-breaking	mischief
bartisan	battlement
basket hilt	sword hilt with a basket-shaped guard
bating	except
bauld	bold
bink	a wooden frame containing shelves; a shelf
birling	carousal
blaud	selection (such as of verse)

blear	blind, deceive
blink	moment
bodach	ghost
bogle	ghost
bogle wark	ghostly happenings
borrel	rough, uncultivated
bower-maiden	(Eng.) chambermaid or lady-in-waiting
brae	a steep bank
braid	broad
brash	a sudden bout of inclement weather (used figuratively)
breacan	(from Gael.) tartan
brockit	an animal with a white streak down its face
brownie	household spirit; goblin
busk	prepare, make ready
by ordinar	extraordinary
callant	young man, lad
callerer	fresher
canny	shrewd, wise; of good omen
cantrip	spell, charm
carles	men
carline	old woman
cast up	turn up
cateran	(from Gael.) marauder
cauld	cold
chaffer	(Eng.) bargain
chamber of dais	the best bedroom
change house	inn
chanter	(Eng.) the pipe of a bagpipe containing finger holes and on which the melody is played
chap	(Eng.) price, purchase
chape	(Eng.) the metal tip of a scabbard
chiel', chield	man, fellow
cinctured	(Eng.) girdled
clachan	(from Gael.) village, hamlet; village inn
clean aff the road	completely wrong
coronach	(from Gael.) lament for the dead, dirge
corrie dhu	(Gael.) black precipice
coup	tumble, fall

GLOSSARY

crawing	crowing
creagh	(from Gael.) raid; booty, spoil
cresset	(Eng.) a metal receptacle usually mounted on a pole and containing grease, oil, wood or coal, burnt as a light source
curch	kerchief
daddle	(Eng.) hand, fist
dang	knock
dargle	(from Gael.) river valley
daur	dare
deasil	(from Gael.) in a sunwise direction
Deil	Devil
Deil scowp wi'	Devil take
Deil speed the liars	quarrel
delation	(Eng.) reporting
deray	wild revelry
dinna	do not
dirdum	blame
dirk	dagger
dispark	(Eng.) convert a private park into common land
distaff	(Eng.) spindle used in the spinning wool or flax
doch-an-dorroch	(from Gael.) a parting cup
doddy	hornless bull or cow
door cheek	doorpost
douce	sober, respectable
dun	(from Gael.) hill fort
dunniewassel	(from Gael.) gentleman
dyvour	bankrupt
éclaircissement	(Fr.) explanation, revelation
een	eyes
eld	elderly people
fand	found
fash	trouble (v.)
fasherie	trouble (n.)
fauld	close
fause	false
fleech	flatter
flirt	flick, jerk
fou	full

frae	from
freat	superstition
gae	gave
gang	go, going
gar	compel
gash	grim, ashen
gate	route, way
gaun	going
gear	goods, property
gie	give
gillie	(from Gael.) male servant
gin	if
girdle cake	a kind of scone or cake cooked on a heavy iron griddle (or "girdle")
girn	snarl
glunamie	a Lowland name for a Highlander
goodman	tenant, husband
grain	groan
grat	wept
greishogh	(from Gael.) glowing ember
gripe	grope
grit	great
grue	creep
grund	estate
grund officer	estate manager
gudeman	(see *goodman*)
gudesire	grandfather
gyre-carlin	witch
gyves	(Eng.) shackles
haill	whole
happed	hopped
hauld	dwelling, home
hesp	a length of yarn
het	hot
hirdy-girdy	topsy-turvy
hog	clip
hooly	slowly
hough-sinews	(Eng.) hamstrings
hout ay	certainly

GLOSSARY

howlet	owl
humdudgeons	(Eng.) sulk
ilk, ilka	each
ill-deedie	mischievous
ill-faured	ill-favoured, ugly
indorsation	(Eng.) endorsement
jackanape	tame monkey
jimply	scarcely
kail	cabbage; broth; food
kaleyard	vegetable patch
katern	(see *cateran*)
ken	know
kenning	(Eng.) view, sight (of something)
kyloe	(from Gael.) a breed of small Highland cattle
laith	loath
lap	leapt
latchet	(Eng.) bootstrap, shoelace
leabhar-dhu	(from Gael.) wallet
leal	honest
leasing-making	lies, deceit
leesome lane	entirely alone
llhu	(from Gael.) calf
loon	(Eng.) rogue, rascal
loup	leap
lum	chimney
mails and duties	rents of an estate
main	(Eng.) cockfight
mair	more
maist	almost
malison	(Eng.) curse
marcat	market
maun	must
mear	mare
merk	mark (a coin worth 13s. 4d.)
messuage	(Eng. from Fr.) a dwelling house with outbuildings
mettle	(Eng.) game, lively
mhor	(from Gael.) great
mind	remember
miscaa'd	slandered

misguider	one who misgoverns
monotroch	(Eng. from Gr.) a one-wheeled conveyance
mony	many
mopping and mowing	(Eng.) making faces, grimacing
moulds	grave
muckle	much
muhme	(from Gael.) nurse; midwife; stepmother
muils	slippers
murrey	the deep purple-red colour of a mulberry
mutchkin	a measure equal to a quarter of a Scottish pint or around three quarters of an imperial pint
nae	no
neist	next
nevoy	(Eng.) nephew
Od	(Eng.) a mild oath meaning "God"
of that ilk	of the estate of the same name
ohonari!	(Gael.) alas!
oig	(from Gael.) young
on the whilst	in the mean time
orra	occasional; miscellaneous
ower	much; too
owerloup	leap over
Pace	Easter
palfrey	(Eng.) a horse for ordinary riding
parochine	parish
peccant	(Eng.) culpable, sinning
peel	(Eng.) strip
penfold	(Eng.) an enclosure for livestock
pibroch	(from Gael.) a form of music for the bagpipes typically played on ceremonial occasions
pickthank	toady, sycophant
plaid	a long piece of tartan worn over the shoulder as part of traditional Highland dress
preferred	(Eng.) proffered
prelatist	(Eng.) supporter of episcopacy
prôné	(Fr.) extolled
prutt, trutt	(Eng.) an exclamation conveying scorn
puir	poor

GLOSSARY

quaigh	(from Gael.) a shallow bowl used as a drinking cup
quean	lass
quotha	(Eng.) said he
raff	(Eng.) scoundrel, worthless person
rant	romp, roister
ripe	search
rood	(Eng.) a measure of land equal to a quarter of an acre
roof-tree	(Eng.) the main beam or ridge piece in a roof
rudas	ugly, hag-like
rug	rake-off, cut
sackdoudling	bagpiping
sae	so
sain	bless
sair	sore
saul	soul
scathed	(Eng.) burnt, scorched
sculduddry	lewd
seannachie	(from Gael.) one who records and recounts history; a storyteller
shieling	shelter, hut
shoon	shoes
sic	such
sidier dhu	(from Gael.) (literally) black soldier (a soldier of the Black Watch)
sidier roy	(from Gael.) (literally) red soldier (a redcoat)
siller	silver
simple	medicinal herb
skene-dhu	(from Gael.) a short-bladed knife with a black hilt
sleekit	smooth
sneeshing	snuff
snuff-mull	snuffbox
sough	tune
Southlander	(Eng.) Lowlander
spaewife	female clairvoyant
speerings	information

spiog	(from Gael.) leg
sprack	lively
spule	shoulder
start and owerloup	(literally) leap and leap over
stend	(of an animal) rear on its hind legs, start
stirk	young bullock
stot	a castrated bullock in its second year or older
strath	wide river valley
supple	cudgel, club
ta'en on	enlisted
tacksman	a tenant of a clan chief, often a close kinsman
taishataragh	(Gael.) second sight
take a lang day	allow a lengthy period for the payment of a debt
tangs	tongs
tascal money	(from Gael.) a reward paid for information (about stolen cattle)
tass	cup
the ne'er a bit	not at all
threap	argue vehemently, maintain insistently
thrum	waste thread
tippeny	(Eng.) weak ale or beer
tod	fox
toom	empty
top-dressing	(Eng.) applying manure to
topsman	chief drover
treillage	(Eng.) latticework; a trellis
trencher companion	(Eng.) fellow diner
tryste	cattle market
turn-up	(Eng.) fist fight
tutelar	(Eng.) protective
twa	two
tyne	lose
unco	strange, out of the ordinary
untented	unregarded
usquebaugh	(from Gael.) whisky
wae	woe
wame	belly (*the worst word in his wame* = the most abusive language)

GLOSSARY

wanchancy	unlucky, threacherous
ware	expend
warrand	(Eng.) warrant
waur	*worse*
weepers	(Eng.) pieces of crape sewn to the sleeves as a sign of mourning
wha	who
wheen	few
whilk	which
whipper-in	(Eng.) assistant to a huntsman who controls the hounds with a whip
worth	betide
writhen	twisted, contorted
wuss	wish
yelloch	shriek
yetts	gates

EVERGREENS SERIES

Beautifully produced classics, affordably priced

Alma Classics is committed to making available a wide range of literature from around the globe. Most of the titles are enriched by an extensive critical apparatus, notes and extra reading material, as well as a selection of photographs. The texts are based on the most authoritative editions and edited using a fresh, accessible editorial approach. With an emphasis on production, editorial and typographical values, Alma Classics aspires to revitalize the whole experience of reading classics.

For our complete list and latest offers visit

almabooks.com/evergreens